RESCUING LILY

Guardian Hostage Rescue Specialists

ELLIE MASTERS

JEM Publishing

Dedication

This book is dedicated to my one and only—my amazing and wonderful husband.

Also by Ellie Masters

The LIGHTER SIDE

Ellie Masters is the lighter side of the Jet & Ellie Masters writing duo! You will find Contemporary Romance, Military Romance, Romantic Suspense, Billionaire Romance, and Rock Star Romance in Ellie's Works.

YOU CAN FIND ELLIE'S BOOKS HERE:

ELLIEMASTERS.COM/BOOKS

Military Romance

Guardian Hostage Rescue Specialists

Rescuing Melissa

(Get a FREE copy of Rescuing Melissa

when you join Ellie's Newsletter)

Alpha Team

Rescuing Zoe

Rescuing Moira

Rescuing Eve

Rescuing Lily

Rescuing Jinx

Rescuing Maria

Bravo Team

Rescuing Angie

Military Romance

Guardian Personal Protection Specialists

Sybil's Protector

The One I Want Series

(Small Town, Military Heroes)

By Jet & Ellie Masters

EACH BOOK IN THIS SERIES CAN BE READ AS A STANDALONE AND IS ABOUT A DIFFERENT COUPLE WITH AN HEA.

Saving Ariel

Saving Brie

Saving Cate

Saving Dani

Saving Jen

Saving Abby

Rockstar Romance

The Angel Fire Rock Romance Series

EACH BOOK IN THIS SERIES CAN BE READ AS A STANDALONE AND IS ABOUT A DIFFERENT COUPLE WITH AN HEA. IT IS RECOMMENDED THEY ARE READ IN ORDER.

Ashes to New (prequel)

Heart's Insanity (book 1)

Heart's Desire (book 2)

Heart's Collide (book 3)

Hearts Divided (book 4)

Hearts Entwined (book5)

Forest's FALL (book 6)

Hearts The Last Beat (book7)

Contemporary Romance

Firestorm

(KRISTY BROMBERG'S EVERYDAY HEROES WORLD)

Billionaire Romance

Billionaire Boys Club

Hawke

Richard

Brody

Contemporary Romance

Cocky Captain

(Vi Keeland & Penelope Ward's Cocky Hero World)

Romantic Suspense

Each book is a standalone novel.

The Starling

~AND~

Science Fiction

Ellie Masters writing as L.A. Warren
Vendel Rising: a Science Fiction Serialized Novel

ONE

Knox

———

The stench of piss, beer, and puke blends with the acrid smell of unwashed bodies, creating a noxious assault on my senses. Half of Alpha team, the bachelors: Liam, Wolfe, and I, troll New Orleans, looking to blow off a little steam after yet another fruitless lead.

We spent the day at the docks in the sweltering summer heat. Now that the heat of the day is lifting, we're ready to grab drinks, find some chicks to bury ourselves in, and basically chill out.

As for the other half of Alpha team, Max is back in California recovering from injuries he sustained when we rescued his woman, Eve Deverough. Axel and Griff work to shake down Carson Deverough, the shipping mogul who bartered his daughter's freedom, for what?

That's the all-important question, and one we don't have answers to as of yet.

Hopefully, Axel and Griff will discover something of value. Meanwhile, Liam, Wolfe, and I look for a contact hinted at in the ledgers Max and I pulled out of Tomas Benefield's operation. That monster is dead. Killed in Colombia when he put a gun to Eve's head. His entire sex-trafficking operation was taken out during that mission, and we obtained the ledgers containing every transaction. Every girl whose life was stolen and every monster who paid to enslave them has been documented.

Those ledgers, something we all thought would be gold, are encoded in a cipher our technical genius, Mitzy, can't unravel. Though, she's hard at work trying to bust that code.

For now, all we have is one name, a date, and a time.

Lei'lani is the name. Tomorrow is the day. Three in the morning is the godforsaken time.

We're still working on the where.

Each nugget of information leads us further down the path of taking down another asshole intent on stealing lives and destroying dreams.

Since Deverough is a shipping mogul, our suspicion is this meeting will happen at one of the many docks. Mitzy's narrowed down the possibilities to a few commercial operations. No surprise, it has to do with shipping containers.

The question is, who is Lei'lani?

What is her role in all of this?

Is she a business partner of Deverough's?

A competitor?

Perhaps, we'll figure something out and solve a piece of the puzzle. Maybe Mitzy will come through, like she always does, saving the day in the tenth hour. Or maybe, our visit to New Orleans will leave us empty-handed, like the last four times Alpha team descended on this town.

"Lots of potential action tonight." Liam watches the crowded street. Eyes alert, head on a swivel, he's not looking for enemies.

"Tone it down." I slug Liam in the arm. His libido is out of control.

"The night is young." He shoves me right back, grinning like a fool. "The possibilities are endless." He returns to checking out the chicks we pass.

The French Quarter, like every night before this one, pulses with vibrant activity. Half the people are stoned, drunk, or otherwise riding one high or another. Festive music pours out of jazz clubs and trickles out of dueling piano bars to mingle with the rhythm of the street and a city coming alive.

It's still early enough that families are out. Moms and dads with eager teens, tweens, and kids with no business being out this late, clutch their children's hands as they drag their young ones to the safety of their hotels for the night.

Couples brave the later hours, seeking one thrill or the next. Boisterous groups of college kids vie for attention from the opposite sex. The bravado of the young men brings a smile to my face. The coy smiles of the girls make me shake my head.

It's barely after nine. This city is only just waking up, which means the skirts get shorter, the dresses grow tighter, and the heels climb higher as chicks eager for a night of partying fill the street.

We pass by a gaggle of sorority co-eds with micro-mini skirts and skintight tops practically sprayed onto their bodies. My gaze naturally drifts to admire what they advertise. Two of the girls aren't wearing bras, and from the look of their skirts, they're not wearing panties either.

It's tempting. Liam takes a long look at them as well, but I yank on his sleeve and pull him along.

"Aw, you're no fun." Liam grumps, but he doesn't resist.

"Those girls are a walking smorgasbord of STDs and bad decisions. Best keep your dick out of those waters." Before I finish talking, a group of guys moves in on the girls, eager for an easy conquest.

"Let's get some chow." Wolfe prowls restlessly beside me.

He, too, scans the crowd, only he's not checking out the chicks. His eyes are on the men and boys with too much liquid courage who are out looking for trouble. They're the ones whose intellect rapidly falls in direct correlation with the alcohol level in their blood.

"We just ate." Restless and growing more agitated by the minute, my senses are on full alert.

"Still, it's better than walking the streets." Wolfe's tired of being on the prowl.

Honestly, I am too.

We're out here because I'm restless. Dinner was beyond

amazing. All New Orleans food is fabulous, but my skin started itching halfway through the meal; I sense something is off. Not that I can put my finger on what's bugging me.

Not that there's any reason to be concerned. The three of us present a formidable force. We're taller than those around us. Broader and more muscled, it's obvious we're either military, ex-military, or bouncers headed to work for the night.

"Still hungry?" Wolfe growls a little, showing his frustration. "Wings and beer? How's that sound?"

"Oysters. I want oysters," Liam pipes in, and I give him another shove.

"The last thing you need is more oysters." Oysters are one of my favorite things, but feeding Liam's raging libido sounds all kinds of wrong.

As we stride down the packed street, the crowd parts seamlessly before us and closes behind us. We attract attention, both good and bad. People are wary of three large men walking around like they own the place.

"I can do wings." With Max on medical hold, due to his injuries, I'm acting commander of Alpha team. The whole team is in New Orleans, trying to dig up some kind of actionable information.

Wolfe rolls his eyes and groans. It's all for effect.

He's the strictest of the three of us when it comes to taking care of his body. Wolfe isn't one to mix business and pleasure. That little bit of fun falls to Liam, the party guy of the group.

"Wings and beer sound great." Liam struts beside me, showing off his physique to any woman who looks, and there are a lot of women who take notice. "Add a little pussy into the mix and I'll call it a good night." He points to a seedy-looking bar. "How about that?"

Three burly bouncers guard the entrance to a strip club. Two girls with dental floss thongs gyrate near the entrance, enticing anyone with a pulse to join them inside.

I consider it for half a second. A bit of a striptease, followed by a lap dance, would be enough to take the edge off, but this restlessness inside of me grows stronger as the evening wears on.

To be honest, I want more of a challenge. A vigorous lap dance simply doesn't cut it for me. Besides, the idea of spending the rest of the night with jizz in my pants is unappealing at best.

"We're not here for cheap hookers." I march right past the strippers and continue on as if I actually have a destination in mind.

I don't. I'm aimless and looking for—something.

Wish I knew what the fuck that was.

"Nothing wrong with a strip club," Liam pouts. He trails behind us, rubbernecking the strip club, but then catches up when it's clear I won't be stopping. "We could stop for an hour …"

Liam is a looker. He's got the Hollywood thing down pat; blond hair, blue eyes, a smirk a mile wide. He's the charmer of the group and never fails to fill his bed.

I'm his complete opposite, dark hair, dark eyes, more of a scowl instead of a smile. I'd like to think I'm easy on the eye, but girls flock to me because I've got the bad boy vibe down pat.

"You can deal with not getting laid one night." I scan the way ahead, looking for something that will satisfy each of us.

"Says who?" Liam joins me in lockstep as we stroll down the crowded street.

"Says me." I jab at him with my elbow, but Liam reads me before I can connect. He dances out of reach, avoiding me while taking a look at the crowd.

We're a triple threat, working as a team until we each have our arm draped over a girl.

A den of sin and loose women, this city is ripe for the plucking, and there are more than enough women intent on riding a stallion for the night to go around.

Too many.

Liam's eager for pussy. In stark contrast, Wolfe's steadfast beside me. More of a stalker, he scans the crowd for something suitable for his tastes. He likes his women wide-eyed and innocent, says it makes it that much more fun when he defiles them, ruining them for any man who comes after him.

I'd say it was all bravado, but I've seen the string of broken hearts Wolfe leaves behind. The man has a magic dick.

As for me, New Orleans suits my tastes just fine. I like my sex nameless and guilt-free. Two consenting adults scratching a mutual itch, with no strings, no connections, and no bother once the sun comes up.

No names exchanged.

No mess to deal with later.

Fuck, then walk away.

Relationships are messy, and I don't need that kind of complicated shit in my life.

The problem with Liam is there's no time to take a woman back to the house we've rented for the duration. After a quick romp in the sheets, most chicks turn bitchy when they get the heave ho' at two in the morning. Liam never lets his women spend the whole night. As soon as he's done, he sets them free.

I get it, but it's not safe for a woman to be walking on the streets at two in the morning. It's also not safe going to a stranger's house either.

Double standards much?

With Max out of action, I've had to step up and take on the lead. The guys look to me to adhere to the rules and keep everyone in line.

They're testing me too, looking to see what they can get away with in Max's absence. I don't like Alpha team being a man down, but for this kind of reconnaissance work, we don't need the whole team.

We pass by a crowded bar. The balcony overflows with a boisterous crowd. Young women eye us.

The girls call out and we stop for a moment to admire the goods. Wolfe sniffs the air while Liam raises his hand. Dangling from his fingers are over a dozen strands of beads.

The girls need no more prompting than that. Liam doesn't even need to ask. Before I know it, half a dozen or so girls flash their tits at us while they shout into the air.

"Come up here!"

"Party!"

"I'll show you a good time."

No doubt they would at that, but Wolfe's not interested. He moves on, and I follow. Liam lingers for a moment to toss beads into the air, rewarding the girls for their little show.

I kind of regret walking away. The only good thing about this assignment is the easy lays. There hasn't been a single night we haven't scored it big. Whether it's hot and sweaty sex in the bathroom of a bar, or hot and sweaty sex twisting the sheets in our rental, none of us lack for female companionship.

Honestly, it's too easy. Boring comes to mind.

Not that I mind getting blown in the back of a bar or fucking some nameless chick in a sketchy bathroom. I do draw the line at doing it in an alley. In New Orleans, that's just asking for trouble.

I have to say it gets tiresome and feels like cheating when women drop their panties with a suggestive crook of my finger or one flagrant wink.

What I wouldn't give for a bit of a challenge.

Music pours into the streets as local bars fill with eager patrons. Beads crunch underfoot, discarded after being tossed from the balconies overhead. The stifling heat of the day recedes as cooler, nighttime temperatures roll in, but that does nothing to quench the smell of stale beer filling the air.

Liam calls out to more chicks partying on the balconies, urging them to flash their tits. It surprises me how many take him up on the offer, especially when he's out of beads.

But that's Liam.

Women turn stupid around him.

We stop to watch street performers, enjoying their incredible acrobatics. I drop cash in the till, and we move on.

An itching between my shoulder blades draws me up short. Liam and Wolfe take a step before coming to a stop. Second time this night my spidey-senses have gone off.

"What's up?" Wolfe scans the crowd, looking for the threat.

"Not sure." I glance around, wondering why it feels like I've got eyes on me.

There's no way three men of our stature, walking together, don't draw nearly every eye. But there's curiosity and then there's *attention*.

Somebody watches us, and I want to know why.

"Hey, how about that?" Wolfe stops in his tracks and points to a bar hopping with activity.

The sign overhead says *Callie's Bar.* Advertisements outside promise cheap shots, rowdy music, and girls dancing on the bar. It sounds just about right.

"You good with that?" I turn to Liam. No need to ask. The devilish grin on his face is answer enough.

"Let's do this." Liam claps his hands together.

People spill out onto the streets. Music pours out of the bar as patrons yell, shout, and grind. The three of us walk in, pushing past the press of people while we head for the bar.

"What's up, handsome?" A pretty woman with golden skin and coffee eyes takes our order. I hand her a fifty up front.

"Tequila shots for me and my friends."

"Sure thing." Her mischievous eyes twinkle. "Body shots?"

"Perhaps in a bit." I peel off another fifty and boldly tuck it in her cleavage, letting my fingertips linger half a second too long.

Her eyes round and her pupils dilate. Give it another few seconds and I bet I can get her to take me to the back for a quick one-and-done fuck.

"You got it, handsome." She plucks the fifty from her cleavage and shoves it deep in the back pocket of her denim shorts.

While I consider pushing for that trip to the back room, that tickling sensation returns. I glance around the room but see nothing out of the ordinary until a flash of white catches my eye.

A crackle of energy whips through the air. A beautiful woman with white-blonde hair and golden eyes stares at me from the back of the room. Like a punch in the gut, I stagger as a bolt of lightning shoots through me.

I turn away to catch my breath and focus on the here and now. Plenty of women have stared at me in my life, but none with ferocity and hunger like that.

The bartender slides over a shot of tequila and I slam it down before turning around for a double take. Sure as shit, the woman's still staring.

I blink and convince myself this weird pulsation isn't real, but the captivating woman continues to stare. It's not a come-hither stare of attraction. It's angry and full of the same shock coursing through my veins. As if she likes what she sees when looking at me yet hates herself for it as well.

Odd.

And not the usual vibe I get from women. For the most part, they're hungry and eager, not pissed off with full, kissable lips pressed into an angry line.

Why the hell would she be pissed at me?

Once she realizes I return her stare, she quickly schools her features, turning that anger into an expressionless mask. She turns to a pretty Latina chick standing beside her and whispers in her ear. The Latina turns toward me, takes me in, then gives a curt nod.

They're talking about me.

I look over at Liam, but he's already talking up some chick. Wolfe scores a seat at the bar. He watches a girl dancing over him on the bar and shamelessly looks up her skirt. With that wolfish grin fixed on his face, no doubt the two of them will be hooking up tonight. He waves over the bartender, points to something on a bar menu, then grins at the chick shaking her ass with all she's got.

With my team suitably entertained, I turn my attention back to my white-haired beauty. Only she's no longer there.

What an odd exchange.

Younger than me, but not by much, she's older than the college co-eds packed shoulder-to-shoulder inside this bar. Curious, I head over to see if I can track her down. A woman like that is hard to lose sight of in a bar.

Then I spy her near the jukebox. Nifty little trick there, getting the patrons to pay for the music blaring over the speakers. Slowly, I wind my way between gyrating bodies, picking my path with determination through the crowded bar.

She turns her back to me, but from the set of her shoulders, she knows I'm coming. Nice way to lure me in, but she doesn't know I'm a master at this game.

I take my time, pause to do a little bump-and-grind on the dance floor with an eager college chick whose eyes turn to saucers when I move in. It's short-lived, however, as I don't stay there long, not when my attention spikes on the woman with the snow-white hair.

My relentless approach doesn't go unnoticed. While my quarry acts like she's unaware of me closing in, her body telegraphs everything as I read her like a book.

Well, I did say I was bored. This is definitely spicing things up. To say I'm intrigued is an understatement. As for my quarry, her skin-tight dress hugs all her curves while leaving the smooth expanse of her back bare. No bra. I like that.

And from the way that red dress hugs her tight ass, I'm pretty sure she's wearing absolutely nothing underneath. I eat up every sensual detail of her bare skin, eager to feel the heat of her body beneath my hands.

She leans against the jukebox, perusing the songs, keeping her back to me. I walk up behind her, lean in close, and sweep the hair off her shoulder until the pearly-white skin of her neck beckons.

"Pick something slow, pumpkin."

A tiny shiver ripples down her spine as my hot breath rushes over her skin, but her spine stiffens and her shoulders roll back. Very slowly, she pivots in her five-inch fuck-me heels. Her head barely reaches my shoulder, which means the broad expanse of my chest is all she sees.

Slowly, her head tips back. Her graceful neck arches. My breath hitches while waiting for her to drag her gaze up my body. The urge to bend down and lick the delicate arch of her neck overwhelms me.

I reach, intent on grabbing her by the waist, when her golden gaze finally reaches my eyes. My hand stops less than an inch from her skin.

Mesmerizing.

I expect her golden eyes to swim with desire and simmer with lust, but those pretty eyes are hard, cold, and brittle. It's a shock to my system, but then her gaze softens as she takes in my face.

"Now, why would I want to pick something slow? Especially when I like it hard and fast." Low and sultry, she issues an invitation laced in a challenge

I lean in and dip down until my lips are at her ear. "So I can hold you close, of course. Lick that elegant neck of yours. Suck on your ear. And kiss you until you forget how to breathe." When I pull back, a smile spreads across my face. "If you like it hard and fast, I can do that too."

Her golden eyes swim with lust and spark with desire. It takes a moment before she realizes it, but then she blinks and takes a step back.

"Does that work on all the girls? I'm surprised you haven't asked me out back for a quick fuck while we're at it."

"I'm not opposed to that." Actually, I'm more and more interested as the seconds pass.

TWO

Lily

____

Knox Wilder is exactly what I expect: cocky, arrogant, and cocksure. Devilishly handsome, he's the kind of man who knocks a woman off her feet and makes other men question their masculinity.

Tall, broad of shoulder, pecs that aren't afraid to pop beneath that tight, black t-shirt, his biceps stretch the fabric of that poor shirt. Intimidating is one thing that comes to mind. It is, however, not the first thing to cross my filthy thoughts.

I'm not opposed to that.

His words ricochet in my head, bouncing around as I decide how far I'm willing to take this.

All the way comes to mind.

Yeah, I definitely want to ride this glorious man. Unlike most women, I'm not afraid of my sexuality, and I frequently indulge myself. Seldom do I wait for the man to come to me, but for Wilder, I'm happy for him to make the first move.

He's got that unknown quantity that attracts women in droves. In that black t-shirt, black pants, and shit-kicker boots, he looks badass, but the perpetual twinkle in his eyes, which carries the slightest hint of humor, makes me take a second look. I can't tell if he's a protective hero who will swoop in to save the day or a bad idea I'll regret in the morning.

Yet again, I'll take it.

He's both hero and bad idea wrapped up in one dangerous package. I'll be frank. I'm not against making a bad decision if it means one, steamy night of twisting in the sheets with this man.

I cock a hand on my hip and roll my shoulders back. "I hate to disappoint you, but you have to work harder than that if you want any of this." I make a sensual gesture down my body.

Research into the man reveals much but hides more. He's an elusive prize I intend to piece together, but right now, taking him down a notch is more pressing. It also brings to mind something other than a simple arrest. He's the kind of man I can have a little fun with first.

"Is that so?" He rocks back on his heels. "Don't mind a challenge, pumpkin, especially when the reward's worth it." Wilder reaches out, touching without invitation, as he grasps a lock of my hair. "Are you worth it?" His inquisitive gaze demands an answer.

"Never had any complaints, but who's to say I'm interested in you? Go find someone else to wet your dick and stroke your ego."

Talk about sex on a stick. My nipples draw tight, putting on a show, and I'm sure there's more than mischief twinkling in my eyes.

"Tell me you don't feel the air crackling between us and I'll walk away. But know this …"

He doesn't back down. Isn't even offended by my taunt. Instead, he leans forward, once again whispering in my ear. His warm breath flutters across my skin, sending shockwaves of sensation shooting through me.

"Know, what?" I hold perfectly still. If I move, his lips will be on me.

"Take a walk on the wild side with me. I promise you won't regret it."

Whoa, Nelly, but my lady bits are on fire. Hot, wet, and wanting, after nothing more than a look and a few words whispered into my ear; Wilder is something.

I'll give him that much.

Focus Lily.

"I don't feel it." I lie right to his face.

The air between us isn't crackling. It's far beyond that—sizzling and snapping as the sexual heat between us electrifies the very air.

"Lie. *Tsk. Tsk.*" He gives a slow shake of his head. "Come on, you can be honest with me. I bite only if you beg."

"What makes you think I'd be up for something like that?"

"Like, what? I'm talking about a dance. What are you talking about?" Mirth crinkles the corners of his eyes. The bastard has me and he knows it.

This is one assignment I can't afford to mess up. Meaning, I need to keep my eye on the prize, and that prize isn't a quick fuck with Wilder in a back alley.

Not that it can't be.

I don't need to justify my actions to anyone. It's a perk of undercover work.

"Nothing." My lips press into a firm line. I'm not happy he got me to jump from a dance to a fuck, and he knows it.

"Another lie. Pumpkin, make this easy on yourself. Admit what you want. You've already thought about what it will feel like when I slide inside of you. Although, I don't think a fuck out back will ever be enough. If you don't want to dance, we can move this someplace much more private." He reaches down to make a crude adjustment. "I can certainly rise to the challenge."

"You really have some nerve."

"Asking a beautiful woman to dance? Since when is that a crime? As for the other, you'll be begging for it. No worries there."

"That's not what you want and you know it."

"What isn't?"

"Asking me to dance."

"I'm very interested in a little bump-and-grind. We start on the dance floor. Heat things up, then move outside."

"Didn't take but a second for your mind to go to the gutter."

"You're the one with the filthy mind. Bet you've already thought of all the ways I might take you. Pressed hard against the wall. Spin you around and take you from behind. I bet you're wild enough to go for a ride and skip the wall altogether? But I only asked for a dance. The rest is up to you."

"Is that so?"

"Yes, when I see something I want, I take it." He licks the seam of his lips, and I practically detonate right there.

How can something like that be insanely sexy? He is full of himself, and he's right. I am thinking about him taking me against the wall, everything else he said, and more. The man is confident as fuck and that's the sexiest thing a man can be.

"I'm a person, not a thing." Still, he needs to be put in his place.

"Are we going to debate this all night? Or are you going to pick us a song to dance to?"

"I thought you wanted to fuck me out back?"

"You should try to get to know me a little better before using me for sex."

"Me? Using you?" My fingers curl into tiny fists, but what am I going to do with them? He's twice my size, and all my training put together isn't going to make him budge.

His eyes spark with mischief. "How about that dance? And you haven't answered my question."

Wilder loops his arm around my waist. He pulls me tight to his chest as his massive hand splays against my lower back. A surprised gasp escapes me, or maybe it's more of a whimper.

"What question?" The words come out in a rush of desire and lust.

"Do you feel me, pumpkin? Do you feel the electricity in the air? Has it hit you yet?"

"What?"

"The inevitable." That roguish gaze makes me wobble in my five-inch heels.

"Holding you close, and fucking you out back, are two things I want to do." His eyes sparkle. "But how about we start with names first? Mine's Knox, and yours is …?" He looks down with lust simmering in his eyes.

This is the part where I'm supposed to make a scene, push against his chest, and tell him to take his hands off me. But the thing is, I don't want to.

I want his hands all over me. Grasping my breasts. Sliding between my legs. Anywhere and everywhere. And all at once.

The heat of his body sinks into me. The scent of masculine virility: dark, sultry, sinful, and forbidden, swirls in the air, overloading my senses.

The man smells incredible. Someone should bottle that scent and sell it to the masses. Women will be losing their panties all over the world.

Okay, maybe that's not such a good idea.

There's something else. Something I can't deny.

The air sparks between us. Tiny jolts of electricity crackle along my skin, raising the fine little hairs of my arms until they stand up and take notice.

"You feel it, pumpkin. I see it on your face." He yanks me closer, pressing the full length of our bodies against one another. "Go ahead, admit it." He's hard and packing, and not at all afraid to show me exactly how aroused he is.

"Admit, what?"

"That you feel this crazy energy." He drags the pad of his thumb from the angle of my jaw down the arch of my neck. "It's more than physical attraction."

"I don't feel it." My reply comes out breathy and unsure.

Most men would back down when directly challenged like this. Not Wilder. He eats it up.

"Now, pumpkin, why would you lie to me again? That's three."

"I'm not lying."

He leans down until our lips are kissably close. His gaze flicks to mine as he closes the distance.

I wet my lips, eager to feel his mouth on mine. His chest expands with each of his breaths, and there's a possessive rumble in the back of his throat, but Wilder holds where he is; our lips a hair's breadth apart, dragging out the moment.

All I'd have to do is shift the slightest bit and we'll be kissing.

"Liars don't get what they want." He suddenly jerks away from me, denying me the kiss I definitely want.

A frustrated growl escapes me.

His mouth moves to my ear again. "Nothing happens unless you say *Yes*, but if you keep lying, I'm not going to ask and you won't be able to say *Yes*. Why deny yourself when you obviously want this?"

I bet he knows how to fuck a woman until she can't think straight. That smoldering look in his eyes says exactly that.

Focus on work.

I need to focus. Getting close to Wilder is my assignment. Might as well have a bit of fun while I'm at it.

Pillow talk never fails to get men to spill their dirty, little secrets. All I need is to figure out who he works for, how the shipments are arranged, and find a way inside his operation.

Well, not *his* operation. Wilder isn't top dog, but he's involved in the shipment of drugs, women, and cash transfers. My job is to figure out how.

Then, I'll take him down.

In between now and then? Working undercover doesn't come without risk, but there are some benefits. I can fuck him without guilt. It's all for God and country, and damn if I'm not a patriot.

But I'm no easy lay.

He can't waltz over here with his filthy thoughts and dirty mouth and expect me to cave just like that.

I've got some degree of respect for myself.

If Wilder wants me, he needs to work harder than this.

Head and shoulders over me, he makes me feel small and vulnerable, two things I absolutely hate. I despise men who underestimate my capabilities. Unfortunately, it happens all the damn time. And his cocky come-on makes me want to take him down a notch.

This could be fun.

What to do? What to do?

"How about we make a bet?" I've officially gone insane. What the hell am I doing?

"A bet? And for the record, you're still dodging my question." His brows pinch together, confused, but then a smile graces his face. "What kind of bet do you have in mind? And just so you know, if I win, you're mine for the rest of the night. Whatever I want …"

"Don't get ahead of yourself."

"Why not?"

"Because you haven't won yet."

"Pumpkin, we both know you're going to let me win."

"Now, where's the fun in that?" Hell if I know what I'm doing right now, but I need to think of something fast.

A quick fuck-and-done isn't going to work. Not if I want to get close to Wilder. I need something that will bring him back to me. Something that will let me wrap him around my little finger until he spills all his secrets.

"Answer my question." Wilder isn't giving up. He's a persistent bastard; I give him that much. "Are you afraid of a simple question?" He traces his thumb from the notch at my throat all the way to the angle of my shoulder until a shiver moves through me.

He's one hundred percent on the money. Something crackles in the air between us, that's for damn sure. It heats the air, stirs desire, and simmers with lust. I want him.

I wish I'd thought to wear a bra because my nipples draw up into tight little peaks of all kinds of a bad idea.

He leans in again, suggestive, aggressive, and sexy as fuck. "You feel it, don't you?" This time, instead of simply whispering in my ear, he nibbles on the tip of my earlobe. "It's going to be explosive."

One of my most sensitive erogenous zones, I about melt into a puddle of need right then and there, but I can't give him what he wants. Wilder needs to work for it before I let him fuck me.

"Promises. Promises." I pull back and regain as much of my senses as possible. "Now, about that bet?" I arch a brow, taunting him. An idea forms in my mind.

It would be too easy to let him have his way. Hell, I'm wet and soaked for him already. Rivers of arousal flow down my legs, making me glad I'm not wearing anything under this dress. He could drag me outside and I wouldn't put up a fight. Although, in my current state, I'm more likely to be the one dragging him outside.

I need breathing space and take a step back. Looking up into his smoldering eyes, I can't help but grin.

"How good are you at darts?"

"Darts?" The confused expression on his face makes me want to laugh.

"Yeah, you know pointy-tipped things you throw at a target? They're played sometimes in bars." And this bar happens to have one.

"I know what darts are, pumpkin." He grabs me again, pulling me against his hard body. "I thought we were talking about a little dirty dancing?"

"When did our dancing turn dirty?"

"From the moment I caught you staring at me from across the room." Wilder releases me. He takes a step back and crosses his arm over his chest. "But I'm game. What are the stakes?"

"Winner takes all."

"All of what?"

"Whatever they want."

"You sure you want to bet something like that with me? When I win, I plan on burying myself balls deep within your sweet heat. After that, I'll take that pert little mouth of yours and stuff it with my cock. I'll ride you all night, and through 'til dawn, until you don't know where you end and I begin."

It's official. I've gone over the deep end. Thoughts of him doing exactly as he says turns me into a quivering mess.

"There's no way you're going to win."

"You've never seen me go after what I want."

"And you've never seen me teach a cocksure prick to eat crow."

"Careful, pumpkin, calling me names only heats my blood, and I'm already on fire thinking about what I'm going to do to you."

"This is how it's going to go. I'll win, and then you'll watch me leave with another man while you go home with a woody and a pair of blue balls."

"Now, why would you want to do that?"

"To teach you a lesson."

"School's been out for years. And for the record, you're not leaving with anyone but me."

"Wanna bet?"

THREE

Knox

———

Darts? When did we go from fucking out back to playing a damn game of darts? Not that I won't dominate the game—Me, darts, and the Navy have a long and fruitful history—but it's a far cry from what I thought we'd be doing.

My first sea tour, all we did on the ship was play darts. Well, that and football. I've got a great eye, steady hand, rarely lose, and made a killing.

This should be fun.

"You really want to play darts?" Maybe I can convince her to take that dance instead? I gesture toward the dance floor and the gyrating couples.

Now, saying Callie's Bar has a dance floor is kind of like saying it's like any other bar. It's not, and it doesn't have a dance floor. But it does have a jukebox. Where there's music and drunken fun, dancing and grinding go hand in hand.

"I do." She flashes a mischievous grin.

"We could just skip to the good stuff." I can't believe we're going to play darts. I'd much rather take her for a bit of a bump-and-grind, then some old-fashioned in and out.

"We could, but why spoil my fun?"

"Remember that comment when I win because after I do, you're mine."

"Not so fast." She places a hand on my chest, leaving it there a bit too long. Her fingers curl, pressing against my muscles, then her eyes widen and her pupils dilate. She's interested all right.

"Thought hard and fast was your speed, pumpkin. Or did I hear that wrong?"

"We've only just begun." There's a look on her face which I should pay attention to, but I don't. I'm not worried about my skill. "And I've yet to state the rules."

"Rules?" I arch a brow. "Other than the obvious ones?" There aren't that many rules in darts, but she's got my interest.

"We play 301. Best two out of three wins. Are you familiar with it?"

"I'm surprised you are."

One of the mainstays of darts is 301. Each player begins with 301 points. Players alternate turns, each throwing three darts at a time. The points the darts land on are subtracted from the starting number, and the first person to reach zero wins the round. There's a bit more to it; strategy when the points grind down toward zero. That's the other rule. You have to hit zero exactly.

"Because I'm a girl?"

"Is that sexist of me?"

"Damn straight, but I'll forgive you."

There's an evil glimmer in her eye, which makes me think I've bitten off more than I can chew.

"Let's play." I clap my hands and rub them together. I'm eager to get this over with and move on to the fun stuff.

"Hold up. I haven't finished with the rules."

"The rules are simple, pumpkin. We start with 301 points and count down from there."

"Well, yes. Standard rules. Three throws each. Subtract from 301. First to zero wins. But let's make it interesting."

"Of course." Her attitude is fucking sexy as hell. There's no doubt in my mind she's playing me, but I'm too committed to back out now. "How do you suggest we do that?" I'm curious what she thinks would make this more interesting than it already is.

"Simple. One shot before each set of throws. Loser takes off one piece of clothing. Their choice. Socks and shoes don't count."

"Strip darts? In New Orleans?" I raise my brows, intrigued, and take another look at her dress. There's no doubt in my mind she's wearing nothing beneath it.

"It's the French Quarter. What happens in New Orleans ..." She spins in a slow, seductive circle. "Of course, if you're chicken, you can back out."

"Pumpkin, there's no way I'm backing out."

A shot between each set of throws? That's a fair number of shots. Even if I lose the first match, which I won't, I can drink her under the table. By the third game, she'll be putty in my hands. That dress is definitely coming off.

"Great." Her coppery eyes sparkle with mischief. "Let's get set up?"

"Of course." We pick our way through the crowded bar.

It's loud, raucous, and I can barely hear myself think over the music blaring through the speakers.

Wolfe and Liam cock their heads, asking if everything's all right. I give them a sign that I'm good, and they turn back to the chicks they're wooing for the night. Wolfe turns his attention back to the woman dancing in front of him on the bar.

My girl goes to the bartender and gets her attention. The bartender, the one I gave the hefty tip to, glances at me and flashes a pretty smile. She reaches under the bar and brings out a box which I assume contains our darts.

Walking around like she owns the place, my girl heads to the dartboard. It's packed at that end of the bar. Boisterous laughter rolls over me as I shoulder my way through, intent on clearing out the space we need to play.

Only, there's no need for me to get people out of the way. I don't know how she does it, but when she opens the cabinet to the dartboard she whispers in a pretty Latina's ear. Before I know it, people step back.

Impressed, I liberate a barstool from some fat-ass bastard and place it next to the throw line. My golden-eyed beauty flicks her lashes and places the box of darts on the stool.

"You ready for this?" Her innocent expression brings a laugh to my lips. Girl thinks she's a shark, but she has no idea how good I am at this game.

"Ready." I open the box and hand her three darts. "You never told me your name."

"You're right." Her lashes flutter as she takes the darts. "I didn't."

"And …"

"We don't need names for this." She pivots in her five-inch heels and steps to the throw line.

"Highest score begins?"

An initial throw generally determines who goes first, but I'm feeling generous.

"Ladies first."

Right as I say that, the bartender comes over with a tray containing two shot glasses and a bottle of whiskey. She grabs the darts box, then sets the tray down on the stool I appropriated. After pouring out two shots, full to the brim, she slips me back the fifty I gave her earlier.

"You're going to need this," she says with a husky laugh.

"It's yours, doll." I take the fifty and put it right back where I stuck it the first time.

My girl and the bartender exchange a look, laughing together at some unknown joke.

Before my unnamed girl throws her first dart, I bring her a shot glass. She takes it with a twinkle in her eye.

"Good luck. You're going to need it," she says.

"To a night of possibilities." I clink my glass against hers and lift it in salute.

"To the winner goes the spoils." She raises her glass, then tosses back the whiskey. Her face contorts with the burn as the alcohol rushes down her throat, but then she hands me back the shot glass. "Let's do this."

I'm all on board with that. The sooner we begin, the quicker I'll get her in bed. She takes in a deep breath and closes her eyes. It gives me a moment to admire her stunning beauty.

Although, that's not her sexiest attribute.

Her confidence is what draws me in. There's something incredibly sexy about a woman who knows what she wants and isn't afraid to take it.

And this little game of darts only heightens the sexual tension between us. Hard, aroused, and ready to begin, I wait for her to throw the first dart.

She holds the dart with familiarity and trust. It's the first sign I've been taken. She winks at me, then tosses the dart. It flies true and hits triple twenty. Damn fine shot. She's either extremely lucky, or …

Her next shot snuggles right beside the first. Two triple twenties.

Fuck me.

The highest score in darts is a ton 80; three triple twenties for a combined score of one hundred and eighty.

Damn if her next dart doesn't strike right beside the first two.

The boisterous crowd roars with the shot. Her friend, the pretty brunette she spoke to earlier, makes her way through the crowd, whispering in the ears of the women.

Something's up.

When my golden-eyed beauty walks to the dartboard and retrieves her darts, I realize I've been had. She takes a little bow, playing to the crowd, then turns to me with a serpentine smile.

Yeah, I've definitely been had.

When she returns, she grabs my bicep for support as she lifts on tiptoe to whisper in my ear.

"You can back out if you want."

No way in hell am I backing out.

"You played me."

"It's just an innocent game of darts." Her lashes flutter. She's no innocent. She's a damn shark.

"Pumpkin, there's nothing innocent about you." I'm going to

lose my shirt, but I don't care. I'm game to play this out to the end. But two can play at this.

My arm wraps around her waist before she can step away. I sweep down and steal a kiss, claiming her lips with the fire and passion burning within me. I dominate the kiss as I'll later dominate her in bed. My tongue lashes out as her first whimper slips out.

Yeah, she feels me.

Honed over the years, my technique delivers results. I fluctuate between exquisitely soft probing to ferocious lashes as I delve in deep and claim her mouth as mine.

She grips my shirt as her back arches, thrusting her tits against my chest. Another whimper escapes her, and I can't help but smile. This kiss is far from over. As I seek out her weakness, and demand her surrender, I give her a hint of what's to come.

I drag her close, melding our bodies. My hands slip down to cup her ass. Fingers digging in, I own the kiss, conquering and demanding her surrender as our hips grind together.

Hard and aroused, I'm eager to strip her bare and complete my conquest. Something tells me we're going to spontaneously combust if we don't take the edge off the passion stirring between us.

Around us, the crowd cheers as I taste whiskey on her lips and stroke the desire blooming on her fluttering breath. She moans, her body accepting the inevitable as I break off the kiss, leaving her eager and wanting.

"Damn." She brushes her fingertips along her swollen lips. Her lashes flutter as she peeks up at me.

"There's more where that came from." Two can play at this game, and while I'm about to go down as far as darts go, I will teach her a lesson. She'll be a quivering mess before we're done.

I step up to the throw line and send my darts flying. I hit two triple twenties, giving me one hundred and twenty points, but then miss the third and hit a single five.

By the time I retrieve my darts, she poured the next round of shots.

"To an interesting evening." She hands me a shot, then clinks her glass against mine. Upending the shot, she downs it in one swallow.

"To unexpected pleasures." I empty my shot glass and wait to be humiliated.

She steps to the throw line. After her, ton 80, which is how the dart community refers to triple twenties—the highest score possible in one turn—she has one hundred and twenty-one points left to get to zero. She raises a dart and it floats straight to the target. Another triple twenty. I rock back on my feet as she throws the next dart and hits the same spot.

Fuck me. Her score is down to one. All she needs is …

She tosses the dart. It sails through the air, and the tip buries on a single one.

Damn, but that's some serious skill.

She doesn't even look at me as she retrieves her darts. At the board, while she's pulling them out, that pretty brunette steps to her side. My girl says something to her Latina friend, who turns and looks at me with an eager gleam in her eyes.

I refill the shots and wait.

My girl returns to me. I hand her the shot.

"Very well played."

"Thank you." She taps her glass against mine. "I believe you owe me a piece of clothing." Her gaze flicks down to my pants.

No way am I removing those. Watching her dominate me in a game of darts is fucking hot. Hard and aching doesn't begin to describe my current state, but I'm no longer a schoolboy with zero control over my body.

I reach down to grab the bottom of my shirt, but then I stop. "You know, I think the winner should have the pleasure."

Her gasp brings a smirk to my face.

In the prime of my life, I'm also in peak physical condition, and I delight in the way her greedy gaze eats me up.

I love it even more when she doesn't hesitate. Her delicate fingers grasp the bottom of my shirt and she slowly lifts the fabric.

She pauses when my abs are revealed. Forget the six-pack. I'm packing eight. Her eyes widen. My abs are cut and defined. Biting at her lower lip, she lifts my shirt to my chest, exposing my pecs. I give a little pop of the muscle, showing off, which makes her jump.

A low rumble vibrates in the back of my throat as she turns her attention up to glare at me.

"That's right, pumpkin, my eyes are up here, but I don't mind if you need to look. I plan on eating you up when I get you alone later tonight."

From her gasp, she guesses correctly at what I mean by *eating her up*.

I'm too tall for her to lift the shirt over my head. Bending down, I shrug my arms through the arm holes and pull the rest of the shirt off my body. She grasps it in her hands, lifting it shamelessly to her nose. With her eyes on me, she takes a long, slow inhale while my dick responds with a jerk and a kick.

I think she's done, but then her gaze drops to my waist. I know what she sees. In addition to a rock-hard eight-pack, deep V grooves angle down and disappear beneath the waistband of my pants. I bet she's mentally tracing a path down, wondering what I'm packing beneath my pants.

She'll know soon enough. I have every intention of shoving my cock past her pertinent, ruby-red lips until she swallows me whole. Yes, there will be payback for this silly game of darts.

I toss back my shot and take the darts. As the loser of the previous round, I'll go first. I won't win, but I'll be damned if I go down like a total loser. She's going to have to work to win this game.

The dart sails into the air and hits the triple twenty. I'm good with darts. Some would say I'm damn good. I loft the second dart into the air, scoring another triple twenty. Turning around, I take in my prize for the night.

She's a knockout in that damn dress. I'm almost tempted to lose on purpose, just to hurry things along. But if I manage to win this round, will she take off that dress? In a crowded bar?

No way in hell will I allow that.

She's mine, and that means nobody gets to see her except me.

But it doesn't mean I don't want to know if she'll follow

through. Not that I'm going to throw this round. I'm far too competitive for that.

My third dart flies directly to its target, yielding me a ton 80 for my first round.

"Nicely done." She inclines her head and waits for me to retrieve the darts.

As I walk to the board, every female eyes my bare chest.

That's okay, ladies. Get your fill. This is as close as you're going to get.

I probably shouldn't have let that thought run through my head. Just like the last round, my golden-eyed beauty wipes me on the mat.

She matches my ton 80. I embarrass myself with my next set, and she closes out the second round with another set of double twenties and a one.

Game. Set. I lose.

Biting her lower lip, she glides toward me. The hairs on the back of my neck lift, knowing I'm in trouble.

"Do you remember the rules, Knox?" I love the way my name rolls off her tongue and hate she has yet to gift me with hers.

"I do." Eagerly, I watch as her hands go to the belt at my waist.

"That's good." She turns her neck and speaks to the crowd. "As promised ladies, the shots are on me." Her attention shifts back to me. Eyes shining in victory, she looks me square in the eye. "Or, I should say, they're on him." She makes quick work of my belt as nearly every female in the room rushes the bar.

"What the hell?" I grip her wrist, stopping her from unzipping my fly.

"We did say winner takes all. Whatever they want?" Her left eyebrow arches. It's seductive as hell.

"And what is that?" I glance nervously over to the bar where women are lining up.

Liam and Wolfe wander over, absent their females.

"What's going on, brother?" Liam's attention shifts from me to the bar. He's not the only man in the place eyeing the line of eager women.

"Can't say that I know." I turn my attention back to the woman standing in front of me. "Care to explain?"

"Oh, definitely, but first, let's get these off."

"Damn!" Wolfe's whistle pierces the air. The boisterous noise in the bar lessens for a split second but then roars back to life. "Why is she taking off your pants?"

"Because your friend made a bet and lost." She looks up at me. "Are you going to strip? Or, are you going to run out on our little bet?"

"What's your name?" No way in hell am I letting a woman strip me down to my boxers if I don't know her name.

She leans forward until the tip of her nose barely touches my chest. Looking up at me through her lashes, I can't help the sudden jolt of electricity shooting through my body. The tip of her tongue pushes out from her ruby-red lips and she licks me from my chest all the way to the hollow of my throat.

A cheer goes out. It's the women, hooting and hollering and banging on the bar. They stomp their feet and begin to shout.

"Body shot."

"Body Shot."

"BODY SHOT!"

Their shouts evolve into a raucous mixture of whistles, stomping, and hands pounding on the bar.

My sultry siren kisses the hollow of my throat.

"My name is Lily." Distracted by her slow, agonizing lick up my body, I miss the moment when she jerks her hand free. "And you're going to let all those women take a body shot off of you."

Before I know what's happening, she yanks my pants down to my thighs, exposing me to the entire bar. Another roar comes from the women.

What the ever-loving fuck?

Wolfe looks at Liam. They stare at each other, then burst out in laughter. And we're not talking a little *Ha ha ha*. Wolfe doubles over, holding his gut. Liam points to me, wheezing as he tries to catch his breath. I can't even understand whatever it is he's trying to say.

What I do know is neither of the fuckers are helping me out.

I glance down at Lily, damn, but I love that name, as she goes to her knees. The look on her face is feisty as shit. She played me all right. She played me good.

That's okay. As she helps me with my boots, I reach down and tilt her face until she looks at me. "Lily, you look damn good on your knees."

Her eyes widen in shock, then a flush heats her skin, turning her cheeks the prettiest shade of pink.

I kick off my last boot and she strips me of my pants. In socks and a pair of black boxer briefs, I lift out my hands and turn in a slow circle for my waiting fans. When I look down on her, she licks her lips and nods vigorously.

"Body shots?" I ask.

"And I get to pour." She licks her lips again.

"Just remember, payback's a bitch."

I can't wait to make her pay.

FOUR

Lily

OKAY, MAYBE IT WASN'T FAIR TO CHALLENGE WILDER TO A GAME OF darts, but I couldn't help myself. Me and darts, we have a long, fruitful history. I'll just leave it at that.

Wilder gets one giant nod for keeping his word. He helps me to my feet and our bodies instantly gravitate toward the other. There's no other way to explain it other than that.

Simply put, we fit.

He brushes his lips across my forehead, soft, gentle, and devastating. My heart kicks into high gear, wondering what it's going to feel like when those lips kiss me in other places as well.

What I will say is this. Lust aside, as much as I ache for him right now, that gentle, feather-light kiss didn't touch just my skin.

It delved deep to brush against my soul.

And that's what tells me I'm in serious trouble.

I know more about him than I should. According to the DEA, which I work for, he's on the other side of the law. My professionalism totally goes out the window the moment he touches me, caressing my skin, holding me tight, and making me believe there's more to him than what I've read in his dossier.

There's a connection between us. It's visceral. Raw.

Overwhelming. And I regret my decision to have a bit of fun with him right about now. I want this man. Which means I'm not eager to share him with the greedy bitches my partner, and best friend in the whole world, Jinx, whipped into a frenzy during that game of darts.

They line up beside the bar, eager for a taste of him.

"You sure this is what you want?" The rumble of his voice settles deep inside of me. "Because I'm thinking you want something else."

He's not wrong about that, but I'm committed now.

"A bet's a bet." I swallow back my regret and give him a little push toward the bar. "Up on the bar."

The women cheer as Wilder swaggers over to the bar. I have to give him credit. He's comfortable in his body, and I swear he eats up all the leering stares from the ladies.

"Here?" He heads to the middle of the bar, where the women pull back the barstools.

"That works." I bite my lower lip, knowing I'm going to regret this.

Wilder moves with sinuous grace as he presses his hands on top of the bar and ever so slowly lifts himself up. Talk about a sexy-assin display of strength. With his eyes on me, he tucks his legs, knees to chest, and pivots until he's sideways.

My friend, Callie, who's bartending tonight, rings a bell. A hush settles over the crowd. Wilder remains sitting, knees drawn to his chest, arms wrapped around them, as Callie calls out.

"All right, all right, all right. Tonight, the ladies are having a bit of fun!" Cheers break out, deafening in intensity, but somehow Callie speaks over the crowd. "Lily?" She calls out to me. "You want to show the ladies how it's done?"

This is the one thing I insisted on. I will be the first to lick the perfection of Wilder's abs and chest.

"Let's do this." I lift my hand over my head as the crowd goes wild.

Like Wilder, I drag out the moment. He sauntered over to the bar, dressed in nothing but black boxer briefs and a pair of black socks. I let him get an eyeful of me in this knockout dress, and boy does he eat me up with his stormy gaze. When I get to him, I flash a grin.

"Have you ever done a body shot?"

My fingers tap the surface of the bar. I want to run them over the entirety of his body, but I keep my hands to myself. Not because it's what I want, but because I don't want any of the eager beavers lined up to think they can touch what's mine.

"I've done plenty, pumpkin, but never from this side of things." His gaze sparks with mirth. At least he's being a good sport about this, but there's a promise of payback simmering in his gaze.

Something tells me Wilder gives as good as he gets. This should make me wary, but I'm excited by the prospect of whatever he comes up with.

"We're doing tequila shots," Callie calls out to the ladies, going over the rules. "Lick, suck, squeeze. You know what to do. And remember ladies, you can't use your hands. No touching!"

"You know I'm going to make you pay for this?" His eyes spark with banked heat.

"I look forward to it."

With that said, Wilder lies back on the bar. All signs of his previous arousal are gone, and I don't know whether to take that as a personal affront or not. Knowing a few dozen women are about to be licking his body, I decide I don't care.

"You ready?" Callie stands on the other side of the bar. She's got a bottle of tequila, a tub of cut limes, and a shaker of salt. The question's for Wilder, not me, but I answer Callie's question.

"Yeah."

A total showoff, which is why Callie does so well with her bar, she makes the whole thing a production. Announcing each and every step along the way.

My attention shifts to Wilder and the simmering heat in his eyes. He makes a guttural sound, nearly below the threshold of my hearing, as Callie sprinkles salt just below his navel. She pours the tequila in his belly button, then places a lime on his chest.

"Come on ladies! Let's hear you roar!" Callie gets the ladies going as my gaze connects with Wilder. With him watching my every move, I gather my long hair to the side and bend to his waist.

Not shy about much really, I place the tip of my tongue just barely above the waistband of his briefs. Acutely aware of what he's packing beneath those shorts, I make a show of slowly licking my way toward his belly button.

I should lick quickly, then reposition to suck the tequila, but I don't. I take my time, loving the way his body twitches. My hands go nowhere near him, even if all I can think about is how much I need to touch and explore every dip and valley of his exquisitely sculpted body.

At his navel, I cover the flat expanse with my mouth and suck slow and seductively. The tip of my tongue licks and flicks, showing him what he can expect later when I do go to my knees before him.

Wilder holds completely still as I suck and swallow. When I lift my head to take the lime off his chest, he blocks me. With a wicked grin, Wilder places the lime in his mouth. He threads his fingers together and places them under his head as those stormy eyes of his dare me to take the lime from his mouth.

Not one to back away from a challenge, I lean down and wrap my lips around the lime. He grasps the sour fruit with his lips, refusing to give it to me. He subtly shifts. Next thing I know, he grasps the back of my head and delivers the most sublimely cruel and delicious kiss I've ever experienced.

This is one bet I'm going to regret because there's a long line of women behind me, and I don't want any of them touching him.

A deep, guttural moan sounds in the back of his throat as he assaults my mouth. The lime falls out as he thrusts his tongue, punishing me with the promise of more. I thought I got one up on him, but all this has done is make me need him more.

But all good things come to an end.

Wilder releases me, and with that, my turn comes to an end. Polite, but insistent, the next woman in line is barely legal. I relinquish my hold on Wilder as Callie takes a wet towel to wipe his chest and abdomen.

At least, this part will be mine. While the next in line moves into position, I join Callie behind the bar. She sprinkles salt, pours tequila, and places a lime on Wilder's chest. As the woman bends down for a tentative lick, Wilder turns his angry gaze toward me.

You will pay for this. He mouths the words. No doubt he will try, but I'm rethinking this whole idea of getting close to my quarry.

The girl finishes with the lime. I take the rag and wipe him down. The muscles of his body ripple at my touch but then settle when the next woman steps up.

For the next fifteen minutes, Callie shakes and pours while I run that rag over his body. It's not hygienic, though nobody but me cares.

A damn good sport, Wilder eats up the attention, laughing with the bold ones, encouraging the shy ones, all the while his gaze heats and promises retribution when he turns it on me.

Once the last woman gets her lick of salt and sucks from his navel, I soap up the rag to wipe all trace of those women from his body. The muscles of his abs tense as I first wash, then dry, his body. Once I'm nearly done, he crooks his finger, demanding I come close.

Now that the spectacle is done, the bar jumps right back into chaos and frenzy, leaving the two of us alone.

I open my mouth, wanting to tell him what a great sport he was, but Wilder gives a sharp shake of his head. My lips press together as I lean down.

A low growl rumbles in his throat as he grabs my hair, yanking me closer. With his lips on my earlobe, he issues his command.

"You. Me. Bathroom. Now."

His words make me gulp. I should refuse. Instead, I step away after he releases my hair. I'm not fucking him in the skanky bathroom. Instead, I do the unthinkable.

His buddies, men I don't know, laugh as Wilder jumps down from the bar. One of them holds Wilder's clothes, while the other clutches the laces of his boots. Wilder snatches his things from the men. His hard gaze follows me as I head to the back of the bar.

With him on my heels, my body burns, my skin tightens, and my entire being aches to feel his hard, ripped physique moving over me, dominating me. Not to mention, I'm acutely fascinated by what he's packing beneath those briefs.

I pause at the door leading to my apartment upstairs. I live above Callie's Bar, and for the very first time in my life, I'm inviting a man into my most private space.

This is happening. I'm both exceptionally aroused and terrified.

FIVE

Knox

GETTING MAULED BY A FEW DOZEN WOMEN ISN'T THE WORST WAY TO spend an evening. Enduring Lily's hands on me in between each shot, however, is nothing short of torture. I employ every trick in the book to keep from getting hard, and barely keep myself in check.

My balls are bluer than blue, and my cock is one hungry fucker. It's pissed off because I didn't let him play.

Hey, I'm not the first man in the history of man to refer to his dick as if it's another person. I swear, I've done some really dumb things because of him. Yeah, I'm talking about my dick.

As for Lily? She's going down.

Now that the entire bar has a fair idea what I'm packing—boxer briefs only hide so much, and I'm the kind of guy who runs on the larger side of things—Lily is going to get one hell of a lesson in payback.

I'm half surprised she didn't say no when I ordered her to the bathroom.

However, she doesn't head to the seedy bathroom. She goes to a door at the back of the bar, hesitates for a second, then opens it and steps through.

Liam and Wolfe help me down from the bar, and by helping, I mean laughing their asses off.

"Fuck if that's not going down in the book." Liam slaps his thigh. "I took lots of pictures."

"Asshole." I take the ribbing. If I don't, it'll only get worse. Once this gets back to the rest of the guys, I'm never living it down.

Liam digs into his back pocket and pulls out a raggedy button. He slaps it against Wolfe's chest.

The button thing came about through my best bud, and Alpha team leader, Max. He let us all think he had a gambling addiction. Since we bet on pretty much everything, instead of using money, we trade these stupid buttons.

After that last mission, I learned the truth about Max and gambling. It's not something I expected, and I got to see him work a poker table like the goddamn pro he is.

"Do I even want to know what the bet was?" I turn to Wolfe, arching a brow.

Liam snickers and gives me his back. Wolfe stares at my crotch and a smirk fills his face.

"Liam didn't think you'd keep that monster dick of yours contained. I told him you were too busy plotting the demise of Miss Red Dress to get hard."

"Fuckers." I grab my clothes out of his hands and take my boots from Liam. At least they kept track of those for me. "Don't wait for me."

"Have fun!" Wolfe calls out as I leave them behind. No doubt they'll have fun tonight, just as I, myself, am planning on doing.

I check the pockets of my pants, making sure the condoms I slipped inside didn't fall out. No worries. I'm good. Then, with all the dignity I can muster, I march after Lily, in black boxer briefs and black socks, ignoring the way my socks stick to the tacky floor.

There are stairs behind the door, heading up, but no Lily. Interested, I climb the narrow wooden staircase, which creaks as I ascend. When I come to the landing, there are two doors. One's painted a garish red with gold trim. The other's a bright, sunny yellow with blue trim.

Since the red door is ajar, I turn toward it. No need to knock. I'm expected. A small apartment, it's neat, tidy, and decorated in the spirit of New Orleans. Bright colors pop and every corner holds something interesting, but I have eyes for only one thing.

And she's sitting at a small bistro table on the balcony with a bottle of whiskey in her hand.

"Wanna drink?" Her sultry voice calls to me, and I don't hesitate.

"It's a start. What're you pouring?" So glad it's not that cheap-ass tequila. My boxers are soaked in the offensive liquid.

"Pappy Van Winkle, but I've got a whole bar downstairs. Tell me what you want, and I'll get it."

"I want you." I close the distance, taking my time. We have all evening, and there's no reason to rush. "And there's no way I'm letting you out of my sight."

"I'm yours."

"You sure about that?"

"You were a good sport down there. Such a thing deserves a reward."

"Interesting."

"How's that?"

"I wasn't considering this a reward-type scenario."

"You weren't?" Her brow arches. "What were you thinking?"

"Punishment." The word comes out as a growl and she flinches just as I expect.

Her eyes widen and there's no mistaking that hitch of breath. She's nervous but trying to play it cool.

The bistro table, barely big enough for one, let alone two, sits on the balcony overlooking the street below. The chairs are half a size too small, but I manage to fold my large frame into the chair sitting opposite her.

At least it's a warm, sultry night. From up here, the stench of the street isn't as profound, and the view of the crowd is definitely worth it.

"Punishment?" Her lids flicker, either from nervousness or second-guessing inviting me up here.

"You disagree?"

She cants her head to the side, exposing the smooth expanse of her neck. The taste of her still lingers on my tongue, but I'm not ready to give her what she wants. I'm going to make her beg.

"I remember winning fair and square." She turns the bottle toward me. "On the rocks or straight up?"

"Straight up will do." Those few shots we had while playing darts were like water, and they're completely out of my system. The burn of a good whiskey sounds just right.

She pours two fingers into two whiskey glasses then looks at me. Our gazes collide, connect, and intertwine. That odd electricity is back, buzzing in the space between us.

"Do you feel it yet?" Tempted to slug back the amber liquid, I take a sip instead. The whiskey burns at first, but then the subtle taste of it fills my mouth. It's a damn good whiskey. When she doesn't answer, I open my eyes. "Didn't you get enough?"

"What?"

"You're staring."

"How do you do it?" Her head tilts to the side again as she studies me.

"Do what?"

"You're so …" She makes a vague gesture with her hand.

"So, what?"

"Secure in your skin."

"I know what I look like if that's what you mean. Women have been dropping their panties around me since my voice deepened and I grew my first chest hair. And for the record, I'm not the only one. You certainly know how to draw attention to yourself."

"You're confident, but not cocky."

"I believe you called me a cocksure asshole downstairs."

"Did I?" She bats her lashes.

Why is that sexy as fuck? I swear, I'm a deranged lunatic around this chick.

Honestly, I can't remember what she said. I look down at my dark socks and kick out my foot.

"What do you think about my socks?" I wriggle my toes and love the way she laughs at the hole in my sock. My big toe sticks out like a sore thumb.

"Definitely something." She turns her attention back to my face. "Not sexy."

"For the record, I usually don't keep my socks on when I strip for a lady."

"A lady?"

"Does *lady* offend you?"

"No." She takes another swig of her drink. "For the record, you're probably the first person to ever call me a lady." Another sip. She does that when she's nervous.

I remember enough about what Max taught me when it comes to reading people. This is why I'm not buried balls deep inside of her yet. She intrigues me. Which means I'm interested in a whole lot more than a meaningless fuck.

"Is that so?"

"Or pumpkin." She looks over the rim of the glass. "What's up with that?"

"I like it." I wink at her and grace her with the most honest smile she'll ever get out of me. "Pumpkin."

She rolls her eyes. "And what should I call you?"

"Knox works for me."

"Knox—such an unusual name."

"Is it?" My name is ordinary. There's nothing interesting about it.

"So, what brings you to New Orleans?" She leans forward, engaging in conversation as if we're here to get to know one another.

We're not.

We're here to fuck.

"Who says I'm visiting?" Answering her questions is not why I'm here.

"Do you live here?" She's persistent. For a second, I wonder if she's really interested in the whole, torrid backstory.

"How is that relevant?" Again, I challenge her.

"Maybe I want to know what my chances are of running into

you again after tonight?"

"Who says I'm staying just the one night?" I'll only be here until dawn, but chicks like to think they're special. As if they have that magical pussy that will stop a man in his tracks.

The reality is cruel and ugly. Men want only one thing, and I'm no different from any of the others who came before.

"Careful, Knox. My hospitality only goes so far." She issues a warning, but there's hesitation. She wants the happily ever after, the whole kit and caboodle, even if she doesn't believe in it herself.

I get that. Her expressions aren't hard to read. This woman's been hurt. Probably by a man just like me. That should make me say my farewells.

If I had an ounce of compassion, I would leave right now. But I'm a hungry fucker—as in *I need to fuck*—and let's not forget, she deserves to suffer for what she did to me.

Compassion only goes so far.

"Is that so? I could leave." No way in hell am I leaving.

"Just curious." She shrugs.

"About?"

"Why are you here? After what I did ..." She shakes her head. "Why?"

"You're seriously asking me that? We both know why I'm here."

"Do we?"

"You're the one who invited me up here. I was good to fuck you in the bathroom. Slip inside. Rut and be done. But you invited me into your home." I glance around the small apartment. "You want me in your bed. More than a quick fuck and be done. Why is that? We could've fucked in the bathroom, or the alley, and gone on with our lives. But you invited me up here."

"Don't get too comfortable."

"Why not?"

"I can kick you out anytime."

"You won't."

Blowing out my breath, I take a look at a city bursting with excitement. The whole town is one big party, and I'm a mess. No way am I twisting the sheets covered in stale tequila, salt, and the rest. I need to wash all those women off my body before I claim the one I really want.

When I suddenly stand, Lily's eyes widen.

"Are you leaving?"

"No, pumpkin. I'm taking a shower."

"I didn't say you could …"

"Don't remember asking permission." I stroll inside her apartment like I own the place and head to the bathroom.

Much larger than I expect, there's no tub. Which is fine. I hate baths. There's an oversized shower with glass doors. As I strip out of my briefs, I wonder what she'll do next.

It's not every day I choose a shower over sex, but this evening is different from normal in too many ways.

The water heats up while I reach down and fist my cock. The demands of my body will be met, but first, I need to rinse off the residue of the bar and the dozens of women who tasted me.

I bet Liam snapped a bunch of pictures. He'll leverage the shit out of them, giving me grief the rest of our stay.

Once a bit of steam builds, I step inside the shower and waste no time lathering up.

No Lily.

I'm a bit surprised. She seemed bolder than this. Thinking about her brings about natural reactions.

Blood races to my cock, lengthening and hardening it as my desire builds. Thoughts of bending Lily over her bed, thrusting into her with punishing force, and taking what I want, are delicious things.

My head tips back as my balls draw up. A tingling of sensation shoots through my body, coiling at the base of my spine. I'm fucking ready to explode.

But then the air shifts and I'm no longer alone. Turning to face the door, nothing but glass separates me from Lily's wide-eyed stare.

"Like what you see?"

I'm pretty shameless when it comes to sex. Nothing surprises me. I'm not afraid to jerk off where a woman can see. In fact, I find it sexy as fuck to watch their eyes dilate and their jaws drop, eager to suck me down and swallow me whole.

Building anticipation is what does it for me.

The filthier the sex, the better.

"I'm wondering how it's going to fit."

"In your mouth or in your pussy?" The corner of my mouth lifts in a smirk. "I'm pretty damn close. You going to stand there and watch? Or are you going to help me take care of this?"

"Is that what you like? Ordering women around during sex?"

"That depends. Does that shit turn you on? If not, my hand does the trick, and I don't mind if you watch. But I'm thinking about that mouth of yours."

Does the dominant shit turn her on? My cock twitches in anticipation.

She makes no move to join me. Not as bold as I thought, that's okay. Her hesitation isn't a hard no.

"You have two choices, pumpkin." She turns her wide-eyed stare to my engorged cock. "Take the dress off, or get it wet. Either way, you're going to your knees."

"Is that an order?" Her eyebrow tics up.

"Take off the damn dress." Fuck me, but she's hot as sin. Talk about a living fantasy; she's begging for it.

"Or, what?" Her haughty attitude persists, but that's okay.

I release my cock and slide open the shower door. As her eyes widen, I step out, dripping water all over the floor. Closing the distance between us, my breath hitches as that scathing electricity returns.

I close the distance until we're toe-to-toe and chest-to-chest. My hand grips her shock-blonde hair as I lean down. We collide in a clashing of mouths and a tangling of tongues. Molten hot desire consumes us, an evening's worth of desire let loose all at once.

She tries to wrap her hands around me, but I growl and grab first one wrist and then the other. Lifting them over her head, I dip down until we're eye-to-eye.

"Take off the damn dress." I wait for her reaction. I'll either walk out of here with balls bluer than blue, or I'll find heaven in her hands, her mouth, and her glorious pussy.

"Make me." She thrusts her chest toward me, demanding, challenging, and hotter than fuck.

I waste no time. Leaning in, I devour her mouth. One hand binds both her wrists. She's so fucking small compared to me. Delicate. Frail. Yet, fucking fierce. It's an intoxicating combination.

I control her head with my other hand. My fingers twine in her hair, pulling, grappling, guiding her where I want. My body burns, tightening with desire, making it damn hard to control myself, but I do.

I back her against the wall, pressing my naked body against hers. She doesn't resist, submitting to my demands as I grind my body against hers, letting her feel every inch of my engorged cock.

Releasing her hair, I yank at the strap over her left shoulder. She doesn't cry out. Doesn't get pissed. Which gives me the green light I need. Growling, I yank at the strap over her right shoulder.

That's all that holds the dress in place. My arm wraps around her waist as I pull her against me.

"You feel that?" I grind my cock against her belly. "I'm going to feed you my cock, and what are you going to do?" I pull back, giving her a moment to breathe. Giving her one last chance to back away and end this.

Her heaving breasts tell a different story. She's turned the fuck on, which only fuels my desire. I yank the fabric of her dress, pulling it down to her waist. Her breasts, now exposed, rub against my chest.

Tight nipples. Strangled breaths. We grind against each other, mindless with need. I cup her breast, showing no tenderness until her breaths hitch in pain.

"You're going to let me feed you my cock, aren't you?"

"Yes." Her lids flutter and her cheeks pink with the flush of her arousal.

"That's right. You like it hard, don't you?"

"And fast." The words tumble from her lips. She looks up at me. "Make me, Knox. No mercy."

"Fuck …" I nearly come right there.

Instead, I pinch her nipple until she lifts on tiptoe and cries out in pain. Releasing her, I allow my hands to fully explore her glorious tits. I palm them. Squeeze them. I torture her nipples, pinching and squeezing until she pants.

The flare of her arousal floods the room. An intoxicating scent I'll never forget.

Lily doesn't just want it hard and fast. She wants domination and control. No problem. I'm versatile when it comes to sex.

I take a step back, giving her room, then I place both my hands on her shoulders. Her eyes widen as she looks up at me.

I say nothing as I put pressure on her shoulders, forcing her to her knees. She resists at first. It's part of the game and her way of testing me. If I don't pass, none of the rest of this happens. But I want to fuck Lily. I want it with undeniable desperation. It's not something I fully understand. Except, I know this is a pivotal turning point.

I force her to her knees, then fist my cock.

Staring down at her, I harden my voice.

"Condom."

I'd use one of mine, but my pants are in the other room. Her eyes flick to the counter beside me. There's nothing on top of the counter, so I yank on the top drawer.

Pay dirt.

A rip and a slide.

While she looks up at me, I sheath myself with the condom, then I brush the tip of my cock against her lips.

"Open. Swallow me whole."

Defiance flares in her eyes, but I push through her bravado. Lily doesn't want me to stop. She needs me to push. I understand this on a gut level.

When she resists, I fist her hair, controlling her head. I place the flare of my cock at her lips, but that is as far as I will push.

All is fun in love and war, but there are some lines I refuse to cross. This needs to be consensual or I'm done and out. To my utmost delight, Lily's shoulders slump in mock surrender. Her mouth parts and her luscious lips take me in.

The moment her lips wrap around me, my entire body shakes. I nearly shoot my load right there. More than a little wound up, I'm primed and eager for release.

But this is where control yields great reward.

I push past Lily's lips, forcing her to take me inch-by-inch. Her hands grip my thighs, part resistance, part surrender.

My fingers curl in her hair, showing her I'm not afraid to fully control this situation. I push in and close my eyes as the heat of her mouth envelopes me.

Fuck, but I've found Heaven.

She presses against my thighs, a signal I pay attention to, acutely aware of her reactions. Slowly, I draw out until the tip is right at her lips. I grasp her hair and, with greater pressure, delve forward, testing her response as I push farther, deeper, harder, inside her mouth.

Lily rewards me with a slow roll of her tongue. She laves me, licks along my length. My control—my dominance—is only for show.

Lily takes over, sucking my cock like a pro. It's all I can do to hold on and sink into the sensations she draws from my body.

But there's only so much a man can handle, and there's no way I'm coming in her mouth. I pull her mouth off my cock and take a step back.

"You're mine now." The growl comes from somewhere deep inside of me. It's primal. I'm not interested in fucking Lily. Oh no. My need is to rut and to claim. To mark her forever.

As mine.

I take a moment to stare down at her. We share a look. A moment passes. She breathes in. I breathe out. It happens again.

Me standing over her.

Her kneeling before me.

It's intoxicating.

Any restraint left within me snaps.

I yank her to her feet, where we collide against one another.

Mouths press together. Teeth clash. Tongues grapple, battling for control. We're a mess of arms and legs. Hands exploring and seeking everywhere at once.

I lift Lily into the air. Her legs wrap around my waist. Our gazes collide, and she gives the slightest nod.

The head of my cock rubs against her inner thigh. It takes only a slight adjustment and I notch the tip at the entrance to her pussy.

"Hard and fast?" This is her last chance to refuse.

Her entire body shakes. She bites her lower lip and closes her eyes. Her chin trembles as she once again nods. That's all the invitation I need.

My hips thrust. I jerk her down on my cock. A low groan escapes me, and a hiss of pain comes from her. I stop, not wanting to hurt her, but Lily's fingers dig into my shoulders. Her golden eyes open, and when she looks at me, all I see is molten heat simmering there.

"Make me burn." Her pussy throbs around my dick, convulsing and flooding with arousal. "Punish me."

Fuck me. It's not possible, but more blood rushes to my cock, turning it hard as steel. I can definitely make her burn. As for punishment? She'll be bruised and aching by the time I'm done.

Two steps and I press her back to the wall. I'm pretty damn strong and can fuck her standing, but to do this right, I need help from the wall.

Her legs clamp around my hips as I lean in.

Then I move. Hard and fast, I plunge into her. My fingers dig deep, grabbing her ass. My hips slam forward as I fuck her against that wall.

Her body amazes me. Every throbbing invitation of her pussy excites me, drives me, and makes it damn hard to hold back my release.

But she wants me to punish her, and I know only one way to do that, which will please us both.

SIX

Lily

The burning demands of my body make me bolder than I should be. Wilder is the enemy, but damn if he doesn't know how to fuck.

My back scrapes against the wall as he ruts and fucks. A flood of arousal fills me, burning, aching, pulsating, and driving me insane. I grip his shoulders, barely hanging on. Not that I need to. Wilder is fully in control.

My heart seizes. It stops for a second, then it's off and racing again, sending pleasure flowing through my body. He drives into me. Long and thick, the intrusion burns as my body accommodates to his impressive size.

He attacks, relentless in his need as my pussy throbs and contracts around his shaft. Impossible to resist, my hands wander where they will, admiring his ripped physique. My fingers trace out the sculpted planes of his muscles as I cry out with each agonizing thrust.

"I'm close."

My body stretches around the invasion as his cock fills me and sends sparks of sensation rioting through my body. My legs shake as another moan escapes me. I tip my head forward, burying it in the crook of his neck as he slams me against the wall and sinks deep.

Squirming in his grip, I need more, and I'm not afraid to ask for it. Not much, but more.

"Harder. I want to feel you. Make it hurt."

His breathing slows, as do his thrusts. Wilder stops and presses a hand against the wall beside my head. Deep breaths pulse out of him as I squirm on his dick.

"Don't stop. I'm almost there." I tremble, right on the cusp of flying over the edge.

When I look into his eyes, there's heat, desire, and raw lust. When I look at his face, I stumble across a nefarious smile.

"Do you know what's the best thing about payback?" The glint in his eyes gives me pause.

"I don't care about that. Fuck me. Fuck me until I scream."

"Oh, I have every intention of fucking you." His hips do this amazing figure-eight roll, sliding his cock slowly in and out, pressing on all the right nerves.

A gasp escapes me. But it's not enough. I need more. Then he does the unthinkable.

Wilder pulls out.

"No!" I let out an ear-piercing shriek. "What are you doing?"

He steps back, lifts my legs off his hips, then settles my feet on the ground.

"Punishing you."

"What?" I mean, that's hot, but *what the fuck?* "I was almost there."

"I know." He winks at me. "And you'll be *almost there* all night long."

"You've got to be fucking kidding me?"

"I'll be fucking. That's for damn sure, but I'm not kidding around."

I grab his cock. My hand slips on my juices as I grip and squeeze, sliding my hand all the way to the base of his shaft before spiraling back up again.

"Tell me you don't want this." Anger edges my tone.

"Anytime your hand is on my dick, you can one hundred percent guarantee I want it there." He grips my wrist, halting the glide of my hand. "Now, turn the fuck around."

"Wha …"

"Hands on the wall." He slaps my ass and spins me around. Nudging just the tip at my opening, Wilder rams home, sinking into me from behind.

He wraps his hand in my hair as he thrusts hard and fast. Yanking my head back, his lips lock on mine. He fucks my mouth the way he fucks my body.

Brutal. Raw. Unhinged.

This is the most deliciously dirty sex I've had in the longest time.

My release builds, climbing higher as my breaths falter and hitch. My body shakes as I cry out.

"Yes. Yes. Almost …"

He pulls out again and takes a step back. Power and fury swirl in his eyes. I glance down. His cock is even more engorged than before, purple and angry, swollen and divine.

My orgasm escapes me for the second time.

"Why did you stop?" Brows pinched together, I don't get what he's doing.

He's close. Maybe closer than me, and his breathing is definitely ragged and barely contained. Wilder points to the floor.

"On your knees." He fists the base of his cock and controls his breathing. When I don't respond, he yanks me from the wall and points to the floor. "Don't test me."

"We don't have to try out every position the first time. We have all night."

"You can either do as I say, when I say, or not." He points to the ground. "But the only way you're getting relief is when I allow it."

It takes a second, but then I get it.

Holy hell, do I get it.

My heart kicks into high gear as a rush of adrenaline and heat runs through me.

Damn, that's hot as fuck. I almost came right there.

I go to my knees, facing him, thinking he wants my lips on him, but Wilder spins his finger in the air, telling me to turn around.

If I'm this close to coming, how is he holding off his release? Then I see it. The clenching of his jaw. The way his lips purse together as he tugs in a breath. The man is the epitome of control, not just of me, but of himself.

I turn around and bend down. On my hands and knees, I tremble, waiting for what comes next. Wilder takes his time, but he settles on his knees and grabs my hips.

"How many women did you let touch me?"

"Huh?" I wiggle my ass. If I position myself just right …

The air whistles as his hand comes down hard on my ass. Pain explodes on my backside, followed by an intense burn. A shriek rips from my lungs.

"How many?" he demands an answer.

"What the fuck?" I twist to look at him and gulp when I see the expression on his face.

"How many women did you let lick me?" His hand comes down again.

Crack!

Fire burns in my ass as the pain delves deep. I try to yank away, but he grips my hips holding me still.

"How many?" The timbre of his voice changes. No longer sultry, it's hard and unforgiving, demanding and commanding. It's sexy as fuck.

A moan of desire escapes me, and with it, another rush of heat flows through my body. My legs quiver and shake. Damn, but if I'm not turned on.

"I don't know."

Crack!

Another swat to my ass.

"I do." He rubs the burn, using his palm, which only makes me writhe shamelessly against his hand.

"Please just fuck me." I turn to look over my shoulder. The first thing my gaze trips on is his monster cock. I ache to feel him filling me again.

"Did you like watching those women touch me? Does that kind of thing turn you on?"

Crack!

"No!" I screech as the pain of the strike settles in and burns, but that's not all that burns. A lick of fire between my legs makes me catch my breath.

Wilder shoves a hand between my legs to stroke my clit. I shamelessly grind against him. Pleasure builds, my climax races toward me, but before I can fly over the edge, his finger disappears.

"Damn you." A whimper escapes me.

"Has it settled in yet?" Low and gruff, his words rumble in the air. "Have you figured out your punishment?"

"Yes." I hang my head in defeat. He's going to keep me on the edge, denying me release. "But that works two ways."

"I don't think you fully get it. I'm not denying myself anything." As if to prove his point, Wilder grips my hips. He pushes past my opening and rams his cock all the way in.

Hard. Fast.

Exquisitely perfect.

An excruciating wave of pleasure runs through me. It mixes and melds with the pain from the spanking, making me cry out.

Wilder presses down on my shoulders, forcing my face down to the floor, which changes the angle of my hips. Each time he slams in, he stimulates my g-spot.

Pleasure builds within me once again. Maybe if I don't let on, he won't deny me release? My skin tightens as sensation overwhelms me. Shimmers of pleasure spark and pulse. Moaning before him, I squirm, trying to get him to hit that spot again.

"Harder." I need more from him. More sensation. More pressure. More of him taking and claiming and driving me insane.

My fist pounds on the floor as the pressure builds. Every time he slams forward, I weep. Each time he pulls out, I swear.

And I demand more.

More power.

More strength.

More violence.

Wilder does all that and more. I'm right there again, needing just a little more. Wilder groans. His punishing thrusts turn erratic.

My release peaks and I ... Wilder pulls out, stealing my pleasure. I cry out. "You fucking asshole. I was right there."

He grips my hair and twists my head. His mouth crashes down on mine. It's violent, unrestrained, and wild as hell. He releases a flood of passion in that kiss. He also fists his dick, rocking in and out of his hand. His body quivers. It tenses. Then his release rushes through him.

Wilder removes the condom, ties it off, and strides into the other room while I collapse on the bathroom floor, but I don't stay there for long.

I rise to my feet and gather the scattered remnants of my dignity. I walk into the room and stand before him, naked, used, abused, and trembling from some of the best sex in my life. Well, best sex without an orgasm.

"You win."

He sits on the bed and arches a brow.

"Whatever you want, I'll do it."

He lifts his hand and twirls his finger in the air, telling me to turn around. I do exactly as he says. He grabs my hips and rubs over my aching backside.

"You're going to bruise."

"No shit. You weren't exactly easy."

"I'm not an easy man, and you said you wanted it hard and fast."

"I did, and I do, but I also want to come." I'm not against asking for what I want. Hell, I'm not against begging. My entire body buzzes with the need to come.

"Is that so?" He lies back on my bed. Fingers looped together, Wilder cradles the back of his head.

"Yes."

"Beg." He gives a little jerk of his head.

"You're a fucking bastard, you know that, don't you?"

"Yeah, but I fuck like a goddamn machine. So, what's it going to be, pumpkin? You going to beg for what you want, or are you going to stare at my dick for the rest of the night?"

His dick is a work of art. Spent, but still hard, it lies alongside his thigh. Red and engorged, it gives a little flick as I stare at it.

"Careful there, or I'll lose my restraint." A low chuckle rumbles in his chest.

"You called what happened in there *not* losing your restraint?" I point toward the bathroom.

"Pumpkin, we just met. I haven't begun to show you what it looks like when I let go."

"And what does that look like?"

"Don't get ahead of yourself. We still have your punishment to discuss." He stares at me with banked heat.

"If you think I'm going to let you spank me …"

"First off, that's not usually my cup of tea. Secondly, you liked it."

"I didn't like it."

"That's not what your body said."

"My body?"

"Pumpkin, you were wet as sin when I pushed back in."

I cross my arms over my chest. "I'm not going to drape myself over your lap and let you spank me."

"The spanking was just for fun."

"I thought that was the punishment?"

"It's not your punishment."

I breathe out a frustrated breath. "Are you going to fuck me or what?"

"I just fucked you."

"You know what I mean." A growl builds in the back of my throat.

"You mean, am I going to let you come?"

"Yes." I roll my eyes. I'd stamp my foot if I didn't think it would make me look petulant. "Are you going to let me come?"

"That depends."

Anger builds within me. "What do I have to do?"

"Now, that's a wonderful question." He gestures, pointing to his semi-flaccid cock. "Kneel."

"You can't just boss me around." I'll totally allow it because it's sexy as fuck. Besides, isn't sex supposed to be fun?

"Why not?"

"Because …"

"Pumpkin, you love it."

"Do not." I press my legs together as a pulse of pleasure runs through me.

"You get off on it." The timbre of his voice changes. "Remember, I can tell when you're lying." He pushes off the mattress until he's sitting again. "Suck me. Show me how much you want to come. Show me how sorry you are that you let all those other women touch me." He fists his cock as it lengthens and enlarges. "Or, do I need to take care of this myself while you watch?"

He'd do it too. I've never known a man to do that, and I hope he doesn't expect that of me. I'm pretty adventurous when it comes to sex, but that may be one of my limits.

Blowing out my breath, I cave. Gently, I lower myself to my knees, kneeling at the foot of my bed. I sweep my hair off my shoulders and rock back on my heels.

"Will this make up for earlier?"

He gives a slow shake of his head. "Pumpkin, I've barely begun."

"I hate you."

"Do you want me to leave?"

And miss out on the best sex I've ever had?

"No."

He shifts his position, moving closer to the edge of the bed.

"Good." His gaze flicks down to his dick, then back to me. The message couldn't be clearer.

A frustrated groan escapes me as I lean forward to take him in my mouth. We have all night. Wilder may take advantage of the situation, but he doesn't seem like the kind of man to leave a woman hanging.

A hiss escapes him as my lips close around his impressive equipment—equipment I hope he'll soon use on me to bring about an orgasm I desperately need.

But Wilder keeps to his word and punishes me. The number, if anyone cares, is twenty-six. I let twenty-six women take a body shot off him. A true master of female erogenous zones, Wilder denies me twenty-six orgasms.

I'm going to kill him.

SEVEN

Knox

Throughout the rest of the evening, and on through dawn, I torture Lily, bringing her close to the orgasm she desperately wants no less than twenty-six times. I told her payback was a bitch. She fumes as yet another orgasm is denied.

Twenty-six is a number I pull out of the air. I have no idea how many women took a body shot off me last night. It was more than ten and less than thirty. Twenty-six seems a fair number.

Not that Lily agrees. Primed and aching, she's had a difficult night, but I've had tons of fun. The best part of the evening is learning her body. I know every inch and am familiar with every one of her erogenous zones.

It's time to put all that into practice and end her misery once and for all. I've got two hours until I need to meet my team. Two wonderful hours to worship Lily's amazing body.

"I hate you." She stares at me, eyes shooting daggers and boiling with fury.

"No, you don't." I walk around the bed, looking down at my handiwork.

About an hour ago, I tricked Lily. I told her if she let me tie her up, I'd let her come. In my defense, I never said I'd let her come right then.

"Yes, I absolutely hate you." She glances at her wrists. "Untie me."

"Nope." I've been having fun teasing and stimulating her, learning everything I can about what she likes and what she loves.

She's adventurous as shit, which is sexy as fuck. I tied her arms to the bedposts and her legs stretch out to either side. The way she squirms ignites something feral and beastly inside of me. I take a moment to admire my handiwork.

Finding something to wrap around her ankles, without causing damage, required creativity, but I managed.

My stomach growls. It's been a really long night, and I'm spent. While I enjoyed this little game of punishment, it's time to reward her for being such a good sport. I came five times last night. Not a record, but that kind of shit takes stamina.

I owe my girl five earth-shattering orgasms. Six if I can manage to come one more time. I'm not a believer in the whole tit-for-tat, an orgasm for an orgasm, kind of thing, but I love watching a woman come undone. Which means the next hour or so is going to be amazing.

"Untie me." Her voice turns serious. There's an argument to say I'm pushing things too far. If she still feels the same in the next sixty seconds, I'll release her.

With her burning gaze on me, I move to the bottom of the bed. She's fully exposed to me, and I take a minute to admire her exquisite features. Features of which I'm intimately familiar with. Which is how I know I'll send her flying in under a minute.

"I will, but first …" I place my knee on the foot of the bed, right between her legs, and I slowly climb over her until my entire body covers hers. "Give me one minute."

"One minute? To do what?" Her eyes suddenly widen as I place the pads of my fingers over her swollen clit. A few strokes and her body's already clenching. "Please, I can't handle another …"

My lips brush against hers. It's a feather-light touch. "Your punishment's over, pumpkin. Are you ready to fly?" The relief on her face brings a smile to mine.

"You're not teasing me, are you?"

My fingers pick up the pace, driving her relentlessly toward an orgasm. She's going to come on my fingers and on my face. I'll let her decide how she wants me to fuck her next. Whatever she wants. It's hers to take.

"No more teasing." I slide down to her breasts, where I lick around her areola until her nipple peaks into a tight bud. Then I wrap my lips around her nipple and suck.

She moans beneath me as I pick up the pace. I shove two fingers into her opening and find that rough spot just inside. Stroking her g-spot with my fingers, rubbing her clit with my thumb, and worshiping her tits, Lily squirms beneath me until her entire body tenses.

"I'm going to …" Her back arches, shoving her breast into my mouth. I stroke her through, and past, her release as her entire body shudders and shakes.

And I don't stop.

She moans and squirms as pleasure races through her body. Before she can come down from that incredible high, I shift positions.

"That was …" Her breathy sigh gets interrupted when I lick along her slit and suck on her clit. "Oh! Ah …"

Her fingers curl and she pulls on the restraints. For a second, I think she's going to snap off one of the bedposts as a second orgasm rolls through her.

I love when I can do that for a woman—send her flying with multiple orgasms. A third wouldn't be out of the question, especially with the way I've kept her on edge all night, but I stick to my plan.

Climbing back up her body, I stare at her as the last tremors of the orgasm run their course. When she opens her eyes, she slowly shakes her head side to side.

"That was …" Her eyes close again and she takes in a deep breath.

"Worth waiting for?" I don't mind completing her sentence. I totally rocked her world.

She peeks open one eye. "Yes. Definitely worth it. I've never had ..."

"Multiple orgasms?"

"Never." She bites her lower lip, and I love the tiniest bit of shyness that it reveals.

Lily is a confident woman. She's beautiful and she rocks that sexy vibe. After our evening together, I gather she's usually the dominant one in bed.

"That's a shame. You should demand more from your lovers."

It's an innocent, light-hearted comment that rolls off my tongue. What's weird is I'm totally unprepared for the possessive vibe rising within me.

The thought of any other man touching her, with the same familiarity and intimacy we just shared—are still sharing—makes me want to throat punch those men and cut off their dicks.

A possessive growl rumbles in my chest. No one is going to touch Lily except me.

Whoa!

I don't do relationships—at least, not anymore.

The life of a Navy seaman, and then a SEAL, didn't lend itself well to maintaining a relationship. Long sea tours put too much time and distance between a developing relationship. The women were either too clingy and couldn't deal. Or, they were too independent and moved on. Either way, I stopped worrying about sticking with one chick a long time ago.

Honestly, there was no reason to put in the effort. Not when I could walk into any bar on the planet and get what I needed. A rough fuck in a bathroom stall. Dirty sex out back by the dumpsters. One night at her place.

I never brought a woman to my home.

I'm the king of one-night stands, but I want more than a single night with the woman spread out before me.

What the ever-loving fuck is wrong with me?

Lily gazes contentedly at me. Her body twists on the sheets. Her arms are tied over her head. She twists and tests the restraints on her ankles as she stretches, arching like a cat in heat, thrusting her tits up while undulating her belly and hips.

My dick takes notice and wakes up. Hungry for more.

"Point taken." Her lids close as she finishes her stretch. "I'll make sure to post my demands the next time we do this." Her sleepy lids slide open and she glances at her hands. "Although, it doesn't seem like I'll be the one making the demands with you." Her attention shifts to me. "You're something else."

"Is that a good thing, or a bad thing?"

"Let's just say that if any other man slapped my ass, tied me to my bed, and denied me that many orgasms, I'd have his balls."

"Not the best visual. Seeing how you're still tied up, I may want to keep you there."

"Your wish is my command." She arches her back. "But, since my punishment is over, how about you do that little trick again."

"Which trick is that?"

"The one with your tongue and those amazing fingers. Or how about you fill me with that monster dick of yours and really make me fly."

"You're not demanding at all."

"Not at all." She bats her lashes at me. "Please?"

"Well, since you begged so nicely."

I kiss her gently, reverently, feeling an odd shift within me.

The next time we do this?

Her words whisper in my head as I bring her to another earth-shattering orgasm. And another. And another. She rolls right through one and onto the next. I consider it a personal challenge to leave her breathless and gasping. Four orgasms later, I release her from the restraints and crawl into bed beside her. With her back curled against my chest, I drape an arm over her waist, and drag her tight against me.

Somehow, this feels right. Yet, I remind myself we barely know each other. In fact, we know nothing at all about the other person. We're strangers who shared an amazing night in bed.

And the day is calling.

In particular, my team.

Lily's breathing evens out, and her body relaxes as she falls to sleep. I'd hoped to fuck her one last time, but my dick will have to wait until later tonight.

As for tonight, I plan to be right here. My one-night, nameless bar fuck, has a name. Somehow, Lily found a crack in my armor and snuck through the opening. She belongs to me now.

I decide whether to wake her, but it's been a rough night. Sweeping her white-blonde hair off her shoulder, I press my lips to her skin. She tastes of sex and sin, my two favorite things.

When I crawl out of bed, she stirs, and I wait for her to wake to say my goodbyes, but Lily is sex-drunk and goes right back to sleep.

Dressing as quietly as possible, I look for a pen and piece of paper. Not a poet by any means, I speak from my heart.

~

PUMPKIN,

You look like an angel when you sleep, but you're a temptress in bed. I had fun last night and look forward to more.

Work calls. I have to go. I'm not sneaking out. I just couldn't bear to wake you.

I leave you hard and aching for more, something I can't wait for you to handle later tonight.

Get it?

Handle?

Yes, pumpkin, I can't wait to feel your hands on me, your mouth sucking me down, and your sweet pussy welcoming me home.

Until tonight …

YOURS,

Knox

~

I sign my name and put the note on the nightstand, where she's certain to see it. I also find her phone and enter my contact number. Then I call my phone from hers. With her number in my phone, I glance once more at my sleeping beauty.

Damn, she's a lot of fun.

I can't wait until I see her again.

For the first time, in a very long time, I wonder what it might be like to have a woman of my own.

EIGHT

Lily

"He left?" My best friend, and adoptive sister, Jinx, takes another look at the note Wilder left by the bed. "After all that wild monkey sex, he left without saying a word? No kiss? No goodbye?" Jinx tosses Wilder's note on the table with disgust. "What a loser."

"He's not a loser." I grab the note and hold it close to my chest. "He left a note." One I've read about a thousand times.

"Yeah, but that's shady. After what you told me about last night? I'm surprised he walked away."

"He said he'd see me later tonight."

"It's a shame *you* won't be here tonight to hook up with him. And for the record, what he said is …" She makes air quotes. "*I can't wait to feel your hands on me, your mouth sucking me down, and your sweet pussy welcoming me home. Until tonight …*" Jinx leans back with a sigh. "At least that bit is swoon-worthy." She recites Wilder's words verbatim after reading it only one time. Her recall astounds me.

"Do you always have to correct me?"

"Only when you're wrong. Besides, you won't be here tonight."

Don't I know that.

A ship scheduled to pull into port tonight carries a shipment the

DEA intends to confiscate before the product hits the streets of New Orleans. I will be there with my team.

"You're impossible. You know that, don't you?"

She's also right.

I'm not going to be here tonight to have monkey sex with Wilder. I'm more likely to be arresting his ass. *If* our intelligence is correct about who's running this shipment.

"Yeah," Jinx flashes me a triumphant smile, "but you love me too much to hold it against me."

"That's true, and you're lucky I do." I pick up Wilder's note and read it one more time. "This note, though …"

Jinx grabs it out of my hand.

"Hey, give it back." I lunge across the table, intent on snatching the note out of her hands, but Jinx holds it out of reach.

She reads Wilder's note aloud. At least the juicy bits. "*I can't wait to feel your hands on me, your mouth sucking me down, and your sweet pussy welcoming me home.*"

"Give it back." I make another grab for it, but she keeps it out of reach.

Jinx holds the note to her chest. "Fuck if that's not the hottest damn thing I've ever read. *Your sweet pussy?*" She thrusts Wilder's note at me and shakes her head. "Tell me again."

"I already told you twice."

"Yeah, but I want to hear it again. Did he really spank you?"

"Yes." My cheeks heat with the memory.

"And the multiple orgasms?"

"Yeah."

"I've never had those." Jinx sighs. "It's like an urban legend. I always thought that was something girls said to make the other girls jealous."

"So did I." I lean back with a dreamy sigh. "You're right, though."

"I am?"

"It's a shame I won't be here later tonight. I'd really like to go another round with him."

"Considering he's your mission objective, I'd say you will. You must." She lifts her index finger and points to the ceiling. "For God and country."

"Really?" I shake my head. "That's a bit corny even for you."

"Well, it is for the good of the country."

"If that's the case, I'll simply have no choice but to endure multiple orgasms again."

"You're not trying to make me jealous, are you?"

"What about your night? I saw you checking out Wilder's friend."

"Yeah, remind me never to go after a guy called Wolfe again, will you?"

"Why? Did something happen?"

"Well, I didn't get multiple orgasms."

"So, you hooked up?" I'm not sure what she's trying to tell me.

"Not exactly."

"Then what *exactly* happened."

She shrugs.

"Come on, I told you. You tell me."

"The man has talented fingers and a mouth that knows how to make a girl fly, but the moment we were done, he hightailed it out of there. Like he couldn't get away fast enough after getting off." She shakes her head. "What can you expect from a random bar hookup?"

I squirm, remembering the never-ending waves of pleasure rolling through me. Right when I thought it was going to end, Wilder sent me back over the edge.

"Phenomenal comes to mind." My evening, evidently, ended much differently than hers.

"And you really did *all* of that?" Jinx looks jealous and sounds wistful.

Jinx and I share everything. I told her every sordid detail. Granted, part of it was for the mandatory debrief. I'm grateful Jinx is my partner on this op instead of Peter-the-Prick.

I was his partner during our last sting, and listening to him drone on and on about his conquests made me want to claw his eyes out.

Or barf.

"We did far more than I've ever done with a guy before, and he's kinky. That was new, and a lot more fun than I ever thought it could be."

My ass hurts from where Wilder spanked me. My pussy throbs from the vigorous pounding it endured. My nipples, abraded and raw from all the stimulation, ache in the best possible way. Plus, my wrists and ankles sport red marks from the restraints.

Is it weird I look at them fondly? Or that my pussy throbs thinking about that spanking? I'm definitely out of my mind insane.

He's your job, idiot!

Yeah, I know. Getting close to Wilder is the objective, and I got very close.

"Yeah, but that was all in one night." Jinx still doesn't believe me about the sex. I can see it in her eyes. "He's going to hate you when we make this arrest. You know that, don't you?"

"I know." I hang my head, but then an idea pops into my head. "We could turn him."

"Make him an informant?" Jinx's eyebrows wing up, interested, but not convinced.

"It's a thought."

"You want to use your magic pussy to get him to turn on his boss?" Jinx gives me the eye. "How confident are you that you could make it happen?"

"Confident enough to try."

I say the words while others spin in my head. The thing is, I don't want to take Wilder down. I want more of what we had last night. And yes, the sex was phenomenal, but it's the connection between us I crave.

That's the hole I feel in my heart right now, as if there's a piece of me missing.

I've never had that kind of sex before because I've never felt that connected to a man before.

Correction, I've *never* felt any connection to any man before.

Maybe that's why it's hitting me harder than it should? When it comes to sex, I'm clinical and detached.

Like, it's something I need. I seek out nameless hookups to scratch the itch when it arises. Some, people who don't know me, would say I'm callous, and maybe a bit cold-hearted, when it comes to relationships.

But that's not it at all.

I've simply never been interested in the personal side of it before. Relationships aren't my jam. Besides, hooking up with the same person over and over again, doesn't excite me. I'm all about the next conquest. It's why I was picked for this job.

My boss knows my views about sex. I'm completely detached. But then, I didn't see Wilder coming.

What we did, and I know how corny it sounds, but it transcended sex. It's almost as if our souls fused into one. It wasn't just intimate. It felt like destiny.

Not that I'm going to say anything about that to Jinx. She doesn't believe in fate, destiny, or psychic connections. Jinx is all about what she can see, touch, feel, and know.

"It's just …" I reach out, grasping at nothing. "He doesn't seem like a bad guy." I implore my friend to understand this thing I can't put into words.

"Don't let his hot-as-sin looks get in the way of your professional judgment." Jinx doesn't get it. She doesn't get it at all.

"I'm not."

It's not his hot-as-sin looks that are getting in the way of my professionalism. It's the way he held me last night. It's in how he made me feel, and how he made even the more adventurous things, like that spanking, feel normal. And when I say normal, I'm talking about not being ashamed of what we did.

"I'm not the one you have to convince." Jinx examines her fingernails and the back of her hand.

"I know." I hang my head.

"You have to convince Harry." She tells me what I already know.

Our boss is the one who needs to buy off on it. To convince Harry Sheldon, I need to tell him why I feel the way I do. That touches on feelings, something neither of us are very good at.

And what am I going to tell Harry? That after one night with Wilder, I've gone insane?

There's nothing about Wilder that should sway my professional judgment, except for my gut telling me there's something about him we're missing.

I'll say *gut*, but because I'm a woman, all he'll hear is that my *feelings* got in the way of my thought processes.

After I tell Harry I slept with Wilder, convincing him that my gut tells me Wilder isn't a criminal will be nearly impossible. He'll think exactly what Jinx is thinking and assume my emotions compromise my judgment.

Which totally isn't the case.

If my male colleagues can sleep around doing their job and still maintain a professional perspective, then I can too.

Except, am I thinking clearly?

"He's protective. Chivalrous almost." If I can convince Jinx, I might have a chance with Harry.

"And you think that's enough?" She leans back and crosses her arms over her chest, testing me. "Harry's not going to play anything off the cuff. He's got the higher-ups breathing down his neck. You need to come up with something better."

"I know it's not enough, but this feels all kinds of wrong."

There's no doubt in my mind Wilder is, in some way, connected to the shipments coming out of Colombia. I'm just having a hard time seeing him as the kind of man who would willingly involve himself in the drug trade.

Protector is a good description, and it fits him well. That kind of person doesn't ruin lives for a living. He's the kind of person who saves them.

Somehow, that image feels right. I rub at my breastbone as it sinks in. That's much easier to believe than him being a part of an upstart cartel moving in on the Colombian drug trade.

After spending the night with Wilder, I feel bad using him. What I said to Jinx is true. Wilder doesn't give off a bad guy vibe. I've been around a lot of criminals, and I like to think I've developed a bit of a sixth sense about the criminal mind.

"Doesn't matter." Jinx taps her finger on the table. "Our intel puts him in Cancun, and then Colombia, right after several shipments of narcotics came into the Port of New Orleans."

"I know. Just like I know there's no record of him entering, or leaving, either of those countries." Jinx and I sat in on the same mission briefs. This is old information. "It could be true but unrelated."

"True but unrelated? What are you saying?"

"He may not be involved."

"His trips to Colombia raise red flags. It's too close to be a coincidence. Especially the last one. Not to mention our informant places him at ground zero."

"That was a total shit show." I lean back and vent a frustrated sigh.

One of our informants spotted Wilder at Tomas Benefield's establishment days before the attack that took out Benefield's operation.

Benefield is, or was, one of the largest players involved in the shipment and sale of illegal pharmaceutical narcotics in Central America and perhaps the largest importer into the U.S.

"Will you indulge me in a little creative thinking exercise?" I can't get it out of my head that we're wrong about Wilder.

"As in?"

"For a second, let's assume what we know is wrong."

"Fine." Jinx doesn't look convinced, but she's willing to play along. It's one of the things I love about her. She trusts my gut, even when she shouldn't.

"What we know." I lift my index finger. "According to our informant, Wilder masqueraded as private security for one of Benefield's guests days before a massive strike was executed on Benefield's compound."

"Correct." Jinx nods.

"Benefield was *the* player in Colombia for the movement of illegal narcotics into the U.S."

"True."

"Our assumption is Wilder went to Benefield's to take Benefield down."

"Right. Wilder executed Benefield in concert with an attack on Benefield's compound."

"According to our informant." I sit back and wait for Jinx to think it through.

"Right. What are you trying to get at?"

"Our assumption is our informant is telling us the truth."

"There's no reason to think otherwise. He's been giving us actionable intelligence for years. The man's been vetted."

"But what if he's wrong? Or what if he's been turned? And why is it that he can't tell us who runs this other operation? Who moved in on Benefield's territory? Not Wilder. We know he's working for a shell operation."

"You think our informant fed us bad intel?"

"Maybe?"

"You think there's another reason Wilder was there?"

"I don't know, but what if there was?"

"What could it possibly be?"

"No clue. But why didn't our informant tell us anything about the man Wilder was with? Wilder was there as a bodyguard. The man he was supposed to be protecting disappeared. That's too convenient."

"Not if that man is the new boss? That would explain his disappearance."

"Maybe." But I'm not convinced. "The outfit that did that job has ex-military written all over it."

No denying Wilder has ex-military written all over him. Very few men put in the time required to achieve that degree of physical conditioning unless they're in the military, or they're muscle-obsessed and a part of the weight-lifting craze.

"That strike undermined years of investigation by the DEA." Jinx blows out a breath, and I feel her frustration.

Jinx and I joined the DEA right out of college. We trained together, built up a reputation as reliable agents, and were assigned to the same task force within months of each other. We specialize in the shipping and distribution of illegally acquired pharmaceutical narcotics into the country.

The past decade has seen an explosion of opioid misuse. The epidemic increases every day, and we're on the front lines, curbing the massive influx of illegal narcotics into the country. Our job's important, and we save lives.

We've each worked on different assignments, building up our experience. This is my first official undercover assignment. Jinx isn't a field operator like me. She works intelligence, and this is her first case as lead intelligence officer.

"Right or wrong, there's a new player in the mix." Jinx is slowly coming around. I've yet to convince her, but she's finally questioning our assumptions. "You've got a long, uphill climb convincing Harry that Wilder wasn't involved in the hit against Benefield."

"I know. And isn't that precisely why Wilder is more important to us as an informant?"

We're looking for who Wilder works for and how they tie into the movement of tons of illegal narcotics into the U.S. every month.

"I don't think you have enough of a case to argue. To do something like that, you'd need something to hold over Wilder's head that he can't walk away from. All you've done is let him fuck you for a night. He's not tied to you in any way."

"What about the note?"

"Not to burst your bubble, but he could've written it just to make himself feel better about walking out on you."

I refuse to agree with her assessment. She wasn't there. She didn't feel the air as it crackled between us. Not to mention, I know Wilder felt it too. More importantly, I know it spooked him. I press my point, intent on getting Jinx to see what I feel.

"Just play this out with me, please?"

"Fine, but you know what Harry's going to say. And if he doesn't say it, Peter-the-Prick will. Your judgment is compromised."

"I know what people will say, but listen."

"I am, Lily. I'm listening to everything you're saying. But here's the thing. We've had our eyes on Benefield for years, trying to locate his supplier, ferret out his transportation network, and figure out how he was moving the product into the country. We finally have a lead on how the drugs get in, but with Benefield gone, our entire operation fell apart."

"That's not all that's gone."

"What do you mean?"

"Your informant is in the wind."

"How do you know that?" Jinx's body tenses, giving me everything I need to confirm a suspicion I've had from the very beginning.

"You just confirmed it."

"You played me."

"No, I put two and two together. After Benefield was taken down, we targeted Wilder pretty damn quick, and we did it based upon thin intelligence. We don't do that. The fact that we did raised alarms in my head. And after spending a night with Wilder, I'm even more convinced we're acting on faulty intelligence. I want to know why we're rushing in when we should be taking a step back."

"The why is easy. Harry's looking for a promotion. Benefield was supposed to be the case that sealed the deal. Losing Benefield jeopardized everything Harry's worked for. He's looking for a quick win."

"So, he sends his field agents out half-cocked?" I raise a brow. "That puts me at risk."

"I'm sorry, Lily."

"I get it, but where does this leave us? You have to feel that things aren't adding up. The case against Wilder is a strawman at best. It's going to come crashing down on us. That, at least, warrants a second look."

"There's no time for a second look. Based on what we know, that ship is transporting several containers of narcotics. Think about it for a minute. We're not talking one cargo container. We're talking several. Getting that product off the street is worth it in the end."

"I'm not arguing that. All I'm saying is it's not worth losing an opportunity to turn Wilder against whoever this new player is. If we arrest him, it does one of two things."

"Such as?"

"We arrest him, convict him, and put him away. That takes him out of play. Or, we arrest him, turn him, and release him."

"So?"

"That puts a target on his back. There's no way to release him without his boss, and everyone else in the operation, curious as to why we didn't charge and convict him. No one will trust him. We lose a massive opportunity."

"And you think, what? That you can turn him?"

"There has to be a way."

"You have to find a reason to convince Harry to offer Wilder a deal."

"We have to catch him first, but it needs to be covert. We can't go in guns blazing."

"So, what are you suggesting?"

"We pull way back tonight. Go in with a SWAT team. Apprehend Wilder. Offer him a deal. If he takes it, we let him go before we make the bust. He can tell his boss he noticed activity and took a step back. That keeps him clean with his boss. Then we make the bust, take all the pretty pictures, and make front-page news. Wilder's boss will see that Wilder keeps cool under duress. There's no other way."

It'll work too. Wilder's been seen around the cargo containers. The first time, he disappeared and showed up again in Cancun and then again in Colombia. As far as our intel can make out, he's made several trips to Colombia, and there's not a single documented exit through customs.

Something's not right. I'd bet my badge on it, and I'm going to prove it too.

My job is to get close, gain Wilder's trust, and figure out how he's connected. From there, we'll send in other agents who'll work their way further into the organization. Once we have enough to build a case, the whole operation will get taken down.

"Did you at least bug his phone?" Jinx rolls her mother's ring on her finger.

"Yes."

Harry didn't anticipate me getting as close to Wilder as I did.

Once again, I'm not the first undercover DEA agent to sleep with someone to obtain information.

Jinx is right about that. Last night, while Wilder slept, I crawled out of bed and swapped out the SIM card in Wilder's phone. His phone is wide open to us, along with all his contacts and whatever else is stored on it.

Despite my blissfully fucked state of mind, I did my damn job. I'm not compromised. Stopping the flow of drugs into my country is my life's mission.

"I'm surprised with all the fucking that you did it." Jinx is quick to judge me.

"I never forgot my objective. You may think my judgment is off, but I'm laser-focused." I tap my head. "I know what's important. Now, are you going to back me or not?"

"We need to be careful in how it's presented." Jinx blows out a breath. "You know how this is going to look, don't you? The first thing that'll go through their minds?"

"I do."

Being a woman means I'll be judged for my actions. Jinx just did it to me now, and she's not only a woman, but my best friend. She knows what's important. I couldn't care less what the guys think, or for that matter. what Harry thinks about me.

I'm not in this for some fancy promotion way down the road. I just want to do my job and do it well.

What I did is no different from Peter-the-Prick Simpson, who slept his way through a prostitution ring until he found how they were moving drugs through that organization. He got cheers for *taking one for the team*. I'll get leers for spreading my legs like a whore.

"I can't believe you let a guy tie you up on the first night you were with him." Jinx falls back into best-friend mode. She'll back me with Harry. "That's some scary shit."

"But it wasn't." How do I explain the instant connection Wilder and I shared? How in tune we were with each other and our bodies?

"It wasn't? I'd have a heart attack if that happened to me. How did you know you could trust him?"

How do I explain the man I took upstairs last night doesn't come across as a hardened criminal?

"He's dominating in bed. No denying that, but there's another side to him." If I can only convince Jinx, it'll make it easier to convince the others. "He didn't touch me until I gave clear consent."

"He didn't?"

"He asked several times if I was okay."

"He asked if you were okay with him spanking your ass?"

"Well," my cheeks heat with the memory, "that first swat did come out of nowhere, but he watched me for any signs I was no longer on board with it."

"I take it you were?"

"I was totally on board, and he knew it."

"You are one kinky bitch, girl."

I can't help but grin. Talking to Jinx, my friend, is a lot more fun than Jinx, my coworker.

An odd dissonance builds.

"I know you don't agree with me, but the man in that dossier isn't the same man I slept with last night."

"Keep telling yourself that. It's still going to be a hard sell."

"Because I slept with him?"

"Precisely because you jumped into bed with him."

Jinx isn't being mean. She's telling me the truth. The rules are different for men and women, but I still feel like something is messed up. Until I can figure out what that is, the mission continues.

As for sex with Wilder, why can't a woman be adventurous or have a healthy appetite for sex?

No big mystery there.

If she does, she's called a slut and shamed. Men get slaps on the back, congratulations for their prowess, and medals. Women receive poor performance reviews and demotions.

It's not fair.

Peter, the self-indulgent prick, got a medal. I'll be shamed, labeled a whore, and potentially demoted for behavior unbecoming of an agent. Nobody will care that I swapped out the SIM card.

The whole male/female double standard irritates me, but it's not the end of the world. It's not worth losing sleep over.

When I complete my job, I'll deserve the same recognition Peter-the-Prick got. I'm out to show the world I can be the best, regardless of my sex. As long as I bring in the criminals trafficking illicit substances into our country, what does it matter if I use sex as a weapon?

All is fair in love and war.

But damn if I wish Wilder wasn't one of the bad guys.

Callie comes downstairs in a pair of loose-fitting pajamas bottoms and a tight-fitting tank top.

"What are you guys doing up so early?" She flits over to the bar, hops up on it, and reaches for an empty glass. She fills it with ice from the ice well then grabs the fountain dispenser to fill it with fizzy diet soda.

"It's almost nine, Callie." Jinx looks at me and we laugh. "You're late."

"Is it?" She pinches the bridge of her nose and rubs at her eyes. "That sucks. We open at eleven. I wanted to grab some beignets. I need coffee, and not the crap I have here." Callie looks between us, sees the smirk on Jinx's face, and props her hands on her hips. "Out with it."

"Lily was telling me about her hot and heavy sex with Mr. Eight-Pack." Despite Jinx's scathing remarks and judgment, she's eager to spill all my secrets.

"Oh God, the body shot man? Damn, he was hot. Tell me about it." Callie turns the nozzle of the dispenser toward me and sprays the air with water. She's too far to hit me directly, and honestly, the fine mist is a break in the heat that is building for the day.

"It was hot."

"I share a wall with you, bitch. I was up all night listening to you go at it with Mr. Sexy Pants. It had better have been better than *hot.*"

"Tell her the best part." Jinx jabs me with her elbow.

"Which part is that?" I rub my arm where she poked me. "Your elbows are boney."

"Lily is now a member of the multiple-O club."

"The what?" It takes a second, then Callie's eyes widen. "No shit." She comes out from the back of the bar and pulls up a chair. "Why don't I ever get lucky like that? It's not fair."

"Nope. Not fair at all." Jinx agrees.

Our conversation takes a pause with Callie around.

The three of us went to high school together and shared an apartment all through college. We say we're triplets separated at birth because we're closer than close. Jinx and I were born and abandoned by our birth mothers on the same day. We were lucky to be adopted by our amazing parents and grew up together as sisters and best friends. Callie came into the picture six months later when our adoptive parents got the surprise of a lifetime. They thought they were barren, but Callie proved them wrong. The three of us were practically triplets.

But where Callie took her bartending skills from college and applied them to running a bar, Jinx and I joined the DEA.

"We can get you beignets while you get the place ready to open." I volunteer to feed Callie's beignet and coffee addiction because I'm feeling a need for fresh air and a brisk walk.

I can't get the image of Wilder out of my head or disperse this odd dissonance in my head.

"You'd do that?"

"I'd rather do that than help you mop these floors." The entire place reeks of stale beer and other noxious fluids I don't want to think too hard about.

Each morning, the first thing Callie does is clean the entire bar. That begins, and ends, with a thorough mopping. Nine times out of ten, at least when I'm around, she guilts me into performing that malodorous task.

"I've got the bar. You get me beignets." She closes her eyes and licks her lips. "I can almost taste them."

I make a show of looking at the floors with the residue of last night's customers. "Anything else you want?"

Callie pulls out a twenty from the till. "Get me enough for breakfast and lunch."

"I'm not taking your money." I get up from the table.

"Oh, come on. It's a business expense. You'll be helping me if you take it."

"Not happening." I kick the leg of Jinx's chair. "Why don't you come with? If you stay, she'll coerce you into cleaning the counters."

In college, Callie had money. She freely shared what she had with Jinx and me. We made it through on student aid and luck. We're years from paying back her generosity.

I need Jinx because we need to go over how I'm going to sell things to Harry.

As for tonight, two ships will be pulling into dock. One is loaded with illegal pharmaceuticals. The owner of the shipping company checks out, but there's no doubt someone is using ships registered to his line to ferry tons of illegal narcotics into the country.

As for Wilder, our operation will likely go on through the night. If he comes looking for me at Callie's bar, I won't be there.

If everything goes off as planned tonight, he won't ever want to speak to me again.

Which sucks.

I'm far from done with Wilder. I need more of his brand of steamy hot sex.

"You're thinking about him." Jinx gives a knowing look the moment we head outside.

"Am not."

"You suck at lying. Your head is totally in the clouds. I hope the sex is as good as you say because it's the last bit of him you're going to get."

"Not necessarily. If Harry agrees, and we turn Wilder ..."

"You really think he'll want to be an informant?"

I really want him back in my bed, but that doesn't help my case one bit. I need to be professional. Nobody said this job would be easy. Using people comes with the territory, especially in undercover work. For the first time since I signed on the dotted line, I regret this part of my job.

"It'll get us into his organization faster." I'm hopeful Wilder will take the offer. Seeing him behind bars ruins everything. Then again, not telling him that I'm investigating him kind of shuts all the doors.

Why did I have to sleep with him?

You know why.

I wish that little voice in my head would shut up.

"Just remember, Peter tried that with one of his marks and got shot down."

"Only because he got her pregnant. There was definite conflict of interest."

Jinx arches a brow. "Right. He got too close. Are you focused on the objective? Or are you too close?"

"I'm focused. One night means nothing, and for that matter, one shipment means nothing. We need to get to the source. We need him working for us."

"Are you sure?"

"Yes." I stop in the middle of the press of morning tourists, feeling like something's off.

Jinx gives me a look and glances back the way we came. Sure enough, the beignet shop is half a block behind us. I completely missed it.

"Fuck."

"You don't say." She turns on her heel and marches back to the beignet shop. "Get your head in the game. You need to focus."

"I know." With my head hanging, I step into line with Jinx. The aroma of freshly cooked beignets fills the air, and I'm not shameless about giving a good sniff. "Best smell ever."

"Isn't that the truth?"

As for keeping my head in the game, the only thing I can focus on is a man with gorgeous eyes, a body cut out of steel, and a night that left me both aching and flying.

Officially obsessed, one night with him will never be enough. If I can't get Harry to buy off on using Wilder as an informant, I'll have to figure out a way to minimize my role in tonight's bust.

But how the hell do I do that?

NINE

Knox

"Howzit going, body shot?" Wolfe elbows me in the ribs as I roll my eyes.

The guys have been on me all day about last night, ribbing me, mocking me—pissing me the fuck off.

Liam and Wolfe put on a show for Axel and Griff, demonstrating exactly how compromised I was on that bar. I have to say; Liam and Wolfe are comfortable in their skin.

No way in hell would I let any of the guys do a body shot on me. Nor would I do a body shot off one of them. But Liam and Wolfe did. They acted out my humiliation in gory detail, hamming it up, acting like a bunch of teenage horndogs.

"You should've seen him in his black skivvies and black socks, one toe sticking out. Fucker had the ladies eating out of the palm of his … Well, they were licking and sucking his …" Liam winks at me.

"I'm going to get even." My glare does nothing to faze Liam.

The prankster of the group, I'll be lucky if I ever get him back.

What I'm not doing is giving them the satisfaction of letting the stupid nickname get under my skin. If I do, they'll be calling me *body shot* for life.

"You totally should've been there." Liam waves a bottle of

tequila in the air while making crude gestures. "All those horny women lining up to take a lick and a suck on his hard body." He proceeds to demonstrate for a second time, slurping up the tequila while pretending to be a chick.

"It wasn't like that." My attempts to tone down the retelling of last night are futile.

Wolfe is no better. He stretches out on the table, pretending to be me, while Liam reenacts the scene. Only Wolfe keeps his pants on and shirt down. There are *some* limits.

Like I said, I love them like brothers, but no way in hell would I do that. No amount of ribbing is worth it.

Wolfe plays it up stuffing a long, black sock down his pants and lets it rise when Liam blows raspberries on his belly. Everyone laughs.

The guys will go to great lengths to make fun of me.

"You should've seen the chick with the double D's," Wolfe jumps in. "She let her tits drag right across his junk. *Body shot* had a hard time taming his monster cock." Wolfe demonstrates with the sock, letting it stand at attention.

I roll my eyes. "My dick didn't even twitch with any of those chicks."

"Damn straight it did." Liam pulls up a video of Lily doing the very first body shot.

There's control, and then there's *control*.

Sure enough, Liam zeroed right in on my crotch, where my dick did far more than twitch. I didn't think anyone noticed, but it's now on video for everyone to enjoy.

"You're supposed to have my back." I swipe at the phone, but he jerks it out of reach.

"We did." Wolfe looks at Liam. "Didn't we hold his clothes?"

"We sure did." Liam nods. "And boots."

"And didn't we make sure to stuff his pockets with extra condoms?" Wolfe turns his wolfish grin on me. "You really should thank us for that."

"I wondered where those came from. And grateful for the assist." I used them all up and need to refresh my supply.

"I got so many great pictures." Liam swipes through the photos on his phone.

I yank Liam's cellphone out of his hand, successful this time, and start deleting all the pictures from last night.

"Dude, you can do that all damn day, but I sent them to everyone." Liam snatches his phone out of my hand right as Wolfe airdrops the whole batch back to Liam's device. Liam mouths *I sent them to everyone! Everyone!*

Well shit.

"You're a fucking asshole." I punch him in the gut. Liam takes it in stride, shrugging off the punch. "I'm totally going to make you pay."

"No, you're not." Liam dodges my next round of punches. He holds up his fists and dances on his feet. He throws a few himself, just parries and jabs. Goofing off as we waste time before our briefing.

As for those photos, they're like those moles on Whack-a-Mole. I can delete to my heart's content, but I'm never living that shit down. Those pictures are out there, and there's not a goddamn thing I can do about it.

"At least you all had an interesting night." Axel lifts his phone, showing me one of the pictures Liam sent him.

It's one of the shy brunettes I had to coax into doing the shot. In the background is Lily. The expression on her face is one of pure regret. I don't remember that, and it gives me pause.

I know she feels bad about last night, and I give her props. My girl has balls. She played me, using my own arrogance to her advantage during that game of darts. I lost fair and square.

That's what I get for being cocky.

"Body Shot isn't the only one who had an interesting night." Liam brags, but then he never fails to bag a chick for the night. "I had fun with that pretty brunette." He points to the picture Axel holds up.

"Dude," Wolfe says, "we all know you had fun. When do you ever *not* have fun?"

"Knox went upstairs with the pretty lady in the red dress. Liam bagged the shy brunette. All I did was swap some spit with Knox's girl's friend."

It takes me a moment to parse through that, but I finally figure he's talking about Lily's friend.

I really was played last night but in the best possible way.

"Her friend?" That must be the girl who worked the crowd, getting all those women keyed up about the body shots. She did it *before* I lost.

"The cute Latina?" Wolfe tries to jog my memory.

I barely remember Lily's friend.

"And you didn't have fun?" I arch a brow. Wolfe rarely bombs with the chicks. He's got a look about him that chicks dig.

"Let's just say she's got a temper." Wolfe rolls his wrist and glances down at the skin. I see four gouges on his inner wrist.

"A temper?" That looks like more than a temper.

"Yeah, didn't pan out. Although, Liam bagged that pretty brunette."

Doesn't surprise me. Liam's a looker and probably has the most interesting sex life of anyone on the planet.

"And her friend. Stayed up all night." Liam preens. He wants to tell us what he did, but I cut him off. I'm not interested in his sexual exploits. You hear about one ménage, you've heard them all.

"Well, I'd still be in bed with Lily if it wasn't for this damn meeting." I regret leaving Lily the way I did, but that's all I'm sharing with the guys.

I turn my attention back to my phone. Liam shared the photos with everyone, including me. There have to be hundreds.

"How many did you take?" I flip through tons of photographs of me lying on the bar.

"As many as I could." He gives me lip but with a grin.

"At least you only sent them to the team."

"Is that what I said?" He arches a brow. "I think I said I sent them to *everyone*. And, dude, I mean everyone."

"When you say everyone, you mean the Guardians, right?" My stomach sinks because I know Liam.

"If you mean everyone in Guardian HRS, then yes."

"Wait a goddamn minute. You sent them to *everyone*?" It sinks in —what he means. "Fucker, you're going down."

"That is what I said." Liam's eyes flash with mischief. His attention shifts to Wolfe, who ducks his head when I swivel to take him in.

"How did you …?" I hold up a hand. "You're just fucking with me." I really hope Liam's just fucking with me. Maybe I've got it wrong?

"I dug up one of the emails from HR." Liam grins. "You know, the blasts about annual COMPSEC training they sent out?"

"You fucking bastard!" I launch at him, tackling him at the waist. We go down in a tangle of limbs. I punch. He blocks. We roll on the floor, trading blows.

"Yo!" Axel calls out. "It's almost time."

Griff looks down at us and gives a slow shake of his head. "Never mind Liam, he's just jealous."

"Jealous?" Liam and I break apart. "What am I supposed to be jealous of?"

"You haven't been bit." Griff turns his stony stare on me. "Knox did."

"I didn't get bit." I climb off the floor and dust off my pants. "What the hell are you talking about?"

Griff and Axel exchange a knowing stare, then they laugh.

"Wanna bet?" Griff gathers around the dining table and pulls out a chair.

"On what?" I look at him like he's grown a second head.

"On whether I'm right."

"Right about, what?"

"You going to take the bet?" Griff crosses his arms and stares down his nose at me.

The man is fucking fierce. He makes others quake in their boots. Those he puts to the question piss their pants and shit their shorts. But I've seen another side of Griff; a gooey, mushy, love-struck kind of side. The man's got a tough exterior, but he's a total softy on the inside.

"Oh, I'm in." Liam dances around the table, staying out of my reach. "What are we betting?"

Here we go with the damn betting again. The thing about bets, in Alpha team, is you can't *not* bet. Especially when challenged, and Griff definitely challenged me.

"Fine." I give in. "I'll take the damn bet." I turn to Axel, who laughs under his breath. "What the fuck are we betting on?"

"In a month," Griff says, "I'm going to ask you if you found your one."

"My one?" I huff with agitation. "I spent one fucking night with a chick I met in a bar. I'd barely call that a fling, let alone finding my one."

"I'm in." Axel turns one of the chairs around backwards and takes a seat. He leans his arms on the back of the chair and stares at me. "Knox has definitely been bit."

"You are full of it." I shove my finger at Axel and Griff. "And so are the two of you." Liam and Wolfe get the same treatment.

Digging into my back pocket, I pull out a raggedy button and toss it on the table. "In one month, you'll see."

Griff flicks a button onto the table. Axel does the same. Liam and Wolfe toss in buttons as well.

"It's a bet then." Since Griff's the one who made the bet, he'll hold our buttons until it's time to collect.

In a month, I'm going to show them exactly how wrong they are.

Lily is great in bed, adventurous enough to pique my interest, but she's a total stranger. We had great sex. It will go down as one of my most memorable one-night stands, and while I told her I'd see her tonight, this briefing will likely force me to break my word.

And that will be the end of it.

Griff's pussy-whipped. He wants the rest of us to fall in line, love-struck like him.

Ever since he and Moira hooked up, the man's been insufferable with how *in love* he is with Moira. Honestly, he makes me sick.

Axel's no better. The two of them go on and on and on about their women. Thank God, Max is keeping a clear head.

Although, come to think of it, he and Eve have been kind of inseparable since our last stint to Colombia.

What the hell?

All I can say is that I'm not ready to give up trolling the bars. I'm a free spirit and there's not a woman on the planet who's going to tie me down.

In one month, I'm going to show these assholes just how wrong they are. I snicker as Griff scoops the buttons into his hand and shoves them deep in the front pocket of his jeans.

Just wait. They'll see.

As for the buttons, there are rules; such as back pockets are for buttons available for betting. Front pockets are for bets in holding. All my pockets are currently empty.

I'm not very good at this betting game.

With that done, we settle in and get serious. It's time for work. We're gathered in New Orleans for a reason. Except, Max isn't with us this go around. Doc Summers finally released Griff from medical hold, only to put Max on the list of those not eligible to operate.

This Guardian business is no less dangerous than being on the teams during our Navy days. Griff took a bullet to his leg during the rescue of Axel's girl, Zoe. Max took a bullet in the leg during the rescue of his girl, Eve. I'm seriously hoping we're not establishing a trend with that.

Wolfe sets up the laptop for our pre-mission briefing with Max, Sam, and the ever-perky Mitzy, our technical genius. I'd say she was our resident technical genius, but that honor truly belongs to Forest Summers, founder of Guardian HRS. His personal mission in life is to eliminate human trafficking all around the globe.

It's a shame to say it, but we'll be employed for a very long time. It's kind of like deleting those pictures Liam took. Knock one down and another pops up in its place.

We jokingly refer to it as job security, but there's no joke about what happens to those who've been taken. Our job is to find them and bring them home. If they have no home, that's not a problem. Forest Summers takes care of all his rescues.

He's also highly invested in the plight of children thrust into foster care. He and his sister, Doc Summers, endured one horror after another as foster children. They call each other brother and sister, but they're not related by blood. Instead, they share a tragedy, which ties them together with bonds deeper than blood. I've never seen a love as fierce as theirs, and I've never seen people more dedicated to saving others as the two of them.

They're the reason I get up each morning. They make life worth living. I've done a lot. Seen a lot. Max and I—let's just say we made decisions no man should ever have to make.

We didn't join the Navy to decide who lives and who dies. We joined to fight the good fight, and yet on a hill somewhere in the godforsaken desert, that's exactly what Max and I did. It's a memory that still shakes me somedays, and I can never tell when that's going to happen.

We all carry scars of one kind or another. We've all been there and done that. But that is in the past. My motto is to move forward. Never dwell in the past because there's not a goddamn thing I can do to change it.

My time on the teams made me feel alive, important, and justified. But that day in the field, when our brothers in arms lay wounded and dying, that's the day I no longer wanted to be a SEAL.

Our missions served no purpose. We were the pointy tip of the spear, a precise, surgical weapon used to bludgeon the enemies of our country.

I got tired of being used, and what we were fighting for got muddier by the day.

This world, it's a haven for all things good. But that's what makes it fertile hunting ground for those born with evil in their hearts. As a SEAL, I executed orders. Completed missions. But the objective always remained remote and unattainable.

I fought the same damn war my father fought before me, and we were no closer to winning. With Forest and the Guardians, things are different. I save lives. That's immediate gratification at work there.

Mission objectives are crystal clear. We save those who've been taken, turning victims into survivors. It's the best damn job in the world, and it's enough for me.

"You almost ready?" Wolfe looks at me.

I guess I daydreamed there for a bit because they all look expectantly at me. It takes half a second for it to kick in. I'm leading this operation.

Max isn't with us on this op. He's still healing from his injuries sustained during our last mission, the one where Eve Deverough was freed from the hands of Tomas Benefield. Max took two bullets during that op.

He walked through miles of jungle, hung out in a tree all night, and nearly ran himself to the ground with a bullet buried in his leg and a wound in his arm. Infection set in, but Max powered through. He never gave up. He said it was because of a connection between him and Eve.

He couldn't let her down.

The only thing that saved him, if we're to believe Doc Summers, was some creative bargaining at a small village for antibiotics. That, and Eve, who took care of him. Their love was something powerful to watch as it developed. From the first tentative looks, glances which lingered, attention that couldn't be swayed, I watched Max fall in love with a woman who, by all intents and purposes, hated him on sight.

I watched him get *bit.*

"Yeah, let's get started."

Wolfe fiddles with the computer, hooking up to the hotspot on his phone. He runs through the security protocols to establish a secure channel.

I grab a chair and sit beside Axel and Griff. They're shoulder to shoulder, thick as thieves, and the bastards are going through all the pictures Liam took last night.

I'm going to kill Liam, but if he didn't take them, Wolfe would've. Actually, I bet half the photos *are* from Wolfe. Now that I think about it, there are two distinct angles from where the photos were taken.

Bastards.

They're supposed to have my back, not glory in my shame.

"Who's the pretty blonde?" Axel leans over, zooming in on a shot with Lily in the background.

Her brows knit together, and I swear there's murder in her eyes. She's looking at one of the women who got a bit handsy and placed her palm on my belly. Her fingers curled over my junk, coping a feel. She wasn't the only one, but she was the only one Lily caught.

A laugh escapes me as I remember the speed with which Lily reacted. She flicked a wet towel, hitting the woman dead on the knuckles.

I remember because my dick wasn't too far from the tip of that towel. From the way the woman jumped, it had to have stung like a bee. That was the last woman who tried to grope me.

Of course, Lily had a part in that. She loudly proclaimed that the next woman to touch my junk would lose her head.

Yeah, Lily is a force to be reckoned with. Her possessiveness turns me on. Her willingness to explore some boundaries, others would pull back from, is hot as sin. I cup my hand over my groin, not willing to let the guys know I get hard just thinking about her.

I still taste her on my tongue, a mixture of whiskey, honey, and spice. She's a tantalizing contradiction. Innocent on the outside. A temptress when we're alone.

"Knox's latest obsession." Liam kicks back, getting comfortable. "Look at the way she looks at him. Like she wants to eat him up."

He swipes on his phone then hands me a picture of Lily bending over me at the bar. She's licking the salt off my belly and her eyes are locked to mine.

"A gentleman never tells." I lace my fingers behind my head. No way am I sharing one damn thing about last night with the guys.

"Fine. Be like that." Liam leans forward, propping his elbows on the table. "I need coffee."

Wolfe finishes up the connection, and the screen flicks to life. Four faces greet us on the screen. Max, our team leader. CJ, head of the Guardians. Mitzy, with her psychedelic hair, is our technical lead. And then there's Sam. He's head over all of Guardian HRS.

Sam opens his mouth, but before he can say a word, Mitzy pipes up. "Knox, what the fuck did you do?"

"Um …" I look around, then punch Liam when he laughs. "I did nothing."

"As if." She rolls her eyes, quite dramatically, and puffs out a breath hard enough to make her purple bangs lift.

"Hey, all I did was lose a bet. Liam's the one who took all the photos. No one made you look at them."

"Ha ha. As interesting as those pictures may or may not be, that's not what I'm talking about."

"Then what are you talking about?"

"I want to know how much of a blockhead you have to be to get your phone tapped."

"Huh?"

Mitzy regales us with another dramatic eye roll. "I don't know what you guys don't understand about operational security, but whatever you did last night, whoever you did last night, she bugged your phone."

"Excuse me?" A sudden chill runs through me, followed by an eerie sense of calm. "What are you talking about?"

"I'm talking about your cellphone. Someone swapped out your SIM card. I'm guessing it's the pretty blonde in the hundreds of pictures clogging my phone."

"How do you know …" I don't finish that sentence because there's no way I can compete with Mitzy and her powerful intellect.

She's crazy smart. It's not something I expect from a chick, and that might make me sexist, but Mitzy isn't just smart. She's a fucking genius and almost as smart as Forest Summers, who created the Guardians, building on what Sam worked to put together during his tenure in the FBI.

"How do you know my phone was bugged?"

"Because I bug all your phones, idiot. When someone tries to piggyback on my handiwork, I take notice."

Notice? More like Mitzy takes offense.

"You bug our phones?"

"Of course, I do." Mitzy doesn't leave anything to chance.

"What do you want me to do?" I pull out my phone and hold it like it's going to bite me. "Remove the SIM card?"

"No, idiot. That would only tell whoever's listening that you found it." She rolls her eyes again. Honestly, I don't know how that doesn't give her a headache. I try it and my head throbs. "I'll figure out who it is soon enough."

"If they're listening, aren't they listening now?"

"Is your phone turned on?"

"No."

"Then they're not listening. But everything you say, every button you press, they're watching you. I already wiped any files linked to the Guardians. You can use it to call 9-1-1, but other than that, keep your phone turned off. If you have to call the team, use some of that code y'all made up for your super-secret hero crap."

Mitzy's funny, but she means every word.

"But won't that make them suspicious?"

"What, that a guy doesn't use his phone? You're too old to belong to the generation that feels obligated to post their every waking moment on social media. But you need to assume that when you turn it on, they have access to your GPS. My advice is to keep the phone off."

"Won't that be suspicious?"

"No. Not everyone in the world is tied to their phone. If she asks, and I really hope you're not planning on seeing her again, tell her you're a professional paranoid. It's plausible."

I am professional. I'm also paranoid.

Right now, I'm embarrassed as fuck about getting my phone hacked. It's like Guardian 101, and I just tanked the test.

"Fuck me." I drop my phone on the table and run my hands over the top of my legs. Lily played me. Not once. But twice. "Why?" The question is to no one in particular as I scrub my face with my hands. When did I become a sucker?

Evidently, all it took was a pretty face, a tight ass, and a little friendly competition to spin me into a frenzy. I lost perspective, and I never do that.

"Why, what?" Mitzy asks.

"Why would she do that?" I don't expect anyone to answer.

"I assume we're talking about Lily Freeman?" Mitzy arches a brow.

"I don't know her last name."

"Of course not. You're the fuck-them-and-forget-them guy. Why would you need a last name?" Mitzy blows out another breath, irritated, not at me, but I'm guessing at men in particular.

I get it. She works in a male-dominated field. Constantly having to prove herself must be tiresome.

"Not only did Lily play me, she screwed me too."

"Loser." Liam coughs a laugh into his fist.

"Oh, I'll *loser* you." I pounce on Liam, digging my knuckles into the top of his head. We go down in another tangle of limbs, trading more punches as we fall.

It's all in fun, but Max cuts us off.

"Knox! Liam! Stop fucking around. We're not here for social hour. Mitzy has new intel."

Liam springs to his feet and lends me a hand. I take it and we clap each other on the back. Wrestling, and trading punches, are just another part of our day.

"The first bit of intel I have is an interesting tidbit," Mitzy speaks to us through the computer screen.

It's hard to really *look* at someone via video conferencing. Depending on where the camera is, and where the person sits relative to it, direct eye contact just doesn't happen.

At least for us mere mortals.

There are only two people I know who can stare me down from the other side of a computer screen. One person is Mitzy. The other is Forest Summers. Right now, Mitzy looks me straight in the eye.

How the fuck does she do that?

"What's interesting?" I try looking straight at the camera, but I know I must look like a fool on her end.

The thing is, Mitzy is baiting me. She could just spit it out, but she wants me to ask. I'm going to bite because I'm curious about the woman I spent the night with. Curious might be a bit of an understatement. Lily has me downright fascinated.

"Lily Freeman works for the DEA." Mitzy leans back with a satisfied smirk and waits for my reaction. I'd like to say I'm calm, cool, and collected, but I'm not. I spit out nonsense.

"What the what?" I'm all ears.

"You heard me. She works for the DEA."

"Why would a DEA agent bug my phone?"

The Guardians have nothing to do with the DEA. We occasionally work with the FBI. Delta team takes on hostage negotiation and rescue assignments when the FBI needs unconventional solutions, but we're not involved with the DEA on any level I'm aware of. A quick check on my team, and they share the same confusion I feel.

"I'm currently hacking into their system to see what she knows, who's on her team, and if they're working an active case right now, or if she's just in New Orleans blowing off steam."

Please be here visiting friends and blowing off steam.

Except Lily lives here. She's not visiting anyone.

Fingers crossed, I don't ask the questions I should, too pissed at myself for being so easily played.

"Is there any reason she would be targeting the Guardians?" We've done nothing that should draw the attention of the DEA.

"Not that we're aware of." Mitzy blows out another puff of air, lifting her bangs out of her eyes. "Don't worry about Lily. I've got my people working on it. But back to business …"

Yes, please, let's get back to business. I need an op right now, something to take my mind off Lily.

"We have good news."

"You do?"

This is why we're here.

Max and I pulled out a set of ledgers when we brought Benefield's operation down. They detail every slave transaction he made. It's in a cipher. Our hope is that it may hold the key to cracking open one of the largest, most sophisticated sex-trafficking rings in the world.

But the intel is only actionable if we act quickly. With Benefield out of the picture, there's no doubt someone else is stepping into the power vacuum left behind.

Some asshole will pounce on the opportunity it provides.

"So, what do you have?" I assume this meeting isn't solely to chastise my mistake.

"I'm working on the cipher, and I've got a date and a time for *Lei'lani's* arrival in New Orleans."

"This is good news." It's exactly what we've been waiting for.

"Good and bad news."

"How's that?"

"It's a trap." Her brows pinch together.

"Why is that?" I'm intrigued.

"It reminds me of when Bravo team got ambushed."

"Wait a second." I look to the guys. "*Lei'lani* is a ship? Not a person."

"You certainly put two and two together fast, Alpha Two."

"Ha ha, very funny."

The Guardians are known as the pointy tip of the spear at Guardian HRS. There's constant rivalry between the tech guys and the Guardians. It's the typical stupid shit. All brawn, no brain.

We're no better.

We call them skinny nerds. The truth is we respect the shit out of each other. The teams couldn't do shit without the intelligence Mitzy and her team provide, and we're not even going to talk about all the cool, cutting-edge tech they create for us.

"*Lei'lani* is the name of a cargo container ship. It regularly makes the rounds between New Orleans, Cancun, and Colombia. Does that route sound familiar?"

"Shit." I draw my hand over my face, thinking about our mission to rescue Zoe.

She was taken off the crowded streets of Cancun in broad daylight. After spending a week in a holding location, her and twelve other girls were loaded into a container and shipped off to Colombia. The details of that mission are morbid. Half those girls didn't make it home.

We weren't fast enough to save them, but we saved Zoe. We later saved one other girl who was in that same shipment. Eve Deverough is now safe and sound, hooking up with Max back in California, while I'm getting screwed by a white-haired vixen.

"Let me guess, the next thing you're going to say is that ship is one of Deverough's?"

"In a roundabout way," Mitzy explains. "It's a subsidiary of a subsidiary. Deverough maintains he's not involved, and there's just enough distance between his shipping company for it to possibly be true." She gives Deverough the benefit of the doubt. We all think he's dirty. He's also Eve's father.

A shipping mogul, he paid escalating ransom demands to Benefield, who was supposed to return Eve. When he didn't, Deverough hired the Guardians to bring his daughter home. Mitzy believes it was all an elaborate money laundering scheme, but she's yet to officially pin that on Deverough.

We rescued Eve, and she's now with Max. Not her father. And she won't be until we figure out the extent of his involvement in the sex-trafficking operation. Max won't allow it. He won't put her at risk.

"So, what's the play?"

Mitzy wouldn't send us into a potential trap. Forest won't allow it. Sam would flat out refuse. CJ would say fuck you. Max will flip out and say, in no uncertain terms, that he won't put us in harm's way. Which is funny considering that's kind of the job description. But then, there's risk associated with the job and risk associated with poor planning and poor intelligence.

"Same play," Mitzy says. "We have reason to believe a new shipment will be loaded tonight."

There's complete silence on my end. None of us move. I stare at the screen, waiting for Max, CJ, or Sam to speak up.

But none of them do.

TEN

Lily

THE CONVERSATION WITH HARRY GOES ABOUT AS EXPECTED. PETER-the-Prick snorts when I mention Wilder spent the night. When I glare at him, the snort turns to a snicker. I know exactly what's going through his mind, but I plant my feet and firm my stance. I dare him to say anything.

Anything.

If I'm a whore, then he's what?

And herein lies the problem. He's a stud while I'm the slut. Yet, we both did what we needed to get the job done.

Fucker.

I harden myself against the slut-shaming, bracing for the pain to twist inside of me. One deep breath turns to two, and the twisting inside of me eases.

Harry, oblivious to the nonverbal exchange between Peter and myself, listens. He's not happy, but I did nothing wrong. In our line of work, the line between good and bad is often fuzzy, especially when we deal in the currency of information.

Jinx backs me up. She argues the points I lay out, detailing why Wilder working for us is better than putting him behind bars.

I meet Harry's gaze head-on. The stare-off stretches between us until his dark-brown eyes soften.

"You think you can get him to work for us?"

"In my vast experience with Wilder, it's a guess at best, but he'd be foolish to throw away a plea deal." I lick my lips and pray the heat I'm feeling doesn't reach my face.

Last night, Wilder rocked my world. My attention shifts down, where it lands on the floor. If I keep looking at Harry, somehow, he'll know. At least Peter's snickers taper off.

He knows what I'm only just now realizing. It was a mistake to jump into bed with Wilder. The man knows how to please a woman. He definitely knew how to please me, as if he's trained in the sensual art of sexual pleasure.

No man is that good.

Right?

Remembering the way his dominance flared, a rush of heat shoots through my body. Only a masterful lover can accomplish such a feat. I'm as good as his, and I hate how much I crave his control.

As for arresting Wilder, and turning him to our demands, technically, we don't have anything actionable which would put Wilder behind bars.

All of our *information* is circumstantial at best. We have him in New Orleans on the days shipments of illegal narcotics entered U.S. soil. We have him in Colombia a few days later, with no record of how he got there.

There certainly appears to be a connection, but it could be true —true and unrelated.

What if we're wrong?

I blink, realizing my mind went off on a tangent, and quickly refocus on our meeting.

"He's involved …" Harry taps his meaty fingers on the smooth wood of his desk. "Either as a courier, overseeing delivery, accepting payment, or transporting it to Colombia. It's a low-level position at best, but all we need is one stepping-stone to get in. You really think you can turn him?"

"I do." Although, after last night, I'm not sure if I still hold the balance of power between us.

Wilder got under my skin. I've thought of nothing but him all day long.

"Let's give it go. If this works, you'll be responsible for cracking this operation wide open." Harry seldom gives praise outright.

That's as close as he'll come to telling me this could very well be the thing that launches my career. It could also be the biggest failure of my career.

Caution is my friend.

But how am I going to keep my head in the game when all I can think about is Wilder and his muscles, honed to masculine perfection? Or how easily he lifted me and fucked me while standing in the middle of my living room.

The man is a fucking machine in every sense of the word.

Hours later, I shift nervously, back and forth, as we get ready to head out.

"You're fidgeting." Jinx jerks on my sleeve to get my attention. "Stop it."

I get it. We're the only two females on our team. Everything we do is hyper-criticized and picked apart.

As far as nerves go, the guys could do the Mexican bean dance and no one would blink an eye. If either of us does it, we're judged as nervous and unsure. The double standard is something I'll spend my entire career fighting.

Not that I fight.

I'm not one of those women out there crying at the top of my lungs about bringing down the patriarchy. I believe good work will be rewarded, which is why I need this operation to be flawless.

"I'm not fidgeting," I whisper back, agitated and fidgety.

Our team gets ready. Armored vests go on over our clothes. Weapons get checked. Magazines are stuffed into the ammo pouches that Velcro to our vests. Flashlight batteries get tested. Beams of light pierce through the darkness, revealing myriads of insects dancing in the night air.

I take a step closer to Jinx. "What if our information is wrong?"

"You doubt the intel?" She checks her weapon, ensuring the chamber's empty.

"I doubt everything." It's a good habit, one I intend on keeping.

"If it's wrong, then you don't have to bear any guilt regarding Wilder." She talks about using him.

"I'll always know." I'm the one who suspects him, and if our intelligence is correct, he'll know I played him yet again.

There will be no more of what happened last night. I've never experienced anything like it; as if all my inhibitions fell away. With him, I could be anything I wanted to be.

I can be apologetically me; the side of me I want to be when I'm with a man.

This totally sucks.

It sucks major monkey balls. The sex was off the charts hot, but what I crave is the connection we shared.

It's what I'll miss.

I haven't stopped thinking about him all day. We started the night as strangers, and while we shared nothing about our daily lives, we shared the most intimate pieces of ourselves.

Most would say I'm more adventurous than is wise when it comes to sex, but for me, sex has always been a release—nothing more than a physical need.

With Wilder?

I don't know what it is about that man, but we bonded. We connected in a way that terrifies me. I let him see a side of me I've never shared with another man.

What if it never happens again?

My jitters aren't the result of pre-mission nerves. When I see Wilder again, and I'm pretty damn sure I will, it's going to be from the opposite side of the law. There's no coming back from that.

"Load up!" Peter calls out as he thumps the side of a van. He's a major asshole, but he's a great team leader in the field.

Harry's in charge of the operation as a whole, overseeing both our team on the ground and the techies who feed us information. They follow in a specialized mobile command center.

Peter's in charge of tactics on the ground. Which is both good and bad. Former military, he parades around like he knows everything, and he does know a lot of really useful stuff. I'm not complaining about that. What I don't like is how he barks orders while looking down his nose at us.

I don't care how much military experience he has, this is a different arena. The same rules do not apply. He likes to think we're his little soldiers rather than the highly trained DEA operatives we are.

Jinx and I share a look, both rolling our eyes in shared sympathy. Then we pile into the van with the rest of our team.

The drive to the docks is quiet.

Tense.

The men we face tonight are well-armed. Our primary mission is to intercept tonight's shipment and have a private conversation with Wilder. This is the trickiest part of the operation.

We can't afford to arrest Wilder. Do that, and whoever he works for will think we turned him, especially after we do turn him and release him back into the wild.

We're working within a narrow window of opportunity. We need to have a conversation that gives Wilder no option but to accept.

Then we let him go.

That's the piece that worries me the most. Wilder knows where I live. If he wants retribution, there's nothing keeping him from coming after me.

That's my mistake.

I should've fucked him in the bathroom of Callie's bar. Instead, I made a bonehead mistake and took him up to my apartment.

After we let him go, one of two things will happen. Either I'll never see him again, or I'll see him immediately after he hunts me down, intent on payback.

I tug at the collar of my shirt. Like most New Orleans summer nights, humidity thickens the air. Somedays, I feel like I'm swimming through the oppressiveness of it all.

The heat of the day lingers in the humid air, making me sweat in all the heavy gear. I'm supposed to say *perspire* because I'm a lady, but I'm sweating buckets. There's nothing ladylike about the sweat trickling down my back, gathering between my boobs, or running off the tip of my nose. My eyes sting from all the sweat beading my brow.

And I probably stink. If not now, within an hour, I'll be a walking plume of funk.

We wear tactical dress with bulletproof vests and helmets fitted with night-vision goggles. I carry a standard-issue pistol, a flashlight, and two clips for my gun.

The cargo container, *Lei'lani*, just pulled into dock. Stacked with thousands of containers, offloading begins immediately. With the speed of the dock workers and crane operators, the entire ship will be offloaded quickly, and hidden amongst thousands of containers, illegal narcotics wait to flood our streets.

Our job is two-fold.

First and foremost, we intercept the containers packed with the drugs. With a street value in the tens of millions, we can't afford for that much product to hit the streets. The opioid epidemic is out of control, growing at a phenomenal rate. It ruins lives, and we won't stand for that.

Our secondary mission is to confirm Wilder's involvement. If he's a courier like we suspect, he'll be here, overseeing the offloading of the drugs, handling the exchange of cash, and then he'll disappear.

We need to get to him before he disappears as we have no jurisdiction in Colombia.

We're laying a trap for him and whoever works with him. Our team offloads some distance away from the busyness of the docks.

"You ready?" Peter stands beside me. He completes a check of his equipment while I do the same. Once done, we turn to each other, performing a buddy check. This routine is drilled into us and prevents accidents from faulty gear.

"I am."

Peter takes in a deep breath and presses his lips together. "Hey, I —um …"

"Spit it out, Peter." I'm still hot from the briefing this afternoon.

"I just wanted to apologize."

"For breathing?" I cock a hip and try to act all badass. It's a constant struggle, working to prove myself to my male colleagues.

"I deserve that." He bites his cuticle, a nervous habit of his, then yanks his finger out of his mouth when he sees me watching. "I shouldn't have …"

"Snorted? Snickered? Undermined me in front of the team?" This isn't something I'm letting go. "I've worked hard to earn my position as a field agent. You outrank me, which means your comments are that much more injurious. I need the team to respect me, to count on me, and to consider me one of them rather than a weak-willed female incapable of breathing."

"Damn." He takes two steps back, hands held up in mock defeat, but then something shifts within him. Peter closes the distance. "You're absolutely correct."

"Excuse me?" The last thing I expect is for him to agree.

He shifts back half a step. "You didn't do anything any of us haven't done before. Nothing I haven't personally done. This job—it can be tough. It doesn't matter if you're male or female. It takes a tough person to make it work. It was wrong of me to act the way I did."

Holy fuck, where is this coming from? My heart just about stops from shock.

Did Peter apologize?

I want to pinch myself.

"That's—um, that's very big of you." Is there cotton in my ears?

"I just wanted you to know that I think you're doing a great job, and I've got your back." He jerks his chin in the general direction of the docks. "I don't want you doubting anyone on your team, least of all me."

"Um …" I'm in shock but impressed. "Thank you."

"Anyway, that's what I wanted to say. Sorry for making you feel less because you're a woman." He barely skates by with the female comment, but I'll give it to him. Peter never apologizes. It's why Jinx and I call him Peter-the-Prick. He really is insufferable.

"Thank you." I'll give him the benefit of the doubt. I can be professional, too, except when it comes to Wilder.

Long, muscled legs. A chest chiseled out of granite. Arms full of sinew and muscle. Images of his naked body fully engaged in sex drive me insane.

Focus on the job, Lily, not your deranged pleasure.

The man definitely got under my skin. His bold stare entranced me. A labyrinth of sin and seduction, secrets and lies, I lost myself in a maze of twisted corners and confusing blind ends.

That never happens. I never lose control like that. My chest squeezes because it knows what I refuse to accept.

Heat pricks along my neck with the memory of his scratchy beard moving between my legs and the magic of his tongue … A groan escapes me as another wave of heat surges through me.

Focus!

I'm trying!

The team moves down the docks, sticking to the shadows. This is an industrial port. Containers waiting for transport fill the docks, creating a labyrinth for us to navigate. It slows us down, but we know exactly what we're doing.

Moving stealthily, our team moves into position. We approach *Lei'lani* from the stern. Massive lines, thicker than my legs, extend out from the back of the container ship to wrap around man-sized iron cleats dockside.

Offloading has yet to begin, but the crane operators are in position. They sit far overhead in climate-controlled cabs where they control the cranes, which will unload containers one by one.

The crew is still dealing with port authorities, going over the crew manifest and cargo listing. The moment that's complete, the crane operators will begin the laborious work offloading over ten thousand shipping containers.

That's ten thousand containers potentially carrying the narcotics we hope to intercept. It still amazes me how much freight moves around the world on these massive container ships. Or is it *in* the ships?

I want to know how many containers are lost at sea. They stack so high; the ships look top-heavy. I could look it up on my phone, but I'm supposed to be focused on the mission instead of stupid trivia facts about container ships. I'll do that later when I'm snuggling into bed.

Tonight promises to be a very long night.

Tonight?

It hits me.

Wilder's note mentioned seeing me tonight. What a fucking putz. He has no intention of seeing me tonight.

Jinx is right. He slipped out on me. What the ever-loving fuck? Next time I see him, you can bet he's getting a knee to the groin.

Nobody plays me like that.

We come to a halt about fifty meters away from the ship, where we hide in the shadows between two warehouses. Between us and the *Lei'lani,* scores of empty flatbeds wait in line. Floodlights shine down on the entire operation, turning the black of night into an odd twilight zone. The docks never sleep, which means getting any closer will be difficult.

Peter sends two of our men to the roof of the building beside us. They'll guide us in, keeping us out of sight. They're also responsible for spotting our mark.

That would be Wilder.

I shift foot-to-foot, nervous about seeing him again. He played me. There's no denying it, yet I still ache to feel him moving over me, sliding in and out, filling me up—making me feel whole.

The team settles in to wait, which only gives me that much more time to obsess over Wilder and build myself up into a frenzy.

ELEVEN

Knox

"Alpha Two, in position." My radio crackles.

One of the wires is loose, filling my ear with static. I adjust the earbud. It does no good, and there's nothing I can do about it.

"Copy that." CJ monitors the team from his position on the roof of a nearby building. He's got a bird's-eye view of the operations on the dock.

He flew in a few hours ago, joined by Max and Sam. Mitzy brought her technical team.

Minutes upon their arrival, they covered all the floors of our rental with brightly colored power cords, cables, and monitors of every size imaginable.

When I left our rental house, it looked like a clown threw up on its floors. Or better yet, a psychedelic arachnid infested our home away from home, spinning a web with its brightly colored silk.

There are wires and cables and cords all over the damn place. Mitzy assures me it's all color-coded. As long as it makes sense to her, what do I care? As the computers came online, the air heated with the smell of ozone. The air conditioner kicked in, laboring to keep up with the extra burden.

While Alpha team kitted out for the operation, the wistful

expression on Max's face didn't go unnoticed. I watched from afar as Griff went over and sat on the bed beside Max. He leaned close, said something, and Max gave a single, slow nod.

No reason to guess at that exchange.

Not too long ago, Griff's injury to his leg sidelined him from operating. Not that Griff let that slow him down. He joined us on a mission to rescue Moira in a support role, and damn if the fucker didn't rappel from a helicopter to pluck her off a cargo container ship, much like the one we're looking at tonight.

That's the thing with Guardians. Nothing slows us down. We'll take a bullet, get knocked down, and we'll keep on fighting.

Our mission in life is to save those unable to save themselves, and we'll go through hell to see it done.

There's no greater gift on this earth than setting someone free, but it's not just about helping those who can't help themselves.

Although, that's how it's generally seen.

It's about lending that hand when it's needed most. It's about stepping up, then stepping down.

We save women, girls, and boys, who've been stolen from their lives. We rescue them, then we show them how to save themselves.

We give them the tools to recover and show them how fierce they can be. We show them how to fight and how to survive. We put control back into their hands.

This is what it means to be a Guardian.

Doc Summers only recently released Griff from medical hold. His first mission back was the one where we pulled Max and Eve out of Colombia.

During that extraction, Max took a bullet to the leg and another to his arm. He then spent a day trekking through the jungle with that bullet lodged in his leg and infection setting in both leg and arm.

Doc Summers patched him up, pumped him full of powerful antibiotics, but now Alpha team's leader sits on the sidelines. Max isn't happy about that.

CJ decided we were good to go a man short. That leaves me to lead Alpha team, and my comm link is a mess of static. Not the best way to start a mission.

We're all in position now.

Max is with CJ, watching over us from the roof, pissed as fuck he's not down here with his team. Sam is with Mitzy back at the house, coordinating the thousands of things that go into a successful operation. Alpha team stops for a bit of on-the-ground reconnaissance to get our bearings and plan how we're going to execute this mission.

Mitzy's intel says a new shipment will be loaded tonight. Shipment? Have I become that jaded over the years?

Those are stolen lives, terrified women who've been kidnapped and are destined for a fate worse than death.

We're usually better prepared for most of our missions; details worked out and planned down to the minute. We couldn't do that this time.

We don't know which of the thousands upon thousands of containers hold the women we hope to rescue. Finding that one container out of thousands is left to Mitzy, her technical team, and her swarm of high-tech drones.

Once we know *which* container, and *where* it's located, we'll head in. Until then, we stay hidden behind a low, concrete barrier, scoping out the scene.

The problem is the size of an operation like this. Not our tiny bit, but rather what it takes to dock, offload, and load a container ship.

"You ready to spring this trap?" Axel stands beside me. We gather behind a low, concrete wall as we decide how to proceed.

"Let's hope it's not a trap. Stay alert."

"Copy that." Axel peers through the sight of his weapon. "It's busy as fuck down there."

"Yeah." I rub at the back of my neck. "We need to blend in, and that's not happening." Alpha team is kitted out in black tactical gear. "I need options."

Griff pulls out his spotting scope and takes a position next to Axel. "The whole place is lit up. Most of the action is at the dock, but we should be able to close in without too much difficulty. There's a nonstop stream of trucks. Not a lot of foot traffic."

The place is a maze of containers waiting for transport, if not for this particular ship, then for the one coming right behind it.

Liam shifts behind me, his agitation palpable. "So much for this operation working only out of Cancun."

"No shit." I agree with him.

The intel Mitzy dug up comes with grave connotations. We thought this particular operation worked only out of Cancun, plucking unsuspecting college co-eds off the street, gathering them until a quota was fulfilled, and only then loading them into a container for shipping to Colombia.

Now, we have action in New Orleans.

"What do you think it means?" Liam hops up on the wall. "Griff, hand me your scope. I've got a better view from up here."

Griff hands up his scope. Liam grabs it and puts it to his eye.

"Did Mitzy say how many girls?" Liam asks.

"It wasn't clear. Only that there's a shipment loading tonight." She's still working on breaking the cipher on Benefield's ledgers.

"Does anyone think it's weird there was basically no halt in operations after Benefield died?" Axel scans the dock through the scope of his rifle.

"I was thinking the same thing." Wolfe leans against the wall, chilling, while we complete our basic scan of the area. "Although, I have a theory."

"What kind of theory?" Griff joins Wolfe against the wall. Axel and Liam continue their scans.

"I'm thinking this is another branch, separate from Benefield's operation."

"But this shipment was in Benefield's ledgers." His logic is flawed.

"Yeah, that's right." Wolfe pauses, but then he gives a shake of his head as if he can't get something out of it. "I've just been thinking about it." He yanks off his black gloves with his teeth. "Working on U.S. soil is pretty damn risky. Not as easy to bribe the cops as it is in Cancun."

"There are dirty cops all over the place," Griff disagrees. "Maybe Benefield was expanding his hunting ground?"

"I keep thinking about Moira and Zoe." Wolfe isn't going to let this go. Something's bugging him.

"What about them?" The timbre of Griff's voice changes. His entire body goes rigid. Griff doesn't like reminders of what Moira went through.

He's not the only one. Axel looks up from his scope, enraged with the memories of what Zoe endured.

I'm curious about Wolfe's train of thought. He's a smart guy with an uncanny ability to make connections between seemingly unrelated things. I used to brush off his hunches, but he's never wrong. My ears perk up.

"What are you thinking, Wolfe?"

"Moira's and Zoe's abductions were the result of specialized orders being placed and fulfilled. What if that's what we're seeing here?"

"Interesting ..." I'm not convinced. "Maybe they're just taking advantage of New Orleans?"

"I thought about that, but this isn't the same kind of place as Cancun."

I think about what Wolfe says.

He's right about Moira and Zoe. Moira was targeted because her buyer specifically requested her. Zoe was also targeted, at least the second time.

The mood shifts within the team as what Wolfe says sinks in.

"So, what? A buyer specifies who he wants? Like how specific?"

"By name for Moira and Zoe," Wolfe answers. "Maybe just by physical characteristics for the others. Who's to say? The order's placed. The girl is picked up, brought here for shipping ..."

"But why take them out of the country?"

"Training." Wolfe kicks off the wall to pace. "Isn't that what you said Benefield did at The Retreat? The girls were brought in, trained over the course of a few weeks, then auctioned off. I bet this is no different. Who wants to go through the trouble of breaking in a new slave when you can have an expert do it?"

On the surface, his words are cold and callous, but they're, unfortunately, very true. I was at Benefield's, acting the part of Max's personal bodyguard. We never saw the training pens, but we did see girls learning how to serve the guests.

"It makes sense."

"Anyway, that's what I'm thinking." Wolfe stops to stretch his shoulders.

"What kind of fucked up shit is that?" Axel spits on the ground. "Fuckers need to rot in jail."

"Agreed."

"We've seen worse." Wolfe shrugs, and he's absolutely right. We've seen some pretty fucked up shit.

The tension within the team escalates. It's in the pinching of Axel's eyes, scribed deeply in the hard scowl lining Griff's face, and etched in the tense expressions shared between Liam and Wolfe.

They say so much with so few words.

"I've got an idea." Liam jumps down from the wall. "Although it means ditching some of our gear."

"Go on." I'm ready to get this show on the road.

Our helmets are pretty high-tech, but they scream special operative. We're five big men, dressed in black, carrying weapons as if we're ready for war.

Which isn't too far from the truth.

There's no way to hide what we are. Ditching our helmets isn't the best plan, but it might make sense. It all depends on what Liam's thinking.

"The workers get bused in from a parking lot." He begins. "I watched two shuttles pull up to the same building. The men file out, go inside, and come out wearing jumpsuits. Different colors, which I'm guessing are specific to each job. The only people I see walking around are those in gray jumpsuits."

"You think we can get our hands on some of those?"

"If we can get in that building."

I patch into command and explain. After a little back and forth, it's agreed.

"Leave your weapons and helmets here. CJ's sending someone

to pick them up. Wolfe and Liam, find us some jumpsuits. The rest of us wait here. Once Mitzy's drones find our target we move in. Axel and Griff, find us a path."

"What do you think about what Wolfe says?" Griff's scowl deepens.

"I don't know what this shipment speaks to. It could be an opportunistic grab."

"How many times has Wolfe been wrong?" Axel chimes in, which is weird. Usually, it's Axel with the weird hunches.

We've all grown used to Wolfe's uncanny ability. He would've made a great intelligence officer if he hadn't decided to join the Navy and become a SEAL, although his hunches served him well as a SEAL.

"I don't know what to think." I shrug, not fully convinced but open to the idea. "New Orleans is a party city. It's just as easy to snatch an unsuspecting female off the streets here as it is in Cancun, but what Wolfe says makes sense."

"If that's the case, we need to find out who's in charge of slave acquisitions. Someone had to have replaced Benefield." Griff's voice rumbles with a growl and his fingers twitch.

"Benefield was a putz, but he was a rich putz. The Retreat was all him. If he wasn't the top dog, I don't know who it could be. We're talking not just filthy rich or stinking rich. He was uber-wealthy. That place was something else."

"But someone had to be helping him. Or, someone set him up as the fall guy, pulling strings in the background." Griff's already thinking about who we need to kidnap to obtain that information. "That could explain why there was no stop in operations?"

If true, the implications transcend everything we know about sex trafficking in the modern age.

What does it mean for a client to be able to pick and choose, either by physical characteristics or personal information, a female he wants to own?

"I really want to know whether these assholes put in an order for a female, age nineteen, five-eight, a buck-twenty in weight, with red hair? Or does he say I want this particular female and get his order fulfilled?" Axel leans his head back and pinches the bridge of his nose.

"Either option is a fucking nightmare," I say. "That asshole did it to get Moira. Maybe we need to speak to him some more."

"That may be a bit complicated." Griff looks at the toes of his boots.

Griff interrogated the man who hired the men who took Moira. I know better than to ask too many questions about why it might be complicated to speak to that asshole again.

I hate sex traffickers, but I hate their clients even more. I'd love to go after those assholes directly and show them what it feels like to have their freedom taken.

I served my time in the Navy, fighting the good fight, but the end objective was never really clear. With the Guardians, I fight the fights which matter. The objective is crystal clear. There's no bureaucracy that muddies the waters and dilutes the impact of the sacrifices I make.

It angers me thinking a man behind a computer screen can tailor the purchase of a slave to a specific individual. It guts me, even more, to know those orders are fulfilled.

It takes less than fifteen minutes before Liam and Wolfe return. They carry dingy-gray jumpsuits and pass them around. While we dress, my gut tells me Alpha team needs a time out.

TWELVE

Knox

I signal for everyone to cut their comms. This is a conversation for the team, and the team alone.

Yes, that leaves out Max, but he's not with us now, and I don't need Mitzy and her tech team listening in. I also don't need CJ hearing anything about what I'm about to say.

Axel cradles his weapon and plants his feet shoulder-width apart. He's annoyed and not opposed to expressing that to me. Griff stands beside him, fingering the knives along his belt.

It's dark, but the anger simmering in their eyes is unmistakable. I get it. Tonight, we're getting upfront and personal with the men who kidnapped their women, tortured them, and worse.

Axel and Griff are personally invested in this operation. That makes their actions suspect. Their abilities are something I will never question, but their focus is off.

It's not on the task at hand.

I turn my attention to Liam and Wolfe. We're a team of six, one man short. Liam and Wolfe, like Axel and Griff, buddy up. It's a testament to the bond we all share. We train and work as a team of six, but on our most basic level, we work in pairs.

"Huddle up, Alpha." I'll keep my comments open for the

moment and will drill down to the shit festering between us if I must.

The gray jumpsuit stinks. It smells of metal, diesel fuel, and sweat. Lots of sweat, and the fabric scratches where it touches my bare skin. There's not much of that with my tactical gear on, but it's enough to piss me off.

The weight of leading this mission drags on me. Max is grooming me to take over the lead of my own team. I'm happy where I am and want to throat punch him for suggesting I'd want anything other than what I have now.

I'm not ready to lead a team into the breach.

What if this is a trap?

What if I'm the one who leads Alpha into the same shitstorm that crippled Bravo team?

With my luck, that's exactly what will happen. Although, Max says I'm far too cautious.

To a fault. His words, not mine.

Is it true? Am I too cautious to be an effective team leader? Am I ready to take on that responsibility?

I'm not.

Max disagrees.

I disagree with him.

I'm a great follower, but corralling a bunch of alpha-fucking men into following my lead?

Totally not on board with that.

It's too much work dealing with all that shit.

Maybe, I'm too touchy-feely? Max doesn't give a shit what other people think. It's his way or the highway. I'm always looking for everyone to buy in to my ideas.

That's what's going to kill me as a leader. Once they realize my insecurities, they're going to walk all over me. Which means, I need to be a fucking son-of-a-bitch when it comes to the mission.

The Guardians are growing with each passing day. We have our international units: Alpha, Bravo, and Charlie. Then, there's Delta, our domestic hostage rescue team who works with the FBI on 'off the books' operations.

Do we need an Epsilon?

Max would say yes.

I say no. Aren't we spread thin as it is?

No idea what CJ, Sam, or Forest Summers thinks, and I don't want to know. I don't want that responsibility. I'm happy as a clam being Alpha Two.

What the fuck would Epsilon do?

How much *more* 'off the books' do you have to be to be Epsilon? It's a good question when the Guardians are, by definition, off the books as it is?

"Why are we doing a fucking huddle?" Liam isn't happy. He readjusts his grip on his weapon. Like the rest of us, his night-vision goggles are on his helmet, flipped up.

We're preserving our night vision while we can, not to mention the night vision goggles will be useless down by the dock, where night turns to day as massive floodlights push back the darkness.

"Why do you think?" Instead of answering Liam, I toss his question back at him. It's an effective leadership technique Max is teaching me.

"No clue." Liam shifts again. "We *are* on a time schedule." He's not happy with the delay and makes no qualms about voicing his opinion. He wouldn't do that if Max was in charge.

Liam's a man of action.

Short on words, he likes to skip ahead to the solution. Generally, this works well for the team, except when it doesn't.

The last thing we need is a hothead. That's the shortest path to disaster. Considering we don't know whether we're walking into a trap or not, now isn't the time to find out. I need Liam to take a step back.

How do I do that?

How do I mimic the power and professionalism Max exudes without him here to back me up?

If the team isn't focused, we're doomed.

That rests on me.

It also means any failure here is all on me. I need Alpha team focused. Instead, Axel and Griff share murderous expressions, thinking about what happened to their women. Wolfe is pondering deep thoughts, abstract ideas we can only speculate at. Liam's agitation is through the roof, and I don't understand why.

I need them to refocus and believe in me.

This crap about why we're here, it needs to disappear. Like, not erased, but obliterated.

If I fail in that, the whole mission falls apart. I've never respected Max's role more than I do in this moment.

As I force the team to huddle, Mitzy's flight of dragonflies scours the dock. That's what she calls the drones she sends out during our missions.

Smaug is the largest of her drones, providing high-altitude support. He's not needed for this. The dragonflies are small, handheld drones, camouflaged and whisper quiet. They're our eyes during a mission.

"You don't feel it?" I glance between my team.

"Feel what?" Wolfe glances toward the ship in the distance. "All I feel is time ticking by. How do we know they haven't loaded it yet?"

"They're still off-loading, that's why. Mitzy will tell us when to move." And where to go.

"She'd better hurry the fuck up before we run out of time." Axel practically growls out the words. He looks to me for support, but I don't give it.

We're here to save lives, not start a war on U.S. soil. I need the guys to focus back in on that.

"It takes well over twenty-four hours to offload and load one of these ships," I say.

"True, but we need to get to that container before it's placed on the ship," Wolfe interjects. "Once that happens, our window of opportunity closes."

"Yeah," Liam chimes in, "then, it's a whole other operation involving more complicated shit like boarding a vessel at sea and rescuing the girls from the ship itself."

He's not wrong. We've done that before, but it's not easy. I feel like all I'm doing is losing their focus rather than reeling it in.

"That's an understatement." Griff pulls one of his knives free and tosses it in the air. It spins, traveling up, while he stares at me. Griff snatches the knife as it falls, without once looking at it. He tosses it in the air. It sails up.

"Regardless of what it means, or doesn't mean." Time to corral them in. "I need everyone to take stock, pack up that shit in your head and shove it down deep. If you're not focused on the mission, you're a liability to the team."

"Who says we're not focused?" Axel takes offense to my comment. "We're totally focused."

"On the girls we need to save, or on taking down the men who put them there?" I look to each of them in turn, fixing them with a hard glare. "Look, I get it. We're all pissed. Axel and Griff, you're closer to this because of Moira and Zoe. But this mission isn't about the men who took them. It's about rescuing the women. I'll call this off if I'm not convinced we're all focused on the objective of *this* mission and nothing else."

"The fuck you will." Griff takes a step back.

"You bet I will." I take in a deep breath and blow it out nice and slow. "Look, no one wants to admit they're not focused. But you're angry, pissed off, and out to slay the bastards who prey on young women and children. That hatred boils in our blood. Mine too. Sometimes that's good. It pushes us further than we could otherwise go without it. But too much of it makes you escalate the risks you're willing to take. I'm not willing to do that, especially after what happened to Bravo team. Or have you all forgotten how they got blown to pieces doing exactly what we're getting ready to do?"

It wasn't at this port, but rather the shipping docks in Cancun. Mitzy got a lead on a shipment going out. Bravo went to free the girls, walked into a trap, and they're still nursing their injuries from that shitshow.

"Need I remind you," I continue, "most of the men out there are innocent dock workers. Honest men out to make an honest living on a questionably honest wage. They aren't the ones we're after, and we're not out to have a video of us splashed all over social media because we were careless and are seen. We're supposed to be invisible."

With the jumpsuits, we're more likely to blend in. It's possible we will be invisible, but there's no reason to mention that.

I expect Griff to hold out the longest. He's personally invested, like Axel, but he can be exceptionally single-minded. In general, I find Axel more willing to listen.

I don't mind Griff unpacking his rage when questioning of a prisoner, but it has no place here.

He tosses the knife once again, and like the time before, he plucks it out of the air without looking at it.

"Got my shit packed up and locked down. I'm good." Griff slides the knife back into its sheath and shoulders his weapon.

"Good to know." I glance at Axel, Liam, and Wolfe, wondering which of them will be next. "Anyone else want to pack up your shit? Leave it here, or we turn around."

Axel's eyes pinch. He's not happy being challenged. This isn't usually my place. Max is the one who holds us together. A look from him and we know we've stepped out of line. The guys trust me, but they follow Max. It's a distinction that means everything.

Wolfe speaks next. "I'm good."

I arch my brow. That's as close to a question that I'll give.

"Focus on the mission." He gives a solemn nod, then ruins it with one of his infamous grins. "We'll do all the touchy-feely emotional shit later. After we take these fuckers down."

"Right," I agree with him. "*After* we take them down."

Liam doesn't speak. He glares at me while stretching out his neck.

"Just another day in the office, right?" Axel's entire body goes from tense and rigid to cool as a clam. He's in the zone now. The whole team seems to be settling it down.

It doesn't take much. I've watched Max for years, learning how he leads. We all know this shit. We know to focus on the mission and leave emotions for later, but that doesn't mean that kind of shit doesn't slip through our defenses.

It's no lie.

Every time we outfit ourselves for a mission, as the gear goes on, our emotions get packed into tiny little packages to be unpacked later.

"Right." Another glance at Liam tells me he's not going to jump on the Kumbaya bandwagon. That's okay. The team is centered and once again focused on the mission. I reactivate my comms and motion for them to do the same.

"Alpha team ready to move." I report our status to command. They're aware of the pause in communications.

Most of the work tonight will be done, not by us, but by the drones flitting over our heads. Mitzy launched over a hundred into the night. One hundred drones powered by her AI technology to search out a needle in a haystack. It's going to be a long night, but if successful, we'll save lives.

Any day we get to do that is a good day.

"Alpha Two, initial sweep of zone one negative." Mitzy's voice pipes through my earbud layered with static.

"Copy that." I turn to the team. "Let's move."

Zone One is the outermost area of containers. Mitzy's working her drones from the outside in. As each zone is cleared, we'll move inward.

We approach from the bow of the massive ship.

Massive cranes move over the ship. They remove containers, lifting them from the deck to place them on a never-ending stream of trucks. Those trucks move out, heading to destinations inland.

Meanwhile, on the dock, specialized trucks move back and forth between the ship and the rows of containers waiting to be loaded. Smaller cranes lift and lower containers onto the backs of the trucks. They feed into the cranes next to the ship. The complex operation is a masterpiece of efficiency, delivering containers to the cranes and into the ship at the same speed containers are removed.

The dock is something which can only be described as organized chaos. It's a massive parking lot, something you'd see at a football stadium, only instead of cars, twenty and forty-foot containers line up in rows upon rows.

Alpha team moves down to the outermost layer of those rows. We'll slowly move inward.

Somewhere, hidden inside one of those containers, a shipment of young women is destined for the slave trade.

Once Mitzy's drones find the container we seek, we'll free those women.

"Anyone want to bet whether this is a trap, or not?" Liam peers into the distance, watching the stream of trucks flowing beneath the cranes.

"I vote trap." Axel pulls a button out of his back pocket.

"Me too." Griff tosses a button into Axel's outstretched palm.

I don't think it is, which goes against what everyone feels. But I've never been one to go with my gut. I rely on what I know, what I can see, and what the facts tell me.

What I see is a dock too busy to risk a disruption a trap would cause. Bravo team activated an explosive, which shut down an entire port in Cancun. The people in charge of this operation are too sophisticated to waste time like that.

They want to fly under the radar, attracting zero attention to their presence. They're hoping to get lost amongst all the confusion, not draw attention to what they're doing.

Wolfe adds a button and glances at Liam.

"We can't all bet the same way."

"I'm fresh out of buttons guys." I lift my hands, up and out. "Sorry."

"Well, if we're all thinking it, what's our plan?"

We're not all thinking it, but I keep my thoughts to myself.

This was discussed back at the house, during pre-mission preparations. The problem is that it's virtually impossible to know until we spring the trap.

Mitzy says she outfitted her drones with special sensors. They should be able to *see* through the thick metal and peek inside. Meaning, not only can they identify humans, but explosives.

"Let's move out."

The guys put the buttons away as we move to the next checkpoint.

We divided the loading area into ten zones. As Mitzy's flight of drones clears each zone, Alpha team moves forward.

That damn static crackles in my ear again. I knock the side of my ear with my palm without much success.

"Any word on the drones?" Axel pauses to ask. I feel his unease. Mitzy's been overly silent since the drones went up.

"Working on it." Her voice sounds through my earpiece. Despite the distortion, there's an edge to her tone. "Nothing yet."

"Copy that."

"What's our play?" Axel looks to me. "We're exposed down here."

Exposed is an understatement, but as long as no one comes along asking questions about five men walking around the containers, we should be good.

Our surveillance revealed little activity on the ground, but there are closed-circuit cameras. Cameras which Mitzy effectively silences as we move in.

Concealed in baggy jumpsuits, we should blend in, but it comes at a cost. We had to ditch our weapons, leaving them with the courier CJ sent in. All we have on us are our side arms and a few clips of ammunition. CJ isn't happy about it, but Max agreed with my improvisation.

"Mitzy, you got anything yet?" Her drones started their search from *Lei'lani's* bow. We cross into zone ten, waiting for permission to proceed.

"Not yet." There's no tension in her voice, but that's Mitzy. Once focused, her OCD makes her a methodical machine. She's probably calculated out all the probabilities regarding which zone we might find the women in.

"Copy that." My earpiece squeals, making me jump. I want to throw the annoying thing out of my ear, but I can't lose communication with the team.

We hold up midway through the current row of containers and wait. Then I notice a problem.

The containers are packed closer together than we thought. In many places, the containers pack end to end, which means we won't be able to open the door to get the prisoners out. I point this out to the guys.

"We need solutions." We huddle together to troubleshoot while Mitzy's drones flit through the air.

"We could always wait until one of the trucks comes by." The pent-up energy in Axel's voice doesn't go unnoticed.

"We could borrow one." Griff ads, finishing Axel's sentence. "If Mitzy ever locates the container, we can drive the truck right up to it."

"And then what?" I like the idea, but there's one big problem. "Do you know how to get one of these containers onto the back of those trucks?"

The whole operation is an intricate dance, highly coordinated by smaller, mobile cranes and the flatbed trucks, which ferry the containers to the massive cranes that load the ship.

I glance at them again, certain the creators of Star Wars used those behemoth structures as inspiration for the AT-ATs on Hoth.

"Zone nine, clear." Mitzy's voice crackles through my comm.

"Copy that." We move and halt again at the border of zone nine.

"How about we wait until the container is loaded, then we hijack the truck?" Wolfe pipes up with a potential solution. "Drive the container right out of here."

It seems an elegant solution. I'm surprised Mitzy didn't think of it first.

"That'll work." Liam nods. "Wolfe and I can secure the truck while Axel and Griff confirm the girls are inside."

I hate how I'm left out, but this is how we're trained to think. Two men, buddies backing each other up.

"I'll provide oversight then."

With our plan revised for the second time, I call it in to CJ. We talk for a bit. Max pipes in. Mitzy's all on board.

"All we need is a target." It's difficult to keep the frustration out of my voice.

"I'm working on it." Mitzy, who's easily annoyed, doesn't appear concerned her drones have yet to identify the container we're looking for. "Initial scan almost complete."

"Copy that." I flinch at the squeal piercing my ear. "Got a lot of feedback on my comm."

"Noted." Mitzy sounds distracted now.

Silence extends between us. It's not clear if she's going to say anything else. Turning my attention back to the guys, we go over how different scenarios might play out. In our line of work, being over-prepared is a necessity.

While we sort through our next steps, I wait for Mitzy and her drones to come through. This allows my mind to wander, and it heads directly to a woman with shock-white hair and a smile, which heats my blood.

The note I left said I'd see her tonight. At the time, I thought I would. However, this mission makes that impossible.

Which is a shame.

I very much want to see her again.

The connection we shared extended beyond the physical release of sex. I want to crawl inside her head, discover her secrets, and make her mine. We touched on a few things last night, secrets she keeps from herself, that I want to explore.

I believe the human mind is the most sexually responsive organ. Getting inside her head, reading her innermost thoughts, the passion and desires she doesn't share with herself, let alone anyone else, is something I desperately crave.

There's an intimacy there, buried deep in her psyche, thoughts and desperate pleas hidden in the nooks and crannies of her mind.

They tell a truth about her desires and her needs. I want to be the one to fulfill her wildest fantasies. Unfortunately, that will never happen.

This is precisely why I don't do relationships. I'm never around long enough to make it work.

"Package located," Mitzy's clear voice calls out through the comms, "Zone four."

I look to my team, making sure they all heard. Tension builds again. We spent too much time waiting around.

"Good. Copy." I acknowledge receiving her communication and that's it's clear. "Move out."

I take the lead, walking quickly toward the container Mitzy indicated.

Once we're close, I separate from my team to scale one of the container stacks. Heat radiates off the metal. It sinks through the leather of my gloves to my palm.

I'll provide overwatch from the top of a container, keeping a look out for any workers who might wander nearby.

Liam and Wolfe will lie in wait for the truck. Once the crane operator lifts the container and lowers it onto the bed of the truck, Liam and Wolfe will take control of the truck.

Axel and Griff will pop the door, not to free the girls, but to release some of the heat that built up inside during the day. They'll provide any immediate medical assistance the women need until we can get them to Doc Summers and her team.

As our team medic, it's the best place to put Axel. The four of them will move off with the truck, driving the container out of here. I'll retreat, meet up with the courier holding our gear, and rejoin my team later.

All we have to worry about is whether it's a trap. My gut, once again, says no. The men who run this operation won't sacrifice their merchandise to get to us.

We get in position and wait.

THIRTEEN

Lily

"Any sign?" I move up the line until I'm beside Peter.

We're a team of eight: seven men and me. Jinx is back with the support team. Because I'm female, I get sandwiched in-between the men.

That's not a point I argue. All for equality of the sexes, I'm acutely aware of the physical differences between them. I'm barely five-foot-four, and that's if I cheat. While an excellent shot, and well trained in defensive combat, if a man gets his hands on me, I lose out every single time.

Right now, all we're doing is waiting for the two guys on the roof of the nearest building to tell us where to go.

Neil and Devon take advantage of the pause to sip from their hydration packs.

"Not yet," Peter answers me, then hydrates.

That's another difference between the sexes. They can unzip and take a piss anywhere they please. For me, peeing is a major production, and there's no way I'm squatting in front of seven men. Not that I would pee out here. Unlike them, I'm civilized and will wait for a restroom.

Despite the sweltering humidity and all the sweat dripping down my body, I lick my dry and cracked lips. I stopped drinking several hours ago when this mission got the official go-ahead. This isn't my first rodeo show and it's going to be a long time before I get to use the facilities.

Peter tilts his head, listening to the radio on the command channel. Mine is tuned into the team's dedicated channel.

"We've got action," he says. "Five men moving fast through the containers."

"You think it's Wilder?" My heart rate kicks up a notch.

Everything about this feels wrong, like it's a betrayal of the worst kind. After the night we spent together, I can't get over the feeling Wilder isn't a criminal.

He took his time last night, devoting himself to making me squirm, both in denying me orgasms and then piling them on so fast I forgot how to breathe.

I existed, entranced in his talented hands, as he took me to another place where I felt him everywhere. From the heat of his body pressed against mine, to the sultry taste of whiskey on his tongue, he somehow settled under my skin, sinking deep until his powerful essence brushed against my soul.

"Looks like." Peter turns to the team. "Come on ladies. Time to go."

I cringe at the slur. He says it means nothing, but it means everything. It does for so many reasons he'll never understand.

Neil follows Peter. Devon goes next. I lope into a jog, next in line. Mark is quick on my heels, pushing me to keep up. Rico, Lucas, and Mateo follow.

I love the guys on my team; they treat me well, invite me to family barbecues, where we drink beer and chill out. But they don't ask me to play on the baseball team. They don't invite me to bowling night. I never get invited for drinks after work. Golf is out.

I work twice as hard as the men, receive half the credit, and miss out on the social scene.

And it's not that it's intentional on any of their parts. I get invites to the office Christmas party at Neil's house. Easter supper is always hosted by Rico and his wife. Mateo hosts Labor Day cookout where we join his boisterous family. Lucas is a fiend for the Fourth of July. He invites us to the bayou where we race airboats, chase alligators, and troll for catfish until nighttime falls and the fireflies come out.

My team is tight. The guys are the best of friends. Their wives and kids get together all the time. But as the only chick on the team, I miss out on a lot. I wish it weren't like that, but I do the best I can.

Which means pushing myself as hard as possible.

Peter moves at a fast clip, getting us into position as he follows instructions from our men on the roof.

Movement in my peripheral vision distracts me. Something dives in, hovers, then moves off again. Has to be a small bird, but I don't know any birds, other than hummingbirds, that can hover like that. I look into the sky, but the strange bird is gone.

Wilder, and his men, if it truly is him, are approaching our position from the bow of the vessel. We come in from the stern. Somewhere in the middle, we'll meet. That's when I'll come face to face with the man I haven't been able to get out of my head all day.

That soft whirring sound returns. It's directly over my head, but nothing's there when I look.

What I don't understand is where Wilder and his team are headed. We shift to converge on them, heading into the part of the staging area which stands thick with containers laid out end to end, and stacked on top of each other, two and three high. Those are the containers waiting to be loaded onto the *Lei'lani*, not off.

Unless … Is it possible Wilder's confused?

The dock is a hectic place, full of what I like to call organized chaos, at least to the uninitiated. I've spent enough time here, intercepting shipments, that it no longer feels disorganized. But I remember feeling overwhelmed the first few times we made arrests down here.

This is the one piece of the plan which runs thin. Containers offload in one of two ways. They are either loaded onto the backs of semi-trucks and immediately exit through customs, or they're placed on the backs of dedicated dock trucks, which move them from the dock to a staging area for later distribution either on a train or the back of a semi-truck.

If the drugs are on one of the trucks headed out of port, Wilder needs to meet up with them in customs. That's the only place the trucks stop. If they're headed for the train yard, he should intercept them there.

But that's not where we're headed.

I'd say something to Peter, except running in tactical gear takes all my concentration if I'm going to keep up with my team. Mark and Rico move up to jog beside me. I think they do that subconsciously, thinking it helps me keep up. Lucas and Mateo's solid footsteps sound a steady rhythm to the rear. In front of me, all I see are the broad backs of Neil and Devon as they hoof it behind Peter.

Peter finally calls us to a halt by raising his hand and making a fist. Neil and Devon lean against the closest container, breathing comfortably. Mark and Rico barely broke a sweat. I bend over, propping my hands on my thighs as I gulp air. Lucas and Mateo come to a stop behind me. Their soft breaths are the only sign of their exertion.

I need to double down on my runs.

Peter carries on an exchange with our men on the roof, then comes to brief us.

"They've stopped and split into three groups. Two pair and then a single man who's climbing one of the containers."

I can't help but wonder which of the five men Wilder might be.

"What's the play?" Mateo asks, looking to Peter. "Any weapons?"

We outnumber Wilder's team with eight against five, but in our line of work, we're often outgunned.

"No rifles that they can see. They stole jumpsuits to blend in, but assume they're armed beneath those jumpsuits." Peter tells us what we can all guess.

Not only are those men armed, but they probably wear body armor better than the cheap government crap we're issued.

There is one advantage. While Wilder and his men carry

handguns beneath those jumpsuits, that fabric will hinder them when it comes to drawing on us.

"It looks like they've stopped." Peter holds us where we are. We can't risk getting too close, or we'll reveal our position and risk blowing the operation. "They're waiting on something."

A truck chugs along carrying a beat-up, orange, forty-foot container. It heads to the dock for loading.

That niggling sensation tickles the back of my mind. Something's off.

One of the small mobile cranes moves toward us, chugging and growling as it puffs blue smoke into the air.

It stops not too far away.

The crane lowers a magnetic claw until it clunks against the roof of the container. The magnetic lock engages, securing it to the roof. Once secured, the container shifts as it's lifted into the air. The whole contraption rotates, moving into position as an empty flatbed comes along.

The driver of the truck stops. The crane operator lowers the container until it settles on the flatbed. With a heavy *thunk*, the magnetic lock disengages and the crane lifts out of the way.

The whole operation captivates me. It's like watching complex choreography, only instead of people, the trucks and cranes perform the dance.

I'm so caught up in my thoughts, I miss the moment two large men jump out from between two containers. One of them opens the driver's side of the truck and hauls the driver out, tossing him to the ground. The other man jumps into the passenger seat.

It takes barely a moment, for the men to commandeer the truck. As they drive off, two more men hop onto the back of the truck, clinging to the side as they work to open the back of the container.

"What the hell?" I look to Rico, who's just as perplexed as me.

The men at the back of the truck get the cargo container door open. It swings wide as they jump inside. I only get a peek inside before the door slams shut.

There are no pallets stacked with drugs. Instead, a frightened young face looks out. No more than a young teen, the look on the girl's face is one of pure terror.

I turn to Rico. "Did you see what I saw?"

"I didn't see anything." His lips press into a firm line. "Did you?"

"Yes." I can't believe he didn't see what I saw. "There was a kid in there."

"A kid?"

"Maybe twelve? Fourteen?" I have no idea how old kids look.

"I didn't see that. Just saw the men jumping in. You sure your eyes aren't seeing things?"

Seeing things? I'll never get that look of terror out of my mind. That degree of abject fear hits where it hurts.

"Peter?" I turn to our team leader. "Did you see the kid?"

"Sorry. My eyes were on the men hijacking the truck." He tenses as the truck picks up speed. It heads down the long row and turns left, away from the dock.

There's no reason to chase it. We're not catching up with the lumbering truck on foot, but we can call it in.

"They're moving out," Peter curses.

Movement across the way catches my attention. A man stands on top of one of the containers. He makes no move to hide himself.

"Peter, the fifth man." I point, and Peter follows my finger.

The air shifts around me as my gaze connects with the man on the roof. A deep, shaky breath rushes into my lungs as the man glares at me with the most terrifying expression. It begins with confusion, then contorts into something ugly and raw.

A chill stabs me in the chest. It cuts through my heart and travels through me until it lodges in my gut

From the crackling in the air, there's no doubt who that is. I know that sizzling charge.

And I suddenly feel as if I've done something terribly wrong.

"Get him!" Peter shouts as Wilder jumps down from the container.

Our team moves out, me one step behind, always lagging. The seething anger in Knox's eyes paralyzes me.

I feel him. I feel his shock, his resonating anger, and a great sense of disappointment. I sense him all around me, strangling my breath as the container walls press in.

"Lily!" Lucas shouts at me.

Peter's already sprinting ahead. Neil and Devon are hot on his heels. Mateo and Mark aren't far behind.

"Lily! Come on." Rico's shout finally gets me moving.

My body, stricken with emotions I don't understand, finally moves. I stumble forward, lurching into a run. I race to catch up with my team and the man who runs from them. Weapon drawn, I run after Wilder, unprepared for the emotional storm raging within me at seeing him again.

Suddenly, the sound of gunfire rips through the air.

Loud percussive pops stab at my eardrums. I round the corner of a container, ten yards behind my team and pull up short.

Wilder stands with his hands over his head, facing away from Peter and the rest of my team. It takes a moment for my mind to register what it sees.

Peter's gun is drawn. It points, not at Wilder, but at men standing in front of Wilder. They not only block his escape, but they aim AK-47s at us, while we train our 9mm pistols back.

That whirring noise returns. I glance up and see a tiny drone hovering twenty feet in the air.

Wilder holds perfectly still.

My hands slick with sweat as I draw my weapon. For some reason I don't understand, I shift my aim from Wilder to these new men.

Dressed as port authority security guards, they're not what they seem. For one thing, port authority doesn't issue AK-47s to their security guards. They carry the same weapons we do.

One of the men steps to the side of Wilder. The muzzle of his gun lifts. It aims directly at Peter.

The concussive report of the AK-47 slams into me. Peter's neck rips to shreds. He falls, dead before he hits the ground. I process everything in slow motion as his body crumples and the man with the rifle turns it on Neil.

Neil staggers as he takes a bullet to the chest. A spray of bullets peppers his vest. The protective gear should save him, but like Peter, a bullet rips through his throat.

Neil drops. Dead eyes stare at the sky as his mouth opens in a soundless scream.

At the same time, another man takes Devon down. He falls to the ground where his body jerks and falls still.

Mark takes a step back. He glances over his shoulder, looking for an exit as he lifts his hands up and out, surrendering. It does no good. A hail of bullets takes him out.

Rico's blood splatters across my face as bullets rip through his throat.

Wilder drops to the ground, going to one knee. I think he's been shot, but no. Two of the men train their weapons on him.

Lucas and Mateo, what remains of my team, fire off their guns, but their shots go wide. They're picked off one by one.

Lucas's leg buckles as they shoot out his knee. Mateo takes a direct hit to his chest. He falls back, landing with a thud, and gasps as his fingers clutch at the air.

The men shooting at us, know exactly where to hit and kill. They aim for the spots our bulletproof vests don't cover.

Wilder doesn't move. On his knees, his hands clasp behind his head. One of the men shouts to another. That man steps forward. He edges around Wilder, wary for good reason. Wilder has several inches on the man and is half again as thick.

Wilder doesn't say a word. He doesn't even resist as the man moves behind him. He yanks Wilder's wrist down, and places it at the small of Wilder's back. He loops a zip tie around Wilder's wrist, then takes Wilder's other hand. Another zip tie comes out, securing both hands behind his back.

The man shoves Wilder forward, until he falls face first to the ground. Wilder hits the hard pavement with his cheek, but he falls such that he looks right at me.

The expression on his face can only be described as fierce as he grits his teeth and turns stormy eyes on me.

As for me, I hold my gun steady. There are ten men total. I have ten bullets. I'm an excellent marksman, but nobody is that good.

One of the men lifts his rifle. I stare down the barrel and know this is the end, but the leader of the group shouts something in Spanish. He takes a step forward and places his hand on the barrel of the rifle, slowly pushing the muzzle down.

"And what do we have here?" He shifts to English, but I barely hear him over the blood rushing past my ears.

My gaze shifts over the scene, landing on the bodies of my teammates. Only Lucas and Mateo move, gasping for breath. The others are eerily still, killed in cold blood.

I shift my weapon to aim at the leader. "Don't move."

"Or what? You're going to arrest me?" He laughs and his men join in.

"I'm not alone." The shaking in my voice messes with my bravado.

"You're a pretty thing." His head cants as his slithery gaze takes me in.

I've never felt so violated. In the time it takes for him to undress me with his eyes, revulsion courses through me. It's all I can do to keep it together.

There is backup on its way. I didn't lie. But he and I both know it won't get here in time to save me.

And why didn't they kill Wilder? Why did they truss him up?

"Seems a shame to waste such a fine ass." He takes another step toward me and it's all I can do not to turn tail and run. The only reason I don't is because there's no escaping this.

I am at their mercy. I know it. He knows it. His men know it too.

"The fucking cunt is DEA scum." Wilder twists on the ground. His words slam into me, slicing and dicing, cutting me to shreds from the inside out. "More trouble than she's worth."

"You think I should kill her?" The leader turns toward Wilder. "Or should I give her to my men?"

"I don't care what you do to her. Kill her. Let her go. If you take her, the DEA will be breathing down your necks to get her back.

Fucking waste of breath, that one." Wilder shifts to his side and pushes back up to his knees.

Every cutting word is like a knife stabbing my heart. Not that Wilder and I mean anything to each other. We shared one night of toe-curling, earth-shattering, soul-melding sex. That was it.

For a moment, I thought it might have been more than it was, but there's no confusion now. Wilder got what he wanted and moved the fuck on.

What a piece of shit.

My gun barrel shifts from the man in front of me to right between Wilder's eyes. My hand squeezes, nice and slow. My finger presses down on the trigger, not enough to fire my weapon. I'm an excellent shot, and I know how to fire a gun.

Wilder pinches his brows and gives a little flick of his lids. Did he just roll his eyes at me?

The urge to kill him recedes, and I realize what I almost did. I'm an agent of the DEA, sworn to enforce the laws of the United States against illegal drugs. What I'm not is an indiscriminate killer. He might be a criminal, but I'm not.

That's a line I won't cross.

But damn if I don't want to put a bullet right between Wilder's eyes.

"What do you think, boys? Do we let *la puta* go? Or kill her?"

My blood turns cold. All those stories people tell about their lives flashing before their eyes. They're full of shit. These may be my last moments and what am I thinking about?

My hands are sweaty. I pray I don't lose grip of my gun. That makes me focus on the trickle of sweat between my boobs and dripping down the small of my back. I'm going to say it, but my crotch is sweaty too. It's not pretty and I probably stink to high heaven by now.

As for my backup, they're easily thirty minutes away, if not more, but I'm sure the cops have been called.

How the hell am I going to get myself out of this?

Something whooshes past my ear. I hear it again, but this time something flies right past my shoulder. The air fills with whirring sounds as scores of flying objects converge on the men surrounding Knox.

The men use their weapons to attack the drones, which takes their attention off me.

Knox rises off the ground. He's a force of nature, single-minded in his attack. Arms secured behind his back, he launches toward me.

"Lily! Run!" He shoulders the man closest to him, pushing him down to the ground.

The man's weapon fires, sending shots into the air. Knox barrels toward the leader, who stands before me. Once again, he shoulders the man, pushing him out of the way.

If I wasn't terrified, the scene before me would be comical. Scores of drones attack the men. They swat at them, using their rifles like baseball bats, but the drones are too fast.

Too agile.

Knox is on me, spinning me around, then shoving me forward when I don't move quickly enough.

Despite the hurtful things he said about me, I'd rather be with him than not. I follow behind him, racing to clear the area.

Knox takes a hard right, running between a row of containers. He moves, full speed, until the next intersection. I barely keep up with him and stumble when I glance over my shoulder.

There is no pursuit, but the shouts of the men aren't hard to pick up. I turn, following the direction Knox ran and race after him.

He runs past three more intersections, before taking a left between a narrow row. The containers here pack shoulder-width apart. He has to turn his body to fit through, but I don't have that problem.

We continue on like that, turning left, then right, then left again, until I'm thoroughly confused. Only then do I realized what he's doing because the sounds of pursuit follow us.

Only the men aren't where we are. They're searching blind. Knox slows, waiting for me to catch up, and that's when I see the tiny drone, not much larger than his hand, hovering in front of his face.

"Where to, Mitzy?"

Mitzy?

The drone takes off again. Knox follows, seeming to be taking instructions from the drone, so I follow him. We weave our way through a labyrinth of containers until coming to the end. Knox pops out and I follow right after him.

Blue lights and sirens sound as port authority and local police converge on the scene. Knox pulls to a hard stop as police vehicles screech.

"Hands over your head." The police siren blares into the night. I lift my hands over my head, still holding the gun, but I release my grip and let my weapon dangle with my finger in the trigger guard.

Knox, with his hands tied behind his back, turns in a slow circle, letting the police see his hands are bound.

Not sure what's going to happen next, I breathe out a sigh of relief when Harry steps out of the lead vehicle.

I lower my arms and secure my weapon. Then I turn to Knox.

"You're under arrest."

Knox glares at me, but he doesn't put up a fight.

"Pumpkin, this is one decision you're going to regret."

And with that, I bury all my fantasies, knowing how silly and foolish I've been. Knox and I are on wrong sides of the law. Last night, as wonderful as it was, is in the past, right where it belongs.

FOURTEEN

Knox

Lily's eyes widen. She'll figure it out soon enough. First, she cons me at a game of darts, subjects me to degradation on top of the bar, then she taps my phone. That should be the worst of it, but this takes the cake.

She's arresting me.

It's cute as fuck. She's all serious. As if arresting me is something she's going to get away with. I'd love to know what's going on inside her head.

I'll figure it out with enough time. If I don't, I'll ask.

And this is the fun part.

My type of questioning will be much different from hers. I imagine her tied to my bed while I grill her about why she thinks she has anything on me.

I'm clean as a whistle. Hell, we're both on the same side of the law. I may work in the gray zones, but I do so backed by the power and protection of the Guardians.

"You have the right ..." Lily rolls her shoulders back, acting tough as shit.

She's so freaking cute I want to eat her up right here. I don't let her finish and speak low enough only she hears me. I'm not out to embarrass her at work, but I will make her squirm.

"I have the right to punish you for bad behavior, lick your pussy until you come so hard you can barely breathe, then I have the right to shove my dick so deep inside of you that you'll be ruined for any other man. You'll never forget me, Lily. You'll ache for me. And you'll have to beg to get what you desperately want." I lean toward her, lowering my voice even more. In a few seconds, we'll have company and I'll need to shut up for real. "Tell me that doesn't turn you on. Tell me you don't ache to feel me inside of you."

"You-you have the right to remain silent." She flushes bright red as her fingers curl into fists.

"There's no way you're arresting me. I've done nothing wrong."

"Please don't make this harder than it needs to be." She peeks up at me through her lashes, begging.

"But you like it *hard*, and *fast*, if I remember correctly. You especially liked it when I fucked you *hard* against the wall, and when I plowed into you as *fast* as I could when you were on all fours. You have the prettiest scream when you come, pumpkin. Damn, but I'm hard right now thinking about giving it to you hard and fast."

"Stop it." She looks over her shoulder as men climb out of the police vehicles.

"Never, pumpkin. I also remember the cuffs belong around your pretty wrists. They don't belong on mine." I give her what I hope is a devastating wink.

"Stop it." Her back goes rigid, but I catch the hitching in her breath.

My girl aches for me. She loves when I'm direct; the filthier, the better.

"Never."

A man approaches and takes over. He's overly familiar with Lily, standing too close. It's more paternalistic than aggressive, so I give the man a pass.

"Agent Freeman, I've got it from here." He gives a jerk of his chin toward one of the cop cars. "Take a break."

It's hard to imagine Lily's a DEA agent. Despite what Mitzy

said, I didn't believe Lily worked for the DEA. If she's arresting me, there must be a drug angle attached, which sucks for Lily.

That's a major miscalculation on her part.

I put up no resistance as I'm loaded into the back of the cop car. The man stands with Lily, their heads close together, as he asks her something and she responds.

For a moment, her breathing hitches, and her shoulders slump. That man wraps his arms around her, pulling her close for a hug.

That's when it hits me—what Lily lost. Her entire team was mowed down in front of her. Five are dead. Two may survive their injuries.

Alarms sound in the distance. Two ambulances pull into sight. I hang my head in shame. It should've been me wrapping my arms around Lily, not that other man.

The worst part is—and this is what I hate—but it never occurred to me how that must feel for her. The chances she's ever lost a teammate must be slim to none. I wish I could say the same, and that's when I realize how cold and callous I've become.

Without a chance to say goodbye, the car I'm in pulls away from the scene. My arrest is a minor hiccup. I'm happy we got to the girls in time. What confuses me is the involvement of the DEA, but that will clear up with time.

Right now, I have time to stew while the NOLA police process me and lock me in a cell where I wait for the Guardians to spring me loose. Sure as shit, several hours later, guards come to my cell.

"Hands." With no preamble, they bark orders at me.

I could be a dick and refuse to cooperate, but that does nobody any good. Without argument, or trouble, I go to the bars and slide my hands through the small opening. They secure my hands in metal cuffs and tell me to take five steps back. I comply, obediently stepping away from the door.

The degree of care they use on me is something to note. They treat me like a hardened criminal, wary and overly prepared should I lash out and try to cause trouble.

There's zero chance of that happening.

No doubt Sam is on the line right now arranging my release; a very quiet release. We try not to advertise what it is we do. After tonight's adventure, there will be questions that don't need to make it into the news.

Forest Summers protects his rescues, and that means making sure his Guardians operate under the radar. Tonight, however, we made a huge splash. Port authority is aware of our activity, as are the police.

As for me, I've got questions. First, and foremost, why is Lily targeting me? No doubt, she believes I'm involved in something drug related. There's no other reason for her to look into my life otherwise.

But why?

Why would the DEA be looking into my activities?

My second and more concerning question is who are the men I ran into? We expected a trap and decided the only way to spring it was to proceed. But nothing happened, or so we thought. Those men were waiting, but they held back, letting us steal their merchandise out from under their nose.

Why?

Why let us get away with the girls?

I've spent the better part of the last few hours thinking about it, and I'm nowhere near finding an answer.

"Come along." One of the guards opens the cell door.

"If you're releasing me, don't you think the cuffs are overkill?" I assume Sam pulled the necessary strings and I'm walking out of here.

"Why do you think you're being released?" The guard's gruff reply takes me by surprise.

"Isn't that what's happening?" I look between the three men sent to escort me. From their hard expressions, they clearly aren't letting me go.

Where are they taking me then?

Curious as to what's happening, I shuffle along, bracketed by my guards.

I'm the most compliant prisoner as they lead me into a small interrogation room. There's a cheap metal chair on one side of a nondescript table. On the opposite side, two more chairs sit empty. On my side, there's a device on top of the table to lock in my cuffs.

It's sad to say, but this whole setup looks exactly the way it's portrayed on TV. I sit my ass down and place my cuffed hands on the table. The guards leave me to wait.

It looks like I'm alone, but there's no doubt in my mind people watch from the other side of the one-way mirror. I could glare at the mirror, but like it is with video conferencing, I'd more than likely be looking at the wrong place.

I decide to do nothing. If they want to watch me, fine. I slouch in the chair, getting comfortable for this first round of interrogations.

They want answers? Well, I have a shit ton of questions. Interrogations work both ways, and I bet I've got more experience interrogating prisoners than anyone in this place.

I settle in to wait. This is the first phase of our game. They'll make me wait, try to get under my skin, see how nervous I might be. Once I show signs of unease, that's when my questioners will reveal themselves.

There are several ways to play this. I decide to dick around with them, just because I can.

My wrists are cuffed and they tied me to the table through a metal ring, limiting some of what I can do. I close my eyes and fall back on my training.

It begins with a breath to center my mind. Those people behind the one-way glass wait for my agitation to build. I do exactly the opposite, freeing my body from all tension.

There's a school all SEALs take as a part of their training called SERE. The initials stand for Survival, Evasion, Resistance, and Escape.

SERE is not fun. At some point, each of us believes it will be different for us. That we're somehow made of stronger grit than the next guy.

Every single one of us is dead wrong.

Resisting physical torture was not the hard part. The body can take a great deal of pain. It's not the body that breaks, but rather the mind.

The whole goal of the SERE is to give its trainees the skills we need to survive with dignity under the most hostile conditions. What I learned was how to escape within myself while enduring the worst torture.

The first week terrified me but was basically a walk in the park. We covered the history of POWs and the lessons learned after World War II and Vietnam.

That first week went by entirely too fast, but we were eager to get to the good stuff; the field exercise. We broke into groups of six, then down to the most basic unit—a buddy pair.

Max and I paired up together.

As far as survival skills go, we had those down pat.

Another deep breath focuses me on the beating of my heart. In my relaxed state, my pulse is low and steady, barely above forty beats a minute. I tune in on the sound of blood rushing past my eardrums, losing myself to the soft susurrations.

I listen for my questioners, but it's too early for them to arrive. They're still wondering what the fuck I'm doing closing my eyes and taking deep breaths.

I take another breath, this one slow. Agonizingly slow. My lungs fill with air, but I don't stop when I can't take in any more air. I force myself to sip and suck and really fill my lungs. Then I hold my breath, counting nice and slow as my mind focuses on the past.

After three days surviving in the mountains with Max, starving and freezing our asses off, we were eager for the evasion part of the exercise to begin. For twenty-four hours, our instructors hunted us down like dogs. The one thing Max and I agreed on was that we were not going to get captured.

Which was our undoing.

At the end of the twenty-four hours of evasion, a loud siren sounded, telling all those who successfully evaded capture to report to the POW camp and turn themselves in.

Max and I encountered a problem, because we cleared the operational area and were out of earshot of the sirens. Which forced us to find our way back. When a truck full of angry-looking men pulled up to us, we weren't sure what to make of it. They didn't look like any of our instructors.

They yanked hoods over our heads, tied us up, smacked us around, and finally delivered us to the POW camp for the final three days of fun.

Turns out those guys had been sent out looking for us and had been out for well over six hours. They were pissed, but we were pleased. Instead of seventy-two hours of POW hell, we had only sixty-six to go. Once we reached camp, they removed our hoods.

The corner of my jaw ticks up at the memory. They beat us to shit, but the first thing Max and I did when we saw each other was grin. That was the last I saw of Max until the end of the exercise, but we knew we'd won a tiny victory. It was enough to sustain me through the worst of the torture.

Back in the interrogation room, where I wait for my questioners, I hold my breath and make it to a count of a hundred before my lungs burn. The urge to breathe becomes overwhelming, but I tamp down that need and continue to count as memories fill my mind.

In the fake POW camp, my captors stripped away my humanity. They took my name, gave me a number, and pressured me every moment from that point on.

Time literally slowed down.

With my lungs aching for air, I release the last residual air from my lungs and take in another breath, reminding myself everything is an illusion.

After getting the shit knocked out of me in the POW camp, I was fed. They tried some diversion tactics to get the prisoners to sign our names in a ledger—which could later be used against us in a forged admission of guilt—and separated us. I got assigned to a small, windowless cell. Okay, it was a standing coffin. They locked me in and left me.

For hours.

I did well at first, but then my body began to protest, demanding to move. Only I couldn't move. I couldn't sleep. All I could do was stand in the stifling darkness.

After a few more hours, there was only one thing I wanted. I wanted them to get it over with already. There was a point where I swear I begged for them to torture me. Anything to get out of that damn box.

More hours crawled by, and that was where I learned how I would survive and resist. Instead of focusing what was outside of me, or the discomfort of my body, I turned my mind inward. I found a place where I could detach from the pain my body endured.

My current circumstance is vastly different from that agonizing week of SERE training. I experience no pain in this interrogation room beyond the slight soreness in my butt from sitting on a metal chair. This is literally a walk in the park.

The door opens behind me. The heavy tread of a male entering grabs my attention. It's the man from before. The one who's close to Lily. He draws back one of the chairs opposite me and lowers himself into it.

Slowly, I open my eyes and focus on him. Before he can say a word, I make my first demand.

"I will only speak to Lily."

"Agent Freeman is indisposed."

"I will only speak to Agent Lily Freeman." I close my eyes and erase the man sitting across from me.

He says something, repeats himself, his tone turns agitated, then frustrated when I fail to respond. I sit there, doing nothing but focusing on taking one deep breath in and letting it out nice and slow.

Eventually, he gets the message. The chair scrapes back. He rises. Heavy steps cross the room. The door opens. It closes.

All I do is breathe.

Lily will be here soon.

FIFTEEN

Lily

"What the hell is he doing?" My gaze once again travels the expanse of Wilder's calm exterior. "How does he just *sit* there?" My comments are aimed at Harry who's been in and out of that room half a dozen times in the past three hours.

As for Wilder, he's easy on the eye. I can't keep from staring, and I secretly want him to look me right in the eye, as if there really is some metaphysical, spiritual, cosmic connection binding us together.

But Wilder never once looks up.

Not that he'd see me if he could, but still …

I can't shake the feeling he knows I'm here. He's certainly been asking for me.

Harry moves closer to the observation window. Hands thrust deep in his pockets, shoulders slumped, his hair is a mess from dragging his fingers through it over the past several hours. He looks more tired than I feel.

It's O'dark-thirty and we've been at this all night. After Harry went to speak to Wilder, that very first time, he tried any number of tactics to get Wilder to speak. Each and every time, the only words Wilder spoke were, "I will only speak to Lily."

"He only wants you." Harry's head cocks to the side. He twists around, brows furrowed, eyes pinched, pensive as hell. "How serious are things between the two of you?"

I will only speak to Lily.

Nothing unless we're talking about the indescribable metaphysical, spiritual, cosmic connection which makes the very air crackle.

Thank God for the one-way glass. I can't face him after what I did. Arresting a man after you have sex with him has to be in some playbook of things a woman should never do.

Regardless of my feelings, those are the only words Wilder says.

That's not the end of it.

He hasn't touched the water. He refused the food. He hasn't asked to use the facilities, even though I've been more times than I can count over the past few hours.

Granted, I escape to the Ladies' Room because it's the only safe place to have a meltdown around here. None of the men would dare follow me in there, and I'd be mortified if they did.

Special operatives aren't supposed to lose their shit, but I lost mine. I lost it and then some. Not proud to say it, but I sat against the wall, not giving a care to the dirty floor, curled up my knees, and cried my eyes out.

I can't stop seeing the bullet rip through Peter's throat. Peter-the-Prick, who turned out not to be such a bad guy in the end. He apologized and encouraged me. Then he died.

He died right before my eyes. As did Neil, Devon, Mark, and Rico. Lucas and Mateo cling to life, but I'm not at the hospital with them. I haven't even called their wives.

Do they know their husbands will never come home?

I know someone's contacted the families, but I need to reach out. I was there. I know their wives. I've played with their kids.

But I also need to be here. Doing my job. Sucking it up and staying strong. Proving to anyone who cares that I'm not a delicate flower, and that I have what it takes to be analytical and focused to get the job done.

My chest still hurts from the sobbing cries, but tears are for women and weak men. Frankly, I don't care. I needed a moment to completely fall apart before I could put myself together again.

I stood my ass up, washed my face, and stared at myself for a good long time before I rejoined the interrogation.

Not that there's any interrogating going on. We're locked in a battle of wills with one clear victor.

Wilder has us exactly where he wants us, effectively rendering us impotent. He knows it too.

How serious are things between the two of you? Harry's comment sticks in my head.

My answer isn't one I'll ever speak out loud. How serious are we? I've known the man less than twenty-four hours, yet I feel as if I've always known him. Or, always knew he would eventually come into my life.

Wilder feels familiar. Comfortable. He feels right.

"Were." I correct Harry. "There's nothing between us." My gaze cuts back to Wilder as I lie to my boss.

"You sure about that?" Harry keeps his voice low, so the others in the room can't hear.

I can't help but bristle at the innuendo in Harry's comment. Wrapping my arms around myself, I walk right to the edge of the one-way glass and peer in at Wilder as he sits tranquilly in place, eyes closed, not a muscle moving. He's calm as shit, and it's terrifying.

"It was one night. Nothing special. Just enough to get close enough to swap out the SIM card on his phone."

"Tell me again what happened." Harry switches from asking about Wilder to what happened to my team. My shoulders hunch as I turn away.

The deaths of Peter and the others are in my *Don't Touch* box right now. It's something I'll deal with later, after this job is done. Except Harry keeps bringing it up.

The ambulances took Lucas and Mateo to the hospital, where they cling to life as surgeons work to save them. The rest of my team is dead.

Dead.

"I don't want to talk about it."

Harry comes to stand beside me. He lets out a deep sigh and wraps his arm around my shoulder.

"Today was a very bad day, Freeman. It'll get better, and we have psychologists you can talk to, if that's what you need. But walk me through it one more time." Harry sounds like he cares about my feelings, but he's one hundred percent focused on the operation that left five of his men dead.

"I don't need a damn psychologist. I need a shower. Then I want to curl up in my bed and sleep forever. Do I have to go over it again?" In the hours we've been interrogating Wilder, or failing to interrogate him, I debriefed my team on what I saw down at the docks.

"Just one more time. Tell me what happened when the drones arrived."

"I'm tired of talking about it."

"I don't mean to press, except, I've got a prisoner in that cell who refuses to speak to anyone but you."

"I don't know what you want me to say." But that's not enough for Harry. I take in a breath and run through the whole clusterfuck of a night for him one more time.

"Why do you think he'll only speak to you?" He drops his arm from my shoulders and takes a step back.

"Because he's pissed at me."

"It's more than that." Harry gives me a look. "Why *you?* Why is he refusing to talk to us?"

"It's a game to him."

"Go on." Harry encourages me to continue.

"It's the only thing he controls. He wants me to know he can make me do what he wants."

"I agree, but what else?" Harry forces all of his undercover agents to think through every possible scenario, examine every nuance, and dig until they get to the truth buried deep. He's doing that to me now.

No doubt, he has his own theories.

"I tricked him in the bar."

"And?"

"I bruised his ego."

"Doesn't seem to be the kind of man who holds a grudge against a pretty woman. There's more. Dig deep, Freeman. Why you?"

"Because I conned him. I beat him publicly, then forced him on the bar for body shots, where I degraded him."

"Did he resist?"

"Wilder played along. He was a great sport about the whole thing."

"And why do you think that was?"

"Because he wanted me."

"I'd say so, but I disagree."

"Huh?"

"You're using past tense, Freeman. The man sitting in that room wants you. Present tense, not past. Why?"

"Do you think he knows about the SIM card?"

"Considering all the drones?" Harry takes a step back. "I'd say whoever he's working for has the capability to detect what we did."

"So, he knows." I saw those drones. "Which means we're not working with amateurs."

"I'd say amateur hour is over."

"If he knows I swapped out the SIM card, he's pissed. He wants revenge."

"That's a fair guess."

Wilder doesn't want revenge. That's not how he thinks. He'll want to punish me.

"If he refuses to talk, what do we do? Do you want me to interrogate him?"

"I'm not sending you in there."

"Because I'm a woman?"

"No, Freeman. It has absolutely nothing to do with the fact you're a woman, although that does play into it."

"That's not fair."

"I agree, but hear me out before you judge too harshly. He knows about the SIM card, which means he knows you lied to him. After everything else you did, that's a lot for a man to let go."

"I can do it. I can remain professional."

"I have no doubt in your abilities, but are you prepared to face him?"

"I am."

"And when he starts detailing the night the two of you spent together?" Harry reaches out to cup my chin. The gesture is paternalistic, but he'd never do that to a male agent. "Think about it. Think about the things he'll say. The things he might make up. All of it goes down on the record, which will be read and reviewed thousands of times by a lot of people you know. He's smart enough to know that. And as fucked up as it sounds, as unfair as it is, you're not coming out of there untouched. He'll destroy your reputation. Even if we know that's exactly what he's doing, it won't matter. As long as everything he says is heard, and recorded, there's no way I'm putting you in there with him."

"I don't mind." I stiffen my spine. "I know the risks."

"And I'm not going to lose one of my best operatives, when I don't have to. Look, tonight—it was tough. It would be tough for anyone. You haven't had a moment to yourself, and you need to decompress and come to terms with what happened."

He's wrong about that. I'd say my meltdown in the women's bathroom was a whole shitload of decompressing.

"Where does that leave us?" I turn toward Wilder and his cool as shit disposition. He sits calmly, meditating, I guess, in an interrogation room. There's not one lick of anxiety, worry, concern, or fear. What does he know that we don't?

"It leaves us with one of two options." Harry turns and paces in the small room. I take a step back, giving him room.

"What's that?"

"We can keep beating this dead horse. I send people in. He turns them away."

"That gets us nowhere."

"He'll have to talk sometime."

"What's the other option?" I'm curious because I don't see another option.

"We let him go."

"Why would we do that?"

"Because, for whatever reason, that man is obsessed with you. Which means …" Harry waits for me to fill in the gap.

"He's going to come looking for me, and if he does that, nothing's recorded."

"Exactly."

"What if he doesn't come looking for me?"

"If there's one thing I've learned, it's that a man like that will come for his woman."

"Harry."

"Like it, or leave it, doesn't matter." He gives a shake of his head. "It's still the truth."

"So, that's the plan? Release him and wait for him to come after me? I'm not so sure that's a good plan."

"Relax." Harry chuckles beside me. "We're not letting him go."

Is it bad that I breathe out a sigh of relief?

The idea of Wilder tracking me down makes my breath hitch. He's great in bed, easy on the eye, but he's a big man. I know how he fucks. I know his strength. What I don't know is what it feels like to face Wilder down, alone, as an adversary.

His intensity scares me. Shit, just watching him sit still in that room terrifies me. The man displays uncanny control.

We leave prisoners alone that first hour of an interrogation for a reason. Everybody gets twitchy. Anxiety builds when they expect to be questioned and it doesn't happen. Usually, it takes less than an hour to agitate our prisoners.

Wilder's been cool as a clam for hours. I'm anxious and fidgety. It's like he's turned the tables on us. I don't know if it's accidental or not, but it's fucking brilliant if this is exactly what he intended all along.

Harry's anxiety is through the roof. This isn't the first time he's paced tonight, and I've never seen Harry upset. He wants answers.

The only man capable of giving them refuses to speak to anyone but me.

Wilder will definitely humiliate me in front of my team.

The things I let him do to me are things no one needs to know about.

"So, what do we do?" I can't help but shrug. "Leave him in there?"

Harry rolls his wrist and checks the time. "That's one option."

"We could always lock him back up. Give him the rest of the night to stew about it."

"We could, but I have a feeling that won't happen."

"Why?"

"Because a man like that isn't one who stays behind bars."

"Why not?"

"Because whoever is working with him has access to things we do not." Harry places his hand over his mouth, then drags it down his jaw. "Go home, Freeman. Get some rest. We'll take care of this and sort it out later."

"We're giving up?"

"I'm going to let him stew for a few more hours, then lock him back up and see who comes looking for him. That's probably the best we're going to get."

"And what about the rest of it?"

"What's that?"

"The men who attacked my team." My voice cracks and it takes everything in me not to choke up. I can't believe they're all gone. "Do you think they're a rival cartel?"

"Unknown."

"I feel like we have more questions now than when we started."

"I agree." Harry takes two steps back and leans against the table. "Go home, I'll catch you up in the morning."

"I need to check in on Lucas and Mateo, see what's happening, then I need to …"

A loud knock sounds and three men in suits enter without waiting for a response. Or rather, I should say two men and a giant.

The palest blue eyes I've ever seen shift toward me. The massive man gives me a hard stare and I wonder if he's thinking the same thing I am.

There aren't too many people in the world with white-blond hair, at least not in this country. In fact, I've never met another person with the same coloring of hair in my life.

His interest in me, however, is cursory. The giant man says nothing as one of the men beside him speaks.

"Who's the agent in charge?" He looks at the men in the room, skipping over me.

"I am." Harry steps up, puffing out his chest and standing tall. "Who are you?"

"Special Agent Samuel Stone. FBI." The Special Agent flashes a badge and turns his attention to the window where Wilder continues with his infuriating internal meditation.

"We're taking over from here." The corner of Agent Stone's mouth tics up in a smirk. "Hopefully, Knox hasn't been too much of a bother."

The third man, who's the same size as Agent Stone, thrusts forward a sheaf of official looking papers.

It's funny. They're both the same size as Wilder, who I consider a big man. My head barely comes to Wilder's shoulders, but standing next to the white-haired giant, they look small. It's an odd dichotomy.

The man with the glacial gaze looks at me and cocks his head. He dissects me with that sharp gaze, cutting through the layers I wrap around myself to shield me from the outside world.

"You must be Lily." His deep baritone rumbles through the room.

Struck dumb by his overwhelming presence, I return his stare with shock and concern. How does he know my name? He says nothing after that, except those pale eyes of his take me in. I feel as if we carry on an entire conversation during that silent exchange

For the life of me, I have no idea *what* we say, except right before he tears his gaze away from mine, I feel as if he approves of me. Like I'm more than enough and don't need to try so hard to measure up.

It takes me back a step. My hand flies to my chest as the power of that thought hits me dead on.

I'm enough.

Damn straight, I'm enough. I suddenly feel stronger, more powerful, more confident.

"Wilder works for you?" I speak up, my tiny voice small in a room filled with the potent effects of alpha male testosterone clotting the air.

"We're not at liberty to say." Agent Stone looks to Harry, who examines the transfer papers. "If that is all …"

"It legit, that's for sure, but we're working a case right now. Multiple homicides."

"I understand, but this is our jurisdiction."

"Is it?" Harry's not letting this go.

"Very much so." Agent Stone doesn't give an inch.

Squabbling over jurisdiction is a complicated matter. What does the FBI want with Wilder?

"I saw a girl's face." I blurt out the first thing that comes to mind. "In that container. Is that why you're here? Is Wilder involved in sex trafficking."

"I'm sorry, but we're not at liberty to discuss the details of our case." Agent Stone turns toward me, eyebrows raised, but lips set into a firm line. "What's your interest in this?"

"We're investigating him concerning a shipment of illegal pharmaceuticals."

"I see. I'm sorry about your men." Agent Stone bends slightly at the waist. "An egregious loss, but that man in there has nothing to do with the transfer of illegal drugs. Wherever you got your information, it's wrong. Consider that a professional courtesy."

Harry says nothing. He stands lock-jawed and stiff as a board at the mention of the men we lost tonight.

As for me, Agent Stone's words cut like a knife. I should've been one of them, but I know why I wasn't. The face of that girl is forever etched in my mind. That man took one look at me and saw opportunity. He wanted to steal my freedom, take away my humanity, and turn me into nothing more than goods to be traded.

If those drones hadn't come along when they did, saving Wilder and myself, is that where I would be now? Trapped in the back of some cargo container headed to some destination unknown?

I'm no idiot. The DEA fights a war on drugs, but that doesn't mean there's not another war being fought out there. It's one that is lost each and every day as children are taken from their homes and fed into a despicable industry.

Unlike Harry, I'm not against fighting for our case. I'm not willing to give Wilder up to the FBI, at least not until I have another chance to speak to him.

"Our intelligence isn't wrong. We tracked your man entering and leaving the country in close association with several shipments of drugs."

"I can assure you," Agent Stone gives me a long hard look, "that man is in no way involved with the shipment of drugs."

"How do you know?"

"Knox is leaving with us." Agent Stone holds out his hand. "The keys to his cuffs, please."

Harry's shoulders jerk at the command, but he doesn't mess around. I totally get his predicament. If the papers are legitimate, and I have no reason to believe they aren't, Harry can't refuse.

We're going to lose Wilder.

I glance back at Wilder. His eyes open. There's a quick scan of the glass then his gaze locks on me, as if he knows exactly where I stand.

I take a shaky step back as a rush of adrenaline spikes my blood. Suddenly, I feel him all around me, but that's not why I'm scared.

His hard gaze fills with a promise.

A promise I'm going to regret.

SIXTEEN

Lily

After the men from the FBI take Wilder, I spend the rest of my day in debriefs where I relive every agonizing detail of the wholesale murder of my team.

I make it through, choking up only once or twice, as they pick apart every detail and ask questions I don't have answers to.

Questions like, who were those other men?

"I don't know."

Where were the drugs?

"I don't know."

Was there really a face inside that container?

The way they ask makes me question what I saw, but I hold firm.

"Yes."

It goes on from there, a constant barrage of questions, which make me feel as if I did something wrong. Thankfully, Harry is right by my side the entire time, supporting me, encouraging me, and being a pillar of support to grab a hold of when the tears threatened to fall.

But I maintain my professionalism. I lock back the tears and sobs, refusing to let them slip past my defenses.

When that's done, I head to the hospital where Lucas and Mateo are finally out of surgery. They're in intensive care, but the doctors let me visit. I leave the hospital knowing they'll live.

My shoulders feel a little lighter, relieved with the news, but I'm not done.

For the next few hours, I make the hardest stops in my life. It feels weird saying it like that, a stop instead of a visit, but there's no visiting going on as I travel to the homes of each of my teammates to give my condolences to their wives.

The entire time I travel around town, a tickling sensation between my shoulder blades has me turning around, checking my rearview mirror, and generally increases my level of agitation. It feels as if I'm being watched.

But there's nobody there. No tail following me as I drive around town. Nobody watching from the street as I comfort distraught wives.

I shrug it off as exhaustion. I've never felt as tired as I do right now. I could sleep for a week and still roll over, reluctant to climb out of bed.

With each stop, the guilt inside of me increases.

Why am I the one who survived? When they lost husbands, and their children will now grow up without their fathers, why am I the only one walking around?

Finally, I park my car and walk the few blocks to my apartment over Callie's bar.

It's dusk in New Orleans. Saturday night has arrived, which means eager tourists pack the streets of the French Quarter.

There's a sense of revelry, an ongoing party that never stops. The legendary magic of the city is in full swing. Jazz music fills the air, covering the streets with their distinct sound. Performers amaze the crowds. People walk around with open containers, enjoying NOLA signature drinks. Couples wander hand in hand. Parents chase bright-eyed kids. Teens congregate for a night on the town with eager faces and fake IDs. The whole place comes alive as the sun dips below the horizon and the lights of the city take over.

But I want nothing to do with it.

I'm the kind of tired that goes bone deep. All I want is to take a long, hot shower and crawl under the covers, never to emerge again.

Harry gave me the next two weeks off—mandatory paid leave. He says it's to *decompress,* but I know what he's really doing.

Harry's worried about my state of mind and how the trauma of losing my entire team might affect my performance at work. Correction, nearly my entire team. Lucas and Mateo will survive.

I would've argued against time away from work, except I agree.

I'm not good—not good by a long shot.

As I thread my way through the crowds, that feeling of being watched returns. I cast about but see nothing concerning. Everyone around me smiles and laughs, having fun on the cusp of a Saturday night filled with endless possibilities.

The energy in the crowd, which is usually infectious, doesn't touch me. I appear to be immune.

Instead of jubilation, I'm despondent. I'm tired, exhausted, and I've been pushing away my grief all day.

A crowd forms outside Callie's bar. Patrons spill out onto the street, carousing and celebrating with friends and strangers alike. I push past the press of partygoers and shoulder my way inside.

Callie sees me and waves me over. I gesture back, telling her I'm headed upstairs to sleep. Her brows pinch together and she gives me a look of concern. I wave dismissively, telling her I'm okay.

Which I'm not.

I've simply run out of the energy to carry on a conversation. Callie will want to talk. She worries about me, but the last thing I need right now is to relive any part of the past twenty-four hours. Callie will want to know what happened. Then, she'll try to console me.

I simply don't have the energy for that.

Once I make it to the back of the bar, I push open the door leading upstairs and trudge up the narrow staircase. That itching sensation between my shoulder blades disappeared somewhere during my walk to Callie's bar, which means I'm a little more relaxed.

Doesn't mean I'm not cautious.

Once inside my apartment, I lock the door, pull the chain across the slider, and shove a chair under the doorknob. Then I take a deep breath in and blow it out slow, releasing the tension in my body.

My air conditioner struggled to ward off the oppressive heat and humidity during the day. I think it's on its last legs. It's humid and stuffy in my apartment. I wander over to the balcony, opening up the French doors to let the evening air circulate through.

A deep breath fills me with the scents of beer, wine, fruity drinks, and the delicious aromas of food. I love NOLA cuisine. The crowds below, boisterous and full of energy, remind me how incredibly exhausted I feel. I feed off what little energy I can pick up from the crowds, getting a little pick me up.

Moving toward my bedroom, I peel off layers of sweat-soaked clothing. Hopping from foot to foot, the boots go, and I strip out of my pants. The stench of blood, sweat, and gunfire turns my stomach.

Whose blood am I wearing?

Peter's? Rico?

Best not to think about that. None of it is mine. I emerged from the whole shitshow without a scratch.

Once I'm under the hot spray of my shower, I take in a slow deep breath. Grief waits for me, patiently sitting off to the side until I'm ready to face it. But I hold off dealing with my emotions for a little longer.

I need a moment to do nothing other than breathe.

Falling apart can come later.

As for my shower, I wash all traces of blood and sweat from my body. Then I sit down in the shower, drawing knees to chest, while the steam builds and the heat soaks in to ease my tired muscles. I huddle and face my grief as my tears mingle with the falling water.

It's only after the water turns cold that I sluggishly climb to my feet and step out of the shower. It's early still. The sounds from the street flow in through the open doors leading to the balcony.

There's a change in the air, a low crackling sensation moves along my skin, an electric charge which makes me suck in a breath. Three things go through my head, nearly instantaneously.

I'm no longer alone. My pistol is in the other room, but this is the kind of danger a pistol can't solve.

He's here.

Which should terrify me. Wilder is dangerous and comes with a warning label. He has the ability to destroy everything I hold dear.

The moment I step into my bedroom, towel wrapped around me, Wilder's presence whispers over my skin, stimulating my nerves, and making my entire body heat and shiver at the same time. I exchange the towel for a long, silk robe to cover my nakedness.

When I step into the living room, he's not there. Instead, Wilder sits casually on my balcony, sipping my whiskey, as if he's perfectly at home. He turns toward me, heat blazing in his eyes. Banked fury, as well as molten desire, licks down my body, stimulating and heating me from the outside in, and inside out.

"What are you doing here?" I stiffen my spine and try my best to keep my lower lip from trembling.

I edge over to the sofa, where I stash one of many pistols for self-defense. Only it's not there.

Wilder's large frame makes the small bistro table look like a child's toy. His sheer size dominates the space, and the scowl on his face gives me pause. It almost takes my mind away from the dark jeans and tight shirt hugging his powerful muscles. And, of course, my pistol sits on top of the table.

Wilder catches me looking at it. He places his palm over the dark metal and leans back, kicking his long legs out in front of him, casually crossing them at the ankles. He lifts the highball glass and looks at me over the rim as he takes a sip of whiskey.

"I was worried about you, pumpkin." He says it casually, as if there's nothing wrong with him breaking into my place and taking my gun.

I should've agreed with Harry and let him put a protective detail on me.

"I'm fine." I gesture toward the door. "If that's all you needed to know, don't let the door slam your ass on the way out."

His sharp gaze sweeps to the door. I regret placing the chair beneath the doorknob. That's the only way out of my apartment, aside from the balcony. I've effectively locked myself inside my apartment, with him.

"How the hell did you get in here?"

"You're magnificent when you're angry, pumpkin, but there's no need to be angry with me."

"Do you need me to count all the ways?"

"You could try, but it's not going to change a thing."

"What the hell does that mean?" I'm too tired for a verbal sparring match with him.

"Only that you know exactly how this is going to end."

"Is that so?" I prop a hand on my hip and stare him down. "Hate to break it to ya' Casanova, but nothing is going to happen between us. This ends with you leaving. You're not welcome here."

"Casanova?" His eyes twinkle with mirth. "We'll have to see about that."

I swallow thickly because he's right. My emotions are all over the place, making me needy and desperate for comfort. This evening has the potential to go down a very dangerous path.

And why shouldn't I let it? What if another night with Wilder isn't exactly what I need to get my mind off everything else?

Because Wilder's dangerous. The voice of reason in my head is one hundred percent correct.

From his strong, corded arms, to his chiseled torso, the man intimidates by existing. His testosterone-fueled masculinity fills the air, potent with promise, clouding my senses, making it hard to focus, and impossible to make good decisions.

He smells too good, heavenly in fact.

From inside my living room, his deep woodsy scent fills my nostrils and floods my senses with all kinds of bad ideas.

A tightness fills my chest as my heart kicks into high gear. The attraction between us is no less than the night we first met, and subsequently spent together, up here, doing all kinds of things.

Sex with Wilder is definitely an experience. It was explosive, undeniable, and unquenchable. My desire for him is no less now than it was then. I feel the need growing within me, to have him hold me close, to feel his hands on me, his lips gliding over mine, his body dominating mine. I ache for him in the worst possible way.

A glance around the room reminds me exactly how that night went. Wilder took me brutally and ruthlessly, *hard and fast*, just like I told him I wanted it.

We did it on the couch, on the floor, backed up against the wall. He put me to my knees and made me fly, fulfilling filthy fantasies I kept hidden from myself. Wilder opened a door, and I stepped through without any care for the aftermath.

This.

This is the aftermath.

An intense longing for something I shouldn't want, but can't deny, fills me with the irrational need for more. I'm like a drug addict searching for my next high.

"You need to leave." I try to shrug off the crazy inside my head which tells me getting fucked by him might be just what I need.

I know it's not. This is why he's dangerous. He's where good intentions go to be twisted into carnal delights.

I square off against him, doing my best to keep the shakiness out of my voice. If he doesn't leave, and soon, I'll regret it.

"Why?"

"What do you mean by why? Because this is my place and you're uninvited. You broke into my apartment. That's trespassing and I could have you arrested."

"You already arrested me, pumpkin. Let's not make that an ongoing thing."

"You should be behind bars."

"That's debatable. As for me being here, I may be uninvited, but I'm not unwanted. You need me, and I'm here." His lip curls as my body jerks involuntarily.

"First off, I don't know who your friends are, but they're definitely not FBI. Secondly, you belong behind bars. Thirdly, I definitely *do not* need you."

"If that's a lie you need to tell yourself, I'm good with it, but it doesn't change a thing."

"What does that mean?"

"That you need me."

"Wilder, I want to be alone. I don't …"

"It's Knox."

"What?"

"My name. It's Knox."

"Whatever, you need to leave."

"I'll leave, but only if you answer one question."

"I don't have the energy to play games."

"It's not a game. If the answer is *No*, I'll leave. If it's a *Yes*, then I'll stay."

"You're not listening." My voice waivers as exhaustion and grief push past my defenses. I really don't want to be alone, and even if I barely know this infuriating man, he feels right. I want him to stay. "I need you to leave."

I hate everything about this no good, horrible, bad day.

"You're a horrible liar." His lips tilt into a grin. "It's just one question."

"It's a trick question."

I don't know Wilder that well, but what I do know about him is there's no way in hell he's leaving me alone. I don't know whether to hate him or thank him.

Regardless of what I really want, I'll never ask him to stay. I'm not that brave.

"Then just say *Yes*."

"Wilder …"

"Knox." He corrects me.

"Fine. Whatever, *Knox*, stay or go, I don't give a fuck. Just leave me alone."

"You were looking around the room, thinking about our first time together, hating how much you loved the things we did and the things I did to you. You're not ready to accept that side of yourself, and that's totally okay. We can take things slow from here on out. That's what I was going to ask."

There's no question in what he says. It's a statement of fact. One which I, unfortunately, agree with.

"I hate you."

"You'd like to think that, but you don't. You need me."

"I really don't."

"I'm here for you. Whether that means letting you cry on my shoulder, or hold you while we share the silence, I'm here, and I'm not leaving you alone tonight."

I ignore everything he says right there. He's absolutely right about all of it.

I hate how my body betrays me. My nipples tighten and there's no doubt he notices. Wilder—Knox notices the tiniest detail. I wrap my arms around my chest. The damn silk reveals far too much.

"That was our first and last time. We're not doing—that again."

"That?" A low chuckle rumbles from his chest. "That was the first of many times, pumpkin, and you know it. You crave it. We're definitely doing more of *that*."

"You've got a lot of nerve." I don't want to talk about sex with him. I definitely don't want to admit he's right. Talking about sex with Knox leads to wanting to do something about it. "I don't want to talk about that anymore."

"Because I'm open about what I want?" He's incredibly open about what he wants. "How about this for a bit of honesty? I desperately want to fuck you again. How does that make you feel, knowing how much I crave what we did? That I can't wait to hold you in my arms again?"

"Is that all this is about? Getting your rocks off?"

"Have you considered I may be here because I'm concerned about you and want to make sure you're okay?"

"Not when all you talk about is fucking me."

"I'm honest about my needs, but I came to make sure you're okay."

"Is any of that even remotely true?"

"You already know the answer to that." He takes another slow sip of whiskey. "But let's lay it out, shall we?" His right brow arches suggestively. "I want to fuck you. I'm hard as a rock looking at you in that robe. Damn, but you're gorgeous. From your body's reactions, you're not against the idea. But let's focus on the last part of what I said."

I don't even know what the last thing I said was. He's got me so wound up, I barely follow our conversation. I'm not sure if we're arguing, agreeing, or if this is some insane type of foreplay.

The only thing going through my head right now is how much I want to feel his chiseled torso and rock-hard abs moving back and forth as he fucks me into oblivion. I need to disappear from myself and the world for just a little bit.

It's time to stop thinking of him as the man who rocked my world and focus on what he truly is.

"You're a criminal." If I say it enough times, I might actually believe it. Hell, even if it's true, it doesn't explain the insane chemistry between us.

"Says who?"

"Says me."

"We're all allowed to have opinions. Doesn't mean you're right."

"Do you deny it?" I've got him, and while he's here, why not try to find some answers?

"I'm not confirming or denying. That's not why I'm here." He cocks his head. "I am, however, curious as to how you came to that particular conclusion."

"Who do you work for?" I fire a shot, digging for information.

"How do you want me to fuck you first?" He shoots back, knocking me off my game and making me struggle to recover. "If you're going to pepper me with questions, I'm going to lob a few of my own. You sure you want to go down this path?"

He's infuriating. My fingers curl until my nails dig into my palms.

"I …" I give a sharp shake of my head, off-balanced by his question. He shook me, and the bastard knows it. "We're not sleeping together."

"I'm ready for a long night of kinky sex, but if you want to sleep, we can put that off until morning. I'd love to keep you tied up in bed all day."

"You fucking bastard."

"Well, I'm not a bastard, but I do hope to be fucking you soon. You're cute when you're angry, pumpkin. Makes my dick take notice. But for the record, I'm arguing for sleep over sex. I haven't stopped thinking about how you feel in my arms, but I have a feeling you need to cuddle more than you need to fuck."

"You're incorrigible."

"I'm concerned."

"Concerned?"

"Is that so hard to believe?"

"Why would you be concerned about me? And yes, it's hard to believe."

"Because I care about you."

"Why?"

"Now that is a very interesting question, one I'm not entirely sure about. Except …" Knox stands and takes a step toward me. The expression on his face is sincere. "You lost your team. They were cut down right in front of you. That's a lot of trauma to process. You shouldn't have to spend the night alone, especially when you have me."

"I don't …" My grief spills over the dam I built and a sob escapes me. My cheeks heat as tears blur my vision.

I hate showing any weakness, and I especially hate showing vulnerability in front of Knox.

"I've been there, pumpkin. I know exactly how it feels, and you don't have to go through it alone." He opens his arms. "We don't have to talk about it. We can unpack that box later, but you definitely will not spend tonight alone."

I want to run into his arms, but I'm too damn stubborn. Fortunately, Knox knows exactly what I need.

He comes to me.

Before I know what's happening, his strong arms wrap around me. He pulls me into an embrace, folding his strong body around mine until I'm cocooned in his warmth. I don't know why, but I suddenly lose all control. Tears fall as gut-wrenching sobs escape me.

Knox holds me for several minutes, saying nothing, while I fall apart, then he picks me up and carries me to bed. He sets me down, while he pulls back the covers, then waits for me to crawl under them.

He tucks me in and turns out the light. I think he's going to leave when he moves to the other room. The lights go out, and I listen for the sound of his departure, but Knox returns. The mattress beside me dips as he crawls into bed.

Knox scoots close. His arm wraps around me and he drags me against him. With Knox wrapped around me, I settle down, emotions run through me and I don't care if he watches me fall apart.

Our bodies touch, and I know I'm exactly where I belong. Sheltered and comforted, I fall asleep in the arms of a man who'll stand guard over me while I sleep.

SEVENTEEN

Knox

LILY'S SOFT CRIES SLOWLY QUIET AS SLEEP PULLS HER UNDER. HER breathing slows until it settles into an even rhythm, telling me she's fallen asleep. Careful not to wake her, I curl around her body, so much smaller and delicate than mine. I take my leg and wrap it around hers, then lock my arm around her waist as I pull her close.

She feels fragile in my arms, as if I could inadvertently hurt her if I didn't take care. Her light scent fills my senses: sweet, sexy, feminine, and unique to her. I can't help but kiss her shoulder and glide my lips along the graceful curve of her neck.

I should sleep. Exhaustion pulls at me, but I stay wide awake late into the night, holding her tight against me. More than once, I wonder what the hell I'm doing.

I'm not the kind of man who holds a woman. I've definitely never comforted one before. I mean, other than those I've rescued, but they are different. They cling to me out of fear and relief.

With Lily?

I cling to her.

If she wakes, I want her to feel my arms around her, holding her, reassuring her—being there for her. I want to be her anchor, a place of safety where fear and worry can't touch her. Not only does she feel wonderful in my arms, she fits.

A wonderfully perfect fit.

Not the kind of man who does the relationship thing, my love life revolves around sex rather than feelings. Meaning I have no love life, but a very active sex life.

Why, then, do I curl protectively around Lily, not as a lover, but as something much more intimate?

Eventually, my body gives in to fatigue, and I sleep curled protectively around her. No matter how exhausted I feel, I wake before the ass-crack of dawn. My body's a well-trained machine and used to adhering to a rigid schedule.

Snoozing fitfully, I crawl out of bed, careful not to wake Lily. While she's still asleep, I ransack her meager kitchen. It's my thought to whip up something amazing for breakfast, but that proves impossible as Lily's fridge contains stale milk, moldy cheese, and something I can't, and don't, want to identify.

What she does have are tea bags. No coffee to be found. I manage to heat up water by the time she stirs from the bedroom.

Lily walks into the living room, looking like shit. Her hair is tousled, bags droop under her eyes, and her shoulders slump as she casually takes a look around.

"You look like you got run over by a Mac truck." I try to keep my voice light, making it a joke, and hope I don't misinterpret her sense of humor.

"I feel like a fleet of Mac trucks ran me over." Her sleepy gaze sweeps to the kitchen. "What's that?" Her attention lingers on the pot of boiling water I've turned into a tea kettle.

"I'm making tea."

"That's not the kind of tea you boil. Boiling makes it bitter."

"How else would you make it?"

"It's sun tea."

"What the fuck is sun tea?"

"You know, you put water in a glass container, set it out so the sun heats it. It makes the best brew, without all the bitterness boiling does to it."

"I'm not a sun tea aficionado." I glance mournfully at the tea I ruined.

"It's okay." Her face brightens with the slightest smile. "I'm not up for tea anyway."

"I tried making breakfast, but …"

"I'm not a good cook."

"What do you eat?"

"I go out."

"For every meal? I checked all the cabinets and your cupboards are literally bare."

"Sorry, didn't get the cooking gene when they were passing them out." She gives a sheepish grin. "And I don't usually have men sleep over." Her cheeks turn the prettiest shade of pink I've ever seen in my life.

I love these tiny moments of vulnerability she shares with me. Or, at least, I'd like to think I'm the only person she's this open with. I want more moments like this; Lily showing me her most private self.

"Are you hungry?" Finding food won't be a problem. There are literally scores of restaurants within a short walk. All of them are fabulous.

"I'm tired." She pushes her hair off her face.

I don't know why, but the way the sun hits the ivory-white strands of her hair mesmerizes me.

"Is that your natural color?"

"You're not supposed to ask women that question."

"I think we passed the polite, social stage when I had my dick shoved down your throat the other night." Her cheeks turn a darker shade of pink and I smile. "Gotcha."

She rolls her eyes. "Is there ever a time you're not thinking about sex?"

"When I'm with a beautiful woman? Never."

She plops down on the couch opposite me with a sigh. "About last night …"

"The only thing we're saying about last night is *of course*."

"Of course?" Her brows pinch together, confused. "What does

that mean?"

"Of course, I stayed with you. I'd never leave you alone after what you went through."

"I don't really want to talk about it."

"That doesn't surprise me."

"Really? Because it seems as if we're talking about it."

"Over the next few weeks, people are going to be all up in your business asking about your feelings and shit. It's going to suck. You're going to get angry. But after enough time passes, you'll find yourself in a place where you can talk about it."

"How would you know anything about what I went through?"

"You really want to know?"

"You sound like you've got it all figured out. So yeah, tell me."

Her challenge doesn't go unnoticed, but I see it for what it really is. Several years ago, I was in her shoes. I know exactly how she feels.

"I used to be in the Navy." I watch her reaction, wondering how much to say.

Back in the day, when I was a fresh baby SEAL, some of us may, or may not, have bragged about being a SEAL; meaning I was the braggart. That kind of bravado got stamped out of me as my betters taught me what it really means to be a SEAL.

SEALs don't mention what they do for a living. We're not the kind of men who need the light of attention shined down on us. After a few ass-whoopings, I figured that out and learned to keep quiet about such things.

Part of being the best of the best is reaching that level of confidence and self-assuredness that boasting about your skills becomes unnecessary. Not to mention it's frowned upon within the community.

I'm not worried about that with Lily. I need her to understand why I want to help her, and how important it is for her to open up. Not that she necessarily will with me, but she needs to unpack that box before it turns poisonous. I see her holding it in and my girl is totally falling apart.

"I'm a SEAL." Again, I wait. She didn't flinch when I

mentioned being in the Navy, and she has no reaction to me telling her I'm a SEAL. "How much do you know about me?"

She flinches and I know she's looked at my dossier.

"How about we try a little open communication, pumpkin? You've got tons of questions you want to ask, so let's trade. Sound good?"

"You're really going to answer my questions?"

"I did say the *only* person I would speak to is you."

"I thought you were just being a prick about it." Her expression lightens, making her eyes sparkle. "You really got under Harry's skin."

"Harry?"

"My boss. He's the one who interrogated you."

"Ah yes. You mean the one who *tried* to interrogate me."

"He was definitely frustrated."

"I didn't have anything I needed to say to him."

"What about to me?" She shifts forward, letting too much eagerness show. Lily's definitely a professional, but all I see is a white-haired beauty needing a comforting shoulder.

And sex.

Lily needs lots and lots of sex. Something to take her mind off what happened yesterday.

"I knew they'd never put you in that interrogation room with me."

"Meaning you played them?"

"Merely wasted time until my team came to spring me."

"You mean the FBI?"

"I don't work for the FBI."

"I knew it. So, who do you work for? Are you a criminal? You didn't answer the question last night."

"That depends on your definition."

"It's a pretty cut and dry definition." Lily leans back with frustration.

"Not as cut and dry as you think."

"How can that be?"

"For example, as a SEAL, I participated in several operations which skirted the law. Did I break any laws?" I watch carefully to see if she picks up on the transition from "I work for the Navy," to "I'm a SEAL." There's definite gravitas to that elite designation.

"Did you?"

"Depends on who you ask, what their security clearance is, and a bunch of other shit."

"But you had the umbrella of the Navy covering you. Your missions were sanctioned."

She completely rolls past the whole "I'm a SEAL thing," which leads me to believe her intelligence is rather thorough. Although, how did they miss that I work as a Guardian?

I'm going to have to ask Mitzy and CJ about that. How much of what we do is black book, or simply not on the books, kind of stuff?

"True, but sanctioned operations and technically legal are two different things. I just want to make sure we're speaking the same language."

"And what language is that?"

"Only that we cut through the bullshit for a second." Her spine snaps straight as a rod, telling me I hit a sensitive subject. "I know you're DEA. You know I'm a SEAL."

"So, it's true?"

"What's that?"

"Once a SEAL, always a SEAL? You said *I'm a SEAL*, like you still are one. Rather than *I was a SEAL*."

"It's the truth."

"Am I supposed to be impressed by that?"

"Doesn't matter what you think, or don't think. I earned the right to call myself a SEAL. I joined that brotherhood and there's nothing anyone can do to take it away from me."

"I didn't mean to say …"

"You didn't have to, but none of this is what I want to talk about."

"What do you want to talk about?"

"Several things."

"Such as?"

"Let's start with why you think I'm a criminal?" It's the easiest thing to move into before getting her to open up about the trauma from last night.

"You just said maybe you were, maybe you weren't."

"True, but I want to know why the DEA is looking into me."

"I can't tell you that." She draws her knees up and wraps her arms around them as she props her chin on her kneecaps.

"Haven't we gone beyond that?"

"I can't share sensitive information with someone under active investigation, unless ..."

"Unless, what?"

"Unless you might be interested in becoming an informant for the DEA?" She sounds serious, and I can't help but snort at the idea of me being an informant.

"Seriously?" Watching the transformation in her from nervous and vulnerable to investigative and hard-core DEA agent is cute as shit.

"What are you smiling at?" Her brows pinch together and I wipe the grin from my face.

"Nothing." I lean back against the counter and cross my arms over my chest. "An informant?"

"We can offer protection ..."

"I'm going to stop you right there." I hold up a hand. "Whatever information you have about me is dead wrong. You're barking up the wrong tree if you think I'll be an informant." I figure it all out now. "You think I was at the docks because of drugs?"

"Weren't you?"

"You already know the answer to that."

Lily's smart, but I've seen plenty of smart people get stuck on stupid because it's what they've been told to think. Once again, her brows tug together. She bites at her lower lip and I see the gears spinning in her head.

"I saw a girl's face."

"Yes ..." I let her think her way out of the box her colleagues built.

"You were there for the girl."

"Girls." I correct her. "We were there for the girls."

"Who is *we?*"

"The people I work for." Just like a real SEAL doesn't brag about his status, a Guardian doesn't either. There's no need to let information like that become mainstream knowledge.

"We thought you were there for the drugs."

"Obviously." I uncross my arms and close the space between us. "Why do you think I was there for drugs?"

Lily's skittish. Last night, exhaustion pulled at her, making her vulnerable. In the light of day, her shields are up, and I'll respect them.

"We've been following several shipments of drugs into this country and matched them up with your comings and goings."

"I'm flattered the DEA thinks so highly of me."

"We traced your movements from NOLA to Cancun and on to Colombia, but there's no official record of you entering or leaving the country. All of your movements coincide with drug shipments."

"Ah, that makes sense."

"How? How does it make sense?"

"I'm a Guardian."

It's easiest to simply put it all out there. Who I am, and what I do, means nothing when it comes to helping Lily deal with what happened to her and her team.

Her fidgetiness stems from that, and I'm working my way around to a position where I can help guide her down the treacherous path toward recovery.

Again, I wonder what the hell I'm doing. If she were any other chick, I'd be long gone by now. I wouldn't still be here, compelled to ease her burdens. With Lily, it's impossible to walk away.

"What's a Guardian?"

I settle beside her on the couch and take her hand in mine. She doesn't draw back. In fact, her delicate fingers curl around my hand. A sudden sense of warmth fills my chest.

This—this right here *feels* right.

"The Guardians are hostage rescue specialists. We rescue those who've been taken."

"I'm confused. So, you do work for the FBI? What's a Guardian?"

"More like the FBI occasionally contracts out difficult cases which require creative solutions to Guardian HRS. The HRS means hostage rescue specialists. Technically, my team doesn't work for the FBI, but one of our teams does, and technically, we're deputized U.S. Marshals, which eliminates some of the red tape when we operate within the U.S. So, we're on the same side of the law."

"Would that be the not-so-legal aspect of the job?"

"Maybe." I lift her hand to my mouth and kiss the back of her hand. Lily's eyes drift closed.

"So that girl ..." She shakes her head. "Girls, you said there were more."

"There are."

"You were there to rescue them?"

"Yes, and that's all I can tell you about the Guardians. It's confidential and shit like that. What I can say is that I'm in no way involved in the trafficking of drugs either into or out of the country. Whoever gathered your intel needs to do better. They're way off base."

"It was thin intel. We knew that, but it all seemed to fit together."

"Which brings us back to what happened yesterday."

I slowly circle back around to what's important. I worry about Lily. I'm concerned with how she's dealing with what went down at the dock. It feels as if she's burying it all, and that's only going to make things fester.

"I don't want to talk about it." She pulls her hand away and tugs her knees tight to her chest. Her attention shifts from me to the floor.

"No need to talk, but I want you to listen for a minute."

"Why?"

"Because it's going to help."

"Nothing will help."

"Do you trust me?"

She lifts her chin off her knees and gives me a dubious look. It's one I ignore as I share what happened to me.

"In the military, we dealt with a lot of heavy shit. The military is good and bad when it comes to dealing with the aftermath. It developed successful processes to identify psychological trauma and treat the results of the PTSD that develops after it."

"Are you saying I have PTSD? That I'm not strong enough to deal with what happened? I'm not traumatized by it."

"It's not my place to say, but, Lily?" I tilt my head and force her to meet my gaze. "Any normal, sane individual would be traumatized if they saw their teammates killed in front of them. I'm not saying you're not strong enough to deal with it. I actually find you incredibly strong, mentally and physically; I merely want to share something that happened to me."

I wait to see what else she'll throw at me to dodge the subject. It's what I did after what happened to me. But Lily gives a soft nod. She's willing to listen, and that's a pretty damn good first step.

"Something similar happened to me, and no matter what the docs told me, I knew I didn't need their help. Not only that, but I got angry when they kept hounding me to take psychological assessments. It pissed me the fuck off. It was as if they didn't think I could deal with my shit. I avoided talking to anyone really, except my buddy, Max, for a very long time. As it turns out, I was dead wrong, as was Max, but we were too obstinate and proud to accept that we might need help. My gut tells me the DEA is not as savvy as the military in offering you the kind of support you need."

"I'm fine, Knox. I've got my shit locked down tight."

"That's what I said, and I got really pissed when people tried to help me. I didn't need anyone's help. Like you, I had my shit locked down tight."

"Is that so?"

"Yes, and my gut tells me I'm exactly what you need."

"You think you can fuck me out of my trauma?" She snorts. It's such a funny sound coming from her.

"I'd love to go another round with you, pumpkin. I'm good, but

I'm not that good." I can't help but laugh. My attention wanders to the bedroom where I kept her tied up our first night together.

The idea of fucking her out of her trauma brings too many images to mind, but we're not going down that rabbit hole.

At least, not yet.

Lily needs a good fucking, something to totally take her mind off what happened, but not now. Right now, she needs to know I care about her as a person; that I'll be right by her side as she navigates all the pitfalls of recovering from something as traumatic as seeing her entire team executed in front of her.

"Sometimes, the best thing to have after losing a teammate is someone who's been in the same shoes. It's easy for people to sympathize after such a loss, but virtually impossible for them to empathize."

Lily stills. After a momentary pause, where I let my words sink in, she slowly unfolds her knees. She scoots to the corner of the couch and grabs a pillow, which she hugs in front of her.

"I know how you feel."

"No, you don't." She stubbornly refuses to look at me, but that's okay. I got her talking, and that's a good first step.

"My buddy, Max, and I lost nearly our entire team on a lonely road in the desert. We made some of the toughest choices a man should ever make. We took the limited resources we had, and saved two lives, while four of our buddies died beside us."

The memory washes over me, just as tense and desperate as ever. That hopeless feeling isn't something I'll ever forget. I still taste the dry desert air, feel the pervasive sand as it abrades my skin, and cringe at the acrid smell of blood filling my nostrils. That shakiness returns. It's the kind of deep-seated fear when you know the shit's hit the fan and it's only going to get worse.

Her head lifts and she looks at me for the first time since sitting on the couch. My words reach her.

"After it all went down, it didn't help in the debriefs when the medical commander told us we did exactly what we should have done. That any other decision would've left six men dead in the field instead of four. The thing is, that kind of math means shit when those buddies are men you trained with, operated with, and spent your downtime hanging out with."

"I can't imagine …"

"I think you can."

I keep my words as soft as I can and she gets what I'm saying. Lily is now a member of a very select group of individuals. It's a club no one wants to be a part of and can't escape. I continue my story, knowing she needs to really understand where I'm coming from.

"If Max and I didn't have each other, the guilt would've overwhelmed us. It would've ruined us as elite operators. Truthfully though, having Max to talk to wasn't enough. We went through the whole damn thing together and felt guilty together about the choices we made. They gave us medals for saving two lives. I'd give anything not to have that damn medal. I'd rather sit with my buddies who died, talking shit about our days in the desert, rather than have that medal. Sadly, that will never happen."

"I'm sorry."

"Thank you, but I've come to terms with what happened. I'm not at peace with it, but it no longer casts a shadow over who I am. Despite how it feels, we did the best we could. And this is the part I really want you to hear. I want you to absorb it."

"Okay?" Her breath catches. I've got her attention.

"It took a guy neither of us knew, who was the sole survivor after a tank rolled over a landmine to get our heads screwed on straight. He sat down with us when we were struggling to come to terms with what happened."

"What did he say?"

"He said life sucked."

"Huh?"

"I'm not kidding. He told us life sucked and that the only way we could honor those we lost was by living the best lives we could. If we didn't, their sacrifice was in vain. So, I'm telling you this now. You can wallow in your guilt. You can play it over in your head a million times. But none of that is going to help you get over it. The docs and shrinks will make you think that's what you're supposed to do—get over it. But the truth is—it's a part of you now. You either embrace it and live your best life, honoring their sacrifice, or you let it eat at you like the cancer it is. So, this is my question for you. How are you going to honor them?"

She lets the pillow fall to the floor and slowly stands. Tears pool at the corners of her eyes.

"Thank you." She wipes at her eyes. "It hurts." Her hand goes to her chest. "Does that ever get better?"

"With time the ache eases, but it's always there. It's a part of who you are now, but the pain will get better."

"I'm just so exhausted. All I want to do is curl up in bed and sleep."

"I felt the same way, but what helped me the most was continuing with my normal routine. I got out of bed, went to the gym. I made sure to eat, even when I didn't want to, and when my thoughts started turning back to that day, I gave myself permission to think about their deaths. But I didn't let it take over my life."

"I don't know if I can do that same thing."

"You're a lot stronger than you know, pumpkin."

"Wil—Knox ..." Her voice shakes.

"Yes?"

"Can you ..." She looks down and to the side and sniffs, but then her teary eyes turn back to me. "Can you just hold me for a little bit?"

Can I?

Hell yes.

I'll hold her for the rest of my life if she lets me.

Without saying a word, I go to her. I wrap my arms around Lily as she rests her cheek against my chest. Her head barely comes up to my shoulders, and she feels perfect in my arms. I lean down to kiss the crown of her head as I do nothing other than hold her in my arms.

We stand there for the longest time and it occurs to me this is the longest I've ever held a female without it turning sexual. That latent sexual chemistry lingers in the air between us. There's no denying the potency of our attraction, but I'll take holding Lily in my arms like this over sex if I had to choose between the two.

This simply feels—right.

A thought pops into my head. Lily needs to do something normal, and I have an idea. But I'm not done holding her. I'll never get tired of this.

Lily sniffs and pushes against my chest. I let her go, needing her to know she's in control. As fun as it was to dominate her during sex, that's not how I want things between us now. She's strong, fucking fierce actually, and she's the first woman I've met who can be an equal partner with me.

"Why don't you take a quick shower, then get dressed. I'm taking you out for breakfast."

She sniffs again, then turns toward the bedroom. Just before the door to her room, Lily pauses and glances back at me. She nibbles at the bottom of her lip as our gazes connect and collide.

"Do you want to join me?"

"I always want to join you, but I'd never push."

She rolls her shoulders back as she takes in a deep breath.

"You're not pushing. I'm asking."

If that's not a total turn on, then I don't know what is. Reaching down, I grasp the bottom of my shirt and pull it over my head.

Lily freezes in place as I cross the short distance between us. This will be nothing like the other night. That was sex, this—this, transcends the simple pleasure of our bodies.

EIGHTEEN

Lily

I MUST BE OUT OF MY MIND ASKING KNOX TO TAKE A SHOWER WITH me, but I feel myself unraveling from the inside out. There's a solidness to him that calls out to me.

I feel adrift and need an anchor.

He provides that, and I can't say why, but maybe it's because of the story he told me about him and his buddy, Max.

I didn't believe him when he said he empathized with me, but it's true. He's been in my shoes before and he's not falling apart. Maybe after it first happened, although he says he was more angry than anything else, but if he got through it, I will too.

I breathe a little easier knowing there's a light at the end of this incredible survivor's guilt.

Honor the fallen?

That sounds like great advice. I'll have to think on how I might be able to do that.

Knox's right about being traumatized. At some point, I'll have to deal with it, just like he said, but right now, all I want is to disappear for a little bit doing something normal.

Not that sex with Knox is normal. The man is sex on a stick. I'm well aware of his impressive talents in bed, which is probably why I know sex is exactly what I need to get out of my head for a little bit.

The moment his shirt falls to the floor, my gaze latches onto the perfection of his body. The strong column of his neck makes me shiver. The broad slope of his shoulders makes me ache. The hard planes of his chest and the most perfect eight-pack I've ever seen speak of sexy, filthy fantasies.

He undoes the fly of his jeans as my mouth gapes. Deep V-grooves angle downward to an impressive member hidden from view.

My fingers clench in anticipation as he prowls toward me, one thought on his mind. It mirrors the thoughts in mine. His virility cannot be denied. His sex appeal fills the air, and I swoon.

Knox is the epitome of masculinity when it comes to sex. His long legs bring him towering over me as my neck arches back to admire the corded muscles twining up his arms.

I shouldn't stare, but there's too much of him to take in. He braces himself against the door frame, gazing down at me. Pressing two fingers under my chin, he forces my chin to lift and my face to tilt upward. While my breaths deepen, his fingers move from my chin to my nape.

"You sure this is what you want?" He dips down, fluttering kisses over my forehead and the bridge of my nose.

My voice fails me, but I give a shaky nod.

His fingers curl in the hair at my nape and gently tug at the roots. "Hard and fast like the last time?"

"Yes." I find my voice, but it shakes, betraying my need.

Knox hauls me close, lifting my lips to meet the heat of his mouth. He feathers a kiss across my lips. It's so light, I'm not sure if we're actually touching or not.

His dark, intoxicating scent floods my senses as I succumb to the moment. He smells good and feels amazing as my hands grip his arms and trace the corded muscles.

He backs me against the wall, pressing his chest against mine. My nipples tighten and peak, stimulated and aroused as his lips drive savagely against mine.

I don't know how he goes from light and caressing to savage and plundering, but the man knows how to kiss until I'm a quivering, moaning puddle of need.

His tongue thrusts past my lips, pillaging my mouth as he sweeps in to claim and take. The tip of his tongue drives me wild as he swirls it inside my mouth. Tasting, he feeds upon my need, stabbing and stroking with his tongue the way he'll soon be inside me, thrusting hard and driving me wild.

Knox isn't a man to take things slow, but I feel him holding back even as he lashes and strikes with his tongue, testing the limits of what I'll allow.

We break apart for a moment. Chests heaving, breaths deepening, I look up at him and tell him exactly what I need.

"Don't be gentle." I need to disappear and he's exactly the man who can make that happen.

Knox's gaze shifts between my eyes, flickering back and forth as he decides if I truly mean what I said. My brows pinch and I bite at my lower lip. My fingers curl and my nails dig into the skin of his arms.

"Please …" I can't help but beg for what I need.

His entire body tenses, nostrils flare, and then he strikes.

Yanking my hair, he jerks my head back, then he attacks my mouth with potent male fury, using his tongue as a weapon to lay claim to my body. He rips the robe off my body, divesting me of the offending fabric, then attacks me with the desperation of a man intent on laying claim to his woman.

My pulse leaps in my throat, flooding my system with adrenaline and a mindless need to be taken.

The heat of his mouth covers my breast. His tongue laves my peaked nipple as his teeth clamp down, biting hard enough to pull a scream from my body.

As if that's the sign he needs, Knox lifts me into the air as he pushes his pants down over his hips. Freeing his thick and engorged cock, a flood of arousal courses through me.

Christ, he's magnificent, engaging his entire body and soul as he ruts and fucks, captivating me with the rawness of his desire. My fingers twitch as they wrap around his neck.

Knox hoists me off the floor, then slams me against the wall as his hard length pushes past my entrance and slams home with one thrust. I cry out with the savageness of the intrusion, but that pain soon morphs into exquisite pleasure.

The full force of his body engages in the act of fucking, stealing my breath as he repeatedly slams me against the wall.

He knocks the air from my lungs with each punishing thrust. But I must be breathing because screams rip from my throat as pleasure courses through my body.

He groans through labored breaths as the first orgasm rips through me. I come down from a delirious high while Knox carries me to the bed.

No softness here and he lets me know we're nowhere near done. Knox slams me down on the mattress.

I scoot back to give him room as he prowls over me. Knox's body covers mine. Our gazes lock together. Staring into each other's eyes, he positions himself between my legs to thrust, driving his hard length into me.

A strangled groan sounds in the back of his throat as he draws back. Then Knox rocks forward, slamming hard, burying himself to the hilt. He builds up speed, rocking hard against me, slamming deeper, thrusting harder.

His grunts fill my ears as I cling to him, opening my legs wider, welcoming him to take whatever he wants. Needing him to fuck me hard and fast until all thought escapes me.

Knox ravages me as he seeks his release, forcing my legs wider as he spears into me. Meanwhile, his hands move over my body, stroking me, mauling me, loving me, while he immobilizes me with his powerful frame.

His thrusting turns savage and raw, building a steady rhythm that makes me writhe beneath him, demanding more.

I need him to be wild and fierce.

He fits inside me perfectly, as if made for me, and fucks me with punishing force, which is erotic as hell and sensual as heaven.

Fully involved in sex with Knox, I realize something profound. I'm not only engaged physically, but Knox makes me feel. He's in my head. He's in my heart.

Emotions spill out of me. Pleasure mixes with pain. Joy melds with happiness. This is nothing like a simple physical release. Every cell in my body engages as he forces me to yield to his need.

He kisses me as he ruts, tasting and consuming as his mouth moves along my neck. My fevered skin reacts, burning and blistering with sensation as he moves up to suck on my ear.

"You feel like heaven, pumpkin." Knox keeps up the demanding pace, burying himself deeper, stretching and filling me, as I surrender to all the sensations he pulls from my body.

He sucks on my ear. Bites along my neck. He torments my breasts. My senses swim, switching from pleasure to pain and back again.

I try to struggle, needing to pretend I resist, but Knox only pins me to the bed. His hands grip my wrists, forcing them over my head as he surges harder.

"You're so fucking tight. So hot. So wet for me. Christ, you feel like coming home."

"Harder, Knox. Please—make me burn."

"Fight me, Lily. All that straining makes your pussy clench around my cock. Squirm all you want, but know that you're mine. I own every bit of you."

I fight him. I squirm and tense. My fingers curl and clench. As I resist, his thrusting turns punishing as he rams in and out, stretching me and making me burn.

A tightness in my belly tells me I'm close. The more Knox takes from me, the higher I climb. His mouth grinds against mine as he takes and takes. Knox plunges mercilessly in and out, groaning in pleasure as I reach my peak.

I've never had a man fuck me with such fury, such virility, such maddening pleasure. Each thrust and every kiss ignites a fire within me. My insides clench and tighten, burn and sizzle, as that crackling energy shoots through me.

No longer able to hold back from the pleasure building within me, my legs clamp around his hips as I cry out. Pleasure washes through me as nerve endings crackle and pop. I feel Knox deep within me, melding with my heart and stirring my soul.

Faster and faster, Knox moves over me, sparking aftershocks of pleasure as my gasps meld with his moans.

The cadence of his thrusts slows. He drags out then slides forward as his hips rock. It feels as if his cock swells, lengthening and thickening, making the burn more intense. He pushes forward one last time. His body tenses, then jerks over mine as pleasure rushes through him.

Knox collapses over me, his heavy body weighing me down. He releases my wrists and I wrap them around his neck as he recovers. His ragged breathing eases, and he starts to pull out, but I grip him tight.

"Not yet." I'm reluctant to let him go. A pulsing ache fills me as my pussy throbs with the aftershocks of my orgasm. I gaze up at him as he lifts his torso and balances his weight on his forearms.

Knox leans down, tenderly kissing my forehead. "You're fucking incredible, Lily Freeman, and I hate to say it ..."

"Say, what?"

"I'm never letting you go."

My fingers play with the hair at his nape. "Don't ever let me go."

His body shifts and he slips out of me. I already feel hollow without him inside of me, but Knox found his way into my heart. He settled in.

"Never." He kisses my forehead, right between my eyes. Then Knox slowly kisses everywhere else until my body shakes with a third, earth-shattering orgasm.

We rest in bed for a little while longer, holding hands and staring at the ceiling, but Knox eventually gives me a light shove.

"Get up, pumpkin. Let's take a shower and find some food."

"Do you like beignets?" They're my preferred breakfast, at least when I eat breakfast.

"Do they taste as sweet as you?" The corner of his lip ticks up in a smirk.

"You'll have to let me know." I lift up on tiptoe to kiss him. "You taste like sin."

He flashes a crooked smile but doesn't otherwise respond.

We shower and dress, then leave Callie's bar hand in hand. Knox towers over me, making me feel small and delicate, but it feels all kinds of right.

NINETEEN

Lily

___

It's early, but that doesn't mean the streets are empty. Tourists are out admiring the street performers who earn a living entertaining the crowds. We stop by a few, listening to soulful jazz for a song or two, then admire the skill of a group of acrobats. Knox tosses bills into their caddies and we move on.

That itching sensation returns, settling in between my shoulder blades, a sense of being watched.

"What's up?" Knox pulls us to a stop.

"Nothing." I glance around, but everything appears to be normal.

"Doesn't look like nothing."

"It felt like someone was watching me. I felt something similar last night, but it's gone now. I think I'm jumpy."

"Hmm ..." Knox's gaze hardens as he looks over the crowd.

"Nerves?" I shrug. I was doing well there for a while, not thinking about what happened to my team. Knox certainly has a way of taking my mind off things I'd rather not remember, but he's right. It's a part of me.

"Could be." He grudgingly agrees, but he takes a keener interest in the crowd as we work our way toward Cafe du Monde and the best beignets on the planet.

"You promise it gets better?" I rub my breastbone as a stabbing feeling shoots through my chest. Images of Peter falling to the ground fill my mind and my entire body tenses.

"Eventually." Knox pulls me into his protective embrace and I lean into him. His heavenly scent fills my nostrils as I press against him.

I love his arms around me, sheltering me, protecting me. He makes me feel safe, as if none of the evil in the world can touch me when he's near.

When we arrive at the Cafe du Monde, the line is long but moves quickly. I usually buy and go, but Knox wants to sit down.

I find a table right by the street. We spend the next hour stuffing our faces with the delectable treat and talking. Knox is curious about me, asking all kinds of questions about my background, my interests, and stuff like that. I shouldn't be surprised. I don't know if I can call us a couple, but we're definitely connected. One of the problems with jumping to sex quickly is that we missed out on the whole getting to know you part of a new relationship.

"How long have you lived here?" Knox licks powdered sugar off his fingers.

I smile, remembering him licking between my thighs not too long ago. The man definitely has skills.

"Feels like forever." I lean back and look over the crowd. Everyone carries on as if it's a normal day, but for me, I'm still dealing with the tragic loss of my team. It feels wrong not to be thinking about them.

"You've got that faraway look in your eyes, pumpkin. Are you thinking about your team?"

"Yeah, sorry." I bow my head, ashamed by how easily my mind drifts.

"Don't be sorry." Knox reaches for my hand. His thumb rubs circles over my skin. "Your thoughts will turn to what happened. Don't apologize for it, but don't let them linger and fester.

Acknowledge the thoughts, don't bury them. Give yourself enough grace to grieve and honor their memories."

"Thanks." I thread my fingers with his, holding his hand. "It just feels too *normal*, like I should somehow …" I gasp and fail to find the words I'm looking for.

"You feel as if the world should stop. That if you could only turn back time, you could somehow prevent what happened."

"Yes." That's exactly what I was thinking. "How did you know?"

"That's all I thought about for weeks. It turned obsessive. I second-guessed every decision I made. If I'd only done something different, I could've saved them all. You can't ignore your feelings. The thoughts will become intrusive. There will be guilt …" He gestures at the people sitting around us enjoying their beignets and coffee. "It feels wrong to do something as normal as eating breakfast, but you still have to live your life. That involves doing normal things. Accept the thoughts. Acknowledge your feelings. Honor your team's memory by doing everything in your power to live the best life you can. They wouldn't want you to obsess and wallow in guilt."

I rub at my chest again. He's right. Everything he says is spot on. "Yesterday, after your team took you, I went to the hospital and then to their homes."

"That must've been very hard."

"I felt it was the least I could do, but when I headed home, I felt like it wasn't enough."

"Max and I did the same thing. The military has a special way they notify families about a service member's death. We knew their families had been notified. We wanted to do it ourselves, but the mission demanded we stay in theater. The day we got back, Max and I visited the widows of our friends. It didn't help either of us, but it meant so much to their wives. Never underestimate the value of compassion."

"You're a pretty good therapist."

"I wouldn't say that. Like I said, I've been where you are now. It sucked. Having someone to talk to, who understood, is what eventually helped me."

"I really appreciate it."

"You're pretty amazing, Lily Freeman." He lifts my hand and kisses my knuckles. "Now, tell me everything about yourself."

"Everything?"

"Yeah," he releases my hand, "we skipped a few dating steps."

"That's funny."

"It's true."

"I know. I just meant that I was thinking the same thing. How we jumped into bed too soon."

"There was nothing *too soon* about it. You and I …" He grasps at thin air. "It feels right."

I definitely agree with him about that.

"What do you want to know about me?"

"Tell me about your childhood." Knox leans back. He crosses his arms over his broad chest, but presses his knee against my leg, under the table, keeping us connected.

"All of it?" I laugh. "There's not much to say."

"Brothers? Sisters? Only child?"

"Adopted."

"Really?"

"Yes."

"Have you ever met your birth mother?"

"It was a closed adoption. I tried, but after a while, I wondered why I bothered. My parents are great. Jinx is amazing."

"Jinx?"

"Yes, she was at the bar when we met. She and your friend seemed to hit it off."

"She's your sister?"

"Partner in crime. We were adopted together, born on the same day. Different birth mothers and fathers, obviously, but same adoptive parents. They're the only parents I've ever known and they're pretty darn amazing."

"That's cool."

"It is. We got to grow up as sisters."

"Jinx? An odd name."

"It fits her perfectly."

We spend two hours talking about nothing and everything, but eventually, we start getting stares from the staff. We're taking up valuable real estate.

"What do you have planned for the rest of the day?" Knox reaches for my hand, helping me up from the table. The moment we thread our way through the crowded restaurant, he wraps his arm around my shoulder.

"Jinx and Callie will want to make sure I'm okay. They're not going to be happy with you monopolizing my time."

"They can have you later. You're mine for now."

I curl into his warmth. I've never belonged to anyone before, and I really like it. I like it so much that it scares me.

There's a reason I don't date. I'm not very good at it.

TWENTY

Knox

I need to get back to my team, but I'm hesitant leaving Lily. She says her girlfriends will check in on her. It's not as if I'll be leaving her alone, but I'm secretly jealous. I want to be the person comforting her.

Not Jinx.

Not Callie.

Me.

The first few days after a trauma like she experienced are critical. The more she's able to talk about it, the better it will be for her down the road. I want to be there for her.

We wander around the French Quarter, popping into tourist shops where we try on masks for each other.

It's fun. Easy. Lily's a blast to be around.

We simply fit.

She's competitive as hell; beats me for the second time straight in another game of darts when we stop for lunch in a bar. Her friends text her. Lily checks her phone each time it beeps but doesn't respond.

I want to think it's because she enjoys her time with me, but I'm hesitant to assume too much too soon.

Unfortunately, I can't ignore the texts on my phone, although I try.

"Shouldn't you answer that?" Lily points to my phone. "That's the third text in as many minutes."

"You're not answering yours."

"That's because it's Jinx and Callie wanting to know where I'm at—and with whom."

"Did you tell them?"

"That was my first mistake." Her cheeks turn the prettiest shade of pink.

"You're cute when you blush."

"I'm not blushing." She presses her hands to her cheeks as the color intensifies.

"Definitely blushing." I grip her wrists and pull her hands away from her cheeks. It's necessary because I want to kiss her until she's breathless.

Without a care as to who can see, I kiss my girl just outside the store we exited. She tastes sweet and innocent, although there's nothing innocent about my girl.

Lily's hands wrap around my neck as I deepen our kiss and move us out of the flow of traffic headed into the store. People stare at our overly indulgent public display, but I couldn't care less what they think.

Her gasps mingle with my low, throaty moans. She makes me crave more, turning me desperate for a little privacy. The way her fingers move along my nape sparks pleasure that shoots straight to my groin. I rock my pelvis against her, letting her know how she affects me as my cock thickens and swells.

"Knox ..." A breathy moan escapes her mouth as I rock reverently against her. "We can't—not here."

"I want you."

"Yes ..."

Her sigh slows the cadence of my kisses, turning them languorous and sultry. I could kiss her for days and never get enough. My phone buzzes with another incoming text.

"I think you really need to get that. Whoever's texting you is persistent." Lily laughs as she pulls away from my kiss.

"No shit."

We separate, and I make a mental note to pound whoever it is into the ground for ruining the most perfect kiss. Which isn't going to happen. Mitzy's the one texting me.

She never texts me.

A quick glance shows dozens of texts from Max, Axel, Griff, Liam, Wolfe, and CJ.

Mitzy's, however, is short and to the point.

~

MITZY: STOP LOCKING LIPS AND GET YOUR ASS DOWN HERE.

~

I SHOULD WONDER HOW SHE KNOWS ABOUT THAT KISS, BUT IT'S Mitzy. She knows everything and is persistent enough to send one of her drones overhead to harass me if I don't comply.

"You have to go?" Lily stands apart, actively avoiding looking at my phone.

I love how conscious she is about not invading my privacy. Although, there's nothing I feel like keeping from her.

"It's work. I gotta get back." My phone erupts with "The Flight of the Valkyries." That's not a ringtone I put in. Mitzy's on the warpath, messing with my phone from behind her computer screen.

~

MITZY: NOW!

~

"EVIDENTLY, NOW." I TURN MY PHONE AROUND TO SHOW LILY.

Lily grabs my forearm to steady herself as she lifts on tiptoe to kiss my cheek.

"Then I'd better let you go. Will I see you again?"

Her question pisses me off and a jealous rage rushes through me. Will I see her again? I'd better be the only man she ever sees again.

I grab her waist and pull her to me. Leaning down, I thoroughly kiss her once more. She grips me tightly as I show her exactly what it means to be mine.

When I finally release her, she sways a little on her feet.

"Wow, what was that?"

"That was a promise. You're mine, Lily, don't ever doubt it. You'll most definitely be seeing me again, and I better be the only person you're seeing at all."

"Possessive much?"

"Damn straight." Mitzy sends another text through, but I ignore it. "Let me walk you home."

We're about four blocks from Lily's place, which means Mitzy is going to have to wait. Another text blows up my phone, making Lily laugh.

"You should really go."

"I will, right after I walk you home."

"It's not that far and will take up too much of your time."

"Doesn't matter."

"I'm fully capable of walking home on my own."

I take her hand, intent on seeing her home safe, but Lily places a hand against my chest.

"Knox, I'm good. I'm going to walk around a little bit more. I'm not ready to go home. Call me when you can, okay?"

I don't like leaving Lily in the middle of the French Quarter, but this is her home, and it's the middle of the day. No one is going to nab her off the street, and I have a sinking suspicion Lily's more than capable of defending herself. I give in, even though I think it's a bad idea.

"I don't know how long I'll be, but I'll call you first thing. I'd love to have dinner with you tonight."

I'm already thinking about something intimate and romantic. New Orleans isn't my town, but I'll figure something out.

We kiss again. Lily pulls back before it goes too far, laughing as she waves goodbye. Her steps are light, joyful, and show no residual trauma. Not that it means her mind won't drift down that dark path again, but it eases some of my concerns.

A little time with her friends will only help. I'm jealous of the time Lily will spend with Jinx and Callie, but I can't monopolize all her time. Not to mention, I still have a job to do.

After spending the night with the police and enduring an embarrassingly piss-poor attempt at an interrogation, I'm out of the loop as far as how our operation went down.

A grin ghosts across my face as I snort with the memory of how easily I played them.

There was no doubt in my mind the Guardians would spring me. All I had to do was stall, and I did that in spades. I hoped they would relent and put Lily in the room with me. However, thinking about that again, I'm glad they didn't. Things would've turn antagonistic between us rather than the way it played out.

And damn, if it didn't play out better than I could've hoped. My steps feel lighter. The air smells sweeter. I'm walking on cloud nine after spending the day with Lily.

After Forest, Sam, and CJ sprang me from the joint, I begged off returning with them, concerned about Lily. I followed her around town the rest of the day.

As someone who's seen their team taken out, I knew she would be headed down a difficult path. I wanted to be the one to guide her through those important first steps.

So, I stalked her, then broke into her place, climbing the railing to her balcony. I'm glad I did and thrilled with how the past several hours played out. Lily and I connected on a level I've never connected with a woman before. It's exciting, thrilling, a little unnerving, but I wouldn't change a goddamn thing.

Unfortunately, it's time to return to my team.

Which means it's time to let Lily go, at least for a little while. Axel and Griff's comments about *getting bit* bring a smile to my face.

It didn't take a month to fall.

I fell for Lily in less than a day.

She's my forever. I feel it in my heart. I know it in my head. I sense it on a soul-deep level.

While I watch her walk away, attention focused on her tight little ass, I make a crude adjustment at my groin, and hail a nearby cab.

Twenty minutes later, I walk into chaos. Our rental house is a mess of people, cables strung out across the floor, over the furniture, and along the walls.

Mitzy brought a team of eight with her. Six of them sit around the dining table, their faces bathed in the blue glow of the monitors. Two huddle around the kitchen island, where four screens display lines of data and code that make my eyes cross.

In the living room, Max hangs with the rest of my team. Griff, Axel, and Wolfe sit on the couch, jammed shoulder to shoulder, while Max and Liam sprawl on the two side chairs.

Max notices me first and waves me over to join the team.

"Have a good night?" His lip turns up in a smirk. Max knows exactly where I've been and what I've been up to.

I reach into my back pocket and toss a shiny button onto the coffee table. While Lily and I were out shopping, I picked up a handful of new buttons.

Griff looks up. His gaze goes down to the button. A huge grin splits his face as he leans forward and scoops it into his thick hand.

"Did I call it, or what?" He gives me an *I told you so* look, but I don't give a damn what the guys think.

"Whatever." With no other place to sit, I plop down on the floor and cross my legs in front of me. "What have you losers been up to?"

It's time to catch up with my team. Although, it's difficult staying focused. My thoughts turn toward Lily, wondering what she's doing.

I hope she's thinking of me.

TWENTY-ONE

Lily

______

People speak about love at first sight, but I never believed in it. There has to be more to it. Like how can a person *know* the first time they meet someone that they've found their soulmate?

I've always kind of chalked it off to superstition, tall tales, myth, and bullshit.

After today?

I may be a believer.

Not that Knox and I fell in love at first sight.

It took a game of darts, an evening of body shots, a night of explosive chemistry, exploratory sex, an arrest, more sex, and a day spent holding hands.

So, not love at first sight, but this feeling in my chest?

I rub at my breastbone and ache now that he's no longer with me. Like, I feel him deep inside of me, wrapped around my heart, settling deeper still, but there's a loss there as well because he's not standing beside me.

He's funny.

I love his mischievous grin. His dominance during sex is pretty hot, not to mention his ability to deliver mind-blowing orgasms. The orgasms are the best I've ever experienced.

He's easy to be around. And there's no doubt in anyone's mind he's confident in his skin.

During our day together, I lost count of the number of swoony looks random women gave him as we passed, or the piercing, jealous glares they shot at me when he held my hand.

Most importantly, Knox isn't a criminal.

So glad we worked *that* out because that would be a serious game-changer. Turns out, he's something else entirely.

A hero.

A Guardian.

He's a rescuer.

Talk about exploding ovaries.

He's the whole package.

And I think he likes me too.

No need to *think.*

Knox definitely likes me. Didn't miss that vibe between us. He's just as shocked and surprised as I am by the instant attraction, insane chemistry, and comfortable as an old shoe feel.

That's what my mom told Jinx and me when we were growing up. When we first started dating, we asked how we would know when we found our one true love. I thought she would tell us sparks and fireworks would be the sign.

But no.

Mom said we'd know because the man we were destined to love would feel like slipping on an old worn shoe.

You slip it on and it just fits.

That was the extent of what she told us about love. It was her great wisdom imparted on the next generation.

I never understood what the hell that meant. I didn't want a stinky old shoe for the love of my life.

I get it now.

I understand what she was trying to tell us.

My thoughts drift during the short walk back to Callie's bar. Knox doesn't know how long he'll be gone, but I secretly hope he'll show up for dinner. I love the way he snuck into my place last night, sitting all mysterious-like in the darkness on my balcony. It was pretty damn cool.

I love that he worries about me. The things he told me about him and his partner, Max, mean the world to me. It makes me feel less alone. I'm nowhere near done dealing with the trauma of watching Peter and the others murdered in front of me, but I'm not alone.

I don't have to go through it on my own.

It was important for him to talk to me, hold me, and let me know things would be okay. He was more concerned about that than hopping back into bed together.

Not that we didn't, but his priorities weren't where I expected them to be. I'm more than a booty call to him, and that matters.

For someone who's all about the one-night stand, it matters more than I thought it ever could.

I should've been afraid or concerned he broke into my place as easily as he did. Instead, my blood heated, and my body woke up.

It said *Hello, sexy!*

It's corny. I know, but that doesn't mean it's not true. So lost in my thoughts, I find myself right outside the bar without realizing it. The door's shut, which is odd this late in the day. It's almost time to open. When I push on the door and enter, all the lights are off.

I also don't notice the tables and chairs. Specifically, how they're tossed haphazardly about. By the time I do, my gaze lands on Callie.

Tied to a chair in the far back corner of the room, she struggles against her bonds and the gag muffling her screams.

A man grabs me from behind, placing his hand over my mouth. My scream comes out a muffled, pathetic sound as the man bodily lifts me off my feet and carries me to the center of the room.

Another man reaches for a chair sitting on its side. He sets it upright, and the man holding me slams me down on the chair. I try to stand, but he holds me down.

I kick and scream, getting off a couple ear-piercing wails before he gags me with one of the rags from behind the bar. The other man grabs each ankle, securing my legs to the chair with zip ties while I buck and struggle to get free.

It's no use. They're both much larger than I am, and they definitely know what they're doing. I can't see Callie behind me, but her soft cries fill my ears.

Once my legs are secure, the men tie my upper body to the chair, binding my arms along my sides.

The first man moves to stand behind me. Which I don't like. I hate that I can't see what he's doing. The second man, the one who set the chair upright, moves to stand in front of me.

His arms cross over a broad chest as my eyes widen. I know this man. He was at the docks. He murdered my team.

A burst of hate-fueled adrenaline spikes in my blood, and I thrash against the bonds holding me down.

He looks at me with a dark scowl, scruffy beard, and waits for me to tire myself out. Once I still—there's no way I'm getting free—he cups his jaw and cants his head sideways.

"You tell me what I want, and your friend keeps her fingers. Lie to me, and she dies."

His threat to harm Callie stirs my anger, and I thrash in the seat. He watches with great patience, waiting me out. Once my struggles cease, he reaches out and curls a strand of my hair around his finger.

"What an interesting color. If you were a few years younger, you'd fetch a good price."

Good price?

What the hell is he—then it hits. I don't know this man, but I know what kind of business he runs. I'm staring at a human slave-trafficker, and I have a fair idea how the rest of this will play out.

How do I protect Knox?

That's what this man wants. I'm sure of it.

Not that I know anything other than Knox somehow works to free those who've been taken.

The gag is probably a good thing. I've already gone through my litany of curse words, calling my captor all kinds of vile things.

"You going to scream if I remove that gag?" He presses his hands to his thighs and bends down, getting eye level with me.

His fetid breath washes over me, making my eyes tear as I heave against the foul stench of not just his breath but a body that's not been washed in far too many weeks.

There are two choices available. I can fight or give him what he wants. No doubt he wants to know about Knox, but when he finds out I know next to nothing, what will he do then?

We stare at each other.

It would be an epic stare-down, except I blink first. Very slowly, I nod, letting him know I won't scream. Doesn't mean I'm not going to pump him for answers to a few questions of my own.

He slaps my cheek, almost playfully, except there's nothing soft and gentle about it. My cheek stings and my head hurts from the sharp slap.

"That's a good girl." He tugs on the towel, pulling it slowly out of my mouth.

My stomach turns at that phrase. I'm not his good girl anything.

"What do you want?"

"A conversation, *puta*."

I don't speak Spanish, but I know what that word means. It's derogatory and vile, meant to put me in my place, dehumanizing me as scum.

"You killed my teammates."

"I took out the trash." He stands to his full height, crosses his arms, and stares down at me. "You were chasing that man."

"Who are you?" I'll ask as many questions as I can, knowing any detail will be vital later when I get out of this.

If I get out of this.

"You don't get to ask the questions." His scowl deepens and I pause.

I'm nothing to this man, meaning there's no value he places on my life other than the information in my head. That means Callie is in serious danger. He'll keep me alive as long as I prove myself valuable. Callie's worth is only in what I'll do to save her.

"Let my friend go."

"And let her run to the cops?" He shakes his head. "What do you take me for? An imbecile?"

"Let her go, and I'll tell you everything I know." It's not much, something he'll soon figure out. Which means I'm worth nothing, but I have to at least try to get Callie free.

"You'll tell me what I want to know, and maybe I'll let her go." His tone hardens and his gaze turns deadly.

It's important to remember this man is a cold-hearted killer, but I need to know who he works for.

"I don't know anything." I'll try that first and see where we go from there.

"Do you work for them?"

"Them?"

"The Guardians."

My eyes widen before I have a chance to school my emotions, giving away my knowledge of that name. I blurt out the first thing that comes to mind, knowing I need to keep what little I know about Knox from this man.

"I don't know anything about guardians."

"And …?" His left brow arches.

Behind me, Callie screams.

I lost track of the man standing behind me, but from Callie's frantic breathing, I know exactly where he is.

"Don't hurt her!" It's not my place to tell these men what to do, but I have to protect my friend.

"Then tell me what I want." My questioner stoops down, shouting and spitting in my face.

My shoulders hunch and I turn my face away. Only, he grips my face, pinching my cheeks, and forces me to look at him.

"Do you work for the Guardians?"

"No!" I glare at him, defiantly. "I don't know what that means."

"You were chasing that man, yes?"

"Yes!" No need to lie about that. He was there. He saw my entire team chasing after Knox.

"Why?"

"We thought he was a courier."

"And you arrested him, yes? Do not lie to me, *puta*. I was there. I saw you take him."

"The police took him." I try distancing myself, playing down any involvement I may have had.

"He was here. Last night." The man looms over me. "Why?"

That itching sensation from the other night? Was that this man? Was he the one following me? I thought maybe Knox had followed me after I left the precinct. But was I wrong?

How do I answer that question? If I tell him Knox and I are seeing each other, I become leverage. I won't let this man use me to get to Knox.

"He wanted payback." That carries enough truth not to be a lie. Our story is far more complicated than that, but that tiny piece is true.

"Payback?" The man laughs. "By sticking his tongue down your throat?" He glares at me. "Tell the truth, *puta*, or your friend pays."

Another strangled scream sounds from behind me.

"Stop!" I twist as much as I can, but the man grips my face again, pinching so hard I cut the inside of my cheek with my teeth.

"Tell me who that man is."

"I don't know!" I scream, terrified for Callie, and growing more concerned by the minute.

Light flickers by the door. My attention shifts to it, desperate and hopeful. Maybe it's Knox?

But I'm not as careful as I think. The man notices the direction of my gaze and spins around. He stalks toward the door, gives the doorknob a jiggle, locking it, then he props a chair beneath the doorknob. It's exactly what I would do if I didn't want someone getting in.

It's what I did last night when I thought someone was following me. Callie and I are screwed. I don't know what to do to save us, except to tell the truth.

"We flirted, that's all."

"You slept with him." His mouth splits into a crooked grin and he gives a knowing look. Spitting on the floor, he curses me, calling me a string of foul things in a language I don't understand.

The man puts a phone to his ear and gives me his back. I look around, desperate to find something I can use. Although, what that might be is anyone's guess. I'm tied to a chair with no way to get free.

Suddenly, a shot rings out. I jerk, looking over my shoulder and see Jinx standing in the doorway to the stairs leading up to Callie's and my rooms. The man torturing Callie falls to the ground, holding his arm where Jinx shot him.

Jinx is a fabulous shot, better than me, and there's one other thing she's an expert at too. Jinx sprints past Callie, slicing at the bonds on Callie's wrist. Something metal flashes in the air, landing on Callie's lap.

Callie grabs the knife, cuts her other hand free, then bends at the waist to free her feet. The man interrogating me spins. His mouth drops as Jinx flies through the air.

She slices one of the zip ties on my wrist, freeing my hand, and drops a second knife in my lap. Like Callie, I race to free myself while Jinx spins and whirls.

An expert in Brazilian Capoeira, Jinx flows through the room. A martial art composed of acrobatics, inverted kicks, and other complex maneuvers; her feet connect with the man's head as she flips through the air.

Behind me, Callie gets free, but the man with the shoulder wound grabs her feet. Knowing Jinx has the first man under control, I go to Callie. Slicing at the man's arm, I get him to release her ankle. Callie scrambles to her feet and I shout.

"Go! Run!"

Callie knows Jinx and I can take care of ourselves. She's also well aware we need backup. No need to tell her to call the police, but first, she needs to get out of here.

She races up the stairs and I turn my attention to the man who hurt her. He's on his feet, looking pissed off and mean as shit.

He's got height, weight, and reach on me. If he gets his hands on me, I'm dead.

Jinx continues to flow around her opponent, kicking him in the gut, the groin, and clocking his chin, making him stagger. He goes down with a roar but grabs Jinx's shirt as he falls.

She spins again, but he's got his hands on her. The man lands on the ground, taking Jinx down with him. She cries out, and in that moment of distraction, the man I fight grabs the wrist of my knife hand. He squeezes until my fingers release the knife. Unarmed, he pulls me to his chest and wraps his hand around my throat.

"Stop! Or she dies." His words stop Jinx in her tracks.

The one she fights lashes out, punching her in the face. Jinx protects her face. She curls into a ball to guard her midsection as his leg draws back.

I get dragged toward the front door, choking and gasping for air.

"We take the girl." He shoves me, pushing me toward the door.

The man who questioned me squats down, staring at Jinx. His arm rears back and slams forward. Her head whips back, knocked out cold. In a flash, he secures her wrists, her ankles, then rolls her to her stomach, where he puts her in a hogtie.

"Get the damn door." The one holding me issues orders.

Black specks fill my vision, moving in from the edges. My body weakens and I sag against the man choking me.

Blackness takes me under as I collapse in his arms.

TWENTY-TWO

Knox

We've got another day, two at most, before wrapping up things in New Orleans. The team doesn't have much to do from this point on except provide the muscle for Mitzy and her team. Which means we lift stuff and move their gear around.

My summons from Mitzy is for a debrief and next steps. It's a high-level meeting, meaning everyone is here.

Forest Summers glowers in the corner, frustration edging his features. He towers over the diminutive Doc Summers, his sister, who stands beside him. They're the founders of Guardian HRS, but not its leader. That distinction belongs to Sam, who leans against the back door leading out of the kitchen.

CJ, head of the Guardians, and Mitzy, head of the technical team, are here as well. All our top players are present and accounted for, which says a lot about how serious they're taking this new development.

Other than the top brass, the worker bees round out the crowd; Mitzy's whiz kid brigade and Alpha team.

It's a lot of people to cram into a small house, but we make it work.

"There's no pattern to the abductions." Mitzy sits on the kitchen counter while the rest of us crowd the dining room and spill into the living room. She uses two computer screens to emphasize her point. "The girls are all between fourteen and eighteen. They were picked up randomly. Or rather, I should say there was nothing common about their kidnappings. One was taken after school, walking home. Another was kidnapped in the parking lot at work. One was pulled to the side of the road by a man pretending to be a cop." She goes on to detail how each of the dozen girls were abducted.

"This isn't like what we've seen in Cancun," Sam interjects. "These aren't Spring Breakers who let their guard down and were snatched off the streets."

"Correct," Mitzy continues. "None of these abductions were opportunities of convenience. Each girl was specifically targeted. Her daily patterns watched. Each abduction came after deliberate planning."

"Not to mention," CJ adds, "all the kidnappings happened on the same day." He lets that sink in before continuing. "This was one team, working over a week to collect girls. It's a highly organized operation."

"How are the girls?" I can't help but ask. Most of the debriefs for the team were done while the DEA held me for questioning.

"Scared. Traumatized." Doc Summers answers. "No major injuries. The men who took the girls were exceptionally careful not to harm them."

"They're valuable assets." Sam folds his arms across his chest. His words hit hard. "Their future owners paid a premium to ensure the girls weren't harmed during the abductions."

No shit, they're valuable assets.

"Do we have anything actionable? Any leads to follow?" It feels like we should be doing more. "How do they have the manpower to execute a dozen kidnappings on the same day?"

Our operation works exceedingly well, but there is always a flow of information which occurs before we spin up to act. The Guardians are nothing without actionable intel from Mitzy and her team.

"We're working on that." Mitzy presses her lips together. I know the fiery pixie well enough to know what that means. She has very little to go on and it's pissing her off. "Our current theory is that the kidnappings are hired out."

"So, they do, what?" Wolfe taps the granite countertop, drumming his fingers against the hard surface. "They get an order for a girl, then advertise it on the local 'kidnappers for hire' bulletin board?" His question, although flippant, is exactly what I'm thinking.

"What about the connection through Deverough shipping?" I hate to bring up Carson Deverough. He's a sore subject around here, but there's a connection we can't ignore. "The *Lei'lani?*"

Deverough hired the Guardians to rescue his daughter, Eve, who now lives with Max. Eve was taken off the streets of Cancun, a target of opportunity, or so we thought, the same time Zoe was kidnapped. We rescued Zoe, but lost Eve and several other girls during that operation.

Months later, we learned about Eve when Deverough hired us. He claimed to have been paying escalating ransom demands after taking out a multi-million-dollar kidnapping policy on his daughter, but when the kidnapper, Tomas Benefield, refused to return Deverough's daughter, he turned to us.

Max scowls beside me.

Benefield held Eve for ransom over several months. Max and I infiltrated that operation. He posed as a buyer and I was his bodyguard. Eventually, we freed Eve from the clutches of Tomas Benefield, along with a score of other girls. During our escape, in addition to the injuries that sidelined Max, which keep him from operating today, we found ledgers detailing all Benefield's transactions as well as information about the clients.

There's one problem.

We haven't broken the cipher on the ledger. I say *We,* but I really mean Mitzy and her team. We also found evidence of Deverough's involvement with Benefield.

Although the shipping mogul tells a different story.

Carson Deverough insists he was blackmailed by Benefield. That's why Eve was taken.

"We're looking into that." Forest's deep voice rumbles through the room. "The *Lei'lani* is not a Deverough shipping asset, but there's a link through subsidiaries." From his tone, Forest's as frustrated as the rest of us.

"As for the girls," Doc Summers addresses the room, "we're tending their immediate medical conditions. Most were severely dehydrated, and we're offering psychological help as well. Forest and Sam are locating family members."

"We're releasing them back to their families?" Max gives a start. "What's to prevent them from getting kidnapped again?"

"Since most of the girls were taken a matter of days ago," Doc Summers explains, "it's best to reunite them rather than let them recover at The Facility."

In addition to rescuing those who've been taken, Forest Summers established The Facility. It's a recovery program, providing lodging, education, and on-sight medical and mental health professionals.

The entire goal is to take victims and turn them into survivors. Part of the inclusive program isn't just access to mental health providers but classes in self-defense. Each Guardian team takes one week a month to train the residents how to evade capture.

"And nothing on how, or why, each of these girls were targeted?" Wolfe looks to Mitzy.

"We're looking into that." She glances at her team, who all nod their heads.

The work they do is different from what the guys and I do, but no less valuable. In fact, I consider them invaluable when it comes to our missions. There's a lot of teasing that goes on between tech and muscle, but we all respect one another's contributions to the mission.

I think back to Max's comment, which hasn't been addressed.

Guardian HRS are hostage rescue specialists. What we do is literally in our name, but the girls who were taken are going to need some degree of protection after they're reunited with their families.

At least until we figure out how the orders are being made,

who's fulfilling them, and where the girls are being taken for training, and eventual delivery to the clients.

Until all that is figured out, they're going to need bodyguards. That's something Forest could farm out, hiring a protection agency to keep watch over the girls, but knowing how the big boss likes to keep things in-house, I'm thinking Guardian HRS will soon be offering protection services.

What will we call them?

Protectors?

I suppose it makes sense.

I wonder who they'll get to head it up?

The briefing continues for several more minutes, ending with Sam telling us to pack up our gear and get ready to return to Guardian HQ back in California.

Because of the size of our group, it'll take two days to ferry everyone and our equipment back on the company jets. I'm relieved to hear Alpha team will be the last to go, but it means I have a day and a half, at most, to spend with Lily before I leave.

With the briefing concluded, Alpha team retreats to the living room. The six of us sit in front of the TV playing classic video games souped up with a Mitzy twist. We're in the middle of epic Tank playoffs.

Forest, Sam, CJ, and Mitzy stay in the kitchen, heads pressed together, strategizing. It's not hard to figure out what they're talking about. The rest of the tech team disburses to the dining table to pour over whatever intel they're working on.

"How much longer do I have to hang here?" I shift my body, trying to find a more comfortable position on the hardwood floor.

"Got somewhere to be?" Griff grabs a peanut out of the nut bowl he's been hogging and tosses it at my head.

"Not spending the night with you guys, that's for sure." I snatch the peanut out of the air and pop it in my mouth.

"Hey, move your fat head." Axel leans to the left, trying to see the screen in front of me.

We're playing old school Tank, quick-fire elimination rounds. I lost my first game to Max and have been chillin' while the guys match up against each other. Axel beat Griff. Wolfe beat Liam. Axel and Max are up against each other. The winner will play Wolfe. There's a stack of buttons on the table for the winner.

"So, what are you going to do about Lily?" Max punches a hole through one of Axel's defensive walls protecting his tank.

"I don't know." I lean back on the coffee table and watch Axel evade Max's attack. "Tonight may be my last night in New Orleans."

"And—what are you going to do?" Max isn't letting up. He's making me face the inevitable. "You're going to face one massive hurdle seeing each other."

"You don't think I can make a long-distance relationship work?"

"Just saying, it's going to be a struggle." Max certainly doesn't sugarcoat anything. "At least you admit this is more than a fling."

"I gave my button to Griff." Damn straight, this is more than casual.

Lily's all I've been thinking about, which is why Max beat me so quickly during our game.

"Long distance definitely throws a wrench in things. But, what do I do?"

"You make a grand gesture." Griff leans back on the couch and watches the Tank battle with the rest of us.

"Like what? I'm a Guardian. It's in my blood. It's not something I can give up. Lily's a DEA agent. We only just met. I can't ask her to pick up her whole life to follow me across the country because the sex is good. This is her home. Besides, who knows what's going to happen down the road? Maybe we don't make it."

"You wouldn't have given me this if she wasn't the one." Griff leans forward and pulls the button I gave him out of his back pocket. He flicks it toward me, and I catch it in mid-air. "You make it work. Whatever it takes."

"Maybe I can get her a transfer? There are DEA jobs all over the country. It'll be easier for her to move than me."

"Easier? Or more convenient? Didn't you say something about NOLA being her home?" Wolfe taps the armrest of the couch, eager to play the final round. He's one competitive bastard. "Who names a kid Jinx?"

His comment seems to come out of left field, but I saw the way his ears perked up when I talked about Lily's friend. I wasn't paying too much attention to him at the bar. Lily had me otherwise preoccupied most of the night. Maybe I missed something between him and Jinx.

"I don't know. Lily didn't tell me."

"Maybe you could ask her yourself." Liam tosses a throw pillow at his buddy. "Maybe up close and personal?"

"Asshole. It's an innocent question." Wolfe tries to downplay his interest, but nobody's fooled. He never talks about chicks. He never remembers their names. Jinx somehow got under his skin.

I told the guys most of what Lily and I talked about. That includes Jinx. A look toward Forest and Sam reminds me both of them have connections that could help.

Sam's ties to the FBI remain as strong as ever. He no longer works for the Bureau, but he personally oversees the cases the FBI subcontracts out to Guardian HRS's Delta team.

Forest seems to have his fingers in everything. If he doesn't have a direct contact high up within the DEA, there's no doubt he knows someone who owes him a favor.

But how do I ask Lily, who I've known a matter of days, to pack up her entire life for me? Especially when I'm not willing to do so for her.

One of our instructors at BUDS used to tell us there were only ever two reasons not to do something. You were either unable to do it, or you were unwilling. If unwilling, you needed to figure out why. If unable, you needed to enhance your skillset.

I know what I feel for Lily. I could stay behind; give up my job as a Guardian. I'm more than willing to do whatever it takes, but being a Guardian isn't just a job. It's a calling, and I consider it my life's work.

If that makes me unwilling, then it is what it is. I could stay, get a job as a bouncer at a bar or security guard somewhere dull and boring, but I know what I'd be missing out on. There's no way I'd be happy.

It seems easier for Lily to transfer, but what if she feels the same way I do? What if she's unwilling to relocate?

"Stop thinking so hard." Max crushes Axel, blowing up his tank after taking out all of Axel's defenses.

"Fucker." Axel leans back with a sigh and hands his controller over to Wolfe. "Beat his ass. Don't let Alpha One win, or his head will get so big it'll explode."

Max and Wolfe set up for the final match. We were going to do elimination rounds for the losers, but I'm eager to grab Lily and take her somewhere amazing for dinner. I don't want to waste any of the limited time I have left with her.

The idea of leaving doesn't sit well with me. I make a decision.

"I'm gonna take a shower and change."

"You heading to Callie's bar?" Wolfe looks away from the screen. A tactical mistake because Max jumps on the opportunity to blow up Wolfe's undefended tank. "Fucker!" Wolfe has two more lives before Max wins the game.

"I was thinking dinner."

"A solo event?" Wolfe asks.

"Solo and romantic. Why?"

"Thought I might join you." He shifts on the couch.

"On my date?" I huff out a laugh. "As much as I love you like a brother ..."

"Ha ha, nothing like that. I was wondering if Jinx might be there. I could cozy up to that sexy Latina all night long."

"You looking for a little action with Lily's friend?"

"Just don't want to spend the night here with the tech brigade." He juts his thumb over his shoulder toward Mitzy's tech team. "You coming?" He looks to Liam, his best friend and wingman.

Since settling down with their women, Max, Axel, and Griff are out of the bar scene. Or rather, they're not interested in one-night hookups when they've got women waiting for them at home.

A few days ago, I would've said I didn't understand, but with Lily.

Gah, everything's different now.

I'm not even interested in anyone else. Why bother when I've got the perfect girl already?

"I could be talked into it." Liam stretches his long legs in front of him. "I think we should all head out. Stir up some trouble as a team. Embarrass the hell out of our love-struck teammate." He folds his arm and makes kissing noises in the crook of his elbow like a damn eleven-year-old.

"Ha ha. Very funny." I get up off the floor and stretch my lower back. "I'm not letting you anywhere near Lily."

"I think that's a great idea." Max pummels Wolfe in the game, but Wolfe's not beaten yet. "I've been cooped up in this house too long. It would be nice to stretch my legs, see a bit of the city."

"Slug back some beers." Axel gives a shake of his head. He taps Griff's shoulder. "What do you say? Up for a night out?"

"Better than the techies stealing our pizza again." He gives side-eyes to the tech team.

I get what he's saying. They're infamous for taking our food.

"Once I'm done kicking Wolfe's ass, let's head out." Max is overly confident.

Knowing Wolfe, he's steering Max into a trap. Not that I can see what the hell he has planned.

"So, everybody's going?" I look to Axel, Griff, and Max. "Don't y'all need to get kitchen passes from your women?"

"Asshole." Axel ignores my dig. "Zoe knows I'd never do anything I shouldn't."

Griff snorts.

Max is too focused on beating Wolfe.

Liam snickers. Between me and Wolfe, he's a major player when it comes to women. I may be king of the one-night stand, but Liam's the true champion, keeping several women at a time. Don't know how he does it.

As for Max, Axel, and Griff, I'm jealous. Things were easier with them. They didn't have to worry about uprooting their women. For example, Max didn't ask Eve if she wanted to live with him.

After we rescued the two of them from Colombia, and with the concerns over whether Eve's father is, or is not, knowingly involved in human trafficking, Max told her she was staying with him. He didn't ask. He just told her how it was going to be.

Eve, Zoe, and Moira are all in college. None of them had to pack up their lives for anything. Moira and Zoe were already living at The Facility, and Eve transferred her courses to make everything work out.

Lily has a job, and from the looks of it, she's destined for great things. I can't do what Max, Axel, or Griff did. I can't force her to move.

But I can beg.

As expected, Wolfe destroys Max in the game, setting up an elaborate ruse to distract Max from the trap he set up.

"Booyah!" Wolfe slams the controller down on the coffee table and leaps to his feet for a victory dance.

I leave him to it, heading upstairs to take a shower and change. As for dinner tonight, I need something to wow Lily. The guys mentioned a grand gesture, but I don't know how grand I should go.

In a display of military efficiency, all six of us are showered, shaved, and dressed in less than twenty minutes. CJ and Sam join us, eager to get some air.

We all gather downstairs and call up two Ubers to take us to the French Quarter.

My grand gesture is not shaping up the way I'd like. All the really expensive restaurants are booked solid, but maybe a dinner out isn't what Lily and I need. I'm thinking a night in sounds like a whole lot more fun.

Only when we make it to the French Quarter, blue flashing lights and a crowd gathers around the entrance to Callie's bar. My stomach drops as I sprint toward the bar. The guys follow right behind me.

Something's terribly wrong.

I feel it in my gut. I feel it in my heart. I pray nothing's happened to Lily or her friends.

The cops keep us back, but after CJ has a word with their

supervisor, we're granted access past the police barrier. Sometimes, it's nice to have friends in high places.

Inside, the place is torn to shit. Jinx and Callie, Lily's friends, are there. One of Jinx's eyes is nearly swollen shut. Bruises cover her face. Her lip's cut and bleeding. Jinx holds a bar towel to her face, while Callie stands protectively around her. Police and paramedics surround both women, taking statements and providing basic medical care.

Jinx's head lifts the moment I enter. She stands and pushes her way past the cops and paramedics swarming over her.

"They took Lily."

Those three words leave me with a hollow, desperate ache. Like a punch to the solar plexus, I find myself unable to catch my breath.

Wolfe approaches Jinx, places his hands on her upper arms, and dips down to look at her face.

"What the hell happened to you?" His gruff tone turns the whole room quiet, but there's tenderness there too. Wolfe reaches up to brush the hair out of Jinx's good eye. Then his knuckles graze her cheek, discreetly wiping away her tears.

TWENTY-THREE

Knox

With my team around me, we go into rescue mode. Sam gets on the phone, letting Forest and Mitzy know what happened. Wolfe sits with Jinx, pushing away the cops and paramedics. He gets her to tell him what happened.

I stomp around, corralling my fear into something I can use. Freaking out does nothing. What we need is actionable intelligence, and that begins with …

"Callie!" My roar pierces the room.

Lily's friend looks up and gapes while I stalk over to her, Jinx, and Wolfe.

"Didn't mean to shout, but closed-circuit TV? Do you have it installed in the bar?"

Callie's eyes widen as she realizes something everyone's forgotten in the chaos.

"Yes, over here." She tugs me to the bar, and we're followed by Sam, CJ, and the rest of the guys, leaving Wolfe to deal with Jinx.

Callie pulls me behind the bar and turns on the monitor, which acts like a cash register, among other things.

"We should have something." She points over her head. "I have four cameras installed."

After a few taps on the screen, four displays show different angles of the bar. We see the men enter before opening. Callie's there, telling them she won't open for an hour.

They push past what she says, stomping around the place like they own it. When Callie protests, one of the men grabs her and ties her to a chair. They yell at her, slap her face, and generally terrorize her.

"Mitzy, are you getting this?" Sam holds the phone near the screen.

"This picture sucks," Mitzy says. "Put Callie on the phone."

Sam hands the phone to Callie, who puts it to her ear. I complain when she takes down the four camera feeds but bite my tongue when I realize what's happening. Mitzy tells Callie how to share her screen, giving Mitzy control of all the data.

The four images come back on and we watch the men pace. They get angry at Callie, who can't give the answers they want, tossing the tables and chairs in a rage.

Suddenly, the images fast forward. Mitzy's in control, moving to what we need.

Lily enters the bar, a dreamy look on her face, but then her expression changes. It contorts as she takes in the disarray. She sees Callie and misses the men.

One of them grabs her from behind and shoves her through the room. I bite my knuckles as everything plays out. One of the men rights a chair, slams Lily down on it, while the other one binds her hands and feet.

They interrogate Lily and damn but she holds her own, demanding answers to questions of her own. My heart lodges in my throat because I know what happens next.

Jinx opens the door to the bar, hears Lily and the men, and closes the door. She appears a few minutes later, coming down from Lily's apartment.

The guys and I look over at her, mouths gaping after we watch her glide through the bar. She somehow manages to cut both Callie and Lily free. Or at least one hand each so they can free themselves.

One of the men grabs Callie. Lily goes to Callie's defense while

Jinx goes to town on the second man. She's a force of destruction, fluid movement and lethal grace. Jinx reminds me of Jenny, lead of Delta team, and moves nearly the same way.

But it's not enough.

Only Callie gets free.

Jinx is knocked out cold while the two men grab Lily and take her out the front door.

My pulse pounds as the feeds inside the bar cut off and there's a ringing in my ear. Then, I hear Mitzy on the line.

"Tying in closed-circuit feeds as we speak. CJ, I'm sending a team your way with the guys' gear. Trying to track those men …" Her voice fades away as I hear shouting behind me.

"No fucking way." Jinx is on her feet, going toe to toe with Wolfe. "No way are you leaving me behind."

"Look, you don't understand …" Wolfe lifts his hands, palms up and out, trying to soothe the angry woman. "We know what we're doing."

"And I don't?" She points toward the rest of us gathered around the bar. "If you're going after her, I'm coming with you."

"Not happening, princess," Wolfe says with a growl.

Sam puts his phone to his ear and gives us the signal to move. Wolfe catches the sudden shift and puts his hand on Jinx's shoulder.

I'm not sure what happens next, except Wolfe winds up flat on his back on the floor with Jinx stepping on his throat. She points at Sam.

"Don't know who you are. Don't really care. But if you're going after my friend, I'm coming with you." She looks down at Wolfe. "Does anyone have a problem with that?"

A grin fills Sam's face. "Name's Sam Stone. Welcome to the team."

"Jenny, but my friends call me Jinx."

"Nice to meet you Jinx." Sam glances over his shoulder. "Let's roll."

Damn straight, let's roll.

"Mitzy's switching to my phone," Sam says. "She's searching for those men via CCT and will let me know when she finds something.

Meanwhile, her techies are inbound with your gear. Anyone have anything to say?" He glances at me.

I have nothing to say. I'm just glad my team's with me and we're headed out.

CJ looks at Max, who glances down at his injured leg. "I'm good to go," Max says with a nod.

"The op is yours, Alpha One."

Happy to have the team back at full fighting strength, I jog beside Max as we race to meet Mitzy's team. We get there before they do. Max limps a little on his bad leg. I give him a look, and he returns a nod.

"Just hurts, but I'm good," he says.

"That's all I need to know." I ran the op at the docks the other day because we were the only team who could, but operating without Max felt all kinds of wrong.

Wolfe and Jinx engage in a massive stare-off. Wolfe's not happy a woman is joining us. Although, I'm not sure if it's because Jinx is a woman or if there's more to it than that.

What did I miss that night in the bar?

Two minutes later, a van pulls up beside us. The side door opens, and we all pile in. It's a tight fit, especially with all of us plus Jinx. One of the tech guys drives. He pulls away from the curb as soon as we shut the door.

"Mitzy's got the men," he says.

I hate that I don't know the guy's name.

Sam transfers his phone to the van's computer system. A visual pops up on the screen. It's a map of the city, with us a blue dot and another red dot on the screen.

Mitzy's voice crackles through the speakers. "They're headed to port."

"The *Lei'lani?*" I can't help but ask.

"No. She departed this morning. This isn't a commercial port they're headed to, but a yacht club near the docks. They've got twenty minutes on you."

I don't bother asking how Mitzy knows where these men are. Most likely, she's hacked into all the closed-circuit cameras in New

Orleans. She's following those men, one street at a time, and extrapolating from there.

"You're my eyes, Mitz." Sam climbs into the passenger seat and buckles himself in. "Destination?"

"Working it. I've got them pulling into the yacht club …" Her voice trails off for a minute, then returns. "Sam, I'm calling in the Coast Guard to assist."

"Explain?" Sam doesn't sound happy.

"Interdiction is their specialty. Every boat in that marina is fast."

"Fast?"

"As in, we don't have a way to catch them once they're on a boat."

"What about air assets?"

"Forest is working on that now, but that's going to take time."

"Tell me what we have?"

"We'll get them." Her confidence doesn't inspire mine.

Granted, it takes seven to eight hours to get from the port of New Orleans to the Gulf of Mexico. Our best bet is to get to them before they get on whatever boat they're planning on taking.

An interdiction on land is a hundred times easier than on water, but we're proficient in hostage rescue no matter the medium.

"Boss." Mitzy's voice pierces the tense silence.

"Go ahead."

"The *USS Charles Sexton* is in the Gulf, right at the mouth of the Mississippi, Commander Erika Fisher has been given the go-ahead to render aid, but …"

I don't like hearing hesitation in Mitzy's voice. Like the other guys, I pause in strapping on my tactical armor.

Once again, I marvel at the efficiency of Mitzy's team. Dealing with our gear isn't a part of what they do. Instead of tossing it all into the back of the van, they were ridiculously meticulous in the thought they put into things.

All six of us have a pile of stuff to put on. Our fatigues, body armor, and weapons are stacked in that order. All I have to do is slip on my fatigues, strap on my armor, and check my weapon.

Everything checks out, which means I've got an ear to follow Sam and Mitzy's conversation.

Jinx scowls at Wolfe as she moves to crouch in the space between the driver and passenger seats.

"Go on, Mitz," Sam says.

"We can commandeer a ship to follow or wait for a helicopter to take you to the *USS Charles Sexton*."

"CJ …" Sam waves CJ to the front of the van. The three of them put their heads together to figure out tactics on the move.

My heart thunders in my chest. Watching the way those men attacked, then questioned, Lily was like pulling out my guts. I'm going to kill the men who dared put their hands on my girl.

No ifs, ands, or butts about it. Their ass is grass.

"Knox …" Max tightens down his bulletproof vest. "Where's your head at?"

It's a check-in.

Max knows exactly what's going on inside my head. He's been in the very same shoes as me when he rescued Eve. Not only did he get Eve safely through a jungle, but kept his cool when Eve had a gun to her head.

"I'm good," I reassure him I've got my shit locked down tight. "Tell me what to do, I'm there." I'm also well aware of the dangers of going rogue.

Max had to stand by, helpless, knowing the team would take the shot that saved Eve. Griff had to do the same, forced to support rather than operate in the mission that pulled Moira off a cargo container ship. Although, due to some questionable communications, malfunctions reported by the pilot of the support helicopter, Griff wound up rescuing his girl anyway.

I've got the best guys in the world to back me up, and I'm not going to let them down by allowing emotions to get in the way.

In this, we're of one mind.

CJ turns around to address us. "Mitzy has them boarding a yacht. It's a fast ship, and they're heading down the Mississippi River to the Gulf. Commander Erika Fisher, captain of the *USS Charles Sexton* is in the Gulf, just outside the mouth of the

Mississippi. She's preparing to interdict. Our chances of overtaking them are marginal at best. Mitzy recommends waiting for a helicopter and boarding the *USS Charles Sexton*. Give me your thoughts."

"Why not just land on the damn yacht?" I can't help it; the comment just bursts out of me.

"You think you can rappel down onto that boat without getting your ass shot to hell?"

The comment doesn't warrant an answer. Max steps in, speaking for the team.

"We assume they took her because she has value to them. The chances of them killing her are minimal," Max says.

"Damn straight they did," Jinx pops off at the mouth. "All they were interested in is who you worked for." Her angry glare turns on Wolfe, accusatory and full of spite. "Who are you guys anyway?"

This woman is fierce. Without too much thought, she attached herself to our team, demanding we take her, and she knows nothing about us.

Max ignores Jinx's outburst, although the corner of his mouth ticks up in a grin. He looks at me. "I say we meet up with the Coast Guard." Max looks at the rest of the team, leaving me out of this decision.

We don't operate by committee, but a good leader always solicits the input of his team.

"Makes sense to me," Axel says. "How long before the helicopter arrives?"

Max turns back to CJ, waiting for an answer.

"We've got an asset not too far away. Ariel Black has helped us before and is already en route. She'll be here within the hour."

"The Angel of the Skies?" Griff gives a nod of approval. "She's fucking badass." Ariel Black is the helicopter pilot who gave an assist to the Guardians during Moira's rescue.

All I'm thinking about is that it's going to take an hour for Ariel to get to us.

That's another hour leaving Lily in these monsters' hands. It kills me, but I don't see any way around it.

"Then it's set," Max says. "We wait for the air asset. Meet up with the *USS Charles Sexton* and go from there."

"You're just going to meet up with the Coast Guard?" Jinx rolls her eyes. "Does everyone jump when you guys call?"

"Pretty much, princess." Wolfe responds. He shoves Max out of the front seat to be close to Jinx.

Max holds back a laugh when he catches me watching the whole thing. Yeah, there's a little bit of tension between those two. The fact Jinx threw Wolfe flat on his back isn't something Wolfe's going to tolerate.

I take note of Sam and CJ, who watch the entire exchange. They always have an eye out for talent. As far as rescuing Lily, interdiction from ship to ship is complicated as shit. We're basically dependent on the Coast Guard crew to stop the boat and hope those men don't use Lily to bargain their way free.

Not that we don't have a few tricks up our sleeves. The best part of the whole plan is something we don't control yet works entirely in our favor.

We're headed into nighttime and there's no moon. While the men on that yacht deal with Commander Fisher and her crew, Alpha team will slip in, under the cover of darkness, and board that vessel.

If we do it right, they'll never see us coming.

Lily, I need you to hang on. I'm coming for you.

I send my thoughts out into the ether and pray she hears me.

TWENTY-FOUR

Knox

I SHOULD NO LONGER BE AMAZED BY THE SPEED WITH WHICH Guardian HRS moves. Mitzy tracks the yacht using *Smaug*, her largest drone. It cruises far overhead, keeping that yacht in sight.

At the speed they're moving, they'll be out of the Mississippi in less than five hours. We're running short on time.

As for our team, we divert to the nearest building with a helipad where we'll meet up with our air asset.

Alpha team, along with Lily's friend, Jinx, pile out of the van, kitted out in tactical dress and carrying our weapons.

"Wait, she can't come with us." Wolfe makes a fuss about Jinx.

"Maybe you don't understand English, Wolfman, but I'm sticking to you, and your team, like glue until we get Lily back. No way are you sidelining me." Jinx rolls her shoulders back and puffs out her chest. Wolfe towers over the woman, but damn if she doesn't remind me of Lily. Those two women have spunk.

"CJ ..." Wolfe implores.

CJ and Sam exchange a look. "Jinx will go with Alpha," CJ says. "Jinx, consider this a courtesy. Do not get in their way."

"I can take care of myself," she says.

"No doubt you can, but they train and operate as a team. You don't want to mess that up. Watch, observe, stay out of their way. If you don't agree to that, then you stay with me and Sam."

Jinx gives us all a long, hard stare, then crosses her arms. "Fine, I won't get in the way, but I'm watching you." She takes two fingers, points them at her eyes, then turns them to us. "Don't fuck this up."

Sam huffs a laugh and CJ turns away with a smile on his face. I'm not sure what the two of them are up two. It's highly irregular to saddle us with a civilian. Not that I pay too much attention to it. Jinx isn't my problem.

"Alpha Six," Max calls out.

"Yeah, boss?" Wolfe replies.

"Jinx is yours."

"Hold up a second," Jinx sputters at Max's command. "I'm not anybody's anything."

Max spins and levels the entirety of his focus on Jinx. "You're his to watch during this operation. He tells you to sit. You sit. He tells you to move. You move. Your presence here is a professional courtesy, but if you get in my team's way, interfere with the execution of this mission, I will personally sideline you. Since I'm in command, Wolfe will be your babysitter. Got any problems with that?"

"No, sir!" Jinx snaps back. Her gaze turns to Wolfe. "Watch yourself."

Not sure what that's supposed to mean, I complete another check of my gear.

CJ and Sam stay behind with the van, while Alpha team, plus Jinx, enter the building. CJ and Sam will return to the rental house where they'll coordinate operations with the help of Mitzy's team.

Two security guards meet us at the front door, letting us in and escorting us to the elevators. They give Alpha team the eye when we enter but keep their questions to themselves. No doubt, they've been briefed. Both of them glance at Jinx and share a look.

We're escorted up to the roof, where we wait for the helicopter to pick us up. Twenty minutes feels like two lifetimes; all I can think about is Lily stuck on that ship.

What are they doing to her? Are they hurting her?

So lost in thought, I don't hear the approach of the helicopter, but I certainly feel the downdraft of the rotors as it lands.

Once we get the all-clear, Alpha team loads up inside the helicopter. We strap in. Wolfe assists Jinx, who gives him the evil eye, batting aside his hands to secure her own harness.

He sits back with a huff and a roll of his eyes, then hands her a headset. I pull on my headset—it quiets the deafening noise of the rotors—and practice my breathing to calm myself down.

"Nice to fly with you again, Ariel." Griff taps the pilot's shoulder, getting her attention. He snags the headset off the co-pilot's seat, slips it on, and slides into the seat while the rest of us take our seats.

"I thought they said you'd be here." Ariel's crisp voice crackles through the headset. "How's your girl?" She reaches across the space between the seats and grips his arm.

"She's doing fabulous. Thanks for asking."

Once we're all strapped into our seats, Ariel takes off and heads south toward the mouth of the Mississippi.

"Forest explained what's going on," she says. "I'm going to take you to the *USS Charles Sexton*. They don't have a helipad on their ship, so I arranged rigging for you to rappel down to the deck." She turns around to speak to us, although it's not necessary. We can't hear her without the headsets due to the overwhelming noise inside the helicopter. She points to several duffle bags secured inside the cabin.

"Check the ropes. There're eight harnesses, so should be no problem letting y'all down. I'll grab the gear later. Commander Fisher is expecting us, and we have an ETA of ninety minutes."

I clench my teeth when she says ninety minutes. Nearly three hours. That's how long those men will have their hands on my Lily. Anything could happen. I don't like sitting around doing nothing, but there's no other choice.

Max signals me to help him check out the ropes. We unbuckle from our restraints and get to work prepping everything. Axel joins us. While Max and I ready two sets of ropes, Axel checks out the harnesses. He taps Wolfe on the knee and they exchange words.

I'm sure it has something to do with getting Jinx onto the deck of the *USS Charles Sexton*. Not my problem. Max assigned babysitting duties to Wolfe.

It takes us the better part of an hour to check and double check the ropes. We secure them in place while Axel distributes the harnesses.

"Ten minutes out," Ariel Black calls out to us.

A look outside reveals a black sky overhead glittering with millions of stars. With no moon out, the stars shine and are absolutely amazing. Down below, there's more blackness, except along the busy waterway that is the Great Mississippi.

Lights shine from boats and barges as they labor up the Mississippi, delivering cargo to port, or head out to the Gulf, transporting goods to other places around the world.

The massive freighters and barges are lit up like Christmas trees, easy to see, but somewhere down there is a yacht running for open water. We're not in contact with Mitzy, but I know her drone, *Smaug*, is keeping pace with that boat.

Ariel shaves off altitude as our objective comes into view. Steel gray, the *USS Charles Sexton* waits for our arrival. Ariel gives us a countdown. Max and I go to the ropes. As Alpha One and Alpha Two, we head down first. Axel and Griff follow. Then Liam and Wolfe will make their way down with Jinx.

I would've given anything to hear the exchange between Wolfe and Jinx when he explained *how* we were getting off the helicopter.

"You boys ready?" Ariel calls out.

"Ready," Max answers.

We remove our headsets and attach ourselves to the ropes. With a thumbs-up, we're ready to go. Axel opens the outer door and we jump out into the night.

The rope whizzes through my carabiner as I fall through the emptiness of space. Max drops with me, our descent precise and controlled on the ropes.

Our boots connect with a solid thunk on the deck of the ship, and we run the remaining length of rope through our carabiners until free.

Max looks up and gives the signal we're off the line. Then we both step back and wait for Axel and Griff to descend.

The two of them jump out of the helicopter and make a smooth descent down the line. They repeat the same process, signaling when they're clear. I'm not sure if it's my imagination or not, but I swear I hear a female's high-pitched scream as Liam and Wolfe lower down out of the helicopter.

Griff goes to help Wolfe, who has Jinx strapped to his harness. Instead of attaching her front to back, according to protocol, he had her face him, wrapping her arms around his neck and her legs straddling his hip. What the fuck is he up to?

Once Griff gets Jinx free from Wolfe, he leads Jinx away while Liam and Wolfe free themselves from the lines.

Once clear, they signal overhead. The helicopter rises, two ropes dangling beneath it, and disappears into the night sky. Once the deafening noise of the helicopter is gone, a woman in a Coast Guard uniform approaches.

"Good evening, gentlemen. Welcome to the *USS Charles Sexton*, I'm Commander Fisher, captain of this ship. Looks like we have a job to do."

Max reaches out and shakes her hand, then makes introductions with the rest of us.

"What's our ETA?" Max doesn't skip a beat.

There's a surge beneath our feet as the ship turns about.

"We're headed upriver now and expect contact in twenty minutes. Let me show you what we've planned." She walks away, expecting us to follow, which is exactly what we do.

I've never been on a Coast Guard ship before. Commander Fisher doesn't waste any time. She shows us the water cannons on board, the guns they have at their disposal, the floodlights and sirens they'll use.

"Now, after speaking with your team, these are my thoughts. Let me know if this works, or doesn't, and we'll come up with another plan."

I listen closely to this. We're not sneaking up on that yacht in this ship. Which means those men will have plenty of opportunity to use Lily as a living shield.

"I understand you're familiar with these?" Commander Fisher stops at a blacked-out Zodiac with a muffled motor. It's a six-man inflatable rib we're intimately familiar with. "Our thought is to close in with the yacht. While we distract with our floodlights, sirens, and water cannons if we must, your boss was thinking to put your team into the water. We'll stop the yacht, which gives you time to approach from the rear and board, hopefully undetected."

Max thumps the side of the rigid inflatable. "Sounds good." He turns to us. "Questions? Thoughts? Concerns?"

"And what do I do?" Jinx is the first to speak.

"You'll stay on board the *USS Charles Sexton*." Max holds up a finger. "This is non-negotiable. Operations on the water, like we're proposing, have no room for someone who isn't trained."

"Just don't fuck it up." Jinx crosses her arms again. "That's my best friend on that boat."

"We'll do our best, and we're very good at our job."

We take a moment to go over the plan, poking holes in it wherever we can. But it's a solid plan which takes advantage of our unique skillset. Best thing about it is the crew of the *USS Charles Sexton* are professionals at interdiction. They've intercepted hundreds of boats. This will be a walk in the park for them.

For us, it's a little more complicated.

Ten minutes out, we load into the Zodiac with an irate Jinx looking on. She doesn't trust us but has no other choice than to let us do our job.

The moment the yacht comes into view, Commander Fisher turns on the floodlights, turning night into day. We slip off the back of the ship and circle around at high speed to insert ourselves at the stern of the vessel.

I say a silent prayer, hoping Lily is all right. I don't know what I'd do if anything happened to her.

TWENTY-FIVE

Lily

I wake in the bowels of a ship. My entire world rises and falls, swaying to the motion of water rushing alongside the hull. They shoved me into a lower bunk in what I assume are crew quarters and left me here, hands and feet bound.

No one is with me.

Zip ties secure my wrists while Duct Tape binds my ankles. This may seem like a problem, but it isn't. If I can squirm out of this bunk, I'll be free in a matter of seconds.

However, it's dark and hard to see. Fortunately, I'm not trapped in total darkness. There's a thin gap between the door and the floor, and a strip of light shines in through that gap. It provides minimal light, but enough for me to make out large objects inside.

The cabin is small. There are two bunks along the wall, one that I'm in and another one overhead. It doesn't look like there's anything else. Although, I expect at least a closet to store personal effects.

My hands go to my head. Interlocking my fingers, I press my thumbs to my forehead. It eases the ache in my head minimally.

How long have I been out?

There's no real way to tell, except I have to pee. That's not a very specific indicator, but it helps. It means it's been several hours since I was taken.

That's a piece of information I'm not happy to discover.

Instead of focusing on the negative, I force myself to think about the positive. That begins, and ends, with Callie.

At least she got free. I watched her run up the stairs. No doubt she worked her way down from the balcony to the street. Callie's smart as a tack. She'll call the cops and get the ball rolling, but what will the cops do?

They're not trained to deal with hostage rescue. Although, there is one man I know who is. I also know his entire team is in New Orleans.

But what are the chances Knox knows about my abduction?

That's a line of thought I squash. Depending on other people to free me is a bad idea. The only person I can count on is myself.

Fortunately, I know what to do. Or rather, I've been trained in what I should be thinking of, how I should prioritize objectives, and I've been given the skills to rescue myself.

So, prioritization.

I lack certain key information, such as where I am, who abducted me, and how many men I'm going up against. The minimum number is two.

The two men from the bar are most definitely on board. But how many friends do they have?

Where am I?

This boat is big. I can tell that from how it moves in the water and by how much motion there is on the deck. From the fit and finish of this cabin, I guess I'm on a luxury yacht instead of a civilian freighter.

If a freighter, or a cargo container, the walls and decks would be made of steel and concrete. The bunk mattress is soft; cloudlike. The walls are warm and smooth, like burnished wood. I'm going with luxury yacht because only those kinds of boats would care about how the crew quarters are fitted out.

Slowly, I continue going down what I know. From that, I'll figure out my next steps.

Other than the rushing of water on the other side of the wall, all I hear are my frantic breaths. I'm thinking through things, but panic rims every thought.

I need to calm myself. Fear has no place here. Without focus, I'm lost. Not to mention, I need to keep my wits about me. Deliberate and intentional are my two friends as I work to free myself.

As soon as I control my breathing, I listen for other sounds. The deep thrum of the engines is more of a vibration than a sound.

Those engines are kicked into high gear, from the low buzzing through the hull. That means we're moving fast.

Which makes sense.

The Port of New Orleans is several miles inland from the Gulf of Mexico. It takes most ships upwards of eight to ten hours to navigate the waterway. That makes the river a choke point. Whoever drives this vessel wants to get free of the constriction of the river as fast as possible.

I want exactly the opposite.

The longer we're on the river, the more time I have to act.

With my hands tied together, my feet as well, getting out of the bunk proves challenging.

I manage to swing my legs around. There's not enough space above my head to sit upright, so I kind of stoop over as I contemplate what to do next.

The sideways rocking motion of the boat picks up, shoving me backward, but then it stops, and I'm able to sit up again. That must've been the boat cresting over the wake of one of the massive ships navigating the river.

Which fits my assumption that we're still on the river, headed to the Gulf of Mexico. It's the only thing that makes sense.

The only chance I have to get out of this predicament is to jump ship and swim toward shore. That's a dicey proposition, considering the Mississippi River is a major thoroughfare with massive ships transiting it every day, and I'm afraid of the water.

At least it's summertime. I won't freeze in the muddy waters of the Mississippi. Getting run over by one of the many barges, boats, and ships is far more likely. It's late, O-dark thirty, which means it's pitch-black outside, not only will the ships not be able to see me, but I'm going to have difficulty finding the shore.

The only thing I know for certain is if these assholes manage to get me into the Gulf, I'm a goner for sure. There'll be no way for me to swim to shore.

As for my hands and feet. I'm not worried about getting free. In the DEA, we train for this kind of shit.

Duct Tape and zip ties appear to be handy for tying people up, but with the right angle and enough force applied, I'll rip myself free.

I wriggle my way out of the bunk until I teeter on my bound feet. Then, I think back to my training, going over it in my head before I try it for real.

The first thing is to rotate the locking bar until it's right in the middle of my wrists. I need to keep my palms facing each other. I use my teeth to move the locking bar where it needs to go.

The next thing is counterintuitive but necessary. I tighten the zip tie. The tighter it is, the easier it'll be to defeat the locking bar. I get it as tight as I can.

This next part is going to hurt. When we trained, our instructors had us wrap our wrists in Duct Tape, of all things. Ripping the zip tie generally cuts into the unprotected skin of the wrists and is painful. Since they had us complete the exercise dozens of times, I was very thankful for the extra protection the Duct Tape provided.

The way to free myself is to be deliberate and forceful. There's no room for hesitancy. The words of my instructors ghost through my mind, and I heed their instruction.

I lift my arms overhead. With deliberate intention, I lower my arms down sharply, chicken-winging my arms, and push toward my midsection vigorously. My instructors told me to think about forcing my shoulder blades together, and damn if it doesn't work like a charm.

The zip tie pops right off. It hurts like a mother and leaves deep gouges in both wrists, but my hands are free.

Now to deal with the Duct Tape around my ankles. This, too, is something I've practiced, training until I'm confident in my skill. That confidence helps me now as my breathing kicks up a notch.

At any moment, someone can come through that door. If they see I managed to free my wrists, they'll make it that much harder to do it again.

To free my legs, all I do is squat down and put my hands together, palms facing each other, right between my knees. The key here is to force my hands down toward my ankles in a really fast, hard action, which stresses the Duct Tape as I force my legs apart.

I take in a deep breath and shove my hands down between my shins. Just like the zip tie, the Duct Tape splits apart. I yank the sticky tape from my ankles, and that's it.

I'm free.

What next?

I didn't hear any voices on the other side of the door when I lay on the bunk, but the low droning of the engines could easily mask the sounds of someone talking. Or, they may not be speaking at all.

I need a plan.

It's going to be me against several men.

Doesn't matter what's outside that door, my only hope for escape is to take out whoever I find immediately before they can raise an alarm that I'm free. Then, it's a matter of making it to the deck unnoticed and jumping into the water for a little swim to the shore of the great Mississippi.

I grab the door handle and give a little jiggle. No surprise, it's locked.

Now what?

A locked door will not defeat me.

Fortunately, I've got a Swiss Army knife in my pocket. Whoever tied me up totally failed to search me for weapons, which will help out in a second.

I don't need a weapon right now. Although, the key to getting out of this room lies in the flat-edge screwdriver of my knife. The door hinges are on this side of the door. All I have to do is pop out the hinge pin and *voila!*

I set to work, feeling with my hands in the dimly lit room. Every now and then, I pause, listening for any noise on the other side of the door that indicates someone might be guarding me. There's nothing, which makes me snicker. The men who took me underestimated me. That is going to cost them their prize.

Me.

Once all the hinge pins are out, I grab the door handle and lift the door off its hinges. Swinging it aside, I find myself in a narrow hallway. There's more light out here than the cabin where they kept me. I look left, then right, trying to get my bearings.

From the looks of things, I'm definitely on someone's posh yacht rather than a commercial vessel. I head toward where I believe the stern of the vessel is because that's most likely where I'll find a set of stairs heading up.

Each step I take is with deliberate intent. Well aware I'm a prisoner here, I devise backup plans to my escape plan. If I hear someone, I'll retreat to the cabin I woke up in, and play possum for the men. It's a thin plan, that won't hold up, but I need something.

Far to the stern, I spy a steep set of stairs leading up. Crouching at the base of the stairs, I listen for the sounds of other people overhead. When I hear nothing, I cautiously climb the ladder until my head is level with the floor of the upper deck. A quick peek reveals an opulent lounging area. To my left, or port, is a bar. To my right, or starboard, is nothing more than a bank of windows looking out into the black of night.

Nobody is here.

Where is everyone?

Slowly, I crawl up the stairs. The bar provides a natural hiding spot, and I hunker behind it as I calm the racing of my heart. All I need is to find a way to jump overboard. This boat moves fast enough, they won't be able to slow down, circle around, and find me.

It sounds simple.

I'm terrified.

Swimming is not my greatest strength. It's the one thing that terrifies me. Anything dealing with me putting my face into the water is a panic-inducing event. But what choice do I have?

It's either deal with my fear of the water or die at the hands of these men.

What I won't be is a victim. If I'm going down, I'll do it fighting.

I hide behind the bar, crouching low, while listening for any signs of life. So far, I've not run into anyone, which helps. It means there aren't that many people on board. Fewer men between me and the rails is a good thing.

A quick peek reveals a shadow moving behind the glass separating me from the outer deck. The only door, however, is toward the bow. Between the bar and that door is nothing but an expanse of nothingness.

I could run, but I'm not willing to act rashly when my life's on the line.

The surge of the engines intensifies, and I grab for a handhold. Floodlights pierce through the windows, blinding me, while sirens sound through the night. Someone speaks on a loudspeaker, but I can't make out the words.

A man rushes into the room, headed down the stairs. I cringe, trying to hide, but the moment he sees me, his trajectory changes. Nearly twice my size, I pop to my feet, knowing this is a threat I can only meet head on.

He charges me, determined to wrap his arms around me, subduing me, and capturing me once again. In this, too, I'm prepared.

This is a move I struggled with, being not only female, but short. For hours, I practiced, and I've never had to use what I've learned outside the practice mat.

The man comes toward me, shouting vile obscenities. I don't give him a chance to get too close, meeting him halfway. Using the weight of my body, I chop at his neck, using the side of my hand to connect with the hard tendons of his neck. Like I was taught, I follow through, using my body's momentum, for maximum impact.

This move challenged me. I trained and trained, getting pitted up against men much larger than me. Performed correctly, it's meant to level the playing field when dealing with a much larger opponent.

There's a bundle of nerves that runs beneath the tendons of the neck. Chopping with the side of my hand should send shockwaves of sensation all the way through my opponent's body.

He closes the distance.

I strike.

The pain in my hand is unbearable, but I follow through as the man staggers back and drops to one knee.

That move is supposed to knock him out completely, but either I'm not strong enough, or I messed it up. He staggers for a moment, wavering on his knee, but then he's up, looking angrier than ever.

I revert to the next move. It's also meant to level the playing field for short people. I rush him, using my open palm to smack him under the chin. This move takes him out, snapping his neck back. Like a lumberjack, he falls back. His bottom jaw hits his upper jaw, and the shock hits his brain, knocking him out cold. He falls back with a thud and doesn't get up.

I turn toward the door, ready to run.

But there's another man standing between me and freedom; a really big man.

He comes at me, a feral grin on his face. I react, not act. There's no other way to describe it.

If I think too hard, I'm going to screw things up. His left arm swings at me. I block, using momentum to shove his arm downward. That opens his neck to me. I wrap my hand around his neck and drag his head down. Then I knee him in the face, knocking him backward.

Out cold, he falls down.

Amped up on an adrenaline high, I race toward the door.

It's dark outside; all I see is inky water and freedom. Behind me, a spotlight sweeps across the deck revealing the shape of a man holding a gun. He swings the weapon toward me.

I race to the railing, say a prayer, and dive into the murky waters of the Mississippi.

TWENTY-SIX

Knox

We execute the plan flawlessly. Commander Fisher's crew interdicts the luxury yacht, stopping it cold. Alpha team hits the water, moving off the stern of the *USS Charles Sexton*.

We make a wide circle, using the cover of darkness to hide our movements, while Commander Fisher's men call for the yacht to surrender and prepare for boarding.

Before I know it, we approach the swim platform at the back of the yacht. No one appears to see us. We tie up and make our way forward, weapons hot and ready.

Max leads. He heads up the stairs from the swim platform to the main level. It's a big boat, with three decks above the waterline, a flybridge, and most likely, two levels below the water. We assume Lily's being kept there.

In the chaos, something heavy falls into the water with a splash. Alpha team holds up, waiting, but no one responds. We move in, tapping each other on the shoulder, as we clear the way ahead and move on.

Max stops at a door. He pauses, taking position to the right. I follow, holding the left side as Axel makes the breach. Griff follows on Axel's heels. We move in behind. Liam and Wolfe guard our six.

Heading toward the bow, we make quick work of searching the vessel.

Far in the back, we find a bunk room door taken off its hinges from the inside. In addition, we find a busted zip tie and Duct Tape ripped in half.

"She was here," I say to Max.

"Did they take her topside?" There's a scowl on his face.

If the men onboard took Lily, they're using her as a human shield, which is the worst possible outcome.

"Doesn't look like it." Axel keeps his voice low. He points to the Duct Tape and the door sitting off its hinges. "Looks like she got free."

"If she did, where is she?"

Our earbuds crackle at the same time. It's Mitzy.

"Guys, *Smaug* caught something falling off the ship."

"Something?" Max and I look at each other, saying the same thing at the same time. "Or someone?"

Holy shit.

"Max, I heard a splash, if that was Lily …"

I don't want to finish that sentence. There are only two reasons Lily would be overboard. Either she jumped, which is reckless in these waters, or her body was dumped, removing any trace of her onboard.

"Mitzy …" Max waits.

"I'm looking," Mitzy responds.

There's an agonizing pause on the end of the line. One where I live and die a thousand deaths. My pulse thrums in my neck, roars past my ears, and makes standing while we wait a nearly impossible feat.

"Got her!" Mitzy's shout makes all of us wince. "She's in the water. Moving. Max, she's alive, but …"

But, what? This isn't the time for buts.

"She's floating downstream. There's a barge headed her way."

A barge?

It's the worst possible scenario. Ships with bows push the water aside. There's a small chance a ship would push Lily to the side.

Barges, however, don't have bows. Tugs push the unwieldy beasts upriver, where they plow through the water.

"Max …" I can't keep the anxiety out of my voice.

Doesn't take Max but a second to make a decision.

"Axel, you're in charge. Take Griff, Liam, and Wolfe, and search this ship. Provide assist to the Coast Guard. Knox, you're with me. We're going to get her."

We don't discuss. We're Guardians, the best of the best. We act.

Max and I rush back the way we came. At the swim platform, I ransack one of the storage holds and pull out two lifejackets. Max and I board, and then we move.

"Where to Mitzy?" Max asks for help.

We need it. It's pitch-black outside with no moon to help us. The muddy waters of the Mississippi don't help one bit. They're black as night.

If Lily jumped out, she's now at the mercy of the main flow of the river. It's been less than five minutes since she jumped, but that translates into a hell of a lot of water to search.

We're hampered because we don't have searchlights, but we do have Mitzy and *Smaug* in the air. While Max follows Mitzy's general directions, I strip out of my body armor and yank off my boots. I'd give anything for a set of fins to help me cut through the water, but I'm a strong swimmer. I'll make do.

"She should be up ahead, twenty yards."

Twenty yards is twenty yards too far. Behind us the Coast Guard cutter takes control of the yacht. What I wouldn't give to have the help of their powerful searchlights.

Then I hear it, the low, nearly subsonic, sloshing of a behemoth barge pushing its way upriver.

"Max?"

"We'll find her. You ready?"

"I'm set."

"You're close," Mitzy says. "You're right on top of her."

"We need better than that." Max responds to Mitzy while I stand in the center of the Zodiac. Some height might help but standing comes with the risk of tipping the small inflatable.

Over my shoulder, I spy the dark shape of the barge. It's a relentless monster moving toward us against an even darker sky. The froth from its bow wave churns as we close in on it, becoming near deafening.

Then I see a shock of white hair.

"There!"

Max follows the direction I point, and we close in on Lily.

The sound of the barge and its powerful bow wave turn thunderous.

Max and I exchange a look. We've only got one chance.

"Lily!" I cup my hands over my mouth.

The spot of white thrashes. An arm flails. She slips under.

My heart leaps in my throat, but I fight back the blinding panic. Keeping my eyes where I saw her go under, I scan for her to resurface.

"We'll have to grab her." Max looks up at the barge. We're close enough to see it. The massive bow wave crashes toward us, pushing the muddy Mississippi water into a five-foot bow wave.

"Grab hold of me," I shout to Max as I lean over the rubber edge of the Zodiac.

Initially, I intended to jump in, grab Lily, and have Max circle around to pick us up. The proximity of that barge makes that impracticable.

We have only one chance. As for Lily, her thrashing speaks to her terror.

I lean over the side of the boat. Max grabs the back of my pants, hooking his hand around my belt, while simultaneously steering. Lily's head breaks the surface. Her mouth gapes as she sputters and gulps.

"Now!" We're too far.

But Max responds, increasing our speed. I reach out as far as I can, leaning perilously over the side. In her panicked state, Lily's as likely to pull me into the water as I am to yank her out.

Max draws near and slows the engine. I reach out. A second passes as her head drops below the surface of the water. I thrust my hand under the surface and sweep for a hand, an arm. Hell, I'll pull her out by her hair if I have to.

My forearm brushes against something. I latch on and yank with all my strength. Lily's head breaches the surface. I pull her in toward the boat as she sputters and coughs.

"We've got to move!" Max angles the boat, turning us around.

With no time to pull Lily fully clear of the water, I cup my hands under her arms. Her skin is cold. Hard to hold on to.

But I don't release my grip. As Max speeds us away from the barge, I hold onto Lily as if my life depends on it.

Her body sweeps alongside the gunnel, getting dragged back as we race to get away from the barge. The muscles of my arms strain. Burning as the ligaments stretch beneath the load. I huff against the pain, but I never let go.

The moment Max gets us free of the barge, he slows down. I hang over the edge of the boat, holding Lily in my arms, as she coughs, sputters, and her movements grow weak.

Once we're far enough from the barge, Max helps me lift Lily up and over the edge of the Zodiac. I sit in the bottom of the boat, cradling her in my arms. Pushed past the point of exhaustion, her body goes limp.

"Is she …" Max asks after Lily.

I sweep the wet hair from her face. Her hot breath blows against my skin. A deep breath in, and I lean back, holding my woman in my arms.

"She's breathing. Exhausted, but breathing."

My Lily's alive.

The massive barge pushes past us, headed upriver oblivious to the life and death battle that played out in front of it.

"You're safe, Lily." I tug her close. "You're safe."

Max leaves me to hold Lily as we head back to the *USS Charles Sexton.*

Alpha team is on the yacht, in control with two hostages under their command. Max pulls up to the stern of the Coast Guard cutter and drives the boat up the launch ramp.

"Lily!" Jinx barely waits for us to come to a stop before she leaps into the boat. "Is she alive?" Her mournful gaze turns to me.

I should let Jinx hold Lily, but I don't. Lily is mine. She belongs to me.

Max gets it. He pushes Jinx aside, getting her to climb out of the Zodiac. Then he waits for me to stand, supporting my awkward climb out of the boat.

Commander Fisher's corpsman directs us to a small medical bay.

"You can put her down here." He grabs a set of vitals, measuring Lily's heart rate, oxygen in her blood, and her temperature.

New Orleans may be muggy and hot, but a dip into the Mississippi River is not recommended. It only takes minutes for hypothermia to set in.

"We need to get her out of these wet clothes." The medic looks at me, probably expecting me to leave the room. No way in hell is that happening. Max departs, leaving me, Jinx, and the medic.

"Are you going to help me, or are you going to stand there and gape." I don't want to exclude Jinx, but my priority is Lily.

It will always be Lily.

Jinx gives a slow blink, but then she hops into action. While I remove Lily's shirt, Jinx works on Lily's shoes. I peel Lily out of her jeans as the medic brings us warm blankets to wrap around her cold body.

She stirs, reaching out a hand. Jinx jumps, moving first, but Lily asks for me.

"Knox—is that you?"

I take her hand in mine and bring it to my cheek. She feels so cold. I kiss the back of her hand.

"I'm here, Lily. I'll always be here."

Jinx gives me the eye as she moves to the other side of the bed.

"I'm here too, Lily."

"Jinx?" Lily's eyes flutter, then slowly, ponderously, she opens them.

"I'm here." Jinx combs Lily's snow-white hair off her forehead. "We both are."

Lily blinks. It takes her a second to focus on me.

"I had a dream you rescued me."

"You seem to have rescued yourself pretty damn well. I just fished you out of the river, although I don't know what to say about jumping into the Mississippi."

"The man had a gun, and I didn't know what else to do."

I lean down and wrap my arms around Lily, pushing Jinx to the side.

"I thought I lost you. I thought you were gone."

I decide right then and there what matters. If it means saying goodbye to the Guardians, there's no question. I'm never leaving Lily's side.

TWENTY-SEVEN

Lily

OKAY, JUMPING INTO THE MISSISSIPPI MAY NOT HAVE BEEN THE BEST idea on the planet, but staring down a gun pointed at me didn't seem like a better option.

Other than sheer terror when I jumped in and my head went underwater, I remember little. There was that initial shock. It was *cold*! So much colder than I thought, which made breathing difficult, if not impossible. My entire body locked up.

Add to that my natural fear of putting my face underwater, and let's just say, I might have done better staring down that gun.

But I think I did the right thing.

I'm alive, thanks to Knox's quick thinking and his friend Max. They fished me out of the water, saving me.

"You're so warm." I curl against Knox's chest, placing my hand against his skin. He's not wearing a shirt, or pants, and I'm a little muddy on the details of how that happened.

But then, I wear nothing except my panties and bra. I am wrapped up in a soft blanket, which feels heavenly against my skin. Jinx hovers, protectively close. There's tension between her and Knox. It vibrates in the air, and I don't fully understand why.

"You need to drink this." Jinx shoves a cup of steaming liquid at me.

"Give her a second," Knox's deep voice rumbles in the air.

"She needs to drink."

"And she will, but give her a second to warm up."

"That's what the drink is for," Jinx argues.

"Jinx ..." His tone is full of warning that she's about ready to step across the line.

I'm feeling better by the second and decide to intervene.

"Give it to me." I reach a hand out from beneath the blanket.

"Here." Jinx leans close, helping me to wrap my fingers around the steaming mug. "How are you feeling?"

"Better." I take a sip then hand the mug back to Jinx.

My hands shake too much, and I'm afraid I'll dump the contents all down my front.

"Knox, why am I naked?"

He laughs. "You're not totally naked. But you're dangerously hypothermic. We stripped you out of the wet clothes, trying to warm you up."

"I feel better now." My body shivers, turning me into a liar.

"Still not letting you go."

"Why are you not wearing a shirt?" I rub my hand down his chest, letting my fingers drag against his skin.

"I'm not wearing pants either." His low, sultry chuckle brings a grin to my face.

"His clothes were all wet, and since he insisted he hold you, I made him strip out of his wet clothes," Jinx answers in a snit.

I love her protectiveness, but I think she's met her match in Knox.

Then I remember what happened and why I thought jumping into the Mississippi was my best option. I crack open my eyes. The first thing I see is Knox's handsome face looking down at me. I lay my head against his chest, burrowing into his heat, but then I peek at Jinx.

"You look like shit."

"Well, you look like a drowned rat." Jinx takes a sip of my hot tea. Her face is a mess of bruises. One of her eyes is nearly swollen shut.

"Hey, that's mine." I poke my hand out of the covers and demand my drink.

"Didn't look like you wanted it." Jinx's attention focuses to Knox. "Especially since you've got that big lug to curl up to. Honestly, girl, it's shameless."

"Shameless?" I laugh. "Give me my drink and get one for yourself." I reposition myself in Knox's lap to sit upright, making it easier to drink.

"Careful, pumpkin." Knox grabs me tight. "Stop wriggling your ass."

"I'm not …" Then I feel the response of his body to my movement. "You're kidding me."

"Still human. Still male." The corner of his lip turns up in a smirk. "Does that answer your question about how often?"

He refers to me asking if there's ever a time he's not thinking about sex. I love his playfulness as much as his honesty. It makes things almost feel normal.

Despite what Knox says, I wriggle in his lap until I'm sitting up. It makes me feel a little bit more in control. When the blanket slides off my shoulder, Knox puts it back in place. I take a sip of the steaming liquid, loving how it burns all the way down my esophagus. Jinx is right. I need this.

"Now, which one of you is going to tell me what the hell happened? How did I get here?"

"What's the last thing you remember?" Knox sweeps my wet hair off my forehead while I cradle the steaming cup and drink.

"I remember Jinx kicking some serious ass."

Jinx smiles at my comment. I think she's going to let Knox explain, but Jinx jumps in. In gory detail, I hear all about her cutting Callie and me free, fighting with the one man while I helped Callie get free.

She doesn't blink when she mentions getting knocked out and tied up. Unusual for Jinx, who hates to admit anyone got the better of her. She tells me about the police arriving. How annoying they were with their repetitive questions and lack of action.

Then she describes, in detail, the arrival of Knox and his team. From there, I laugh when she tells me how she wouldn't let them go without taking her with them.

I totally see that happening. Jinx is fierce when she's got a mind to do something. Again, I love her protectiveness. Although, as I snuggle up against Knox, shamelessly stealing his warmth, I realize Jinx has someone else who will claim that spot.

She mentions something about *that guy from the bar*. It takes me a moment to figure out who she's talking about. It's one of Knox's teammates, if I'm not mistaken.

For the next twenty minutes, I get a full debrief. Knox speaks up, only to add details of my rescue out of the water.

The door opens, and a woman in a uniform enters. She takes a look around the room, then smiles when she sees me sitting upright, drinking the hot tea. She carries a bundle under her arm.

"It's good to see you up and about." She approaches me, hand extended to shake. "Commander Erika Fisher."

"Um, nice to meet you." I manage to free a hand to shake with her.

Commander Fisher's attention shifts to Knox. "Your team is in the wardroom, waiting for you."

"Sorry, pumpkin." Knox kisses the top of my head. "I need to debrief with my team." He lifts me effortlessly and sits me down beside him. I gather the blanket around me, feeling uncommonly self-conscious without him holding me. "I'll be back as soon as I can."

Knox leaves me and Jinx with the Commander who holds out the bundle.

"I think these will fit."

"Thank you." I take the stack of clothes from her. It's a pair of sweatpants, a t-shirt, a pullover sweatshirt, and socks.

"Unfortunately, there isn't much to choose from. I'm the only woman on board. You might have to roll up the pants. I'm a good deal taller than you and a bit heavier in the chest. I didn't think my bras would fit."

"I'm thankful for this." And I have no problem going braless or stripping out of my wet panties.

"You've got some interesting friends." She takes a seat while I let go of the blanket and put on the clothes she brought. "They moved Heaven and Earth to get you."

"Yeah, I'm pretty lucky." The sweatpants are a bit too long, but they roll up without a problem, and I practically swim in the sweatshirt. "I can't thank you enough for the loaner." I gesture to the clothes. "I'm not exactly sure what happens next."

I'm totally out of my element.

"We're arranging transport now. Any idea who those men are who kidnapped you?"

"None really. I think it has more to do with the Guardians." I cover my mouth, not sure if I'm supposed to mention that.

Commander Fisher laughs. "I know all about Forest's Guardians, which is why I didn't hesitate when the call came in. I'm just glad we were in a position to help. I think they're trying to figure out what to do about our prisoners."

"Do you think we could join their debrief?" I gesture to Jinx.

"It's my ship. You can do whatever you want. Come, I'll show you the way."

I like Commander Fisher. It's cool to see a woman in a position of leadership. Captain of a U.S. Coast Guard vessel? I like that.

The wardroom falls silent as Jinx and I enter. Knox pulls me down into his lap while Jinx stays by the door.

"Where are the others?" I'm pretty sure Knox mentioned six men in his team. I see Liam and Wolfe, knowing them from the night Knox and I met in the bar. The other man feels familiar, but I don't remember him.

"Lily, do you remember Liam and Wolfe?" Knox makes introductions.

"I do. Um, thank you …"

The other man in the room laughs. "I'm Max. It's nice to see you up and about."

"Max helped me fish you out of the river," Knox says. I must look confused because he continues. "Axel and Griff are down below, questioning the prisoners."

The way he emphasizes *questioning* makes me feel as if there's more going on.

"It feels like *thanks* isn't quite enough, but thank you."

I don't know what else to say and kind of curl into myself as the men pick up with the debrief. As an agent in the DEA, debriefs are familiar to me. They're not much different from what I expect.

It does fill in some of the holes in my memory and gives direction for the next steps.

The *USS Charles Sexton* will be pulling into port with the confiscated luxury yacht. Not in New Orleans. A boat is coming for us, us being Knox and his team, along with Jinx and me. The prisoners are staying with the Coast Guard. There's some kind of subtext I don't appreciate about Axel and Griff needing to get what they can out of the prisoners before our ride gets here.

After yawning for the tenth time, Commander Fisher takes Jinx and me back to her quarters.

"The two of you look exhausted. It's going to be a bit before your ride gets here. In the meantime, looks like the two of you could use a breather. Make yourselves at home. If you're tired, please lie down. I'll send someone to get you when it's time."

"Thank you." Jinx closes the door behind Commander Fisher, then turns to me. I hold out my arms. Jinx runs to me, and we embrace.

"I was so scared. I thought I lost you." Tears fall from Jinx's eyes, a rare event, it tells me how scared she was.

"I'm here. We're both okay. You were something fierce, you know. If you hadn't come and freed Callie and me like you did, this might all have turned out differently."

"When they took you, I was so scared. That man you found is pretty damn sweet too. A bit overprotective." She slugs me playfully in the arm.

"Knox is pretty amazing."

"*Le sigh* ..." Jinx puts the back of her hand to her forehead and drops back onto the Commander's bed with a sigh. "If only I had a hottie like you."

I lie down beside her on the bunk with a yawn. "Yeah, Knox is fucking hot."

We talk for a bit, but then I drift. Exhaustion pulls at me, and it's all I can do to keep my eyes open. Jinx holds my hand, and we lie side by side on the bed as sleep overcomes me and I drift. My dreams fill with images of Knox and the future I want.

TWENTY-EIGHT

Lily

THE NEXT TWENTY-FOUR HOURS ARE A WHIRLWIND OF ACTIVITY. A boat arrives to take us off the *USS Charles Sexton*. We don't return to NOLA, but instead pull into port at the closest marina. From there, we load into two luxury vans and drive to an airport, where we board a private jumbo jet.

Jinx and I find ourselves flying across the country, kidnapped it seems, by a very unusual group. Unlike my previous kidnapping, I don't mind this one at all.

Jinx and I pretty much cling to each other as we take in the organized chaos that appears to be Guardian HRS's state of normal. I meet up again with Forest, Sam, and CJ. Just like at the precinct where they liberated Knox, they're all as much, or more, intimidating than Knox's teammates.

I'm also introduced to two amazing women. Skye Summers, Forest's sister—who looks nothing like him—is a doctor. Mitzy is a young woman in her early twenties, who seems to have no problem putting everyone in their place. Her psychedelic hair is a hoot and gives me an idea for spicing up my whiter than white locks.

My attention keeps landing on Forest, a man with the same coloring as me. I itch to know his background. Knox and I sit together, near the rear of the plane, but as soon as we get to altitude, Jinx pulls me to the front of the plane to talk with Mitzy.

"So, this is where all the magic happens, and this is *Smaug*." Mitzy gives Jinx and me the rundown on her team's capabilities.

"So, all those drones at the dock were you?" I remember the swarm which saved Knox and me during that standoff.

My chest pinches. That memory comes with the pain of losing my team. My breath hitches as I rub at my sternum, trying to do what Knox says. *Let the moment roll over me; embrace it but don't hold onto it. Live my best life.*

It helps. Not much, but it's better than a paralyzing flashback.

"Not exactly me," Mitzy says. "It's an AI program Forest and I built, driven by my guys."

She introduces us to her entire technical team and tells me all about how she used a much larger drone, with its night vision capabilities, to locate me in the water.

If it wasn't for *Smaug*, Knox and Max would've never found me. I would've been drowned and crushed by that barge, and no one would've known what happened.

I owe several people thanks for my rescue.

Mitzy's crew is right up Jinx's alley. I swear Jinx looks like a kid in a candy shop. She's more tech than operations, which is why we make a good team. I operate, and Jinx feeds me the information I need. Not to mention, she's a cyber expert.

I leave Jinx and Mitzy to gab and wander to the back of the plane. Knox plays cards with Wolfe; the two of them appear intent on the game. An odd stack of buttons sits on the table between them.

Needing a moment alone, I head to the middle of the plane and hide out in one of the lavatories. Very much unlike the lavatories found on commercial planes, this one comes with a full-sized shower. Not to mention the sink and commode.

I splash water on my face and do my best to finger comb out the tangles in my hair. Appreciative of Commander Fisher's sweats, I look tired and frumpy in the oversized clothes.

And what exactly am I doing on a plane headed to California? I need to talk with Harry and do my own debrief with my team. Except, I have no team.

Not anymore.

The tears appear out of nowhere. Since I'm alone, I wrap my arms around myself and sit on the edge of the tub and allow myself to fall apart for a few moments.

It's only when someone knocks on the door and jiggles the handle that I realize I've been in here for too long.

Another look in the mirror and I splash water on my tear-streaked cheeks. My eyes are puffy. Red mars my cheeks, and I look miserable.

I feel lost.

I need my anchor.

With a deep breath in, I gather myself together and go in search of Knox. Instead of him, Sam and CJ wait outside the lavatory with Forest towering behind them.

"We were hoping to have a word with you." Sam gestures to a room behind us. The door is open to a conference room. Jinx waits inside, as does Knox.

He stands when I enter, coming to me and draws me into his embrace.

"Just breathe, pumpkin. It gets better with time."

Not sure how he knows about my little private meltdown, I lean into him, drawing strength from him.

"I look a mess, don't I?" I wipe at my cheeks.

"You look perfectly imperfect." Knox draws me around to the other side of the table, where I take a seat next to Jinx.

"What's going on?" I look to him. "Are we in trouble?"

"No trouble at all," CJ says as he sits opposite Jinx.

Sam takes the middle seat, opposite me, and Forest sits beside him. The room suddenly feels ten times smaller.

"We wanted to sit down with the two of you and discuss possibilities." Sam leans forward, fingers splayed against the tabletop.

"Possibilities?" I ask.

"I want you to work for me." Forest cuts off whatever it is Sam was going to say. I get the feeling he's blunt and to the point.

"Nice way to ease in there, Forest. I thought you were going to let me take the lead."

"Just don't like wasting time. What do you say? I've looked at your portfolios. Harry says you'd be a great fit. Jinx, you totally rocked whatever it was you were doing. I'd love for you to show my Guardians some of those moves, and Lily, I hear you not only escaped, but took out two men before my Guardians ever boarded that yacht. You need to work for me."

"Work for you?" Jinx sounds excited. "Like, what does that mean?"

"Did they say yes?" Mitzy flits into the small room. She squeezes around Sam and CJ and sits on the table facing Jinx. "Please tell me you said yes. There is way too much testosterone in this group. I need some badass chicks to even some of that growly-man-crap out."

"Um …" I glance over at Jinx.

From the smile on her face, she's eager for a job change. I'm a little more reserved. It took a lot of time and effort to get where I am in the DEA. It's a big deal to be a special operative, but I do see one immediate benefit. It answers a lot of questions.

If I do this, it means being close to Knox. I didn't know how, or even if, we could pull off a long-distance relationship.

"Can we think on it?" I say because Jinx and I made a pact very early on to stick together through thick and thin.

There's some karmic chaos binding us together. Two girls, born on the same day, both abandoned by their mothers, and adopted into the same home.

We're not to be separated.

Sam, CJ, and Mitzy lay out what we might expect if we join the Guardians. Our actual roles are to be determined, but it's good to know there's a team with female operatives on it. I don't know if I could join an organization where women weren't valued for what they can do.

Sam and CJ appear really interested in Jinx as an operator, but I saw the light shine in her eyes while talking to Mitzy. They're going to have a tough sell on that one. As for me, it's intimidating to join such an accomplished team. I'm honored to be considered, but feel like there's so much to learn.

"Can we have a moment alone?" I need to corral Jinx and figure this out before we commit to something we don't fully understand.

"Sure thing. It's a lot to take in. And no pressure for an answer right away. We'll send you information about Guardian HRS, and the offer with all the important stuff." Sam stands, and the others file out of the room behind him.

Mitzy is last; she turns and clasps her hands to her chest. "It's seriously *the best* place to work. I need more females!" She gives a little finger wave and flits out of the room, leaving us alone with Knox.

"Should I leave?" He appears hesitant and shifts in his seat as if he's going to stand.

I reach for his hand and thread our fingers together. "Did you know about this?"

"They mentioned something during our briefings. I knew it was likely."

"And what do you think about it?"

"Do you have to ask?"

"I need to know." I need him to tell me to stay.

"Love," he takes both my hands in his, "if you don't move to California and work for Guardian HRS, then I'm quitting and moving to NOLA. I don't know what this is between us. I've never felt it before, but the thought of you living all the way across the country feels all kinds of wrong. I've got three spare bedrooms in my place. You're both welcome to crash there until you figure things out." His grip tightens on my hand. "Although, if you wanted to stay, I'm totally cool with that."

That last comment is for me alone.

"It's an incredible offer. A lot to take in." I lean back and glance over at Jinx. "What do you think?"

"I need to know more." Jinx props her elbows on the table. "But it sounds amazing." Her brows pinch together. "You don't happen to live with Wolfe, do you?"

Jinx knows nothing about subtlety.

"I do not, but his place is literally a stone's throw away." Knox laughs. "What the hell happened between the two of you?"

"A dare that he still owes me." Jinx bats her eyes innocently at Knox, but there's nothing innocent about Jinx.

"You didn't tell me anything about that." Jinx tells me everything. "I'm curious."

"Well, you've also been a bit preoccupied." She pushes back from the table. "I'm going to leave the two of you alone for a bit to *discuss* what this means. Should I stand guard outside, or are you going to lock the door?"

"Lock the door?"

"Come on, Lily, you've always wanted to be a member of the mile-high club. I'll just stand guard outside."

"Oh no, you don't." I push her out of the conference room and twist the lock behind her.

Jinx jiggles the handle with a laugh, then slaps the door.

"Have fun, my friend."

"She's just joking." I turn around, feeling self-conscious. "Jinx doesn't mean anything by it."

The heat smoldering in Knox's eyes makes me take a step back. Only, there's nowhere to go. The door's to my back, and Knox is up and on his feet.

Coming to me.

"Up to you, pumpkin, but I am not yet a member of that particular club." Low and sultry, his words turn my knees to jelly and hijack my pulse.

TWENTY-NINE

Knox

Two weeks later

INCREDIBLE AND AMAZING ARE TWO WORDS THAT FAIL TO
adequately describe my girl. She and Jinx stay with me, moving in
with zero fuss. Next week, their things will arrive from New Orleans,
and the move will be official.

There are three spare bedrooms in my house. I didn't want to
assume anything with Lily, thinking she and Jinx would take a room
each, and knowing women, I figured the third room would turn into
an unofficial closet.

I'm not wrong about the closet. Jinx packs it with her stuff. Lily
is more modest with her things, and best of all, she moved into my
room.

Just assumed.

It's the best, most perfect assumption anyone ever made. I'm
thrilled to fall asleep with her by my side. Lily simply fits. She fits in
my bed. She fits in my life. She's also officially, the worst cook on the
planet.

Cooking remains my task, but she and Jinx help out where they can. My house has never been so clean. Who knew you had to vacuum that often?

We sit outside on the deck. Wolfe and Liam join us, along with Max and Eve, Axel and Zoe, and Griff and Moira. It's fun watching our team grow from six steadfast bachelors to what we have now.

The ribbing the guys gave me over getting bit irritated me at the time, but I'd change nothing about the past month.

"Dinner was delish!" Lily turns in my arms and plants a sexy kiss on my lips. "I'm gonna help Jinx with the dishes."

I yank on her hip, keeping her close. When Jinx started clearing everyone's dishes, Wolfe joined her in the kitchen.

"I think Jinx has more help than she needs."

"Why?"

I gesture inside, where Wolfe and Jinx are obviously embroiled in yet another argument.

"Lord, those two …" Lily sits back with a sigh. "They need to take that in the bedroom and work it out of their system. This is getting ridiculous."

I agree with Lily, but it's not my place to interfere. Besides, there are other things well worth my time.

"Speaking of the bedroom, how about we sneak out?"

"You're the host of this party." She sounds scandalized, but it's not like it's a big secret we're screwing each other's brains out. Besides, the guys won't mind.

"We'll be quick." I keep my voice low as I trace the edge of her shorts with my finger.

"There's nothing quick about you in the bedroom."

"I do aim to please." I nuzzle her neck, licking a path that makes her quiver. Sucking gently on her earlobe, I tease her with a promise.

"Stop!" She giggles and pulls away.

I continue to tease her over the next few minutes. Max notices and gives Eve a little nudge. Without me having to say a thing, the guys slowly file out with their women in tow.

Liam looks for Wolfe, but when he sees him in the kitchen arguing with Jinx, he gives a shake of his head.

"Dude, I'm calling it a night." He tips his beer toward me and Lily. "You two have fun. Don't do anything I wouldn't." With a snicker he leaves, which means Lily and I are finally alone.

Or rather, almost alone.

"Come on," I whisper in her ear. "Let's make a break for it."

"Don't you think Jinx and Wolfe will find it weird everybody's gone?"

"I don't think those two are thinking about much other than themselves right about now."

My place is a sprawling single-level dwelling perched over the rocky coastline of California. Which means, there's a door leading off the master bedroom to the massive porch. I lift Lily out of my lap and lead her to our bedroom.

I love the sound of that.

Our.

But what I love even more is the woman with me.

Before I can shut the sliding door, Lily has her hands on her top. She lifts it in front of me, revealing the creamy expanse of her stomach to my hungry eyes. With a shake and a shimmy, her shirt falls to the floor.

Her hands go to her waist, where she plucks the button of her shorts free. With a sensuous glide, the zipper draws down as blood races to my cock. A low growl escapes me. I take a step forward, advancing. Eager and wanting, I'll never get enough of my girl.

The more time I spend with Lily, the more a part of me she becomes. Honestly, I don't know how I breathed before she came into my life.

Tilting her neck, her gaze unerringly finds its way down to my groin and my eager cock. Her hungry eyes flare, and her tongue darts out to wet her lips.

Despite the few feet of distance between us, we engage in our intimate dance. She teases. I react. Then she submits.

I'm in no hurry to race to that finish line. One of the things I love the most is the chase. Can never get enough of that. Her seductive striptease burns me alive, sending flicks of heat searing my skin. Her gaze never leaves my eyes.

Since we met, Lily's become bolder in taking what she wants, and she wants to disappear within the fiery caldron that is what making love to her has become. We both burn as one, disintegrating to ash, only to be reborn stronger as a couple.

Her gaze blisters my skin and manipulates the flow of my blood. It races to fill my needy cock, and I love that about her. I love how she can go from simmering to boiling hot.

She rouses the darkest, most sinful parts of my nature. The parts which urge to take, to claim, to devastate, and adore. My desire builds, blooming outward in a rush of heat. My cock swells, and I reach for it.

"Is this what you want?" I grip my hard length, fisting it where she can see what I promise.

The feelings she unleashes within me are monstrous and impossible to contain. When we're alone, absolutely alone, I let loose the raging beast within me, a dangerous rutting feral thing that gives it to her just the way she likes it.

"Hard and fast?"

Lily gives a slow nod. Her shorts join her shirt on the floor, and she steps free, but she doesn't give in.

Lily's lusty voice reaches straight for my groin, encouraging and challenging. "Make me."

"Oh, you're damn straight. I'm going to make you." I take a step toward her, prowling with the assurance she belongs completely to me. These feelings are powerful, but unwieldy as well. The masculine urge to rut and fuck consumes me, but it's the beating of my heart that tells the truth.

I'm irrevocably and forever bound to this woman. Desperately in love and completely at her mercy. I exist to please Lily. It's the only thing that matters.

Right now, I know exactly what she needs. That's not tender or gentle. We save that for later. For intimate moments where the world stops and it's just the two of us sharing one moment within a lifetime of moments.

"I'm going to make you beg, and then I'm going to make you scream."

I'm going to do all of that, but first, I need a little relief. I won't make it through the next hour if I don't take the edge off.

"On your knees." My voice deepens. Grows hoarse. It's commanding and demanding. As she falls to her knees, I close the distance, shredding my clothes along the way.

She looks up at me from the floor, cheeks flushed, tits pink with arousal. Nipples standing up for torment and pleasure alike. I'm going to get to all of that, but first.

I tap the head of my dick against her lips. "Take me, pumpkin. Show me how much you want my cock."

Her lashes flutter as her gaze turns inward. That's Lily sinking to her happy place. We play in the bedroom, games only adults enjoy, and damn if we don't have the best time.

Her lips wrap around my cock, and my toes curl as pleasure rushes through me. Sparks of electricity shoot through my body, gathering at the base of my spine as she licks and sucks and drives me wild.

Lily likes when I take her hard and fast, but when sucking my cock, she needs to be in control. We played with that, finding limits which surprised us both. No matter, I'm putty in her hands.

And Lily is amazing when she sucks my cock. She also knows I need this too. I need to see her willingness to go to her knees. I need to feel her love and adoration. And she knows I'll return that a thousand-fold.

We give, and we take. Each serving the other's needs. Loving each other with the entirety of our souls.

She drives me toward oblivion until I strain to breathe. I'm holding on, only because the pleasure rushing through me moves too quick. But I can only hold off the flood of arousal for so long.

My hand goes to the crown of her head, gathering her hair in my fist as my hips rock and thrust.

The only sound in the room is the sound of my deep breaths and the low throaty groan as I come in her mouth. Lily licks me clean, leaning back with an impish grin on her face, pleased with her ability to take my pleasure with such ease.

I shake my head.

"Better wipe that grin off your face. It's my turn now. Do you remember the night we met?"

"No!" Her eyes widen, and she shakes her head. "Please, not that. Anything but that."

"Again, and again, and again, until you beg me to let you come." Dominance comes in many forms, and I love exploring them all.

"Knox—please, I'm begging. That was torture."

"I remember you loving it in the end."

"In the end, but …"

"If you don't want to …" I make a grab for my shirt, totally teasing her and having fun.

"Don't you dare leave me like this."

"Like what, pumpkin?"

"Needing you." Her eyes plead with me.

Not that I'd ever leave Lily in the lurch. It's just fun to mess with her a bit and have some fun. She's going to get me back. She's done it before, keeping me hard for hours with a seductive touch here and there.

I lean down and lift her into my arms. "I'd never leave you wanting, but if you want to come, you have to do one thing first."

"Anything."

"You sure about that?"

"Anything but the butt sex." She bites her lower lip.

That the one thing she's put her foot down about. It's a hard no, but I don't care about that.

I lift her and carry her to the bed. Placing her down gently, I go to my knees. While she watches with wide eyes, I open the drawer to the nightstand. We keep a wide assortment of new toys in there. Some she likes, and some she claims to hate. Those are my favorite toys.

I pull out the set of nipple clamps she's yet to let me try, saying they're too scary, but that's just to put her off her game.

"Knox, I'm not ..." She scoots away, but I grab her left hand and hold her in place as I draw out the velvet box I bought the day after she moved in.

With one hand pinning her wrist in place, I pivot on my knees.

"All I need is for you to say yes."

"Yes, to what?"

I release her and bend on just the one knee. I'm sure I look comical as fuck, buck naked, semi-hard, holding a ring case in my hands. As what I'm holding hits her hard, her eyes widen as I open the box and reveal the solitaire diamond I intend for her to wear for the rest of our lives.

"Lily Freeman, will you do me the honor of being my wife?"

"Get out!" She screeches and sits up in bed, swinging her legs around and folding them in front of her. She shoves her left hand forward, wriggling her fingers as tears streak down her face. "Yes— Oh my God. Yes! Yes! Yes!"

"I love those words on your lips." With her answer loud and clear, I slip the ring over my fiancée's finger.

Before she can lift her hand to admire the ring, I grab her legs and slide her ass to the edge of the bed, where I proceed to show her exactly how devoted of a husband I intend to be.

I tighten my grip on her thighs as I bury my face between her legs. Decadently teasing her, I torment her without mercy until she begs so sweetly to come. Only one goal is on my mind, and that's to wreck her as thoroughly as she's wrecked me. There will never be another woman for me, and there sure as shit will never be another man touching my woman.

Hard and aching again, blood rushes to my groin, swelling my turgid cock until I weep for her. My desire for her goes deeper than physical lust. It's a visceral need. I swell and harden for her as she comes on my face and on my tongue.

Before Lily drifts down from her insatiable high, I lift her in my arms and do what I do best.

I take her hard and fast. Her scent fills the air and carries through my nose where her essence imprints itself on my soul. She feels good. Fits just right, like the comfort one feels when slipping on a pair of old shoes.

Our gazes latch and lock as I carry her through the bedroom. I love making love to her in bed, but the soft mattress limits some of my more vigorous moves. I like it best with my woman wrapped around me, legs clenching as I pound into her with nothing but the primal need to rut and fuck.

I slam Lily against the wall. Her gaze socks me in the chest. She's everything I never thought I wanted and now find impossible to live without.

She's viciously fierce, unstoppable, and the most beautiful creature I know. A glimmer lights her eyes on fire. Lily looks at me, breathless, ravenous, and overtaken with the need rushing through my veins.

"Hard and fast, Knox. Don't you dare hold back."

I thrust upward, burying myself to the hilt as Lily lays claim to my cock. Her body's strong. Her lips are soft. She's perfect for me.

Hard and fast, I thrust into her, pounding hard, going deep. I almost lose myself to my fury, but I regain control. There's no way I'm going to last, but this time I want us to come as one.

I adjust my angle, hitting her inner walls the way I know she loves and register every twitch of her body. When her fingers dig into my skin and her legs wrap tightly around my hips, everything fades around me except for the gliding of flesh on flesh.

Our mouths collide and clash, tongues meeting with the same frenzy as our hips. We explore as if this is our first time, but there's only so much I can take.

Panting, grunting, I hold off my release until I feel her cresting alongside me. Her tongue darts out, sharp jabs that lose their fierceness as her entire body jerks and clamps down around mine. It's just the stimulation I need.

My release slams into me with such incredible force, it feels as though I'll die from the pure agony of the pleasure rushing through me. My legs shake as she folds herself around me, panting with her own release. With throaty groans, I ride the wave, hips pumping until I'm spent. I crush my face against the side of her neck, thoroughly in love with this woman in my arms.

Shouts from the other room disturb our union. Something large crashes to the floor. Glass shatters, and the sound of objects falling to the floor has Lily and I breaking apart in a flash.

I grab a towel to wrap around my nakedness and grab my gun from under the mattress. Lily runs to the bathroom and shoves her arms through my robe. She, too, grabs her gun from under her side of the bed.

We meet up by the door. She reaches for the handle and waits for my signal. I give a sharp nod. Lily yanks the door open and I barrel through, gun sweeping the room, looking for intruders. Lily's right on my heels, adapting well to the training she's receiving as a Guardian.

Then we both pull up short when we see Jinx standing over Wolfe in the middle of the living room. They've torn down two bookcases, shattered my glass coffee table, and destroyed basically everything.

"What the fuck?" I lower my weapon and run my fingers through my hair.

Wolfe stares up at Jinx, a murderous glare in his eyes.

"He's paying for this." Jinx points down at Wolfe. She lifts her hands and takes a step back.

"What the hell, Jinx?" Lily lowers her weapon. "What happened?"

Jinx points again at Wolfe. "Ask your fucking buddy what happened." With that, she turns in a huff and walks out of the room.

I give Wolfe a hand up and look at the destruction of my living room. "Do I need to ask?"

Wolfe's gaze follows Jinx as she retreats down the hall. Lily goes after her friend. Once they're out of sight, he turns and smiles with a cheeky grin.

"I think she likes me."

"Likes you? The two of you destroyed my living room. What the fuck did you do?"

"Nothing much."

"Doesn't look like nothing."

He rubs at the back of his neck and twists to get out the kinks. "I may have kissed her."

"You did, what?"

"She definitely likes me." He glances at the towel around my waist. "Looks like the two of you had a bit of fun. Did she say yes?"

"Yes, to what?"

"You asked her, didn't you?"

"Asked her what?"

"To marry you, bro." Wolfe takes a step back. "Did she, or didn't she?"

"How do you …?" I shake my head. "Never mind, I don't want to know."

Wolfe dusts off his clothes. "For what it's worth, the two of you fit."

He leaves me, waltzing out the door as if he didn't destroy my living room. I don't bother the girls. Lily and Jinx are as tight as girls can be.

Instead, I grab a beer from the fridge and head outside to watch the sun set over the horizon.

"To the perfect ending of a perfect day."

I raise my beer and toast my brothers in arms, who never made it home. "I'm living my best life, brothers. I wish you were here."

THIRTY

Jinx

"Jinx, are you okay? What happened?" Lily follows me into my room, concerned and worried for my sanity. Not that I blame her. Wolfe and I demolished the living room.

I live with her and Knox, moving to the bedroom farthest from their love nest where I swear they bang each other fifty-thousand times a day. Honestly, the two of them are shameless, going at it like rabbits day and night.

Meanwhile, my sex life is as dry as the Sahara. That is the fault of the frustrating man who knows exactly what buttons to push to get me riled up.

"I'm fine." I stomp into my room, arms folded across my chest, and heat rising in my cheeks. It's not just anger.

I'm bothered, hot, and aroused; turned on by the only physical contact I allow myself to have with the wolfish Wolfe.

What an appropriate description.

The man is a mangy halfbreed; if we're calling mangy halfbreeds the sexiest man alive. The bastard is good-looking and he knows it. Like, drool worthy good. Lord knows I've spent far too many nights salivating over the bastard.

"You don't look fine." Lily looks tiny in Knox's robe.

No doubt that little spat between Wolfe and I broke up another of Lily and Knox's sexcapades.

I turn on my best friend in the whole universe, needing an outlet for my anger. Not that she deserves to bear the brunt of this messy situation.

"Really?" I pointedly check out her attire. "You couldn't wait for the party to be over before fucking each other's brains out?"

"Jinx, that's not…"

"Not true? Or not fair?" I give her an out, but she won't deny the truth to my face.

"It's not fair." As expected Lily's cheeks flush, moving toward bright crimson as I point to her boobs which are trying their hardest to escape the Terry cloth robe.

"I knew it."

"We *were* fucking each others brains out when you and Wolfe started World War III in the living room. What's up with the two of you, anyway?"

"Nothing." I stomp over to the window and pull back the drape.

I keep it closed as much as possible, opening it only to drive Wolfe crazy. Fucking perv likes to jack off while watching me undress, and I get off on him getting off on me.

It's some fucked up twisted shit. Lily's not wrong about that.

How many nights have I resorted to yanking out my vibrator after watching him shamelessly jerk off in front of me?

Too many.

That's the long and the short of it.

I hate how I ache for him, but I'm not some bimbo to use and throw away. He did that once and he's never doing it to me again.

Never.

"Nothing my ass." Lily closes the gap in the robe with a sharp yank and plops down on my bed. "You two are going to have to work things out."

"Not happening."

"But if you're placed on Alpha's tech team, you're going to see a whole lot more of him."

"I'm not getting assigned to Alpha."

"You're not?" Lily's mouth gapes. "I thought…"

"You're not on Alpha. Why would I work with them when you and I are a package deal?"

"You know why." Lily cocks her head. "They're getting close to cracking the cypher in those ledgers. You have to be on that team. No one knows about that kind of shit like you."

"The only way I'll work with Alpha team is if they put you on that team. Then, I'll consider it. But no way—no how—am I getting any closer to that asshole." I jerk my thumb over my shoulder, pointing toward Wolfe's house.

He and Knox are neighbors, a stone's throw away from each other, and my bedroom window happens to face Wolfe's master bedroom. It's annoying as fuck, because I can't keep my eyes off of him when he thinks I'm not looking. My view looks right into his bedroom. Directly at his bed.

Where he sleeps.

Where he tosses and turns.

Where he stays up late reading on his phone.

The only time I can't see him is when he leaves the lights off. When he does, all I see it the reflection of my window in his.

Wolfe rarely leaves a light off.

He enjoys me watching him.

Lily picks at nonexistent lint on my comforter. She curls her legs up under her bottom and breathes out a sigh. "Knox won't have it. He knows I can take care of myself, but says it would be too much of a distraction for him and the rest of the team."

"Fuckers. So where are they going to place you? Delta?" That's the only Guardian team with women on it. Jenny is Delta-One and a firecracker of a woman. Charlene is Delta-six.

"You've got the filthiest mouth on the planet." Lily loves my colorful language.

"I'm not the only one who knows how to swear like a sailor." I prop my fists on my hips and give her the eye. "Especially when you fuck."

"Jinx!" Lily grabs one of my pillows and throws it at me.

I dodge it without thinking. I've got the reflexes of a cat, and I always land on my feet.

"Don't deny it."

"I'm not denying it, and if you would get your head out of your ass, you'd be doing the nasty with Wolfe." Lily shakes her head, tired of the same discussion we've been having since we moved here from New Orleans. "That man wants you."

"He wants a quick fuck and that's all."

"You're kidding right?" Lily makes a show of rolling her eyes, showing her growing frustration. "He devours you every time he looks at you. *De-vow-ers.*" She emphasizes each syllable.

"Does not."

"Girl, the air ignites when the two of you are in the same room."

"Does not."

"Does so." Lily blows out an exaggerated sigh. "We're all just waiting for the two of you to get your heads out of your respective asses and fuck each other's brains out already. The tension is that thick."

"Is not."

"Just jump his bones, Jinx-y." Lily flops back on my bed. She peeks up at me. "Seriously, fuck him already."

"No."

"You're insufferable." Lily scoots to the edge of the bed. "I've never seen you this obsessed with a man before. One of you has to give the first inch. It's inevitable. Might as well be you."

"Not happening." I turn away because it's my turn for my cheeks to flush crimson.

"If you do, you can set the ground rules." Lily gives an exaggerated huff of frustration. "You seriously don't want him setting them."

She's not wrong about that. It's something to think about.

But how?

How do I set ground rules?

I hate how the thought of having sex with Wolfe turns me on. That deep-seated ache returns. It pulses within me. Flushes my cheeks. Makes my pussy throb. My nipples tighten into heartless betrayers. I've lost control of my body.

Because of a man.

Fucker.

We didn't do nearly as much as I would've liked in Callie's bar. After I ran up to Lily's place to put myself back together, and checked Callie's apartment to make sure it wasn't a complete disaster, I headed back downstairs to collect Wolfe.

The plan was to bring him upstairs where we could do the nasty all night long. I was really looking forward to it, because a man like him doesn't just have sex.

He has crazy monkey sex.

I just know it. And it's driving me crazy *not knowing* it.

But when I returned to the bar, I found him with his tongue down another chick's throat, minutes after giving him a blow job in the bathroom. A jealous rage boiled up inside of me. Righteous fury followed right on the heels of that rage until I couldn't see anything but red.

"Wolfe's an asshole." I stomp my foot, emphasizing my point. I will not budge.

"He may be, but you're stuck on stupid if you don't march over there right now and take what you want from him."

"He's a straight up A-S-S-Hole." I turn to Lily like she's crazy.

With his cocky walk, that roguish grin, and those dark, mesmerizing eyes, he's sex on a stick, and the man is most definitely a wolf out on the prowl.

"So? When have you ever been against a little casual sex? Just because you fuck him doesn't mean you have to like him. You most definitely don't have to keep him." She slips off the bed and gathers the robe around her slim body. With a tug, she cinches the robe tight, and gives me a shake of her head. "Use him for sex. He won't be the first guy you've used to scratch that itch."

"You just don't get it." My shoulders slump.

The problem with Wolfe is there won't be anything casual about it. He's the kind of man who fucks with his whole soul, burning the memory of him into a girl's mind, leaving all other men feeling less as a result.

We haven't fucked, yet I already know it'll be true. Honestly, it terrifies me. If I'm this obsessed after a bit of heavy petting and a blow job, what kind of crazed lunatic will I turn into once he fucks me with that monster cock of his. The man is hung. I've seen the whole package, choked on him as he rammed his cock down my throat, I held his balls in my hand.

"What I get," Lily says, "is the insane chemistry you two share. You're still butt-hurt from New Orleans. You don't know if he actually fucked that girl."

"I know what I saw."

"So why don't you call him out on it?"

"Because."

"Because you're too chicken shit to talk about it?" She heads for my door. "It's called communication for a reason, Jinx. Tell him what you saw. See what he says. Verify before jumping to conclusions."

I'm not against casual sex.

I'm not against wild monkey sex in the back of a bar.

I'm not against getting finger banged and giving a blow job to a virtual stranger as a warm up to some of that crazy monkey sex.

What I'm not is a girl a man fucks and leaves; stranger or not, for another chick.

That's why I detest him as much as I do.

Not five minutes after we hooked up in Callie's bar, he found another chick to seduce and fuck. When I came down, he had his nose in some bitch's ear, nuzzling and licking her throat with his tongue.

The man has no shame.

No shame at all.

And he wonders why I can't stand him?

Like he doesn't know I saw him trailing that chick when she went to the bathroom? The very same bathroom where he blew my mind with the deft skill of some extremely talented fingers?

I had a mind to go after him then, and show him exactly what I thought of his whorish ways, but I stomped out of the bar and headed home, before the tears pooling in my eyes had a chance to fall. I haven't been with another man since.

No kissing. No petting. No fingering. No nothing.

Fucking putz.

And he keeps getting under my skin.

Each time I tell myself I'm done, he does something to piss me off. As my temper flares, I lose all sense of self-preservation, going after him like a cat in heat, only to be pissed at my lack of control later.

That's my biggest issue right now.

I.

Can't.

Resist.

Him.

And I hate that. I hate that my defenses crumble. That I'm the one yelling at him, and then my hands are all over him. That I kiss him like a deranged madwoman. All that does is make the cocksure asshole even more frustratingly annoying.

I bet he does it on purpose.

He gets me hot under the collar and waits for that heat to boil over. I don't even want to continue down this vein of thought. So what do I do?

I do what I always do. I head to the window and draw back the drapes, hoping for a chance to see him.

He's not in his bedroom. I've got the best view of that, but there's movement on his deck. He catches me spying on him. How does he do that? Invariably, he catches me every damn time.

But I'm not backing down now. I'm too pissed to run and hide.

And what does he do?

The fucker stands, takes off his shirt, and kicks off his shoes. Then he pulls out his phone and sends me a text.

My eyes widen at the blatant invitation, then my cheeks heat as desire sweeps through me. I'm going to regret it, but I can't help myself.

This needs to end.

My grip on the phone is tight enough to turn my knuckles white. I storm out of my room, rage down the hall, and stomp over to his place. With my fist raised to bang on the front door, I stop.

His text. The arrogance. I'm so hot, I'm livid. I turn toward the camera guarding his front door and give him the finger. Then I turn about and march right back to my room.

Lily's right about one thing. I need to get laid. It's just not going to be Wolfe, even if the thought of sleeping with any other man seems like settling for a whole lot less.

Back in my room, I close the drapes, dress in my sluttiest outfit, grab my keys, and head to the closest bar I can find. Let's see what Wolfe thinks when he sees another man's hands on my skin. Another man's lips on mine. Another man taking what Wolfe almost had.

Two can very well play at this game.

THIRTY-ONE

Wolfe

A FIERY SPIRIT, JINX IS HOT AS SIN AND A SEDUCTIVE AS A SIREN. She's a Grecian goddess sent by the gods to torment unsuspecting men who can't help but fall to their knees in reverent adoration.

She's a tantalizing temptress and a total cock tease, sending mixed messages until my head feels like it's going to explode.

Both heads.

She kissed me in New Orleans, dragged me to the bathroom where she climbed my body like a cat in heat. I fingered her to an ear-splitting release, then she blew my mind with her hot mouth, talented tongue, and hands that took me to the brink and beyond.

Those kind of things make a guy think a chick's into him.

I'm not wrong about that.

But ever since she and her best friend, Lily, moved to California, and joined forces with the Guardians, she acts like none of that happened.

As if she didn't hump my leg.

As if she didn't shamelessly grind against me and come all over my fingers.

As if she didn't wrap her silky lips around my cock to suck me like the temptress she is.

For some reason, she's pissed, yet I've done nothing wrong.

Perfect angel here. I've treated her with nothing but respect.

Her explosive temper should drive me away, but fuck if it's not a goddamn siren's call, drawing me in, heating me up, making my mind spin, and my body come alive.

When I catch her looking at me, I'm instantly hard. Each and every time, without fail, the moment she realizes I've caught her staring, she turns away with a dismissive snort.

She desperately fights her attraction. I don't mind watching that battle unfold, because I know something she's yet to accept.

Jinx wants me with desperate hunger. She can be angry, pissed, and annoyed, but that's a war she's doomed to lose.

And I have the best weapon in my arsenal. I shamelessly use in my quest to claim her as my own. I feed that volatile temper of hers until she's boiling hot, primed to explode, then, I kiss her. I did that in Knox's kitchen.

I love the way she fights her nature.

How she refuses to accept the inevitable.

Even as she twirls, flowing in that lethal Brazilian fighting dance of hers, getting in three hits to my one, the girl can't help herself.

She always kisses me back.

Always.

She rises on tiptoe, hands lifting until she cups my face. Eyes simmering, she presses her silky lips against mine. Her kiss silences my protest, steals my breath, and sends my heart into overdrive. Adrenaline spikes, racing around my body, making me take notice even as I get lost in the tenderness of the kiss.

My heart skips a beat. My fingers curl around her tiny waist. I devour her intoxicating essence like a man starving for what he can't have. She ignites a firestorm that burns like the sun, turning everything to ash as it sweeps through me.

Then the space between us explodes. Jinx pulls back, anger building as if I'm responsible for the kiss. She slaps me and storms off in a huff.

We tore up Knox's living room. Destroying bookcases and

shattering his glass table. Fixing that is going to put a major dent in my wallet, but the kiss was worth every penny.

I've kissed before, but those kisses were weak, empty things. They didn't burn through me like Jinx's tantalizing teases.

I'd love to end one of our fights by tossing her over my shoulder, loudly proclaiming *"You. Me. Bed. Now."* But to do that, I need to win one of our fights.

So far, I'm zero for two.

I meander back to my home; frustrated and aroused.

My house is literally a stone's throw from Knox's place. Although, it's not as big, or as nice. I've got something of a 70's bungalow perched on the side of the cliff. It has two bedrooms. Perfect for a bachelor to call home.

Once through the front door, I head outside to watch the sun go down. It's my favorite time of day.

Grabbing a cold one from the fridge, I lounge in a chair and stare out over the glittering sea.

It's a calm, cloudless day, which means the sunset won't be nearly as spectacular. Not that I mind. A light breeze blows off the ocean, ruffling my hair. Down below, the slow, steady rhythm of waves hitting the beach synchs with the beating of my heart.

Not one to meditate, I've been told there's power in such a thing. My eyes drift closed as I hone in on the sounds around me.

Seabirds call overhead, screeching to one another as they hunt their next meal. Light gusts ruffle the sparse foliage clinging to the cliff wall beneath me. The wind chimes on my deck tinkle, adding randomness to the world around me. The surf below rolls relentlessly onward, churning the rocky coast to sand one powerful surge at a time.

Out on the water, a solitary surfer bobs in the water beyond the breakwater. The surf along this part of the coast is deadly, but this isn't the first time I've seen that particular surfer brave the waves.

One of our nearby neighbors, Noodles plays keyboard for Angel Fire, one of my favorite bands. His zen-esque lifestyle is one I don't understand, and if the rumors are true, he's not out there to surf.

He's there to talk to Old Joe, a great white shark who hunts these waters and happens to be Noodles' friend.

My eyes snap open as I fail, yet again, to meditate.

That zen state eludes me with the distractions around me. I tip the bottle to my lips and swallow down the cold brew. To my left, a window opens next door. I turn, instinctually feeling her eyes on me.

When Lily and Jinx joined the Guardians, they moved in with Knox. Jinx's window faces my bedroom, which complicates things as much as it enhances the crazy attraction pushing and pulling us apart.

She leans out of the window. Her long, dark hair blows back from her angelic face, and she tilts her head back and closes her eyes. Her honeyed skin takes to the California sun, deepening her tan to a golden brown. Long, black lashes frame her face, highlighting the sculpting of her cheeks, and her tiny upturned nose. Her pillowy lips, soft as sin, sexy as silk, curve upward into the most serene smile I've ever seen.

She knows I'm out back on my porch. The girl watches my every move. She also knows, I've got an unobstructed view of her bedroom. It's something she uses to tease and torment me, a nightly ritual we began the first night she moved in.

Lily and Knox know nothing of the games we play. They're blissfully unaware, too wrapped up in themselves to take notice of what happens beneath their own roof.

Jinx's eyes slowly open. Her head turns until our gazes connect and instantly clash. Less than an hour ago, I held her in my arms, stealing a kiss, which prompted a fight in Knox's kitchen. That fight extended to the living room where mayhem and destruction followed.

I still taste her on my lips.

With her eyes on me, I place the beer down on the table beside me. Then I stand and slowly turn toward her. She doesn't turn away as I peel my shirt over my head, tossing it to the deck. I eye her, waiting for her to retreat, but Jinx won't. She takes my challenge and stands firm.

Pressing my fingers to my lips, it's a reminder of that kiss in the kitchen. Her eyes flare, widening momentarily, and her pert lips part. I make a show of kicking off my shoes.

She knows what comes next. We've danced this dance for weeks.

The first time she stripped for me, Jinx didn't know I could see right into her room. Our bedroom windows face each other. She didn't know because the lights were off in mine. When I came home after sparring practice with the guys, I froze when I realized I could see everything.

I remember that day vividly, as does my cock. Already, the fucker wakes up, lengthening and hardening as it weeps for her. That first night, not wanting her to think I was a perv, I turned on the lights, letting her know our bedrooms faced each other.

Okay, I'm a little bit of a perv, because I waited until she slipped out of her pants before I flicked on the lights. Her head snapped up as I stepped to the window. Our gazes locked, much as they do now.

She didn't try to hide from me. There was no shock. No anger. No indignation. Instead, she held my gaze, almost as a challenge. That night, I closed the curtains like any gentleman would, then fucked my hand with her tantalizing image filling my mind and all kinds of filthy thoughts.

For the next week, she kept her drapes closed. Then one night, when I again came home late, I walked into my bedroom and came to a sudden halt. She was in her room, light on, facing me.

I turned on my lights, letting her know I was there. If she was going to undress in full view, then I would watch. I made several concessions for her, holding back my advances, but there's no way I'm going to keep my drapes pulled out of respect for her privacy.

I was here first. This is my home. And I sleep with the windows and doors open.

What happened next, will remain between us forever. I slowly took off my shirt, letting my muscles ripple and flex. Then I dropped it on the floor and waited.

Half a beat later, Jinx grabbed the bottom of her shirt and drew it over her head. I kicked off my shoes, much as I just did, then slid free of the constraint of my pants.

Hard and aroused, I waited to see what she would do next.

Pull the curtains? Turn off her light? Would she sneer at me in disgust? Or was this yet another tease?

She removed her jeans as my heart lodged in my throat, beating like a stallion in the last leg of a race. I gripped the waistband of my briefs, lifted it over my engorged cock and stepped free. With no shame, I fisted my cock, letting her see how hard I was for her.

Jinx watched me glide my hand from root to tip, leaving her bra and panties in place. I stared at her half naked state with fantasies spilling through my mind. Jinx on her knees, blowing me. Jinx bent over the side of the bed as I rutted into her from behind. Jinx in my arms, back braced against the wall, as I buried myself deep into her wet heat.

I masturbated while she watched, turning to the side as my release slammed into me. My hips bucked and jerked with my release. When I turned back, the corners of her lips turned up into a smirk. She reached behind her to unfasten her bra strap. Before letting it drop she closed her curtains, bringing a strangled moan of frustration to my lips.

The next morning I looked out my window. There, taped to the glass, were two numbers with a slash between them. She gave me a 4 out of 10.

Bitch.

Each night, thereafter, I've upped the stakes, eager to improve my score. I'm up to 7 out of 10, but I want more.

And I've been preparing my revenge.

Picking up my phone, I tap out a simple text.

THE FRONT DOOR'S UNLOCKED. COME IF YOU DARE.

WITH THAT, I SAUNTER INSIDE, FULLY EXPECTING HER TO IGNORE ME.

But that's not the point.

There's a chip on Jinx's shoulder, which means she rarely backs down from a dare.

It'll be fun to see which way she jumps.

Rescuing Jinx is waiting for you!
To see what happens between Wolfe and Jinx, get your copy today!
Get my Copy of Rescuing Jinx

Please consider leaving a review

I hope you enjoyed this book as much as I enjoyed writing it. If you like this book, please leave a review. I love reviews. I love reading your reviews, and they help other readers decide if this book is worth their time and money. I hope you think it is and decide to share this story with others. A sentence is all it takes. Thank you in advance!

Click on the link below to leave your review
Goodreads
Amazon
Bookbub

ELLZ BELLZ

ELLIE'S FACEBOOK READER GROUP

If you are interested in joining the ELLZ BELLZ, Ellie's Facebook reader group, we'd love to have you.

Join Ellie's ELLZ BELLZ.
The ELLZ BELLZ Facebook Reader Group

Sign up for Ellie's Newsletter.
Elliemasters.com/newslettersignup

Sybil's Protector

The One I Want Series
(Small Town, Military Heroes)
By Jet & Ellie Masters

EACH BOOK IN THIS SERIES CAN BE READ AS A STANDALONE AND IS ABOUT A DIFFERENT COUPLE WITH AN HEA.

Saving Ariel

Saving Brie

Saving Cate

Saving Dani

Saving Jen

Saving Abby

Rockstar Romance

The Angel Fire Rock Romance Series

EACH BOOK IN THIS SERIES CAN BE READ AS A STANDALONE AND IS ABOUT A DIFFERENT COUPLE WITH AN HEA. IT IS RECOMMENDED THEY ARE READ IN ORDER.

Ashes to New (prequel)

Heart's Insanity (book 1)

Heart's Desire (book 2)

Heart's Collide (book 3)

Hearts Divided (book 4)

Hearts Entwined (book5)

Forest's FALL (book 6)

Hearts The Last Beat (book7)

Contemporary Romance

Firestorm

(KRISTY BROMBERG'S EVERYDAY HEROES WORLD)

Billionaire Romance

Billionaire Boys Club

Hawke

Richard

Brody

Contemporary Romance

Cocky Captain

(Vi Keeland & Penelope Ward's Cocky Hero World)

Romantic Suspense

EACH BOOK IS A STANDALONE NOVEL.

The Starling

~AND~

Science Fiction

Ellie Masters writing as L.A. Warren

Vendel Rising: a Science Fiction Serialized Novel

About the Author

ELLIE MASTERS is a multi-genre and best-selling author, writing the stories she loves to read. These are dark erotic tales. Or maybe, sweet contemporary stories. How about a romantic thriller to whet your appetite? Ellie writes it all. Want to read passionate poems and sensual secrets? She does that, too. Dip into the eclectic mind of Ellie Masters, spend time exploring the sensual realm where she breathes life into her characters and brings them from her mind to the page and into the heart of her readers every day.

Ellie Masters has been exploring the worlds of romance, dark erotica, science fiction, and fantasy by writing the stories she wants to read. When not writing, Ellie can be found outside, where her passion for all things outdoor reigns supreme: off-roading, riding ATVs, scuba diving, hiking, and breathing fresh air are top on her list.

She has lived all over the United States—east, west, north, south and central—but grew up under the Hawaiian sun. She's also been privileged to have lived overseas, experiencing other cultures and making lifelong friends. Now, Ellie is proud to call herself a Southern transplant, learning to say y'all and "bless her heart" with the best of them. She lives with her beloved husband, two children who refuse to flee the nest, and four fur-babies; three cats who rule the household, and a dog who wants nothing other than for the cats to be his best friends. The cats have a different opinion regarding this matter.

Ellie's favorite way to spend an evening is curled up on a couch, laptop in place, watching a fire, drinking a good wine, and bringing forth all the characters from her mind to the page and hopefully into the hearts of her readers.

FOR MORE INFORMATION
elliemasters.com

facebook.com/elliemastersromance
twitter.com/Ellie__Masters
instagram.com/ellie_masters
bookbub.com/authors/ellie-masters
goodreads.com/Ellie_Masters

Connect with Ellie Masters

Website:
elliemasters.com
Amazon Author Page:
elliemasters.com/amazon
Facebook:
elliemasters.com/Facebook
Goodreads:
elliemasters.com/Goodreads
Instagram:
elliemasters.com/Instagram

Final Thoughts

I hope you enjoyed this book as much as I enjoyed writing it. If you enjoyed reading this story, please consider leaving a review on Amazon and Goodreads, and please let other people know. A sentence is all it takes. Friend recommendations are the strongest catalyst for readers' purchase decisions! And I'd love to be able to continue bringing the characters and stories from My-Mind-to-the-Page.

Second, call or e-mail a friend and tell them about this book. If you really want them to read it, gift it to them. If you prefer digital friends, please use the "Recommend" feature of Goodreads to spread the word.

Or visit my blog https://elliemasters.com, where you can find out more about my writing process and personal life.

Come visit The EDGE: Dark Discussions where we'll have a chance to talk about my works, their creation, and maybe what the future has in store for my writing.

Facebook Reader Group: Ellz Bellz

Thank you so much for your support!

Love,

Ellie

Dedication

This book is dedicated to you, my reader. Thank you for spending a few hours of your time with me. I wouldn't be able to write without you to cheer me on. Your wonderful words, your support, and your willingness to join me on this journey is a gift beyond measure.

Whether this is the first book of mine you've read, or if you've been with me since the very beginning, thank you for believing in me as I bring these characters 'from my mind to the page and into your hearts.'

Love,
Ellie

THE END